THE
EDITORS'
CHOICE:

NEW AMERICAN STORIES

VOLUME II

THE EDITORS' CHOICE:

NEW AMERICAN STORIES

VOLUME II

COMPILED BY
GEORGE E. MURPHY, JR.

A BANTAM/WAMPETER PRESS BOOK

BANTAM BOOKS
TORONTO • NEW YORK • LONDON • SYDNEY • AUCKLAND

THE EDITORS' CHOICE: NEW AMERICAN STORIES, VOLUME II
A Bantam Windstone Trade Book / January 1986

ACKNOWLEDGMENTS

"Two-Head Fred and Tree-Foot Frieda" by Robert William Antoni. First published in *The Missouri Review*. Copyright © 1984 by Robert William Antoni. Reprinted by permission of the author.

"The Salt Garden" by Margaret Atwood. First published in *Ms*. Copyright © 1984 by Margaret Atwood. Reprinted by permission of the author.

"The *"New Yorker"* Story" by Martha Bayles. First published in *Harper's*. Copyright © 1984 by Martha Bayles. Reprinted by permission of the author.

"Monologue of the Movie Mogul" by Michael Covino. First published in *The Paris Review*. Copyright © 1984 by Michael Covino. Reprinted by permission of the author.

"Land Where My Fathers Died" by Andre Dubus. First published in *Antaeus*. Copyright © 1984 by Andre Dubus. Reprinted by permission of the author.

"Saving the Dead" by Kurt Duecker. First published in *Shenandoah*. Copyright © 1984 by Kurt Duecker. Reprinted by permission of the author.

"Fire Ants" by Gerald Duff. First published in *Ploughshares*. Copyright © 1984 by Gerald Duff. Reprinted by permission of the author.

"All Set About with Fever Trees" by Pam Durban. First published in *The Georgia Review*. Copyright © 1984 by Pam Durban. Reprinted by permission of the author.

"Julius Caesar and the Werewolf" by John Gardner. First published in *Playboy*. Copyright © 1984 by the estate of John Gardner. Reprinted by permission of the author.

"Here Comes the Sun" by Janette Turner Hospital. First published in *Cosmopolitan*. Copyright © 1984 by Janette Turner Hospital. Reprinted by permission of the author.

"The Quickening" by Lisa Interollo. First published in *Seventeen*. Copyright © 1984 by Lisa Interollo. Reprinted by permission of the author.

"Harmony" by Janet Kauffman. First published in *Vanity Fair*. Copyright © 1984 by Janet Kauffman. Reprinted by permission of the author.

"The Rise, Fall, and Redemption of Mooski Toffski Offski" by James Howard Kunstler. First published in *Tendril*. Copyright © 1984 by James Howard Kunstler. Reprinted by permission of the author.

"City of Boys" by Beth Nugent. First published in *The North American Review*. Copyright © 1984 by Beth Nugent. Reprinted by permission of the author.

NOMINATING MAGAZINES

Antaeus, 1 West 30th Street, New York, New York 10001

The Atlantic Monthly, 8 Arlington Street, Boston, Massachusetts 02116

Cosmopolitan, 224 West 57th Street, New York, New York 10019

Esquire, 2 Park Avenue, New York, New York 10016

The Georgia Review, University of Georgia, Athens, Georgia 30602

Harper's Magazine, 2 Park Avenue, New York, New York 10016

Mademoiselle, 350 Madison Avenue, New York, New York 10017

The Missouri Review, Department of English, 231 A & S, University of Missouri, Columbia, Missouri 65211

Ms., 199 West 40th Street, New York, New York 10018

The North American Review, 1222 West 27th Street, Cedar Falls, Iowa 50614

The Paris Review, 45–39 171st Place, Flushing, New York 11358

Playboy, 919 North Michigan Avenue, Chicago, Illinois 60611

Ploughshares, Box 529, Cambridge, Massachusetts 02139

Redbook, 230 Park Avenue, New York, New York 10017

Seventeen, 850 Third Avenue, New York, New York 10022

Shenandoah, Box 722, Lexington, Virginia 24450

Tendril, P.O. Box 512, Green Harbor, Massachusetts 02041

TriQuarterly, 1735 Benson Avenue, Northwestern University, Evanston, Illinois 60606

Vanity Fair, 350 Madison Avenue, New York, New York 10017

CONTENTS

INTRODUCTION

The Editors' Choice: New American Stories, Volume I, was an experiment, an alternative design for a new anthology of stories. The collection was the result of a simple, though previously untried, idea: I asked the fiction editors of both commercial magazines and select independent literary journals to nominate what they felt were the stories they were most pleased to have published that year. The response of readers, reviewers, editors, and authors has been overwhelming—as well as gratifying. The experiment, it seems, was a success. As such, it brings me even greater pleasure to introduce *Volume II.*

To avoid the possibility of overlapping authors or themes, and to create as varied and eclectic a collection as possible, I asked each of the nominating editors to contribute as many as three stories, from which one would be selected. Making the selections, editors said, is a very difficult task. Many tried to choose stories which, to them, represent the editorial ideal of their publications. Others chose to endorse talented new writers whose work they found striking and exceptional. As *The Atlantic*'s editors noted, "Since we don't publish stories we don't think are among the best we've seen, we hate to single out any one of them as the 'best' for that year. Even so, we're always pleased when we have the chance to introduce a new and able writer, and so don't mind calling attention to work we think particularly original and distinctive."

Reading the various magazines' nominations, I was struck by both the high quality and enormous diversity of short stories being published. Arriving at the final decisions for this anthology was a difficult task. Yet I believe that each of the stories gathered here is among the very best of 1984. As in *Volume I*, I'm delighted to include new work from well-known writers as well as from lesser known, younger writers.

Included here is the last published story of John Gardner, whose untimely death halted what many consider to be one of the most significant literary careers of recent decades. Here, too, are stories from such well-established authors as Margaret Atwood, Andre Dubus, and Trevanian, as well as first published stories from Robert William Antoni, Kurt Duecker, Lisa Interollo, Ilene Raymond, and Brent Spencer.

From the stark desperation of Beth Nugent's "City of Boys" to the antic humor of James Howard Kunstler's "The Rise, Fall and Redemption of Mooski Toffski Offski," from the poignant realization in Gayle Whittier's "Turning Out" to the satirical twists of Martha Bayles' "The *New Yorker* Story," this is indeed a wide-ranging collection.

For sure, a notable change is occurring in terms of the popularity of short fiction, a trend that *Newsweek* recently recognized and referred to as "A Silver Age of Short Stories." More collections of stories are slated for publication by major publishing houses in 1985 than has been true in years. As well, there is a wider acceptance of the notion of short stories as an art form which, in terms of precision and impact, may, at its best, be closer to the poem than to the novel. As Raymond Carver recently said, "A well-made short story is worth any number of bad novels." And it is the well-made short story we are all hoping to find, the story which, to paraphrase W. H. Auden, "closes like the click of a well-made box."

I think you will find such stories in this volume.

George E. Murphy, Jr.
Key West, Florida
April 1985

THE EDITORS' CHOICE:
NEW AMERICAN STORIES
VOLUME II

ROBERT WILLIAM ANTONI

TWO-HEAD FRED AND TREE-FOOT FRIEDA

FROM THE MISSOURI REVIEW

ς

I LOVED ZOE because she helped raise me, because she let me pinch her breasts when my mother wasn't around, and because she told me she ate Barbados rat for whooping cough. I loved Jook Jook because he helped raise me, because he let me sip from his rum bottle when my father wasn't around, and because he told me he ate Whatlin's Island iguana for grimps. I'd never been to Barbados, never been to Whatlin's Island, never seen an iguana, but I'd seen enough rats to prepare myself for sudden death should I ever get whooping cough or grimps.

"Who dat pretty young gal you all bring wid you dis time?"

"Zoe?"

"I ain' know she name, but dat gal get tottot fa so!"

"What are tot-tots?" I asked.

Jook Jook laughed. "Boobie, boy." He let go the tiller to squeeze a nipple of mine between a thumb and forefinger of each hand. "Tottot is tittie."

"That's Zoe with the tot-tots," I said. "She's our maid."

The thought of spending a month of my summer vacation at Deep Water Cay was anything for me but exciting; this was only the first day. The island was tiny, desolate, sandfly-

1

infested, and surrounded by sea. The bigger I grew, the smaller Deep Water Cay shrank. I cannot tell you how small an island two miles long and fifty yards wide can feel to an eleven-year-old. It would require the full measure of my persistence and whatlessness to find any excitement on the rock. I had lots of time on my hands; ideas were already taking shape in my head.

"So how do you like Zoe, Jook Jook?"

"I ain' know she yet. How long she work wid you fambly?"

"She's lived with us since Christopher and I were babies."

"How come you nevah bring she here before?"

"She always wanted to stay at home. Besides, our house here is too small."

"She Bahamian?"

"No. She's from Trinidad."

"Oh-ho."

"She even eats rats!"

"Dat musie why she so pretty."

"And has those nice tot-tots!"

The only good reason to come to Deep Water Cay, as far as I was concerned, was to see Jook Jook. He would come across from McClean's Town to do odd jobs for my father, and sometimes to take Christopher and me with him fishing, conching, and misbehaving. Jook Jook was the greatest conch and woman jooker in all the world. For years he'd taken the title of King Conch Jooker at the Conch Jooking And Slopping Contest held at McClean's Town every Boxing Day. For even longer, Jook Jook had been sought after by every woman from Pelican Point Village to End Of The World Rock and farther.

"How's that three-legged woman from White Sound doing?"

"She be fine. Except now she get corn on she big toe."

"Which one?"

"Middle foot, I tink it is."

"How's she ride her bike then?"

"I ain' know."

"If it was one of her outside feet, that'd be fine."

"No mattah. She still ridin' good 'nough."

"How's her toe jam business?"

"Goin' strong."

"Did you ever buy any of her toe jam, Jook Jook?"

"Fa what? I not 'fraid a no jumbie, dat I needs to stink up meself wid Tree-foot Frieda toe jam."

Jook Jook stood on the bench in the back of his boat steering, and I sat looking up at him. The tiller had an extension of shaved pine limb attached by a couple of hose clamps. Every Bahamian dinghy had the same extension, the same hose clamps: for some reason they could never sit and steer. Jook Jook seemed a giant as I looked up at him. He was in his late thirties, muscular and handsome. He was wearing an old pair of my father's white pants which he'd cut off into shorts. Jook Jook had not let the ends fray, but had hemmed them neatly. He owned the only block house in McClean's Town, which he'd built himself. Besides the King, Jook Jook was known as *de one wid de concrete house.*

Christopher sat quietly in the front of the boat looking at the water google-eyed; my brother was the only ten-year-old I have ever come across who deeply appreciated nature. I'm sure he even found pleasure in coming to Deep Water Cay. Christopher could sit and admire an entire sunset without getting bored; I'd look for about thirty seconds, then for a bird to throw a rock at.

Jook Jook's Abaco dinghy had a tiny diesel engine which puttered and puffed away as seriously as a locomotive, propelling us at no miles an hour. The boat was very heavy and built of hand-hewn pine boards in the Abaco way: the boards were not sealed; when wet they expanded to become watertight. If an Abaco dinghy went into the water dry, it would sink. Jook Jook always spoke of his boat as though it were one with the water. He had inherited the dinghy from his father and, even though it was slow and old-timish, he refused to part with it for a Boston Whaler and a Johnson outboard.

"So how's your dog doing, Jook Jook?"

"He be fine."

"Does he still fight over his food?"

"I done solve dat problem."

"How?"

"I find out one like fish, one like macaroni pie. So I give he bowl a each."

"Good idea."

"But still big big problem when people give he bone."

"Really?"

"Z-bell give he bone las' night, an' almos' get eat alive."

"Z-bell should have known better."

"Fa true. Only a fool gon give Two-head Fred one bone."

Jook Jook had taken me to the sunken jeep, and a dozen little white croakcrows were already trying their best to swim in the water sloshing about in the bilge. None had been speared cleanly through the head, and some trailed a silver and purple ribbon from their stomachs; I was hardly strong enough to pull back my Hawaiian sling, far less aim at a fish. That was why Jook Jook took me to the sunken jeep. It lay on its side in about ten feet of water, and the fish would be huddled in the front seat. I could float on the surface, pull back the sling, and let the spear fly through the window on the driver's side. Sometimes I'd get two at once. Only when I speared the rusted metal would I have a problem, and I'd have to make several dives before I could dislodge it. Like most Bahamians, Jook Jook refused to go into the water when there was no need; he could sit in the dinghy and catch three times as many fish as I could spear. He'd told Christopher and me he'd never learned to swim, and if he ever fell into the water we'd have to save him, but we were not sure we could believe him. Christopher did not care about spearfishing; he'd stay in the boat and play with the croakcrows, throwing back the stronger ones while I wasn't looking. When we got home we'd give the little fish to my father, and he'd fry them up for himself and Jook Jook. The two would sit down to feast for an hour, picking them apart bone by bone.

Jook Jook weaved his way through the intricate channel which ran between the sandbars on the western end of Deep Water Cay and the small mangrove island off the point. If you didn't take the channel, you had to go a mile out to sea to get around the reef. Every time my father tried to negotiate the channel in our Whaler he ran aground off the mangrove island; we'd all have to get out and push. Jook Jook had once told Christopher and me that the island was unnamed, and so we had made a flag out of a pair of my father's boxer shorts and christened it Pain-in-the-butt Island.

As we rounded the point, our little house came into view, perched on the hill and shining in the sun. The bright red shutters and black trim were my father's attempt to make the original gray house a bit more quaint. The eccentric Lord Brooksfield had had the house built during the days of colonialism, when the Queen had offered him the tip of the island for his fiftieth birthday. But Lord Brooksfield had come from England only once to be bitten from head to toe by sandflies, and to swell up like an enraged porcupine. The tiny house remained vacant for several years until my father bought it from Sir Max Hashkins, sweet-skinned sovereign of the second generation, complete with an assortment of first-aid creams, mosquito nets, and a case of imported, giant-sized cans of Bedbug Bully. Our skin, however, was of a tougher making, and we began to come to Deep Water Cay on weekends and for a month each summer.

The rest of the family and Zoe were still asleep, and the house was without activity; Jook Jook had awoken Christopher and me an hour after sunrise to go fishing with him.

We began to make our way slowly along the beach in front of our house. The morning breeze was strong enough only to ripple the water, and the sun hung just above the horizon laying pieces of light on the water around us, like long, unbroken strips of orange peel floating on its surface. In the distance bright sparkles popped like jumping beans.

"Where are we going now, Jook Jook?"

"I hadie check some me traps."

"Where?"

"Lightborn's Cay."

"Then what?"

"Den we gon get some conchs."

"Then do you think I could do some more spearing?"

"We gon see. Day still young."

After Deep Water Cay came Sweeting's Cay before Lightborn's; it would take at least an hour to get to Jook Jook's traps. I decided to go sit with Christopher on the front of the boat.

Christopher's legs hung over the bow with his feet dragging in the water. I sat next to him and let my feet hang the same way.

"Are you making blood?" I asked.

He nodded.

If you held your toes just below the surface of the water and pointed them exactly right, purple bubbles formed and it looked like blood oozing out. The trick was to keep your toes the same distance below the surface as the boat moved through the water, and so to maintain a constant flow of blood.

I stared down at my feet. "Did you know Three-foot Frieda has a corn on her big toe?"

"That's great."

"Aren't you going to ask which big toe?"

"There isn't any Three-foot Frieda."

"That's not the point," I said.

"What is?"

"Forget it."

We continued making blood.

"I've got a great idea," I told Christopher.

"What?"

"I think Jook Jook likes Zoe."

"Yeah."

"He thinks she's pretty. *Especially* her tot-tots."

"What's that?"

I smiled. "Boobie, boy. Tot-tot is tittie!" I reached over and squeezed his nipples.

"Cut it out, faggot." He shoved me away. "So what's your idea?"

"You know how Jook Jook's the world's greatest jooker?"

"So?"

"So how'd you like to see him in action?"

"I've seen him clean millions of conch."

"I mean *jooking*, stupid. Maybe him and Zoe will do it, and we can trail 'em and watch!"

"Trail them where?"

"I don't know. Wherever people go to do that stuff."

Christopher concentrated on his toes again.

"So what do you think?" I asked.

"I think your idea is dumb, and I'm not interested in spying on anyone. It's not right."

"Are you kidding?"

"No."

We went back to our toes. I managed to keep mine bleeding for about a full minute.

"Did you see that one?" I asked.

"Yeah. Pretty good."

"You really don't like my idea?"

"No. It's wrong."

"What people don't know can't hurt 'em."

"That's not the point," Christopher said.

"What is?"

"Forget it."

I kicked my feet up hard, filling the air in front of us with a spray of water. The motion of the boat carried us into it, showering Christopher and me.

"Thanks a lot," he said.

"Any time." I got up to go back to Jook Jook, climbing over a jumbled pile of fish netting and a big sheet of tarpaulin used as a tent when Jook Jook went on long fishing trips.

"How far to the traps?" I asked.

"We be dere jus' now."

"The shallow ones?"

"Shallow trap furs'."

I looked around to see where we were, but couldn't tell. "Where's Lightborn's?"

Jook Jook pointed at a bright sandbar which interrupted the rocky coast to our left. I remembered the beach at the end of Lightborn's Cay. Behind it, in the distance, I found a couple of television antennas and the water tower belonging to Sweeting's Cay Village, where the island curved behind Lightborn's.

"Do you want me to dive down and check the traps?" I asked.

"Tink you here fa you good looks?"

"Are they shallow enough?"

"Some be. If not, I haul dem."

"How soon will we get there?"

"Soon soon."

I put on my diving gear. The world looked odd through the mask: small and distant in the center, stretched and curving toward me at the edges. I tilted my head back to look up at the clouds, and felt as though I were speeding up to meet them. I unfolded my wings and rolled my head from side to side. My mask began to fog up. Jook Jook tried to wipe a circle clean on the glass, but the fog was on the inside. He leaned closer.

"What you doin' inside dere, boy?"

I took the snorkel out of my mouth. "I don't know."

"Good ting I ain' bring no rum today."

"How come?" My voice sounded nasal in the mask.

Jook Jook laughed. "You done kaponkle up. I give you rum, no tellin' what you might do."

"No way. I know how to hold my rum."

"You evah drink more den a sip?"

"Not really." I put the snorkel back in my mouth.

Soon we got to the first float marked JJ. Jook Jook picked me up and tossed me overboard. I pulled myself down to the trap along the float line, stopping once or twice to purge my ears. The trap was empty. I swam up, told Jook Jook, and he lifted me out of the water into the boat. I checked all the shallow traps, just beyond the first reef, in fifteen or twenty feet of water. Most were empty. One had a margate fish and a couple of yellowtails. Afterwards, Jook Jook checked the deeper traps off the second reef. He didn't have to haul them all the way up; Jook Jook could tell whether the traps were empty by lifting them a few feet off the bottom, checking the weight, and feeling for the vibration of the fish moving about in the traps. He could have checked the shallow traps easily enough by looking through his glass, but he made it clear that that was my job. One of the deep traps had a large Nassau grouper, and Jook Jook hit it over the head with his bootoo before he threw it into the bilge.

On our way back to Deep Water Cay Jook Jook stopped at a grassy patch for conch. Christopher and I jumped overboard. Jook Jook cut the motor and let the dinghy drift with the tide. While we dove up conch and threw them into the boat, he removed the conch from their shells and cleaned them, throwing the empty shells back into the water. Sometimes I hung onto the side and watched, amazed at his fluidity and speed. I admired nothing in the world so much as Jook Jook's ability to jook and slop a conch. After we'd filled two old paint buckets with conch, Jook Jook lifted Christopher and me into the dinghy, and we started off again.

"Where to now?" I asked.

He smiled. "I ain' know."

He headed for the gap between Sweeting's Cay and Deep Water Cay. He steered between the islands, and then along the mangrove on the northern side of Sweeting's Cay. Suddenly he turned the boat hard into the mangrove trees and cut the engine.

"What are you doing?" I asked.

"I ain' know."

"You'll crash into the mangrove!"

"Bes' duck you head den, boy. Hear, Christopha?"

We all crouched below the gunnel. The dinghy skidded between two huge clumps of mangrove, and the leaves and branches brushed our shoulders as the trees swallowed us up. Beside us, thick brown banyans arched out of the water as eerie as charmed snakes. Above and around us, only bright leaves. I lifted my head and found we'd entered a kind of interior river which weaved its way through the mangrove. The trees nearly enclosed us, here and there a patch of sky showing through. The world hidden by the mangrove trees was cool, silent, and secret. Everything was still. Even the current which carried us along was invisible. The blues and greens were as bright as stained glass.

"Up here!" Christopher called, and I climbed forward.

Fish darted away from the bow and buried themselves, creating puffs in the mud where they entered. On the surface needle fish slashed back and forth. Along the sides, among the mangrove banyans, hundreds of snappers and grunts swam in slow procession.

We drifted with the current for about half a mile, shoving off the mangrove trees where the stream twisted. Jook Jook grabbed a branch, walked toward the bow as the current swung the stern around, and tied the anchor line to a mangrove limb.

"What are we doing now?" Christopher asked.

"You gon see. Come." Jook Jook picked up my spear and climbed out onto the mangrove banyans. We followed, walking on the smooth curved roots. Jook Jook found a mangrove snapper wedged between the banyans and called us over. He raised the spear shoulder height, threw it at the fish, and tipped it up with the fish wriggling on the end.

"See how to stick dem?"

"Wow," I said. "It's so easy."

Jook Jook laughed. He removed the fish. "Here, Christopha. Take de spear."

"That's OK," he said. "Let Addy do it."

"Well go-long wid he den, an' make sure de boy don't jook up he foot. I gon skin some de conchs."

Christopher and I took off between the trees in search of more mangrove snappers. I was so excited I became careless with my steps; my foot slipped off a mangrove banyan into the water, and my leg sunk knee-deep into the mud.

"Over here!" Christopher called; he'd found a snapper.

I struggled to pull free from the mud sucking at my leg and rushed over. I raised the spear quickly, high over my head, and brought it down, missing the fish by about a yard. The snapper scuttled away between the roots and buried itself in the mud, leaving a cloud behind it. Christopher laughed. I tried to spear several others, missing every time, until Jook Jook whistled.

"No way I'm going back without a fish," I said.

"Come on, Addy."

"Look, I found a puffer fish." The chubby little fish lay between a couple of banyans. It seemed to be playing in the mud by expelling water through its mouth, blowing cloudy circles like smoke rings.

Christopher came over, and we watched for a while. He laughed.

"I'm gonna spear him."

"What?" he asked.

"Just what I said."

"That's stupid. What can you possibly do with a puffer fish?"

"Spear it, that's what."

Christopher left as I took a stab at the puffer fish and

TWO-HEAD FRED AND TREE-FOOT FRIEDA 11

missed. It moved over a little. On my third try I got him. I lifted the little fish, and it began to inflate by sucking in short hard breaths of air. I hurried with my fat prize toward Jook Jook's dinghy.

"Look what I got!" I climbed into the dinghy.

"Why you do dis, Addy? Why you do dis?" Jook Jook's voice was not harsh.

"I don't know. I wanted to spear something."

He took the puffer fish off my spear and threw it into the bilge. Christopher picked it up and laid it on the bench next to him. Jook Jook went to the bow, untied the anchor line, and we began to drift again. When he got to the back of the boat, Jook Jook grabbed a branch so that the bow swung around, and we continued bow first into the heart of the mangrove.

After a while Jook Jook spoke quietly. "Nevah do dat by me again."

"Let me throw it back in then!"

"No, no. He dead. I gon find some use fa he."

The fish lay on its side, deflated now. Its loose white belly was sprinkled with red. On flat calm moonlit nights, Christopher and I would often go down to the beach to look for puffer fish. We'd find groups of four or five, attracted by the moonlight, lying on the sand at the water's edge. It was as though the moonlight hypnotized them; if we were very gentle, we could handle them without scaring them away.

Christopher picked up a leaf from the bilge and brushed it once along the little fish's speckled belly. I watched. In the cool stillness of the world hidden by the mangrove trees, I was sweating. Jook Jook spun the boat around and started the motor. It seemed to grow louder and louder as we worked our way out, and I began to feel better and better. Not until we broke into the hard sunlight again, could I put the little puffer fish out of my mind. Jook Jook headed his Abaco dinghy in the direction of home.

"Well, it sure smells funny."

Zoe sucked her teeth: she chupsed. "Don't mind 'bout de smell. I dis rub lil olive oil in me joints every mornin'."

"Really?" I asked.

"Dat dis keep de hinges from stickin' an' painin' me."

The rich smell of Zoe's olive-oiled knuckles mingled with the green smell of the shelled pigeon peas which fell from her fingertips like rain. Zoe was the fastest pea-sheller in all the world. No contest had been held to determine this, and she didn't have to tell me: Zoe's fingers moved over the flat, brown legumes so quickly you couldn't see them, couldn't keep count of the small, white peas dropping into her lap if you tried. The trick was *not* to think about what you're doing, and *never* watch. *Causin soon as you put your mind in you fingah, dem can't move.* But I was sure it had something to do with the olive oil.

It was the last day of our stay at Deep Water Cay, and the month had been uneventful and particularly unexciting. Jook Jook had been coming to see Zoe regularly during the last couple of weeks. At first he seemed almost shy; Zoe did most of the talking. She asked him to take her in his dinghy to catch flying fish. Jook Jook had never heard of eating flying fish, nor did he have any idea how to catch them. Zoe assured him that in Trinidad they ate them all the time, and catching them was simple enough. *Onles ting is sit in de boat at night wid a torch-light, an' wait fa dem to jump pon you lap.* Jook Jook laughed at this, saying he'd never heard of such fishing in his life. But when they came back that first night with a dozen flying fish, and Zoe fried them for us all the next morning for breakfast, Jook Jook admitted that they were the best fish he'd ever tasted. For me, even the thought of eating fish first thing in the morning was disgusting.

I'd followed them a few times—keeping to the sea oats so as to remain undetected—when he came over, and they went for walks down the beach. So far, I'd seen nothing that looked like jooking, but I hadn't given up hope.

"Isn't Jook Jook coming over tonight?"

"He comin' to carry me 'cross to McClean's Town fa some fête oh de oddah dey havin'. But I ain' gon let he stay long. Is nothin' in de worl' I like worse den a party where I ain' know de people. Besides, we got plenty bettah tings to do in we private."

I smiled. "Like what?"

"Don't play de fool wid me, chil'. You know jus' what I talkin' 'bout." She chupsed.

"What kind of party is it?"

"Somebody gettin' marry, oh somethin' so."

"When is Jook Jook coming to get you?"

"Guess roun' seven o'clock."

"Is he picking you up at the dock, or in front of the house?"

"Say meet he at de dock. Why you so full-up wid questions dis mornin'? Wha fa you needs to know de houah an' wherebouts oh de mahn comin'?" She chupsed again.

"I don't know."

"You bes' not be plannin' no mischief! Hear me? I don't want no mischief from you, chil'!"

"I only wanted to know in case Jook Jook comes to visit Chris and me."

"Well don't worry 'bout dat. He ain' studyin' you tonight."

"*That's* for sure."

Zoe chupsed.

The rest of the family had gone shell collecting earlier that morning, and Zoe and I had gone to a place near the center of the island where pigeon peas grew wild. There were dozens of trees on a small plateau, and when they were in bloom you could see the mass of yellow flowers from far out at sea. We'd picked for about an hour, Zoe collecting three floursacks full to my one. I'd begged her to let me dump all the peas in a single big pile, and the mountain of peas lay at our feet, almost blocking my view of the ocean where we sat on the front step.

Between Zoe's spread thighs her brightly flowered dress formed a net which caught the falling peas. Zoe had only to shell the peas, but I had two jobs: to make sure she always had a fresh supply of pods next to her, and to fill the plastic Bahama Bread bags she had collected with the shelled peas from her lap. Zoe would give some of the peas to her friends, and she'd dry some in the sun to be used for peas 'n rice and pêlau during the winter.

Zoe had huge brown eyes and no lashes. Her mother had drunk too much sea water while pregnant with Zoe because she had canker sores—Zoe called them gum boils. The salt water had washed Zoe's lashes clean off. Somehow, the bald lids accentuated the size of her eyes. She had fat red cheeks, as though she were sucking a canap seed under each one. She was short and round. And although she scarcely looked old enough to have two children, Zoe was a grandmother.

She'd had no use for husbands; Zoe refused to be dependent on any man. When Zoe had decided she was ready to have children, she hand-picked the fathers: a pretty man for the girl, a smart one for the boy. She must have had some way to determine the sex of her children, although I never thought to ask her.

"Are you glad you finally got to come to Deep Water Cay?"

"I pass de time pleasant enough. Sometime dat big house at home dis get lonely, when me one inside."

"Don't you think this place is pretty boring?"

"Is all right. But I ain' know why you all dis leave you nice home, to come to dis lil board house."

"Jook Jook has a concrete house!"

"Tink I ain' know."

"Where *is* Jook Jook's house?"

"You plannin' on goin' McClean's Town?"

"No, but just in case."

"Is near de sea. Jus' by de public dock. Jook Jook get a very nice house. I mus' say dat fa he."

"I bet you'll miss him when you go."

"Don't worry 'bout dat, chil'. Is not me to hang 'bout no mahn. Onles ting I gon miss is de flyin' fish."

"Wouldn't you like him to come with us?"

"Not me. Leave he right here where he belong."

"Well *I* wish he was coming with us. Then I could get some rum!"

"Don't worry 'bout no rum; worry 'bout you job. You slackin' off, chil'. Look, I out a pea to shell, an' my lap full. How you could neglec' you job fa me so?"

I smiled. Zoe sucked her teeth. I always thought it funny when Zoe tried to sound cross with me. She couldn't do it. Whenever she got vexed with me—and there were plenty of occasions—we'd end up hugging one another. If I got in trouble with my parents, I went to Zoe; she'd always be ready to console me.

I dug my hands into the pile of unshelled peas and placed a bunch on the step next to Zoe. She reached and took up a branch of pods without looking. Zoe began opening them, slipping her thumb along the inside ridge where the pod halves joined, and breaking the tiny umbilical cords which connected each pea to its chamber. The freed peas fell into her lap like hard, green-edged raindrops. She was looking at the sea, and her eyes did not shift once to her hands. The mountain of peas had much diminished. I studied Zoe's profile against the aquamarine background, thinking that I just might lean over and plant a wet kiss on the fat rosy cheek nearest me.

"Bag de peas, chil'!"

"All right," I said.

Zoe chupsed.

While Jook Jook went to the house to get Zoe, I hid beneath the tarpaulin and pile of fish netting in the bow of his dinghy. I'd told my mother I wanted to go shark fishing at the dock. She told me to tell my father. He told me to take Christopher. I told Christopher I was going to hide out in Jook Jook's dinghy. He told me he'd tell my mother and father. I told him I'd sock him in the jaw.

I waited for a while after we got to McClean's Town, and Jook Jook cut the motor, before I stuck out my head. I'd not been able to hear much of their conversation on the way over due to the engine, and I did not know how they'd failed to notice me in the front of the boat. Jook Jook had tied the dinghy to the dock, beneath a tremendous tamarind tree which stretched out over the water. Some of the branches reached right down into the boat, keeping me well camouflaged. I watched Zoe and Jook Jook walk down the dock, cross the street, and enter a pink house. There were about ten houses which I could see, and from the house where the party was obviously being held, I could hear a lot of racket: talking, laughing, loud music. People came and went. Sometimes they stopped for a while to talk in front of the house. A man and woman came out, danced for a minute in the street, and went back in.

First I thought I'd wait for Jook Jook and Zoe to leave for the party before I got out of the dinghy. Then I thought they seemed to be taking a long time; maybe they were doing a quick jook before they left. But just as I took hold of the tarpaulin to throw it off, they walked out. I crouched down and watched them go to the house where the party was being held.

When the coast was clear, I shot down the dock, across the street, and ducked behind some bushes at the side of the pink house. I tapped on the wall to make sure: concrete. Because I'd seen Jook Jook lock the front door, I knew I had to find another way in. I checked a large window above the bushes. Like most of the Bahamian houses, there was no screen— only a wooden shutter hinged at the top of the window, held out from the wall by a stick. I hitched myself up onto the windowsill and lay across it with my feet hanging out. I ducked my shoulders and tumbled in, knocking the stick out from the shutter and landing on my head. The shutter slammed with a *whack,* and the stick came down with another, giving me a matching lump on the other side of my skull.

I sat quietly until my head stopped pounding and my eyes adjusted to the darkness. It was the bedroom. There was an uncanny stillness and silence about the house. I pushed open the shutter and put the stick in place, letting in a cool breeze and a narrow strip of light. I decided to hide under the bed. I stared up at the coiled springs for some time before I realized I would see nothing from there, and slid out.

I looked around. Across from the bed a tall box stuck out into the room: a self-contained hanging closet constructed of pegboard. I slid the hangers aside to make a gap in the middle, stepped in on top of several pairs of shoes, and closed the door. A couple of belts hung on the inside of the door, just in front of me. I unhooked them. They slipped out of my hand to my feet and seemed to squirm about my ankles. I kicked them away and took several deep breaths. The closet rocked gently.

After I calmed down, I began a careful selection of that hole in the pegboard which would give me the best view of the bed. I found the perfect peephole, but I had to crouch to look through it. I waited. Soon I began to feel tired, so I put my little finger in the hole and leaned against the back wall of the closet. And I must have dozed off, even while standing; at the sound of Zoe and Jook Jook's voices I jumped, knocking over something on the floor of the closet. I felt a wetness with my toes. The bottle had not been capped properly, and I reached down quickly and righted it before much spilled out.

I had already swallowed several mouthfuls of rum when Jook Jook and Zoe entered the bedroom. My eyes were watering. I wiped them clean on my sleeve and looked through my peephole just in time to see a pair of large tot-tots go by. I blinked and took another big swallow of rum. I looked through my hole again, smiling to myself. I took another swig. Then I couldn't find my peephole, and I began to feel dizzy. I shut my eyes: fat rats and big slippery lizards. I began to sweat. Thinking the rum might calm my nerves, I took another big swallow. The closet began to spin. I closed my eyes: Two-head Fred snapped at me, *Why you do dis, boy? Why you do dis to me?* I screamed. Zoe screamed. "Tief in de house! Tief!" I tried to shove out of my closet. It flopped over, trapping me inside, rum spilling, Zoe screaming. Tree-foot Frieda kicked me. *How you could do me dis mischief, chil'? How you could neglec' me so?* Commotion filled the house: the sounds of people rushing, crying, yelling.

Eventually, someone turned the closet over, and when the door opened I saw that it was my father, who had come looking for me. Zoe sat on the bed with the sheet wrapped around her, crying. Jook Jook had put on white shorts. The room was filled with people, all staring at me. Christopher was among them. One woman wore a wedding dress. I stood up in my closet and fell over.

When Jook Jook awakened me the next morning, I felt terrible. I could not be sure what had happened the previous night. "What am I doing here?" I asked. I'd slept on an old car seat in Jook Jook's living room.

"You don't know?" He was cooking something on a Coleman stove in the back of the room.

I thought for a while; my mind began to clear. "How come Dad didn't take me home?"

"We lie you on de bed when you fall. An' I tell you daddy not to wake you, dat I carry you cross dis mornin' when I bring Zoe."

"I'm so sorry, Jook Jook!"

He did not answer. After a couple of minutes he came over and told me I needed to put something in my stomach. He led me to the table where he'd set a bowl of boiled fish and a small Johnny cake. He handed me a spoon and sat opposite. We looked at each other.

"Eat, boy."

"Where's Zoe?"

"I gon wake she jus' now. She up de whole night cryin'."

"She'll never talk to me again!"

"Eat!"

I'd never eaten fish soup before, and I didn't want to that morning, but I ate. Jook Jook watched until I finished, then he went to the bedroom to get Zoe.

For the first time I did not mind the slow speed of Jook Jook's dinghy. The water and the air were still, the sky vacant. He stood beside me on the bench steering, and she sat at my other side, looking away at the sea. As the little engine struggled on in vain to conquer the silence, I wiped my eyes clean and reached into the bilge for a leaf. I stared at it in my hand for so long my fingers began to feel numb. Not until I closed my eyes for a moment and allowed my thoughts to find a center, could I brush the leaf along her bare shoulder. She allowed me this, and I put the leaf on my tongue and imagined that it could melt slowly in my mouth, could cool my hot insides.

MARGARET ATWOOD

THE
SALT GARDEN

FROM MS.

§

ALMA TURNS UP THE HEAT, stirs the clear water in the red enamel pot, adds more salt, stirs, adds. She's making a supersaturated solution: remaking it. She made it already, at lunchtime, with Carol, but she didn't remember that you had to boil the water and she just used hot water from the tap. Nothing happened, though Alma had promised that a salt tree would form on the thread they hung down into the water, suspending it from a spoon laid crossways on the top of the glass.

"It takes time," Alma said. "It'll be here when you come home," and Carol went trustingly back to school, while Alma tried to figure out what she'd done wrong.

This experiment thing is new. Alma isn't sure where Carol picked it up. Surely not from school: she's only in Grade Two. But they're doing everything younger and younger.

Alma has racked her brains, as she always does when Carol expresses interest in anything, searching for information she ought to possess but usually doesn't. These days, Alma encourages anything that will involve the two of them in an activity that will block out questions about the way they're living; about the whereabouts of Mort, for instance. She's tried trips to the zoo, sewing dolls' dresses, movies on Saturdays. They all work, but only for a short time.

When the experiments came up, she remembered about putting vinegar into baking soda, to make it fizz; that was a success. Then other things started coming back to her. Now she can recall having been given a small chemistry set as a child, at the age of ten or so it must have been, by her father, who had theories in advance of his time. He thought girls should be brought up more like boys, possibly because he had no sons: Alma is an only child. Also he wanted her to do better than he himself had done. He had a job beneath his capabilities, in the post office, and he felt thwarted by that.

He'd tried to interest Alma in chess and mathematics and stamp collecting, among other things. Not much of this rubbed off on Alma, at least not to her knowledge; at the predictable age she became disappointingly obsessed with makeup and clothes, and her algebra marks took a downturn. But she does retain a clear image of the chemistry set, with its miniature test tubes and the wire holder for them, the candle for heating them, and the tiny corked bottles, so appealingly like doll-house glassware, with the mysterious substances in them: crystals, powders, solutions, potions. Some of these things had undoubtedly been poisonous; probably you could not buy such chemistry sets for children now. Alma is glad not to have missed out on it, because it was alchemy, after all, and that was how the instruction book presented it: magic. *Astonish your friends. Turn water to milk. Turn water to blood.* She remembers terminology, too, though the meanings have grown hazy with time. *Precipitate. Sublimation.*

There was a section on how to do tricks with ordinary household objects, such as how to make a hard-boiled egg go into a milk bottle, back in the days when there were milk bottles. It's from this part of the instruction book (the best section, because who could resist the thought of mysterious powers hidden in the ordinary things around you?) that she's called back the supersaturated solution and the thread: *How to make a magical salt garden.* It was one of her favorites.

Alma's mother had complained about the way Alma was using up the salt, but her father said it was a cheap price to pay for the development of Alma's scientific curiosity. He thought Alma was learning about the spaces between molecules, but it was no such thing, as Alma and her mother both silently knew.

Her mother was Irish, in dark contrast to her father's clipped and cheerfully bitter Englishness; she read tea leaves for the neighbor women, which only they regarded as a harmless amusement. Maybe it's from her that Alma has inherited her bad days, her stretches of fatalism. Her mother didn't agree with her father's theories about Alma, and emptied out her experiments whenever possible. For her mother, Alma's fiddling in the kitchen was merely an excuse to avoid work, but Alma wasn't thinking even of that. She just liked the snowfall in miniature, the enclosed, protected world in the glass, the crystals forming on the thread, like the pictures of the Snow Queen's palace in the Hans Christian Andersen book at school. She can't remember ever having astonished any of her friends with tricks from the instruction book. Astonishing herself was enough.

The water in the pot is boiling again, it's still clear. Alma adds more salt, stirs while it dissolves, adds more. When salt gathers at the bottom of the pot, swirling instead of vanishing, she turns off the heat. She puts another spoon into the glass before pouring the hot water into it: otherwise the glass might break.

She picks up the spoon with the thread tied to it and begins to lower the thread into the glass. While she is doing this, there is a sudden white flash, and the kitchen is blotted out with light. Her hand goes blank, then appears before her again, black, like an afterimage on the retina. The outline of the window remains, framing her hand, which is still suspended above the glass. Then the window itself crumples inward, in fragments, like the candy-crystal of a shatterproof windshield. The wall will be next, curving in toward her like the side of an inflating balloon. In an instant Alma will realize that the enormous sound has come and gone and burst her eardrums so that she is deaf, and then a wind will blow her away.

*   *   *

Alma closes her eyes. She can go on with this, or she can try to stop, hold herself upright, get the kitchen back. This isn't an unfamiliar experience. It's happened to her now on the average of once a week, for three months or more; but though she can predict the frequency, she never knows when. It can be at any moment, when she's run the bathtub full of water and is about to step in, when she's sliding her arms into the sleeves of her coat, when she's making love, with Mort or Theo, it could be either of them and it has been. It's always when she's thinking about something else.

It isn't speculation: it's more like a hallucination. She's never had hallucinations before, except a long time ago when she was a student and dropped acid a couple of times.

But none of it had been like this. It's occurred to her that maybe these things are acid flashes, though why would she be getting them now, fifteen years later, with none in between? At first she was so badly frightened that she'd considered going to see someone about it: a doctor, a psychiatrist. Maybe she's borderline epileptic. Maybe she's becoming schizophrenic or otherwise going mad. But there don't seem to be any other symptoms: just the flash and the sound, and being blown through the air, and the moment when she hits and falls into darkness.

The first time, she ended up lying on the floor. She'd been with Mort then, having dinner in a restaurant, during one of their interminable conversations about how things could be arranged better. Mort loves the word "arrange," which is not one of Alma's favorites. Alma is a romantic: if you love someone, what needs arranging? And if you don't, why put in the effort? Mort, on the other hand, has been reading books about Japan; also he thinks they should draw up a marriage contract. On that occasion, Alma pointed out that they were already married. She wasn't sure where Japan fitted in: if he wanted her to scrub his back, that was all right, but she didn't want to be Wife Number One, not if it implied a lot of other numbers, either in sequence or simultaneously.

Mort has a girlfriend, or that's how Alma refers to her. Terminology is becoming difficult these days: "mistress" is no longer suitable, conjuring up as it does peach-colored negligees trimmed in fur, and mules, which nobody wears any more; nobody, that is, like Mort's girlfriend, who is a squarely built young woman with a blunt-cut pageboy and freckles. And "lover" doesn't seem to go with the emotions Mort appears to feel toward this woman, whose name is Fran. Fran isn't the name of a mistress or a lover; more of a wife, but Alma is the wife. Maybe it's the name that's confusing Mort. Maybe that's why he feels, not passion or tenderness or devotion toward this woman, but a mixture of anxiety, guilt, and resentment, or this is what he tells Alma. He sneaks out on Fran to see Alma and calls Alma from telephone booths, and Fran doesn't know about it, which is the reverse of the way things used to be. Alma feels sorry for Fran, which is probably a defense.

It's not Fran that Alma objects to, as such. It's the rationalization of Fran. It's Mort proclaiming that there's a justifiable and even moral reason for doing what he does, that it falls into subsections, that men are polygamous by nature and so forth. That's what Alma can't stand. She herself does what she does because it's what she does, but she doesn't preach about it.

The dinner was more difficult for Alma than she'd anticipated, and because of this she had an extra drink. She stood up to go to the bathroom, and then it happened. She came to covered with wine and part of the tablecloth. Mort told her she'd fainted. He didn't say so, but she knew he put it down to hysteria, brought on by her problems with him, which to this day neither of them have precisely defined but which he thinks of as her problems, not his. She also knew that he thought she did it on purpose, to draw attention to herself, to collect sympathy and concern from him, to get him to listen to her. He was irritated. "If you were feeling dizzy," he said, "you should have gone outside."

Theo, on the other hand, was flattered when she passed out in his arms. He put it down to an excess of sexual passion, brought on by his technique, although again he didn't say so. He was quite pleased with her, and rubbed her hands and brought her a glass of water.

Theo is Alma's lover: no doubt about the terminology

there. She met him at a party. He introduced himself by asking
if she'd like another drink. (Mort, on the other hand, introduced himself by asking if she knew that if you cut the whis-
kers off cats they would no longer be able to walk along fences,
which should have been a warning of some kind to Alma, but
was not.) She was in a tangle with Mort, and Theo appeared to
be in a similar sort of tangle with his wife, so they seemed to
each other comparatively simple. That was before they had
begun to accumulate history, and before Theo had moved out
of the house. At that time they had been clutchers, specialists
in hallways and vestibules, kissing among the hung-up coats
and the rows of puddling rubbers.

Theo is a dentist, though not Alma's dentist. If he were
her dentist, Alma doubts that she ever would have ended up
having what she still doesn't think of as an affair with him. She
feels that the inside of her mouth, and especially the insides of
her teeth, are intimate in an antisexual way; surely a man
would be put off by such evidences of bodily imperfection, of
rot. (Alma doesn't have bad teeth; still, even a look inside with
that little mirror, even the terminology, *orifice, cavity, mandi-
ble, molar . . .*)

Dentistry, for Theo, is hardly a vocation. He hadn't felt
called by teeth; he told her he picked dentistry because he
didn't know what else to do; he had good small-muscle coordi-
nation, and it was a living, to put it mildly.

"You could have been a gigolo," Alma said to him on that
occasion. "You would have got extra in tips." Theo, who does
not have a rambunctious sense of humor and is fastidious about
clean underwear, was on the verge of being shocked, which
Alma enjoyed. She likes making him feel more sexual than he
is, which in turn makes him more sexual. She indulges him.

So, when she found herself lying on Theo's broadloom,
with Theo bending over her, gratified and solicitous, saying
"Sorry, was I too rough?" she did nothing to correct his
impression.

"It was like a nuclear explosion," she said, and he thought
she was using a simile. Theo and Mort have one thing in
common: they've both elected themselves as the cause of these
little manifestations of hers. That, or female body chemistry:

another good reason why women shouldn't be allowed to be airplane pilots, a sentiment Alma once caught Theo expressing.

The content of Alma's hallucinations doesn't surprise her. She suspects that other people are having similar or perhaps identical experiences, just as (for instance), during the Middle Ages, many people saw the Virgin Mary, or witnessed miracles: flows of blood that stopped at the touch of a bone, pictures that spoke, statues that bled. As for now, you could get hundreds of people to swear they've been on spaceships and talked with extraterrestrial beings. These kinds of delusions go in waves, Alma thinks, in epidemics. Her light shows, her blackouts, are no doubt as common as measles, only people aren't admitting to them. Most likely they're doing what she should do, trotting off to their doctors and getting themselves renewable prescriptions for Valium or some other pill that will smooth out the brain. They don't want anyone to think they're unstable, because although most would agree that what she's afraid of is something it's right to be afraid of, there's a consensus about how much. Too much fear is not normal.

Mort, for instance, thinks everyone should sign petitions and go on marches. He signs petitions himself, and brings them for Alma to sign, on occasions when he's visiting her legitimately. If she signed them during one of his sneak trips, Fran would know and put two and two together, and by now not even Alma wants that. She likes Mort better now that she sees less of him. Let Fran do his laundry, for a change. He goes on the marches with Fran, however, as they are more like a social occasion. It's for this reason that Alma herself doesn't attend the marches: she doesn't want to make things awkward for Fran, who is touchy enough already on the subject of Alma. There are certain things, like parent-teacher conferences, that Mort is allowed to attend with Alma, and other things that he isn't. Mort is sheepish about these restrictions, since one of his avowed reasons for leaving Alma was that he felt too tied down.

Alma agrees with Mort about the marches and petitions— out loud, that is. It's reasonable to suppose that if only everyone in the world would sign the petitions and go on the marches, the catastrophe itself would not occur. Now is the time to stand up and be counted, to throw your body in front of the juggernaut, as Mort himself does in the form of donations to peace groups and letters to politicians, for which he receives tax receipts and neatly typed form letters in response. Alma knows that Mort's way makes sense, or as much sense as anything, but she has never been a truly sensible person. This was one of her father's chief complaints about her. She could never bring herself to squeeze in her two hands the birds that flew into their plate-glass window and injured themselves, as her father taught her to do, in order to collapse their lungs. Instead, she wanted to keep them in boxes filled with cotton wool and feed them with an eyedropper, thus causing them—according to her father—to die a lingering and painful death. So he would collapse their lungs himself, and Alma would refuse to look, and grieve afterward.

Marrying Mort was not sensible. Getting involved with Theo was not sensible, Alma's clothes are not and never have been sensible, especially the shoes. So, in the face of Mort's hearty optimism, Alma shrugs inwardly. She tries hard to believe, but she's an infidel and not proud of it. The sad truth is that there are probably more people in the world like her than like Mort. Anyway, there's a lot of money tied up in those bombs. She doesn't interfere with him or say anything negative, however. The petitions are as constructive a hobby as any, and the marches keep him active and happy. He's a muscular man with a reddish face, who's inclined to overweight and who needs to work off energy to avoid the chance of a heart attack, or that's what the doctor says.

Theo, on the other hand, deals with the question by not dealing with it at all. He lives his life as if it isn't there, a talent for obliviousness that Alma envies. He just goes on filling teeth, filling teeth, as if all the tiny adjustments he's making to people's mouths are still going to matter in ten years, or five or even two. Maybe, Alma thinks in her more cynical moments, they can use his dental records for identification when they're sorting out the corpses, if there are any left to sort; if sorting will be a priority, which she very much doubts. Alma has tried to talk about it, once or twice, but Theo has said he doesn't see any percentage in negative thinking. It will happen or it won't, and if it doesn't, the main worry will be the economy. Theo makes investments. Theo is planning his retirement. Theo has tunnel vision and Alma doesn't. She has no faith in people's ability to pull themselves out of this hole, and no sand to stick her head into. The thing is there, standing in one corner of whatever room she happens to be in, like a stranger whose face you know you could see clearly if you were only to turn your head. Alma doesn't turn her head. She doesn't want to look. She goes about her business, most of the time; except for these minor lapses.

Sometimes she tells herself that this isn't the first time people have thought they were coming to the end of the world. It's happened before, during the Black Death, for instance, which Alma remembers as having been one of the high points of second year university. The world hadn't come to an end, but that wasn't the point. Believing it was going to had much the same effect.

Some of them decided it was their fault and went around flagellating themselves, or each other, or anyone else handy. Or they prayed a lot, which was easier then because you had some idea of who you were supposed to be talking to. Alma doesn't think this is a dependable habit of mind any more, since there's an even chance that the button will be pushed by some American religious maniac who wants to play God and help Revelation along, someone who really believes that he and a few others will be raised up incorruptible afterward, and therefore everyone else can rot.

Or you could wall yourself up, throw the corpses outside, carry around oranges stuck with cloves. Dig shelters. Issue instructional handbooks.

Or you could steal things from the empty houses, strip the necklaces from the bodies.

Or you could do what Mort was doing. Or you could do what Theo was doing. Or you could do what Alma was doing.

Alma thinks of herself as doing nothing. She goes to bed at night, she gets up in the morning, she takes care of Carol, they eat, they talk, sometimes they laugh; she sees Mort, she sees

Theo, she looks for a better job, though not in a way that convinces her. She thinks about going back to school and finishing her degree: Mort says he will pay, they've both agreed he owes her that, though when it comes right down to it she isn't sure she wants to. She has emotions: she loves people, she feels anger, she is happy, she gets depressed. But somehow she can't treat these emotions with as much solemnity as she once did. Never before has her life felt so effortless, as if all responsibility has been lifted from her. She floats. There's a commercial on television, for milk she thinks, which shows a man riding at the top of a wave on a surfboard: moving, yet suspended, as if there is no time. This is how Alma feels: removed from time. Time presupposes a future. Sometimes she experiences this state as apathy, other times as exhilaration. She can do what she likes. But what does she like?

She remembers something else they did during the Black Death: they indulged themselves. They pigged out on their winter supplies, they stole food and gorged, they danced in the streets, they copulated indiscriminately with whoever was available. Is this where she's heading, on top of her wave?

Alma rests the spoon on the two edges of the glass. Now the water is cooling and the salt is coming out of solution. It forms small transparent islands on the surface which thicken as the crystals build up, then break and drift down through the water, like snow. She can see a faint white fuzz of salt gathering on the thread. She kneels so that her eyes are level with the glass, rests her chin and hands on the table, watches. It's still magic. By the time Carol comes home from school, there will be a whole winter in the glass. The thread will be like a tree after a sleet storm. She can't believe how beautiful this is.

After a while she gets up and walks through her house, through the whitish living room which Mort considers Japanese in the less-is-more tradition, but which has always reminded her of a paint-by-numbers page only a quarter filled in, past the naked-wood end wall, up the staircase from which Mort removed the banisters. He also took out too many walls, omitted too many doors; maybe that's what went wrong with the marriage. The house is in Cabbagetown, one of the larger ones. Mort, who specializes in renovations, did it over and likes to bring people there to display it to them. He views it, still, as the equivalent of an advertising brochure. Alma, who is getting tired of going to the door in her second-best dressing gown with her hair in a towel and finding four men in suits standing outside it, headed by Mort, is thinking about getting the locks changed. But that would be too definitive. Mort still thinks of the house as his, and he thinks of her as part of the house.

She reaches the white-on-white bathroom, turns on the taps, fills the tub with water which she colors blue with a capful of German bath gel, climbs in, sighs. She has some friends who go to isolation tanks and float in total darkness for hours on end, claiming that this is relaxing and also brings you in touch with your deepest self. Alma has decided to give this experience a pass. Nevertheless, the bathtub is where she feels safest (she's never passed out in the bathtub) and at the same time most vulnerable (what if she were to pass out in the bathtub? She might drown).

At one period, long ago it seems now, though it's really just a couple of months, Alma indulged from time to time in a relatively pleasant fantasy. In this fantasy she and Carol were living on a farm, on the Bruce Peninsula. She'd gone on a vacation there once, with Mort, back before Carol was born, when the marriage was still behaving as though it worked. She'd noticed the farms then, how meager they were, how marginal; it was one of these farms she chose for her fantasy, on the theory that nobody else would want it.

She and Carol heard about the coming strike on the radio, as they were doing the dishes in the farm kitchen after lunch. (Improbable in itself, she now realizes: it would be too fast for that, too fast to reach a radio show.) Luckily, they raised all their own vegetables, so they had lots around. Initially Alma was vague about what these would be. She'd included celery, erroneously, she knows now: you could never grow celery in soil like that.

Alma's fantasies are big on details. She roughs them in first, then goes back over them, putting in the buttons and zippers. For this one she needed to make a purchase of appro-

priate seeds, and to ask for advice from the man in the hard-
ware store.

"Celery?" he said. "Up here? Lady, you must be joking."
So Alma did away with the celery, which wouldn't have kept
well anyway.

But there were beets and carrots and potatoes, things that
could be stored. They'd dug a large root cellar into the side of a
hill; it was entered by a door that slanted and that somehow
had several feet of dirt stuck onto the outside of it. But the root
cellar was much more than a root cellar: it had several rooms,
for instance, and electric lights. Anyway, when they heard the
news on the radio, she and Carol did not panic. They walked,
they did not run, sedately to the root cellar, where they went
inside and shut the door behind them. On the shelves built
neatly into one wall were rows and rows of bottled water.
There they stayed, eating carrots and playing cards and reading
entertaining books, until it was safe to come out, into a world
in which the worst had already happened so no longer needed
to be feared.

This fantasy is no longer functional. For one thing, it
could not be maintained for very long in the concrete detail
Alma finds necessary before practical questions with no answers began to intrude (ventilation?). In addition, Alma had
only an approximate idea of how long they would have to stay
in there before the danger would be over. And then there was
the problem of refugees, marauders, who would somehow find
out about the potatoes and carrots and come with (guns? sticks?).
Since it was only her and Carol, the weapons were hardly
needed. Alma began to equip herself with a rifle, then rifles, to
fend off these raiders, but she was always outnumbered and
outgunned.

The major flaw, however, was that even when things worked
and escape and survival were possible, Alma found that she
couldn't just go off like that and leave other people behind. She
wanted to include Mort, even though he'd behaved badly and
they weren't exactly together, and if she let him come she could
hardly neglect Theo. But Theo could not come, of course,
without his wife and children, and then there was Mort's
girlfriend Fran, whom it would not be fair to exclude.

This arrangement worked for a while, without the quarreling Alma would have expected. The prospect of imminent death is sobering, and Alma basked for a time in the gratitude her generosity inspired. She had intimate chats with the two other women about their respective men, and found out several things she didn't know; the three of them were on the verge of becoming really good friends. In the evenings they sat around the kitchen table that had appeared in the root cellar, peeling carrots together in a companionable way and reminiscing about what it had been like when they all lived in the city and didn't know each other, except obliquely through the men. Mort and Theo sat at the other end, drinking the Scotch they'd brought with them, mixed with bottled water. The children got on surprisingly well together.

But the root cellar was too small really, and there was no way to enlarge it without opening the door. Then there was the question of who would sleep with whom and at what times. Concealment was hardly possible in such a confined space, and there were three women but only two men. This was all too close to real life for Alma, but without the benefit of separate dwellings.

After the wife and the girlfriend started to insist on having their parents and aunts and uncles included (and why had Alma left hers out?), the fantasy became overpopulated and, very quickly, uninhabitable. Alma could not choose, that was her difficulty. It's been her difficulty all her life. She can't draw the line. Who is she to decide, to judge people like that, to say who must die and who is to be given a chance at life?

The hill of the root cellar, honeycombed with tunnels, too thoroughly mined, fell in upon itself, and all perished.

When Alma has dried herself off and is rubbing body lotion on herself, the telephone rings.

"Hi, what are you up to?" the voice says.

"Who is this?" Alma says, then realizes that it's Mort. She's embarrassed not to have recognized his voice. "Oh, it's you," she says. "Hi. Are you in a phone booth?"

"I thought I might drop by," says Mort, conspiratorially. "That is, if you'll be there."

"With or without a committee?" Alma says.

"Without," says Mort. What this means is clear enough. "I thought we could make some decisions." He means to be gently persuasive, but comes through as slightly badgering.

Alma doesn't say that he doesn't need her to help him make decisions, since he seems to make them swiftly enough on his own. "What kind of decisions?" she says warily. "I thought we were having a moratorium on decisions. That was your last decision."

"I miss you," Mort says, letting the words float, his voice shifting to a minor key that is supposed to indicate yearning.

"I miss you too," says Alma, hedging her bets. "But this afternoon I promised Carol I'd buy her a pink gym suit. How about tonight?"

"Tonight isn't an option," says Mort.

"You mean you aren't allowed out to play?" says Alma.

"Don't be snarky," Mort says a little stiffly.

"Sorry," says Alma, who isn't. "Carol wants you to come on Sunday to watch 'Fraggle Rock' with her."

"I want to see you alone," Mort says. But he books himself in for Sunday anyway, saying he'll double-check it and call her back. Alma says good-bye and hangs up, with a sense of relief that is very different from the feelings she's had about saying good-bye to Mort on the telephone in the past; which were, sequentially, love and desire, frustration because things weren't being said that ought to be, despair and grief, anger and a sense of being fucked over. She continues with the body lotion, with special attention to the knees and elbows. That's where it shows up first, when you start to look like a four-legged chicken. Despite the approach of the end of the world, Alma likes to keep in shape.

Theo lives in a two-bedroom apartment in a high rise not far from his office. Or at least Alma thinks he lives there. Though it makes her feel, not unpleasantly, a little like a call girl, it's where she meets him, because he doesn't like coming to her house. He still considers it Mort's territory. He doesn't think of Alma as Mort's territory, only the house, just as his own house, where his wife lives with their three children, is still his territory. That's how he speaks of it: "my house." He goes there on weekends, just as Mort goes to Alma's house. Alma suspects he and his wife sneak into bed, just as she and Mort do, feeling like students in a 'fifties dorm, swearing each other to secrecy. They tell themselves that it would never do for Fran to find out. Alma hasn't been explicit about Theo to Mort, though she's hinted that there's someone. That made him perk up. "I guess I have no right to complain," he said. "I guess you don't," said Alma. It's ridiculous to Alma not to go to bed with Mort. After all, he is her husband. It's something she's always done. Also, the current arrangement has done wonders for their sex life. Being a forbidden fruit suits her. She's never been one before.

But if Theo is still sleeping with his wife, Alma doesn't want to know about it. He has every right, in a way, but she would be jealous. Oddly enough, she doesn't much care any more what goes on between Mort and Fran. Mort is so thoroughly hers already; she knows every hair on his body, every wrinkle, every rhythm. She can relax into him with scarcely a thought, and she doesn't have to make much conscious effort to please him. It's Theo who's the unexplored territory, it's with Theo that she has to stay alert, go carefully, not allow herself to be lulled into a false sense of security: Theo, who at first glance appears so much gentler, more considerate, more tentative. For Alma, he's a swamp to Mort's forest: she steps lightly, ready to draw back. Yet it's his body—shorter, slighter, more sinewy than Mort's—she's possessive about. She doesn't want another woman touching it, especially one who's had more time to know it than she's had. The last time she saw Theo, he said he wanted to show her some recent snapshots of his family. Alma excused herself and went into the bathroom. She didn't want to see a picture of Theo's wife, but also she felt that even to look would be a violation of both of them: the use, by Theo, of two women to cancel each other out. It's occurred to her that she is to Theo's wife as Mort's girlfriend is to her: the usurper, in a way, but also the one to be pitied because of what is not being admitted.

She knows that the present balance of power can't last. Sooner or later, pressures will be brought to bear. The men will not be allowed to drift back and forth between their women, their houses. Barriers will be erected, signs will go up: *Stay Put Or Get Out*. Rightly so; but none of these pressures will come from Alma. She likes things the way they are. She's decided that she prefers having two men rather than one: it keeps things even. She loves both of them, she wants both of them; which means, some days, that she loves neither and wants neither. It makes her less anxious and less vulnerable, and suggests multiple futures. Theo may go back to his wife, or wish to move in with Alma. (Recently he asked her an ominous question—"What do you want?"—which Alma dodged.) Mort may want to return, or he may decide to start over with Fran. Or Alma could lose both of them and be left alone with Carol. This thought, which would once have given rise to panic and depression not unconnected with questions of money, doesn't worry her much at the moment. She wants it to go on the way it is forever.

Alma steps into the elevator and is carried up. Weightlessness encloses her. It's a luxury; her whole life is a luxury. Theo, opening the door for her, is a luxury, especially his skin, which is smooth and well-fed and darker than hers. Theo amazes her, she loves him so much she can barely see him. Love burns her out; it burns out Theo's features so that all she can see in the dimmed apartment is an outline, shining. She's not on the wave, she's in it, warm and fluid. This is what she wants. They don't get as far as the bedroom, but collapse onto the living room rug, where Theo makes love to her as if he's running for a train he's never going to catch.

Time passes, and Theo's details reappear, a mole here, a freckle there. Alma strokes the back of his neck, lifting her hand to look surreptitiously at her watch: she has to be back in time for Carol.

"That was magnificent," says Alma. It's true.

Theo smiles, kisses the inside of her wrist, holds it for a few seconds as if listening for the pulse, picks up her half-slip from the floor, hands it to her with tenderness and deference, as if presenting her with a bouquet of flowers. As if she's dying, and only he knows it and wants to keep it from her.

"I hope," he says pleasantly, "that when this is all over we won't be enemies."

Alma freezes, the half-slip half on. Then air goes into her, a silent gasp, a scream in reverse, because she's noticed at once: he didn't say "if," he said "when." Inside his head there's a schedule. All this time during which she's been denying time, he's been checking off the days, doing a little countdown. He believes in predestination. He believes in doom. She should have known that, being such a neat person, he would not be able to stand anarchy forever. They must leave the water, then, and emerge onto dry land. She will need more clothes, because it will be colder there.

"Don't be silly," Alma says, pulling imitation satin up to her waist like a bedsheet. "Why would we?"

"It happens," says Theo.

"Have I ever done or said anything to make you feel it would happen to us?" Alma says. Maybe he's going back to his wife. Maybe he isn't, but has decided anyway that she will not do, not on a daily basis, not for the rest of his life. He still believes there will be one. So does she, or why would she be this upset?

"No," says Theo, scratching his leg, "but it's the kind of thing that happens." He stops scratching, looks at her, that look she used to consider sincere. "I just want you to know I like you too well for that."

Like. That finishes it, or does it? As often with Theo, she's unsure of what is being said. Is he expressing devotion, or has it ended already, without her having been aware of it? She's become used to thinking that in a relationship like theirs everything is given and nothing is demanded, but perhaps it's the other way around. Nothing is given. Nothing is even a given. Alma feels suddenly too visible, too blatant. Perhaps she should return to Mort, and become once more unseen.

"I like you too," she says. She finishes dressing, while he continues to lie on the floor, gazing at her fondly, like someone waving to a departing ship, who nevertheless looks forward to the moment when he can go and have his dinner. He doesn't care what she's going to do next.

"Day after tomorrow?" he says, and Alma, who wants to have been wrong, smiles back.

"Beg and plead," she says.

"I'm not good at it," he says. "You know how I feel."

Once, Alma would not even have paused at this; she would have been secure in the belief that he felt the same way she did. Now she decides that it's a matter of polite form with him to pretend she understands him.

"Same time?" she says.

The last of her buttons is done up. She'll pick up her shoes at the door. She kneels, leans over to kiss him good-bye. Then there is an obliterating flash of light, and Alma slides to the floor.

When she comes to, she's lying on Theo's bed. Theo is dressed (in case he had to call an ambulance, she thinks) and sitting beside her, holding her hand. This time he isn't pleased. "I think you have low blood pressure," he says, being unable to ascribe it to sexual excitement. "You should have it checked out."

"I thought maybe it was the real thing, this time," Alma whispers. She's relieved; she's so relieved the bed feels weightless beneath her, as if she's floating on water.

Theo misunderstands her. "You're telling me it's over?" he says, with resignation or eagerness, she can't tell.

"It's not over," Alma says. She closes her eyes; in a minute she'll feel less dizzy, she'll get up, she'll talk. Right now the salt drifts down behind her eyes, falling like snow, down through the ocean, past the dead coral, gathering on the branches of the salt tree that rises from the white crystal dunes below it. Scattered on the underwater sand are the bones of many small fish. It is so beautiful. Nothing can kill it. After everything is over, she thinks, there will still be salt.

MARTHA BAYLES
THE "NEW YORKER" STORY

FROM HARPER'S

§

WILLIAM HAS COMPLETED one paragraph of his new short fiction about a young woman who works in a J. C. Penney's department store. Striving for an atmosphere of depthless banality, he is imagining a shopping mall in one of those Midwestern states, Kansas or Indiana, where he might have ended up if his teaching position hadn't come through. He is still so relieved to have landed a decent creative-writing teaching job on the East Coast that he actually feels drawn to the idea of writing about a plastic, meaningless shopping mall: a palace of materialism surrounded by nothing but featureless wheat fields. It thrills him just a little to think how narrowly he's escaped.

Thanks to the editors at the *New Yorker*, William's talent was recognized in the nick of time. He probably wouldn't have gotten this great job if he hadn't been able to say casually that, oh yes, the *New Yorker* was going to print "Fred," his short fiction about a middle-aged, Midwestern Middle American who pumps gas, regular and diesel, at a 76 truck stop somewhere out there in that endless, anomic, checkerboard flatness: that heartland without a heart to which his imagination keeps returning.

Leaning forward in his chair, William looks over his opening paragraph.

Betty waits at the cash register, even though there is no one in her checkout line. Buffing her Honeybee Pink nails, she watches Mr. Schmidt dust the Home Glassware display. The display takes up an entire aisle, and Mr. Schmidt keeps it arranged by color. First the red, then the blue, then the yellow, in neat rows. All the glasses are the same shape, with a nubbly surface for easy grip. E-Z GRIP, the sign says. Betty wonders what it would be like if one of the glasses broke, whether the nubbles themselves would shatter or whether they would roll like little marbles across the floor.

Pretty good, thinks William. But "linoleum floor" would be better. He whites out "floor," ponders a minute, and then types "Congoleum no-wax floor." After another minute he adds, "the kind with the imitation mica."

Now he is ready to begin a new paragraph.

From the plastic rack next to the cash register Betty takes a stick of Vaseline Lip Balm and applies it to her Honeybee Pink lips. It is cola flavored. Mouth watering, she licks it off. Then she has to apply more Honeybee Pink.

Perfect, thinks William. There she is, out in consumerland; and the more she consumes, the emptier she feels. Eagerly, he goes on typing.

Her lips are drawn full, with a symmetrically tapered line, as though the makeup artist's hand had just withdrawn before the camera. Her face is an immaculate oval as delicate as an eggshell, defined by the smoothly plucked hairline and brows, the subtle trace of rouge underscoring the cheekbones, and the gold spirals of the Monet earrings. Her eyes are as brilliant as star sapphires in their cups of eye shadow and dramatically accented lash.

Her whispering mouth forms an elegant rosebud: "Lancôme, Paris."

Astounded, William pulls back. The page is almost full, which is good. But how oddly he has digressed! For a moment he considers whether to give rein to this impulse or to go back to his original conception. Before he can decide, another impulse carries him further.

Betty's expression does not change as Mr. Schmidt walks forward with a single goblet that, although it refracts all the colors of the other glassware through its richly faceted surface, is itself beautifully clear. He speaks in a deep brogue: "What is apparent to the cognoscenti is the affinity between the old and the new Waterford. Centuries have not altered . . ."

The deep brogue fades as the crystal grows larger, then fragments into seeds cut by a master hand to flash smaller, more numerous sparks. Arrayed across a black marble table-top, they dazzle, juxtaposed to a cameo portrait of Betty gazing over her black velvet shoulder. Her swelling pageboy and reproachfully arched brow bear a strong resemblance to Lauren Bacall, in whose husky voice she says, "Food, shelter, and diamonds are the essentials. The rest is luxury."

Now William has to stop. This is getting out of control. The Betty he started with wears an ankle chain linking the fake gold letters of her boyfriend's name, not 122 marquise diamonds. Concentrating hard, he tries to go back to the shopping mall.

It's not yet ten-thirty, but Betty goes early for her coffee break. Nor that it's much of a break to sit at the empty lunch counter with nothing to look at but the Tropical Punch circulating in its cooler. Betty wonders if they ever empty it out, or whether that same Tropical Punch has been circulating since the store opened five years ago.

Easing back against the striped canvas of her beach chair, Betty digs her toes into the sand. Under the thatched roof of her private cabana, which casts a cool lavender shade fretted with pink-gold sunlight, she gazes at a dark fringe of coconut palm and a brilliant turquoise ocean.

"Here we are," she says to Mr. Schmidt, who is ensconced in the other chair. "At home in our very own villa, all pastels and privacy. With Evangeline to pamper us: she's going shopping soon, to surprise us with a lobster for dinner."

"Madly extravagant?" asks Mr. Schmidt.

"Not at all," replies Betty. "There are hundreds of villas for rent, all over Jamaica."

"*Damn!*" cries William out loud. "What the hell is going on?" He is very surprised when Betty answers. No longer in the canvas chair, she now appears against the towers of Manhattan, seen at night through a glass wall on the fiftieth floor. In a beaded black gown, with her hair swirled sideways, she offers William a Hennessy V.S.O.P.

"Nothing." Her smile is alluring, her voice cold. "I'm just waiting for you to get started."

"I *am* started!" exclaims William.

"No you're not. You haven't even got a character."

"I've got *you*, a cashier at J. C. Penney's. You're wearing J. C. Penney imitation designer jeans and a red, white, and blue smock that says DOLLAR DAYS SALE."

Betty turns, revealing the graceful cut of her gown. "Is that all?"

"Certainly not," William snaps, and begins to describe the tacky merchandise she rings through the register all day, her boyfriend's four-wheel-drive pickup, the Denny's where they go for patty melts and thick shakes, the remote-control color television on which Betty's parents watch *Family Feud* . . . "I merely describe, I don't judge. You ought to appreciate that, at least."

She doesn't appear to. While he is talking, she strolls over to a baby grand piano and kicks off her gilt evening sandals. Pouring herself a Martell, she throws back her head. "So where is this going to be published?"

William feels a twinge of anxiety, but refuses to let it show. "Probably in the *New Yorker*."

"Oh, like the other one. Poor Fred."

"You know Fred?"

"Of course. To you, our town is just a cloverleaf on Route 80. But to us, it is the center of the universe. You may not

THE "NEW YORKER" STORY

know us, but we know each other. Fred, for example, is my oldest uncle on the German side."

"How do you know he's German? I didn't give him a last name."

"Oh, the town's full of Germans. Look at Mr. Schmidt. Do you know, we're having our centennial this year? One hundred years since our great-great-grandparents came from Russia."

William suppresses a smile. "Germans from Russia?"

"Oh yeah," she says, her voice beginning to warm up and take on a Kansas twang. "You see, this empress in Russia, Catherine the Great—you've heard of her? Good. Well, she got them to settle some scrubland by passing this law—"

William interrupts. "Please, please. I'm sure it's all very interesting, and I'm glad to see you talking with an authentic accent. But family sagas have nothing to do with my kind of fiction. I'm not James Michener."

Betty looks blank, so blank that William has to move closer. But even then all he can detect is a fragrance with that most exceptional of qualities: presence. "Only one woman could have created it," murmurs Betty. "Estée Lauder."

"Oh, knock it off!" shouts William.

"Sorry," says Betty, getting up and walking over to a chrome supper table set with black-and-gold-rimmed vichyssoise plates and flawless stemware. From the center of the table, against the delicate pinstriping of the dove-gray Levolor blinds, rises a tall, twisting bouquet of red poppies, pink orchids, and white flowering quince. Betty displays her bare back, warm and creamy smooth in the indirect track lighting. "Perhaps," she says huskily, "I can make it up to you by letting Lenox express my world."

William slams down his Hennessy. "*I'm* expressing your world, goddamn it!"

"Oh," says Betty, looking blank again.

William waits, but she doesn't do anything. Together with the chrome supper table, she is starting to fade. "Wait," he says. "You're out of place here. Tell me some more about Kansas."

"Bet I know what you want to hear about. My boyfriend.

He works for the phone company, and gosh, does he get jealous. I mean, real jealous. One time I was talking to this other guy, and later on that night my boyfriend *hit* me. Oh, he was real sorry, but still, he *hit* me. Isn't that awful?"

"Please," says William. "Go find one of my scribbling female colleagues, if all you want to do is criticize men."

For a moment, Betty dims. But then she brightens again, evidently because this is a story she wants very much to tell. "Uncle Fred has this buddy who hauls cattle. He's from Arkansas, and real scary-looking, with a patch over one eye? But Fred says he's been every place you'd care to name. Guff—that's his real name. 'Guff don't take no guff'—he's always saying that. Um—do you really want to hear this? It gets kind of weird."

For once, William doesn't try to hush her up. "Yes, yes. Go on."

"OK. Well . . . Guff kind of likes me. Like a father, I mean. So when my boyfriend hit me, you know what he told me to do? He said next time my boyfriend gets jealous, I ought to cuddle up real close, like I'm going to whisper sweet nothings. Then bite off a hunk of his ear and spit it out in his face. Guff says that'll teach him."

"Terrific!" exclaims William. "Bizarre! Emotionally flat, symbolically ambiguous! What a pure gesture!"

Betty just looks at him, eyes filling with tears. "You know, when Guff said that, I realized a whole lot of things. Like how much I love my boyfriend. I don't want to hurt him, but I realized, making somebody jealous is like biting them with your teeth—it's painful."

"Oh no," groans William, "not the moral of the story!"

"I realized something else, too. I think it's because my dad ran off when I was small . . . I expect the worst from my boyfriend. It's like I *try* to make him jealous, because I'm scared to get close. I'm scared he'll run off, too. Deep down, I'm just so afraid of love!"

The expression on her face is too mawkish for William, and he pulls back. "Please," he says levelly, "don't ask me to be a psychologist. Save that for the potboilers."

"Then what do you think I should do? My mom says talk

to Father Tim. But I can't apply religion to my problems. All I
know is, if I had to die for my boyfriend, I think I would. And
I know he feels the same way about me."

"*Stop! Please stop!*" Now William is shouting. "I'm a
postmodernist writer! No epiphanies, no romanticism! You
have to realize, I've accepted the void!"

"The what?"

William tries to calm himself. He picks up his Hennessy.
"Look. I like the part about Guff and the ear, but the last thing
I want to do is *explain* it. I want to *present* it as an utterly
pointless experience that *seems* to have meaning but is really
absurd. Like the rest of your existence."

"Oh," says Betty, turning slowly to look at him through a
pair of emerald-and-aqua-stippled glasses frames, curved to
emphasize the shape of her eyes. "Exotic," she breathes, "is
your Dior."

"Oh no, not *that* again. Look, Betty, dear. Will you do
me a big, fat favor and go back to J. C. Penney's where you
belong?"

Thoughtfully, Betty picks up a remote-control transmitter
and flicks on the Pioneer stereo system. Given the surroundings, William expects Kraftwerk, or possibly Schoenberg. But
no, it is the same mindless, sappy Muzak that has been playing
in the mall.

William leaps forward. "There, you *see*?!? *That's* why I
want you back in J. C. Penney's! Because you have no *taste*!"

Betty turns up the Muzak, then smiles. "Let me get this
straight. There's no meaning in the world, so all experiences are
equally pointless."

William waves his arms. "If you want to discuss my world
view, you're going to have to turn down that *garbage*!"

"Can I play something else?"

"Sure, if you can find anything tolerable."

Through her glasses Betty studies the tuning device, then
switches to a station playing one of Beethoven's last quartets.

"Much better," sighs William, "although I'm sure it's pure
luck. You know, you shouldn't fixate on all these expensive
luxuries if you don't know how to relate to them."

"Why not, if they give me pleasure?"

"Because they're just *objects*. They don't *define* you if you're not a certain kind of person to begin with."

Betty glides toward him on the polished floor, voice full of icy seductiveness. "How can you say they don't define me? Look at me."

"I am looking at you. And those glasses actually make you look intelligent. Maybe someday you'll figure out that a character is more than a collection of possessions. Don't you see? I could describe every jet bead on your evening gown, every imported wine in your closet, and it wouldn't add up to a human being. People are more than the sum total of their commercialized surroundings!"

"Even in this day and age?"

"Especially in this day and age."

"Well," says Betty sweetly. "In that case, I'll go back to J. C. Penney's."

MICHAEL COVINO

MONOLOGUE OF THE MOVIE MOGUL

FROM THE PARIS REVIEW

§

NO SOONER HAD I FINISHED WORKING, finished assembling the final cut of my movie, finished adjusting, finished revamping, finished splicing the last two images together, finished mixing the last two sets of sounds, finished adjusting the last two images to the last two sets of sounds, no sooner had I finished all this and resolved not to shift a single other image, nor to heighten or lower a single other sound, not even the merest chirp of a background cricket which can be so absolutely indispensable in the extramarginal manipulation of the poor moviegoer's mood—the placement of the merest chirp, or of the wrong quality of chirp, over the wrong image, over a hardwood forest (say) instead of over a pine forest, or making that chirp too loud, or too soft, or too shrill, or too deep, can be devastating to the whole effect of the most lavish, big-budget movie, can create a vibration that shakes and rattles the whole structure of the movie, that causes that structure to sway, shudder, and splinter asunder—yes, no sooner had I brought the movie to as satisfactory a state of completion as possible, as coherent an order of images and sounds as I would ever find, than I had to turn my full attention *immediately* to the preparations for the big weekend party that I was throwing

the next night at my country estate to celebrate the completion
of this very picture. I felt spent. Indeed. For a year I had
sequestered myself in my editing room with my editors and
sound people, and after having pressed my crew to work first
ten-hour days six days a week, then twelve-hour days seven
days a week, and then sixteen-hour days for months on end,
after having driven them like cattle, yelled at them like they
were dogs, shouted at them that this cut doesn't measure up,
this confluence of dialogue and melancholy patter of rain falls
miserably short, that this image of a single sickening tree against
the dusk sky—so poetic when isolated—is found wanting in the
larger context, after having made them do and then undo the
previous night's work not once but dozens of times, *hundreds*
of times—and there were times when the slightest distraction
would send me into a fury, when I locked into the movie
with a singlemindedness they found frightening, but I found
exhilarating)—for I worked without stopping, without pause,
with a mania and an obsessiveness for detail that is legendary in
the industry (and legends can always press for more money),
cloistered there in my editing room like a mad monk, because
nothing matters to me but my work, others work to live but I
live to work, indeed I am never happier, never more in love
than when I'm working, and love comes from my finest work;
yes, after having done all this and then, this past week, thanked
all my technicians and ushered them out and then *truly* focused
myself for a final one week stint of frightening intensity, of
furious concentration, a week during which I barely slept,
cutting, recutting, arranging, rearranging, not shaving, not eating, not washing, not changing my underwear, not moving my
bowels for days on end, *for the whole week,* reducing my life
to the utmost simplicity in order to complete this most complex, this most concentrated of movies, after all this—well!
—after all this I felt ready to relax and party a bit.

I telephoned my personal aide, my trusted lieutenant, who
had had the good sense, the great tact, the tremendous *decency,*
not to disturb me during the past and final week, even after the
five hundred invitations for the party had gone out and it
wasn't at all clear that I would emerge from my editing room
with a can of finished film in time to attend the party celebrat-

ing my having emerged from the editing room with a can of finished film, yes, I spoke to my lieutenant and told him that I was about to drive across town *from* my editing room *to* my house, where I would then attend to some neglected business matters (the possible collapse of my independent studio if I went any further over budget, some niggling actor's litigation over the profits from my last movie in which he had some points, overdue notes on my mortgaged country estate where the party was to be held, other minor irritants) and afterwards spend the night before driving up the next day to my country estate for the party, and he said, "Good," then mentioned in passing that a young visiting documentary director was staying at my house, had in fact been staying there the past few days while his film was screened at the local film archives and some other places. I said, "Fine, I'll be driving over myself," and hung up.

Actually, I already knew that this young filmmaker was staying at my house—I knew because I'd read about it in the so-called society column of our local newspaper's "society columnist," that prattling scandalmonger, that insufferable bilgebag, that *war correspondent* with his daily dispatches from the dinner tables of the very rich, forever issuing his snide or stupid or "clever" items about me from his regular column, from his little plot of turf in that weed patch he writes for, whether it's to hint at my latest mistress (he makes me green with envy of myself), or to dispense the opinions of an "informed industry source" on my latest not yet released—always "unreleasable"—film. Let's change the subject.

The ride across town was a pleasure. After the ardors and rigors of the past few months holed up in the airless, windowless basement editing room, it was a sheer pleasure to be negotiating nothing more complicated than traffic lights and wayward pedestrians in the cool afternoon sunlight. I felt like hitting a few—expendable extras in the over-budget production of life. So a young out-of-town director, a supposed up-and-comer, was staying at my house! I was not looking forward to company. When visiting directors are in town they are always welcome to stay at my house, it is a common courtesy I extend to all without expectation of repayment of any kind—certainly not monetary (I don't need it), still less veneration or idolization (hero worship nauseates me)—it doesn't even matter whether I am home; in fact, to be frank, I prefer *not* to be home since these visiting directors—inevitably younger, poorer, unknown, and a bit on the touchy side—usually end up, usually *start up*, asking me for production money, one director I put up later complained bitterly that despite his international reputation in art film circles, *in the art house ghetto,* I wouldn't even spare him ten minutes, which was true enough, his films disgust me, they reflect a certain crepuscular sentimentality, a hidebound romantic insularity—

Nonetheless, my maid is always present, the large refrigerator is kept well-stocked, and they are given the complete run of the house, the ingrates, and my lieutenant even arranges to screen a film or two of theirs in my comfortable basement screening room with all my staff invited.

But now I had to go home and attend to last-minute odds and ends before driving up to my country estate, and a young documentary filmmaker from out of town was staying over, his first film was being screened that week and, according to my lieutenant, had received extraordinary notices in the film quarterlies, which I could care less about. No, I was not looking forward to company. Most of these visiting directors are hopeless young hotheads bubbling over with powerful convictions, staunch theoretical beliefs, art directors who film an interview in which a single person talks in a monotone directly into the camera for a fortnight; and then the director has the nerve to babble to me after the screening about how the uncompromising neutrality of the camera in his film forces the viewer out of his old, easy, comfortable, bourgeois viewing position *blah blah blah*—the poor unsuspecting viewer for whom we should show more love—yes, these directors run on as if boredom is beneath them, is too banal for them to even consider.

Then another one, a very earnest young political filmmaker, starts telling me that the recurring images of women and violence in my pictures cannot be used, however critical my intent (and he assured me he did believe my intent was critical!), without some degree of complicity, a certain collusion that reeks of the brothel slaughterhouse. Of course, at a party that very evening, after prevailing upon me all afternoon to look at his film, our young political director was prevailing quite drunkenly upon the young beauty whose beauty I had made capital of in my last box office smash. Bad faith! It is easy to grow cynical in my position, where the supplicant's contradictory demands on his master justify the king's contempt. Yes, these artistic directors speak of how their concerns necessitate their making films that are strictly unviewable, and then they come and sniff around my mansion, poke their noses into my wine cellar, remove their boots and socks in the dead of winter to stick an experimental toe in my heated outdoor pool. For art and business, which might seem separate, are insolubly linked, you cannot separate the problem of finance from the problem of the frame, legal tender from the long take, cash from cutting, or the dollar sign from the dolly shot. Money is articulate. Something else: I find bankers more honest than your average "artistic" director, or your average *cinéaste*, or your average film archivist. At least the banker will let you know in no uncertain terms when your film stinks—money invested is money watched, that is, money whets the senses. Unlike purists and artists, bankers are not contaminated by quaint notions of purity and art.

But neither was this visiting documentary director, according to my lieutenant, who laughingly had told me how this young man had received a large government humanities grant and then one week later received a duplicate check in the mail by mistake, which he did not return but immediately cashed. "A man after your own heart," my lieutenant had chortled, but my lieutenant had better watch it.

I arrived home, parked my car, and went directly into the kitchen for a beer—there were none. The visiting director wandered in—sipping a beer. He was tall but walked swaybacked, no, *hunchbacked*, he had incredibly poor posture, in fact despite his height he gave exactly the *opposite* impression, the *contrary* impression, that of being a gnome, and his blue right eye, which was dead, drifted aimlessly in its socket while the blue left one simply, *coolly*, fixed on me; to be frank, this unsymmetrical, misshapen, ill-proportioned, *twisted* human form looked like a cretin, a natural idiot if I ever saw one. He mumbled, "Hello," then shambled past me, tossed the beer can in the wastebasket, opened the refrigerator, muttered disappointedly—and was gone. I stood there dumbstruck.

Nevertheless, I got on with my afternoon's business. And over the course of the rest of the afternoon, whenever we would brush past one another, be it in the hallway, or in the living room, *or in the kitchen*, he would sort of shrink back—I won't say he was exactly intimidated by me, but in his shrinking back I sensed a curious, mixed-up disdain, as though he scorned not just me but himself—and not because he was too timid to hustle me, but because he was weak enough, status-conscious enough, *ambivalent* enough, to be there in the first place instead of just putting up in some anonymous suburban motor lodge.

My lieutenant had recommended, very gently, that I view this young director's film before driving up to the party; it wasn't even a feature film but—of all things!—a documentary about the chicken industry and methods of fattening chickens. I made inquiries. An industrial short? Another tiresome exposé of merchandising practices? No, my lieutenant said cautiously, not exactly; but then all he could do was mumble something about "rigorous" and "insidious" and "very funny" and "highly original." But "rigorous" is a word only restaurant reviewers should use, *This rigorous steak.* . . . My lieutenant didn't really push me, he knows when to push and when not to, he himself obviously felt diffident and defensive about it. Besides, he won't go out on a limb for anyone unless he knows there's a safety net spread taut beneath him, and anyway I was incredibly busy that afternoon what with money matters and calling the labs to arrange for answer prints of the film, which was already nine million dollars *over budget* and six months *behind schedule*, the studio executives were howling as usual; but as an older filmmaker once told me, "The eye that knows its business won't be told to edit better or faster." Let the interest on the bank loans accumulate; making films and making money are two different things, though to be honest my films have made a bundle. At any rate, this younger director didn't try to sell me a bill of goods so much as skulk and slink around my house, and this to tell the truth got on my nerves worse than if he had been hustling me.

Night fell. Soon I was tired and decided I wanted to sleep in the second floor corner bedroom with the northeast exposure affording a view of the bay—no one bedroom is mine and depending on the seasons, and the weather, and the moon, and my mood, I will sleep in whichever bedroom pleases me. Actually, the more homes I own in different parts of the country the less I feel at home *anywhere,* the more I feel like a vagabond, a rootless wanderer, a forlorn nomad. But this is neither here nor there. I told my maid which bedroom to prepare, and she hesitated just an instant but an instant long enough to make me ask, "What's wrong?" and she explained that nothing was wrong, nothing at all, it was just that the young visiting director had been sleeping in that room, but of course it was no problem, no problem at all, there were more bedrooms to spare—twelve of them in fact—and I nodded and said, "Don't forget to change the sheets."

That night however I felt *uneasy.* The corner bedroom, besides its own bathroom, has two doors which swing open into it, one from the hallway and the other from the adjoining bedroom—into which the visiting director had moved himself— and both doors have keyholes which yield *full, unimpeded views of the bedroom.* For some reason, as I sat up in bed late that night reading over company finance reports, I imagined that damned documentary director's single blue eye fixed on his bedroom keyhole watching, scrutinizing, analyzing, *registering,* my every move. I put down the reports. I got up. I turned off the light, climbed back into bed, and then burrowed deep down under the thick, heavy blankets. In the dark I kept *absolutely still.* Nonetheless, I couldn't shake the feeling that his single damned eye was still glued to that keyhole, as if the eye came outfitted with an infrared scope. What a nightmare! Nor could I get up and check, for what if I should put my own eyeball to my side of the keyhole and suddenly find myself eyeball to eyeball with that screwball, *then what*? I pondered my dilemma carefully. I thought about it long and hard. *And then it came to me.* I got up, tiptoed into the darkened bathroom, groped in the medicine cabinet for the box of adhesive bandages, and removed two one-inch strips. Darling Band-Aids! I taped one of these over the keyhole to his bedroom, and the other over the keyhole to the hallway—just in case. There! Not for nothing am I considered one of the most resourceful filmmakers in the business. Now I would be able to sleep untroubled.

But I didn't sleep untroubled. *I couldn't sleep.* I started thinking about the film and one cut in particular—from a shot of a seagull flying over a lake at dusk, to a shot of my protagonist staring out the lakeshore window—a cut I'd arranged and then rearranged and *deranged* dozens of times, to no avail, a cut I'd agonized over, and which now, thinking back, I realized was simply execrable. I had to get that damn film out of my head. I thought of the gross of my last movie, of my country estate where even now my dear wife was overseeing the last-minute preparations for tomorrow night's big party in celebration of the movie I had finished this afternoon, that even now I was agonizing over, *that I was just beginning to realize I hadn't yet finished.* I thought of my vast real estate holdings, restaurants, bowling alleys, suburban motor lodges, my investment portfolio, my liquid assets, my frozen assets, the numbered overseas accounts, the gold coins and jewels secreted in various safety deposit vaults all across the country, and how everything was riding on the success of this movie—and I felt frightened. I remembered the days when I was a mere script reader and often found myself at the mercy of stupid superiors, *inferior* superiors, and how easy it is to be broken in such situations, how much self-determination and will it took to stay strong, to maintain my own vision, and how now it was *my* task to stay receptive to anyone around me who, though my inferior, might well indeed be my superior, and how I mustn't destroy such a person but help him. And often had my wife professed that she recognized me in the strong-willed protagonists of my movies, be they gangsters or renegade soldiers or just a young boy coming of age, yes, my wife saw me, her husband, in my movies, she detected a vestige of personal flavor, of an intensely private sensibility, in those huge, impersonal, expensive, commercial blockbusters that I'd directed. If my gangster looked a police officer straight in the eye, *expres-*

sionlessly in the eye, then my wife would claim that that was exactly how I went about intimidating her, not to mention the various studio executives I was always bullying into signing over more checks whenever I went over budget.

There is no peace for me anymore. And sometimes I think it would be so nice just to be a quiet, inconspicuous nobody, some anonymous editing technician with no ambition or drive; but of course it is far too late for that. Yet other times I think that nothing would make sounder investment sense than to purchase some small tropical nation on the verge of bankruptcy and simply transform the whole country into one enormous studio, a gigantic soundstage with video cameras all over the place—atop mountains, in trees, rotating in the middle of the desert to capture the vulture as it roosts in the cactus—ready to capture *everything*, night and day, with all the rain forests wired for sound, *the incessant melancholy patter of the rain*, and with tall transmitting towers set up on the country's highest mountains so that I could then beam, by way of my own privately owned—*nationally* owned—series of telecommunications satellites, the ongoing movie, the ongoing *story*, of this country, *my* country, to the rest of the world outfitted with its own series of satellite dishes—imagine!—the movie of a country's life—I couldn't sleep. I was all excited. I got up and paced the room. I checked to see that the Band-Aid was still in place over the keyhole to the adjoining bedroom. I tiptoed up to the hall door and—flung it open. No one. It was four in the morning. I decided to telephone my wife. Sleepily she got on the line, but I was pleased to note that despite the hour she did not sound annoyed. I told her that I had finished the film, no, I hadn't quite finished it, one cut was still troubling me, but that I was looking forward to the weekend-long party, that after being cooped up in the editing room for so long I was looking forward to sleeping outdoors in the pine forest beneath the starry skies, and that I hoped all my guests, all five hundred of them, would bring their sleeping bags too as suggested on the invitations and camp out in the woods instead of putting up in nearby motor lodges or at friends' cabins in the area, and my wife said she and our children were looking forward to sleeping outdoors too. Then I mentioned that some one-eyed cretin was staying at the house, a young documentary filmmaker, and my wife, my darling wife, who loves movies and knows nothing about them, asked me how in the world the young man could make movies if one of his eyes was dead, so I explained to the simple, dim dear that that might well be to the young man's advantage, that he sees the whole world as though through a camera lens, which is to say, flattened out, with less depth perspective, that the way we see images on the screen is how he sees everyday life, *that with him life itself is nothing but a vast movie perspective*, the whole world not a stage but a screen, and my wife said, "Oh, that's nice," and that was the end of that dismal exchange. I said good-bye and hung up more anxious and depressed than before.

I climbed back into bed. I burrowed back down under the blankets. But I couldn't get that one execrable cut out of my mind. I remembered an old silent gangster movie that contained a cut that suggested a solution to my problem—from a shot of a cormorant flying over the sea at dawn, to a shot of the gangster staring out his seaside bungalow window—and though I had this film in my private archives downstairs I hadn't looked at it in ages. So I decided I'd run it in the screening room before anyone else was up. Outside, the sky was just beginning to grow light. There would be time enough before people started drifting down for breakfast.

But after making a pot of coffee in the kitchen and taking it downstairs, I found—*him*!—the one-eyed cretin at the foot of my basement stairs gazing with his *one damned eye* at the framed photostat of my first check from a major studio for over a million dollars, right there on the wall, next to my fire engine red antique soda machine, which appeared briefly in my second film. He was scrutinizing the check with obvious bewilderment, no doubt trying to figure out if it was the real thing, and if so how I could stand not cashing it; and I have to admit, judging from the expression on his face it wasn't even envy or professional curiosity but simple unadorned metaphysical bewilderment—but then he heard me padding down the carpeted stairs and looked up—*with that one damned eye!* —obviously startled and embarrassed, and he muttered, "Good morning," and I just nodded, and he proceeded to slink away, but then suddenly swung around and asked if there was a bathroom downstairs, "Yes," I said, *"but there are no towels on the rack,"* and he said, "Oh," and stumbled off—

I set up the film.

I ran it.

But I couldn't see anything in perspective; for ninety minutes I sat there dazed, the images racing before me, I wanted to create images that didn't yet exist—and I couldn't even look at the ones in front of me. Finally I shut the projector off and went upstairs for breakfast; but, yes, *he was there*, sitting at my dining room table, sipping orange juice freshly squeezed by my maid, reading the morning edition of my newspaper, which he had roughly folded back to the comics. He glanced up and barely nodded, and I barely nodded back, and then he turned the page to *the racing results*. I wondered if he was calling his bookie back East on my telephone.

The maid brought me a fresh cup of coffee and I sat there sipping it, staring out at the sunlight dancing on the water in my backyard pool; I felt confused, I didn't know what to do; he was reading *my* paper; finally he looked up and asked if I would like the news section; I shook my head no, of course I didn't want it, if I wanted it I would just come right out and say so; after all, it was *my* paper; but then someone else—a young woman—my lieutenant's newest girlfriend, joined us and started chatting with me; she completely ignored him, and soon he put down the paper and began sniffing for an opening in the conversation, an entranceway into our little chat, a place where he could rend it apart and enter, triumphantly—but I left no such place, I kept up a steady patter of small talk about people who were friends of both me and my lieutenant, people whom *he* couldn't possibly know.

Finally he said to me, slowly and reticently, "You know, I've been your house guest for close to a week now and I'm not even sure you know who I am or what I'm doing here." I remained impassive. "In fact," he went on, "I'm not even sure you know I've made a film." I turned and looked straight at him, straight at that *one damned eye*, and then I spoke softly, reassuringly, though without smiling. "I know you've made a film. I know who you are." I paused and waited for him to fill

the pause, to say, "Do you plan to look at it?" or, "I'd
appreciate it if you looked at it," or, "I'd be indebted to you
for life if you looked at it," but he said no such thing, he didn't
say anything, he just let the pause hang there, yawning, gaping,
spreading—"And," I added, "I plan to look at it as soon as
possible." Which wasn't true. One way or the other didn't
seem to matter to him though. He just nodded, a bit puzzled,
he wasn't completely satisfied or reassured by my answer, but
he took it as the end of the matter, and so resumed reading the
paper, *my* paper, roughly folded back to the racing results.
"Who were you calling this morning?" He looked up, startled,
as if he hadn't heard me correctly. "Huh?" "I heard you on the
telephone. You dialed eleven numbers—long distance. Where
to? The other side of the continent?" "If I make any long
distance calls," he said carefully, "which I haven't, I have every
intention of paying you back." Whereupon he resumed reading
the paper, *my* paper, with an air of wounded pride!

I needed fresh air, *immediately,* so I rose, excused myself,
and went out for a walk. I walked around the block. I strolled
leisurely around the block. I paced the pavement around the
block. But no sooner had I rounded the block for the third
time than I saw coming my way the wife of the local newspaper's scand almonger, *that bilgebag;* she is a petite, attractive
woman in her late forties, and she talks too much, way too
much, and too much of what she says is gibberish, and I cannot
stand, I cannot stand, her husband, that pest. Once I even sent
an inner-office memo around expressly forbidding any em-
ployee to talk to him or her, and sure enough the memo turned
up the next day in his column, while his wife protested to
mutual acquaintances of ours that she had nothing to do with
it, which I didn't believe for one minute, still don't; but at least
I have the satisfaction of not inviting our so-called society
columnist, that minor irritant, that insufferable bilgebag, to the
best parties, the best "social events," in town, *my* parties, and
what's more he and his wife can see the lights of my mansion
through the swaying tree tops outside the second floor bedroom window of their *smaller* mansion which is set slightly
lower on the hill; and if the wind is blowing in the right
direction, if the wind is blowing from the northeast to the

southwest, then the merry laughter and music from *my* party should carry right into *their* second floor bedroom, as they're tossing, and turning, and yanking their pillows over their ears—

But now here she was, that gossip columnist's wife, coming straight toward me, not *straight* toward me, no, she was on the inner part of the pavement, and I wasn't sure what to do, in fact I was about to turn around and head back, or else cross to the other leafy side of the leafy street, but it may already have been too late, I think she'd spotted me and was hoping I'd say hello, or even just nod brusquely; actually she wishes that I and her husband would make amends so she could start attending these parties that so disturb her sleep—

Suddenly it came to me—in a flash! It was so simple I nearly laughed out loud; but I didn't; instead—here's what I did—instead of steering away from her I steered straight *towards* her, that is correct, I made a beeline directly towards her, I *aimed* myself at her, yes, and even as I was doing so I could see her eyes widen in momentary disarray, in surprise, in *disbelief;* nor did I smile, I didn't even look at her, in fact even while I was steering straight towards her I was pretending not to notice her; I was *actively* ignoring her, ignoring her existence, *canceling out* her existence—

And then—*bump.* I knocked my shoulder into her shoulder, not hard enough to knock her down or anything, after all I am a large man and she is a slight, diminutive lady, no, I didn't send her sprawling to the pavement or anything like that—but I did bump her hard enough to knock her off course, to upset her own delicate gyroscope, to *startle* her, to make her wonder if this signaled some new, nasty escalation of hostilities, to give her something to *think about*—

And let me tell you a secret. I had my trusted lieutenant check the "society" column the next day and no item appeared about a *nationally known* film director rudely bumping into *local* columnist's wife on the street, nor did any righteously angry husband come banging his fist on the door of my more stately mansion, yes indeed, *for I am bigger and younger and stronger,* call it physical intimidation if you like, call it terrorization—and that's the long and the short of it.

Now I felt better. Now I felt ready to tackle that trouble-

some cut. I did *not* feel ready to face that moronic director
with his one damned eye. So without even bothering to report
back to the house I got in my car and began driving across
town to my editing room. I would do it alone. *I have always
been doing it alone.* It was a beautiful day and I noticed
nothing. And while it may well be true that I'm an extraordinary salesman, that I know how to talk up a storm of enthusi-
asm, that I radiate and infect others with my self-confidence
and vitality, that I've counseled and sponsored and bankrolled
and produced the most promising young directors of my generation, it's equally true that there've been times when I've been
short of friends and low on funds, when I've had to mortgage
everything in sight including the lawn in front of my house—
the autumnal lawn with my son's blue tricycle lying overturned
on it, one rear wheel still sentimentally turning—and if later I
could buy everything back, even buy into the banks I had been
mortgaged to—well, what of it? The truth is, I care nothing for
worldly goods, nothing for security, *I don't need it.* If I have
only a dime left in my pocket, I'm still not in anyone else's
pocket. The idiots who envy me my "opportunities" think that
it is a simple question of rubbing my hands together and
shouting, "Okay gang! Time to make another movie, another
blockbuster!" But it's sheer idealism, sheer *madness,* to believe
that you're going to get exactly what you want out of your
camera men, your sound recorders, your editors, actors, set
designers, art directors, wardrobe supervisors, *animal trainers*!
for all of them are used to doing things in their own way, *in the
old rut,* and if you're to do anything at all new you must break
their habits, destroy their *wills,* you have to write the new laws
yourself. Because to place one image after another, to lay one
sound over another, is the most terrifying project in the world,
is fraught with hidden dangers at every step of the way, is the
most maddeningly *rational* poetic enterprise imaginable. I shape
the movie and the movie shapes me. And afterwards it is very
hard for me to leave the shelter of the editing room and assume
my upright position among other vertical human beings, to
recover my tremulous sense of self, or even a small sense of
self.

I parked in front of the building, unlocked the door, and

descended the stairs to my editing room. *I got right down to work.* I worked for hours on end, I reviewed outtakes, put the image of the gull flying over the lake *before* the image of my protagonist staring out the window, I put it after, I faded out the *caw caw caw* of the gull, I heightened it, I superimposed the *caw caw caw* over my protagonist staring out the dusk window, I arranged a whole new sequence of the shots, I rearranged them, I *deranged* them, for hours and hours I worked in a mad frenzy, cutting, taping, fiddling with the dials, I tossed in the sounds of ocean waves crashing with a roar along the rocky coast even though this was a placid, inland lake, I subtracted them, I tossed in flashback shots of a young boy splashing happily at a lake shore—outtakes from a sun tan lotion commercial I'd directed as a young man—I subtracted them, I worked relentlessly, throwing myself completely into it, stepping back from it as far as possible—

And finally—toward the end of the day—I arrived at what I wanted, at the exact confluence of sounds and images that I *needed,* and to be perfectly frank *it was precisely what I had started out with,* but do not laugh, do not snicker, for in truth it wasn't what I had started out with, for by working so long and so hard at it, by pressing myself so relentlessly, by arriving at the same thing through so intensely a concentrated ten-hour work stint, I had arrived at something *new,* something better, something different, something *more assured,* yes, I had arrived at *the same thing* but by virtue of the new burst of work, the new meditations, the new elucidations, the new arranging and rearranging and deranging, by virtue of all of this the same thing was, quid pro quo and tit for tat, *something different!*

The door broke open. My lieutenant burst into the room. He looked at me in horror, then without a word hustled me into my jacket and up the stairs and into my car so that we could get to the party—we were already late—celebrating the completion of the film I was busy completing. It had slipped my mind!

We arrived just after sunset. The party was well under way. The sign I had requested had been posted at the gateway to my estate: *Your presence on these grounds implies consent to appear in a film being made of this party.* No one wins a lawsuit besides lawyers. My second unit director would be filming the whole event for my private archives—call it a documentary, call it a home movie, call it what you will, I have an aversion to categories. It was a cool summer night and hundreds of people strolled at their pleasure over the gently rolling wooded hills; in the clearings campfires had been built and beer kegs and wine jugs set up on the tables, while in the large central clearing, over the open barbecue pit, sausages were bursting their skins and enormous kettles of beans were simmering. I had hired some country-and-western musicians and they roamed from clearing to clearing playing their songs like wandering minstrels of old; actually I am sure they were like no such thing; I despise their crooning but my lieutenant had recommended them, they had just crooned a few songs for a friend's forthcoming movie that was already all the talk of the industry.

I detached myself from my lieutenant and drifted around on my own. Friends, guests, employees smiled shyly at me. Yet no one approached me. *No one approached me.* Not one script reader from my story department wishing to advance to script writer approached me with a first draft for a film that would put the company back on its feet; not one film editor wishing to advance to film director approached me with an idea for a movie that would break all box office records and win critical acclaim to boot. No. They knew I was exhausted and anyway, I intimidate them. So I wandered through the woods from one campfire to the next, from one knot of people to the next—*and I felt lonely.* I would approach the campfire through the dark quiet of the woods, see the people gathered around it, hear their voices and their laughter borne aloft on the gentle night breeze, and then as soon as I stepped out of the woods, as soon as I stepped into the light of the fire and smiled—well, they would smile back but a bit timidly, and then fall silent or continue to talk but in more subdued tones—*and I felt lonely.*

I wandered forlornly through the woods. I passed someone's tent pitched on a bluff overlooking a creek. I stumbled over a pair of sleeping bags spread on a poncho on a bed of dry pine needles. Contrary to rumors my woods are not wired for sound. Then as I approached another clearing I espied my second unit director, that imbecile, shooting some thoroughly mediocre footage, standard stuff, of the country-and-western singers backlit by the fire. I remained hidden at the edge of the woods. Some wonderful horseplay was going on at the other side of the campfire—a young woman whom I didn't recognize had taken a long string of linked sausages and in a delightful pantomime of a pedantic boy-scout master was demonstrating overhand knots and timber hitches with them—but do you think my second unit director picked up on this? Of course not, all he could see were those crooning cowboys, those philharmonic wranglers—and that is why he will always be second-unit.

I continued through the woods. At the next clearing I spotted a young woman whom the gossip columnist, that bilgebag, had recently reported I was dating—and she saw me and smiled shyly, and I smiled shyly back. I noticed she was talking with someone who stood just in the shadows at the edge of the clearing, I couldn't make out who it was, but he appeared to be tall, yet swaybacked, no, *hunchbacked,* he had incredibly poor posture, there was something about him, but I couldn't quite put my finger on it, I couldn't quite place this . . . unsymmetrical . . . misshapen . . . ill-proportioned . . . grotesquely deformed . . . *twisted, one-eyed cretin*—horrified I fled back into the woods.

I continued to wander forlornly. Then just as I arrived at the edge of the next clearing a long black limousine bounced up the dirt road and stopped right in front of the campfire. The chauffeur opened the door and from it stepped the blond female lead of my new movie—I was sick of looking at her—in tight-fitting blue jeans and a gray silk blouse; and from my spot in the woods, from my *hiding place,* I overheard another woman, an old friend, say to her companion, "Leave it to that idiot to show up in a rented limo." And I might have written this remark off to the average woman's petty jealousy of a starlet—except this woman was the head of my story department, an articulate woman, an intelligent woman, an educated and cultivated woman, exquisitely beautiful in her own right, and I knew that she was speaking the truth—*and I felt lonely.* I drifted away before anyone discovered me, before the actress came over fishing around for my opinion of her in the final cut (not secure enough to feign indifference, not famous enough yet to ask me outright, though the movie would fix that).

I drifted away. I plunged into the woods, far from the voices and laughter of the campfires. Soon, the party had faded to the merest background murmur, indistinguishable from the soft murmur of a creek whose stony bank I had arrived on. For a long time I simply stood there, admiring a stand of tall dark pines on the opposite bank silhouetted against the night sky. Then—I heard a cricket. It did not sound right. Its chirp was too soft. I looked at the creek, at the silhouetted pines, the pebbles of the creek bed, farther back the rounded hills, higher up and to my right the moon; it was as coherent a picture of nature as one could ever hope for—but that damn cricket chirp was too low, it threw everything else out of kilter; I stepped closer to the clump of bushes from which the chirp seemed to be emanating so that it would sound louder—but in doing so the creek slipped behind a boulder, the rounded hills disappeared behind the silhouetted pines, the moon vanished behind a larger hill—yet it was absolutely essential to see the moonlight shimmering on the waters, and the rounded hills off to the left of the silhouetted pines, and the moon, all at the same time that I was hearing that damn chirp, otherwise the woods got boring, the starry sky turned commonplace, the whole sum total panorama of nocturnal nature would be all shot to hell. I stepped to my left. That adjusted the cricket chirp to the right level, and the moon even slipped back out, but the rounded hills and the creek continued to elude me. I took two steps backwards and the creek jumped back out but now the moon slipped behind the hill again. I stepped forward—moon, no creek—backwards—creek, no moon—three steps sideways—moon, creek, but no silhouetted pines—turned to my right—hill eclipsed moon—farther to my left—pines eclipsed hills—sideways again, backwards again, a giant step forward, a giant step backwards, *moon, creek, hills, pines*—

"Daddy, are you all right?"

I looked blankly at my youngest boy, then patted him on the head, smiled paternally, and allowed him to take my hand

and lead me through the woods to our campsite. My wife was already there, tucking our other children into their bright blue and orange sleeping bags. She looked up and smiled wearily, and I smiled back. I had been afraid that at the last moment she'd make a big production, insist on sleeping in the manor; but she didn't, she just smiled wearily, acceptingly—and I was grateful.

The next morning I was up at dawn. I was one of the first people up. I could have used another twenty hours sleep but legend has it I am bounding with energy—so bound out of the sleeping bag I must. In the main clearing coffee makers had been set up on the tables, along with platters of rolls and muffins, and boxes of oranges and apples. A few people were already drifting in, and my lieutenant had revived the campfire. It was chilly and people sat around the fire on logs and stumps, warming their hands around their coffee cups. I wandered about. I sniffed the piney air. From a clear bubbling brook I splashed water on my face. Then as I knelt on the bank drying my head with my towel, through the wet tangles of my hair I saw *him*. That damned documentary director with his *one damned eye* was standing off on the edge of the woods chatting with the head of my story department and her boyfriend. Still rubbing my wet hair furiously with my towel, I went right over and wished her and her boyfriend good morning, studiously ignoring *him*, canceling out *his existence*. I asked her if they'd slept in the woods, and she laughed and said no, they'd slept in the camper on account of her boyfriend's bad back—she slapped him jovially on his bad back—but I felt sad, even my old trusted friend, the head of my story department, hadn't bothered to sleep in the woods, hadn't really gotten into *the spirit of the thing*. To be frank, I felt a bit irritated, a trifle peevish, I began wondering how many other people had sneaked off to motor lodges and friends' weekend cabins. Then I turned to that damned documentary director; I just looked at him and he just looked at me *with his one damned eye!* and I figured he'd slept in the woods, he'd slept in a motel, he'd sneaked back to the city and slept in *my* bed, to tell the truth I didn't want to know where he'd slept; but then he rubbed his good eye, as though to get the sleep out of it, and said, offered, volunteered, *thrust forcibly upon me*, the unsolicited information that he hadn't slept anywhere, quite the contrary! he'd been up all night troubled by a cut in the documentary he was currently completing; it was a cut from a shot of a giant chicken squawking in pain, to a shot of the teenage scientist gazing sadly through the bars of his bird's cage, or maybe it should be vice versa, or maybe the squawking should be played over the close-up of the teenager's mournful face, or—anyway, unable to sleep he'd wandered along the creek that winds through my estate, had in fact followed it *off* of my estate (which wasn't as big as he'd originally thought, he added) for miles and miles in the dark, and at one point had startled a paunchy raccoon pawing through the creek for fish, *why in the world was he telling me this drivel?* I said good-bye and stalked off.

I drifted over to the campfire and sat on a log, facing a group that had grown to a dozen or more. A few people smiled sleepily and nodded hello, but I was beginning to feel depressed; but just then the beautiful young actress came over, still wearing her tight-fitting blue jeans and her gray silk blouse—not a wrinkle or a crease in the blouse, she hadn't slept on a bed of pine needles!—and she was carrying a Kodak pocket camera and she smiled, and I smiled back, then she grinned, said "Cheese!" and snapped my picture. Whereupon I reached for her camera which she flirtatiously surrendered, expecting me to snap *her* picture—she went instantly professional with the mock-sexy pose and smile—but instead I cupped my hands around the camera like it was a harmonica, brought it up to my lips, and pretended to start playing it; and everyone around the campfire laughed genuinely, and I began to feel better. Then I held up the junky automatic for everyone to see and said, "Here we have it, folks. State-of-the-art for the early eighties," and again everyone around the fire laughed nicely. Upon which the actress, still laughing (she'd recovered capitally from her unphotographed pose), installed herself in my lap; and immediately, without even thinking about it, I began working invisible marionette strings, pretending to move her arms and legs this way and that, and right away her arms and legs began to move floppily *this way and that*, as if hinged like a puppet's—she was acting quite nicely, better than she had in the movie, more spontaneously—and again everyone laughed. But then I noticed, standing on the edge of the growing crowd, my dear wife, her arms crossed, smiling grimly. "Darling," I yelled grinning, "this beautiful young actress isn't really sitting on my lap. We're really discussing photography," and all at once *the spell was broken*, everyone around the fire suddenly looked confused, a bit embarrassed, as if some country bumpkin, *me*, had deviated from the script; and even more suddenly I had an idea; *I would remove the actress from my lap, jump to my feet, and rubbing my hands together, yell, "Okay early birds, let's see if there're enough of us to get some volleyball going!"* but then I noticed, on the other side of the crowd, that damned documentary director studying me with his one damned eye, and right behind him with the video camera, *shooting blithely over his shoulder*, was my second unit director, that oaf, cheerfully shooting away, oblivious to everything; and *he* looked at me scornfully, with a look of contempt, of deep repugnance, of vast ontological disgust—

And just then I noticed the sun rising over the soft green hills, and I filled my lungs with the resinous scent of the dewy firs, so tall and so motionless in the cool dawn light, and far away a cricket chirped, and even farther away a creek was murmuring, and I faltered—

ANDRE DUBUS

LAND WHERE MY FATHERS DIED

FROM ANTAEUS

For James Crumley

GEORGE KARAMBELAS

IT WAS A COLD NIGHT, AND I WAS DRUNK. I couldn't get a ride at Timmy's when they closed, and I had a long way to walk. It was after one o'clock, and I kept thinking of my warm bed. I could see it in front of me, like it was ahead of me on the sidewalk, like those guys in a desert that see water that isn't there. A mirage, it's called. You can see it some time on a highway in summer. I thought about summer.

I lost my car. It was an old Pontiac, eight years old next year, that sucked gas. First the exhaust system went, rusted out, and I paid for that. Then it was a new starter, then the carburetor had to be rebuilt and I paid for all that and was broke. Then the transmission started to go and I said fuck it and sold it for junk. Fuck them at Timmy's. Fuck Steve. Fuck Laurie. Fuck George, they say, let him walk a hundred miles in fifty below just to sleep. Well, fuck them too, I said.

Maybe out loud. I was that drunk. I wished I wasn't. I wished I had gone right home soon as I got all the dishes washed and the pots scrubbed out and hung from the beam. I still would have frozen to death walking home, but I'd be in bed. And Timmy's is on the other side of the river so it was a longer ways to walk and I had to cross the bridge going and coming back, and the bridge is long on foot, and the wind was coming down the river. It's the chill factor. You never know how cold it is. The thermometer outside the window will say nineteen, but then you go outside and the cold comes blowing and it's like twenty below. That's the story: it's nineteen but it's *like* twenty below.

I tried to walk straight, looking down at the sidewalk like it was a board over a big hole, but I was zigging and zagging from one snow bank to another. Once I slipped on ice and landed on my ass. I thought about if I had hit my head I could have stayed there and froze to death. But still I couldn't get sober. I walked through the square about a mile above the river. Even the pizza shop was closed. We got a lot of pizza shops in this little town, mostly Italian, some Greek.

When Steve gave last call at Timmy's I started asking around for a ride. Nobody going my way. Who are they shitting? A night like this you can go out of your way for somebody. Up above the square I was walking past houses. Trees were in the yards in the snow and next to the sidewalk. Face it, George, I said to myself. Nobody's ever gone your way. I didn't like hearing that. I'm twenty-three. I started thinking about people that liked me. I got back to eighth grade, there was this Irish kid, but nobody liked him either. I got very sad walking under the big trees. No girl, not ever, and I don't know why. I look in the mirror and I don't know why. I've been laid, sure, but with sluts. It's a wonder I never caught herpes or something. I saw the light on in Dr. Clark's office. I was walking past it, and it was on my right, the road on my left. Then I stopped because I saw that I was seeing the light through the window but through the door too. Hey, I looked around: up and down the street, no cars, and up and down the sidewalk, of course nobody was out. Who would be but Eskimos and a dumb Greek.

I went up his walk slow and casual like a dude coming home. There was salt on it. I was doing everything but whistling, a Greek dishwasher coming home to sleep in a doctor's office. It was a one-story brick building set back in the trees, a

small office, a one-man operation. This was a neighborhood of
big old wooden houses. They were dark. At the two front steps
I stopped and looked again. I went up the steps and in the
door, breathing hard with the booze. Everything was hard to
do. This was the waiting room, and it was dark. Or the lights
were off, but I could see the desk by the office door and the
chairs along the walls; because the light was coming from the
office and that door was open. I could see part of his desk in
there, a corner and some of the top. To this day I don't know
what I had in mind. I was thinking money, but I think about
money all the time. Every day, every night. I think I was
hoping for drugs. But I was too drunk for any of it to make
any sense and if I hadn't been drunk I would have walked right
on by. If I hadn't been drunk maybe somebody would have
given me a ride, maybe that's it, maybe I drink too much. But
that's not it because in high school I wasn't drunk or not much
of the time and it didn't matter. I'd go to the smoking area
outside where the faggots made us go even if it was a blizzard
and I'd look at the girls shivering around their cigarettes and
they'd either look at me like the smoke made them blind or like
instead of a mouth I had a boil under my nose. I'd go over to
the guys and they'd start busting balls on me. Sometimes it's
friendly, it depends how you say things. Bob the chef busts
them on me all the time, but it's friendly; he likes me, and he's
an old man. The guys at school weren't friendly. *So George,
you going to ever shave, or what? He plucks them. All three,
every week.* I'd laugh with them. But I wouldn't say anything
back.

   I was still not walking straight. I got across the waiting
room on a slant toward the door and stepped in and saw a dead
man. I knew he was dead when I saw him. I've only seen my
grandparents, all four, laid out in their coffins. But I knew he
was dead. I think I said something out loud. I remember
hearing somebody. It did not get me sober but it got me sober
as I could get. He was on his back, dressed up in a suit, and
there was blood dried on his mouth. It was open. I've never
seen a mouth look so open, looser than somebody sleeping.
His eyes were closed. One hand was resting on his belt buckle.
He was not a very big man, on the thin side. I had never been

to see him, we always went to Papadopoulos, our family, but I knew it was Dr. Clark. I had seen him around town in his Mercedes, and sometimes when I was washing dishes I'd look through the window to the dining room and he'd be there eating lobsters with his scrawny old lady. I started to get out of there when I saw the big pistol on the floor. It was lying right beside his face. I bent over and picked it up and I kept my eyes away from his that were shut. I put it in my coat pocket, a pea coat. A prescription pad was on his desk and I put that in the other pocket. Then I got out of there.

I turned off the light switch by his door, and the office was dark. I had to feel my way across the waiting room. I think I was walking straight then. I had my arms out in front of me and moving, like a breast stroke, like I was swimming through the dark. My hands hit the front door. I opened it a little and looked at the street. A car passed. Then it was empty, and I was gone, shutting the door, and down the steps, holding the metal rail cold under my glove. Down his walk to the sidewalk.

I didn't think about the cold anymore. I didn't feel it. I didn't see my bed either. I saw his face on the floor looking up at the ceiling except his lids were down and there was nobody behind them. I saw his hand covering his belt buckle. The pistol was heavy in my pocket, and I was weaving again. I live in an old house that used to be one family's house, all three stories, and now it is a lot of apartments. I went up to mine on the second floor and pissed, shivering, for a long time. Then I swallowed some anisette from the bottle and drank a beer while I took off my clothes. I put the coat over a chair, and left the gun in it. When I got in bed I could still see him and I was tense and breathing fast, curled up on my side under the covers, and I thought I would not sleep. Next thing I knew the sun was in the room and I had a dry mouth and a headache and I had to piss but I lay there remembering everything and thinking here I was with a dead doctor's script pad and a big pistol I didn't want to see. Then I got up and took it out of the coat pocket. It was an Army .45, and the hammer was cocked. I looked some more. The safety was off.

ARCHIMEDES NIONAKIS

Because it was probably not murder—someone hit Francis Clark on the jaw and apparently his head struck the desk as he fell—and because it seemed to involve bad luck more than volition, I sometimes thought George had done it, but it was a thought I could only hold in the abstract, for a few moments, until I imagined him in the flesh. Then I could not believe it, could not see George Karambelas punching anybody, much less a man with a loaded pistol.

Then I believed the story he had just told me. I could still smell his story as I drove back to town from the prison. My car windows were up, and my clothes smelled of George's cigarette smoke trapped in the counseling room, and also the vanished smoke, and words and breath it seemed, of the others who had sat or paced in that room with its two straight wooden chairs and old wooden desk with an ashtray long overflowed, and butts scattered on the desk top with burns at its edges where live cigarettes had lain, and burns on its top where they had been put out. I did not sit at the desk. I leaned against a wall without windows, and said: "I can't believe how dumb you are."

"Don't say that," he said. "You got to make the jury believe it."

He did try to smile, as he tried to be friendly, but in his circumstance it is hard to do either. I don't mean simply incarceration; or being charged with second degree murder. George is one of those people who have nothing specific wrong with them, except that they are disliked, and it's difficult to understand why. I don't even know why I don't like him. He is not very bright, but it isn't that. So I stood breathing in that room and told him I would represent him, and that is why: I couldn't bear disliking him for no just reason, and seeing him in that room too, and imagining him in the cell where probably already his cellmates didn't like him either. I did not mention money, any more than I would look for a fish in a tree, but he said he would raise it. He did not go so far as to ask how much he ought to raise. I told him we'd talk about that when the time came. I listened to his foolish story again, and congratulated him again on at least burning the prescription pad, forced my hand into his, and fled.

In my old Volvo, once I had opened a window a bit to cold air, and got past the weariness I feel when I do something good that I don't want to, I was suddenly glad he had called me. This surprised me, then disturbed me, for at thirty-three I should not be able to surprise myself. But there it was: that part of me I can't silence or even fully please, that will sometimes, while I'm in bed with a woman, leave us and stand dressed in the room, laughing or scowling: the little bastard was active again. I know he's the one who makes me an insomniac, when I'm too tired to read, and have no worries about money or family: I have money because I don't have a family, and I live alone by choice so am not lonely; still he keeps me awake, feeling that I'm worrying. Though I'm not. Except about getting to sleep. Now he hoped for some complicated work. Probably, for him, there had been too many times lately when I would stop what I was doing and look around me at my life—or the little bastard would—and feel it was not enough. Not enough for what? was the question I couldn't answer, except to say it wasn't using enough of me. I run a lot.

In the detectives' office, Dom Schiavoni sat on the secretary's desk. He sat on its edge, profiled to her; in winter clothes he looked even bigger, a V-necked blue sweater pulled tight over his belly and chest, his shoulders looking squeezed into an old dark suit coat. His complexion, in winter, changed from dark to pale olive, so he always looked like a swarthy man who had just had the flu. He introduced me to the secretary, Roberta Ford, a buxom woman in her fifties with fleshy cheeks and probably arms too under the sleeves of her sweater; her hair was red, and looked like it had been done by one of my brothers, who had colored it for her too. Dom introduced me, and she said: "Your brother Kosta does my hair."

We came over on the boat when I was five, the youngest; my brothers own their shop and work very hard, from seven in the morning till six or seven at night, every day but Sunday; they tell me they could have women in the chairs at five in the morning if they wanted to start that early. There are many

Greeks in beauty parlors in the Merrimack Valley; it was work they could learn quickly and could do in Greek while they were learning English, and it paid well. My brothers put me through school and they turn, in seriousness, to the stock exchange section of the *Boston Globe*.

"You still running?" Dom said.

"Yes."

"You look like it. You going to run the Marathon again?"

I told him yes and that I was representing George. I watched his mouth, waiting for the smile; but there was none in his eyes either. Then he said: "Good."

"Why?"

"Somebody ought to."

"You want coffee?" Roberta said.

I told her I hadn't had breakfast and would take anything.

"This is early for him," Dom said. "Maybe there's a doughnut left." He looked at his watch. "Nine-thirty. What's it feel like?"

"Dawn. You don't think he did it?"

Roberta gave me a Styrofoam cup of coffee and a glazed doughnut.

"I *think* he did it. Problem is, I don't *know* he did it."

Then he told me how it took less than forty-eight hours for the arrest because the receptionist found him when she opened Thursday morning and later in the day did a quick inventory for Schiavoni and told him the gun and a prescription pad were gone. Schiavoni found the receipt for the pistol in a desk drawer, and talked to Mayfield, the narcotics officer. Mayfield started talking to punks, and on Saturday one told him who had bought a .45 Thursday.

"So we went to see the new owner. He never heard of the .45 till I told him the name of the previous owner, then he's giving me the gun, seven rounds of ammo, and the name and address of George Karambelas."

"Who didn't even deny it."

"No."

Roberta shook her head, repeating the no.

"The dumb bastard," Dom said. Roberta nodded.

"Why was Clark in his office at night? And on a Wednesday?"

This town has an old custom: a lot of stores close on Wednesday afternoons, and no doctors work. Neither do I.

"The receptionist doesn't know. Maybe his wife will tell you."

Then he smiled.

"They're separated, right?"

"Why do you say that?" He smiled again.

"Because the receptionist found him."

"Archimedes," and he reached out and laid his big hand on my shoulder, smiling that mischievous way, and said: "They're not separated."

"Where was she? In Moscow?"

"About five miles from here."

"So you went Thursday morning and told her why her husband didn't come home last night?"

"Kind of grabs you, doesn't it?"

"What did she say?"

"She designated a funeral home."

Roberta was nodding.

I drove to the address Dom gave me. It was a clear February day, with deep snow bright on the ground in the sunlight. The downtown part of our city, on the riverbank, is ugly, and there's nothing more to say about that. They tell me this place used to thrive; that was back when my uncle brought us over and put my brothers to work in his factory. They made parts for women's shoes: bows, and an arrangement of straps called vamps; these vamps and bows, when attached to an arched and high-heeled sole, formed an absolutely functionless shoe. My uncle shipped the bows and vamps my brothers helped make to another factory in another state, and there they were attached to soles.

There are neighborhoods of big, old houses that prove someone was making money, but I don't believe this town ever thrived; I think people mean the shoe business was good and the factory owners made a lot of money and most of the poor were employed poor. They still are; there are no union facto ries, and unskilled workers, many of them Greek and Hispanic and now, since the war, some Vietnamese, work for minimum wage. Our better neighborhoods have many old trees, and these places are lovely when the leaves change colors in the fall. As I drove under them on the way to Lillian Clark's, there were enough pines to scatter green against the blue sky, and sometimes the sun glinted from ice on the branches of naked trees. I skirted a frozen lake bordered on one side by a public woods that has a good running road under its trees, following the bank of the lake. I entered countryside: woods, and fields of snow with tufts of brown dead weeds above it. Dr. Clark had a rural mailbox at the road, at the entrance of a paved driveway that curved up through evergreens. I shifted down and went up it, thinking of the good smell he had had in spring and summer, when a breeze went from the pines into his house. It was not an old one but one he had either built or bought from its first owner: two stories of stones and brown wood and A-shaped peaks enclosing windows. The garage was built onto one side, its door was raised, and inside, in one of the two spaces, was a fucking Porsche. The little bastard got excited by that sculpted-looking piece of steel that could feed a family across town in the tenement streets for five years or more; he liked knowing that the big surprises of pain and death infiltrated so impartially. I told him to show some compassion for Christ sake, and got out and pressed the cold button for the bell.

Lillian Clark had bags under her eyes, and they were not the recent kind that let you know someone's had a bad night. They were permanent knolls on the landscape of her face. She was a thin woman who could have been dissipated in her forties or poised in her fifties for a final decline. There was gray in her brown hair; her eyes were brown and angry, so that I apologized and felt my cheeks flush as I introduced myself and asked if I could speak with her; then I realized the anger was permanent too. Or guessed it, because of the rest of her face, its lines in her cheeks and about her eyes, that appeared set in some epiphany of bitterness. You have seen them, when you spy on people in airport lounges or pedestrians walking toward you: their eyes focus on things, and you wonder what they could be looking at to cause such anger; then you know it is being fed to them from inside their skulls. Her skin was the pallid tan of Dom's, but hers was not genetic; this was a woman of the sun and had probably had a winter vacation a month ago in Florida or the Caribbean. Wherever it is they go. Her voice was soft, though a bit crisp at the edges, and probably that was permanent too, a chord telling the world that was all the control she could muster. In the living room I sat in an armchair that was too deep and soft, so only my toes touched the floor. She sat opposite me; our chairs were half-turned toward a cold fireplace with ashes between the andirons. She drank sherry from a stemmed glass, and flicked a hand, as though backhanding a gnat, toward a bottle of Dry Sack on the table beside her, and asked if I wanted some. There was no question mark in her voice, so the invitation had the tone of a statement like: Your socks don't match. I said no and repeated the condolences I had offered at the door, while she sipped and gazed at the fireplace. I offered to light a fire, and she said: "I can make fires."

I said something about chimney drafts and the trick of holding a torch of burning paper up the chimney to start it drawing, and I began telling her about a bricklayer I knew who built a chimney for a man with a bad reputation for paying bills, and halfway up the chimney he laid a plate of glass across it, but her head jerked toward me, and this time her eyes glared. I liked the story and had believed it when I heard it, though it was one of those I stopped believing the first time I told it; still, I wanted to tell her about the man calling to complain about the smoke backing up in his living room and the bricklayer telling him he would fix it when he got paid for the chimney, in cash, and driving to the man's house and, with the money in his pocket, going up his ladder with a brick in his hand and dropping it down the chimney. But I said: "Can you tell me why your husband was at his office on a Wednesday night?"

"He took Wednesdays off."

"The afternoons?"

"Yes. He went to the hospital in the morning."

She was looking at the fireplace. So did I. I kept seeing

George in prison, suspended in dismay, but not one sentence, not one word, came to me.

"Why did he do it?" she said.

I looked at the side of her face, and an attractive streak of gray above her left ear.

"George didn't do it."

"You don't think so?"

"No."

"Would you defend him if he had?"

"No."

"Really? Why?"

"I couldn't enjoy it."

"You couldn't enjoy it."

"No."

Now she did look at my socks, which matched and were folded over the tops of hiking boots. Her eyes moved up my legs, or slacks, and shirt and coat to my face.

"I like you with a mustache."

I was about to ask when she had seen me without one, but caught that in time and said: "He didn't know Dr. Clark."

"He could be angry at him without knowing him."

"Is that why your husband had a gun?"

"Probably."

"Did he see patients on Wednesday nights?"

"That's what he said."

She was looking at my eyes, and I wished she would turn to the fireplace again.

"Because they needed him?" I said. "Because of the afternoons off?"

"Some. He said."

"So why not work on Wednesday afternoons and take the evening off?"

She was watching my eyes. I had heard or read about recent widows being angry at their husbands for dying. I had not understood it, though I recognized that it must have something to do with grief; but those were widows of husbands who had died of what we call natural causes. Their husbands had not been murdered. Yet there was nothing of sorrow, of memory, in Lillian Clark's eyes.

"For the receptionist?" I said. "So she could have time off? Or did she work on Wednesday nights?"

"You could ask her."

"You don't know, then?"

"I never phoned the office on Wednesday nights."

"Was she a nurse?"

"You mean is she. Francis was killed, not Beverly. Yes, she's a nurse."

"She would have to be there, wouldn't she?"

"Would she?"

"For female patients. Doesn't there have to be a nurse in the examining room?"

"I suppose."

"All this is very strange."

Finally she looked away, back at the fireplace. So did I.

"Did he ever talk about trouble with a patient?"

"Trouble?"

"Someone who might have got angry and hit him. I think it was an accident. His death, I mean."

"Depends on what you call an accident."

"I suppose it does. Are you the executrix of the estate?"

"That's funny."

"What is?"

"My new title. Yes."

"Could I look at his files?"

Looking into the fireplace, she called Teresa, with Spanish pronunciation, and my thighs jumped taut. I looked behind me, stretching to see over the back of the chair, at the sounds of footsteps. Teresa was young and too thin.

"Bring my purse down from the bedroom."

She left, and I listened to her climbing stairs and walking above us, and I looked around the room. A model of a yacht was on the mantelpiece. In one corner was a small bookcase with a glass door; the corner was dark, and I could not read the titles. More furniture was behind us and against the walls. The floor was carpeted, and Teresa crossed it now with the purse, then was gone. Lillian took out a key ring, and worked one of them to the top.

"Where's the other car?" I said.

"He had a Mercedes. I gave it to my daughter."

"What was his practice?"

"Internal medicine. Here."

I took the key and thanked her.

"Mrs. Clark?" I stood up, looking down at her face gazing at the fireplace. "Did you call anyone when he didn't come home Wednesday night?"

"I was asleep."

"What about next morning?"

"I slept late. I always do."

"So Detective Schiavoni woke you up?"

"No."

"I don't understand."

She looked at me.

"You don't understand what?"

"Why you didn't know."

"I always woke up alone. He got up at seven."

"You couldn't tell he hadn't slept there?"

"How?" She was still looking at me.

"The blankets. The way the pillows were. Teresa must make a tight bed."

"Why are you upset?"

"I'm not."

"Yes, you are. I suppose I didn't look."

I thanked her, told her I'd bring back the key, and left. In the car I felt I had a hangover: the weariness, the confusion. On the way to my office I bought two meatball subs and four half-pint cartons of milk. My office is small, the waiting room no larger, and the receptionist's desk was empty, its surface bare save for a covered typewriter. I did not have a regular secretary, and was using interns from the small college in town. I gave them work to do and even taught them, and the college paid them with credits. My intern was Paula Reynolds, a lovely girl with healthy skin and long blond hair. I opened the office door. She was lying on the leather couch my brothers gave me. She wore a sweater, and jeans tucked into high boots, and was smoking a French cigarette.

"Jesus," I said, and opened the window behind my desk. A pack of Gitanes was on the floor beside her. Sometimes she does this, shows up with Gauloises or Gitanes, and I accuse her of affectation; but the truth is she spent a year in France before college, and now and then she has the urge. While she finished smoking I told her about my morning, then she took her milk and sandwich to the couch, managed to eat daintily, a good trick with a meatball sub, and she was smoking again as we left the office and I drove us to Dr. Clark's.

He was either a yachtsman or simply loved boats. What had been a model of a yacht, painted white, was on his desk, the bow split and crumpled, the masts snapped in two and held together by sails; it looked as though a storm had driven it against rocks. I thought of all the concentration he had put into it and the one on his mantelpiece at home. Then I imagined the ocean rushing through the hole with its splinters, unpainted on the inside, and I looked away. On the wall were three color photographs of the same yacht, at anchor. Paula stood beside me, looking down at the yacht, and when I turned, our arms brushed, her sweater and my jacket and shirt-sleeve padding our muscles and bones. I unbuckled her belt, turned her toward me, and kissing her, slipped her jeans down her hips. Her pants were pale blue and already moist. We undressed and, as she lay on the floor, she said: Isn't this where—and I said Yes, and was in her.

We dozed for half an hour on the carpet, then dressed and stood at the filing cabinets against one wall. Paula started with the A's, on my right, and I crouched to the Z's, three of them, and sat on the floor and read about a man named Zachary who was fifty-eight years old, had seasonal allergies, got an annual physical, and since five years ago, when he had asthmatic bronchitis, had either not been sick or had treated himself at home. Paula went to the reception room to look for an ashtray and came back empty-handed except for her unlit cigarette and said: "Goddamn doctors."

"Just chew it. Then I can breathe."

"Goddamn joggers."

"I'm not a *jogger*."

"Goddamn runners then. Why don't you put pictures of running shoes on your office wall. And a bronze pair on your desk."

"My bronze pair is between my legs."

Then she was bending over me, her fingers coming like claws at my crotch, and I quickly shut my legs. She put the cigarette between her lips, untied my hiking boot, pulled it off, took it to her end of the cabinets, and set it on top of the A's. I put away Zachary and opened Zecchini. Florence Zecchini was not doing well: she was sixty-three and had high blood pressure, bursitis in the left shoulder, and every year, from November to April, she contracted a mélange of viruses.

"The Z's are all old." I watched her flicking ashes into my boot. "What happened to wastebaskets?"

"It has paper in it. What are we looking for?"

"Are you going to put it out in my boot?"

"The toilet." She went there, through the examining room beside the files. When she came back, I said: "I don't know. Anything that'll help George. The poor fuck."

She looked at me over a file. She was still standing, working at the top drawer.

"You're not a poor fuck," she said.

"Neither are you."

I was thinking about the endless money from her parents, but her eyes looking at me were brown and lovely, so I did not clarify.

I was in the P's, still wearing one boot, when the sun shone on the windows behind Clark's desk and on its glass top, and the bow of his broken white boat. The sun was very low, and I had missed my run. When we finished, Paula's smoke lay in the air, and the sun was behind the houses and trees beyond the windows, a rose glow beneath the dark sky. In the car I said I would run before dinner, and Paula told me I was crazy, that I would twist an ankle or slip on ice or get hit by a car; I said I needed a run after an afternoon shut up in an office reading files, and she said it wasn't *all* reading files, and a drink would do as well. I have never run at night, for the reasons Paula gave, and I crossed the bridge over the Merrimack as the last glow of sunset faded to dusk, and stopped at Timmy's, where we stood at the bar and had two vodka martinis, and talked with Steve Buckland, the bartender, who has a long thick reddish-blond beard and is one of the biggest men I've ever known; he is also a merry one.

We had planned to go to my apartment and cook steaks and spend a quiet evening; she had her schoolbooks with her, and I was reading *Anna Karenina*, although I meant to watch a Burt Reynolds movie on television at eight. I had not told her this because she might have the discipline to go to the dormitory to study. I was going to glance at the paper after dinner and say Oh: *Hustle* is on; then she would watch it with me, tensely for a while, but she would stop worrying about her work and after the movie, because the television is at the foot of my bed, we would make love, and soon she would fall asleep studying beside me and I would read *Anna Karenina* until two or three, when I would sleep. But we had our third martini at an Italian restaurant south of town, and the young woman tending bar made them so well that we violated the sensible rule, whether we had one or not, about martinis, and drank a fourth. We shared a bottle of chianti with dinner; Paula eats well and does not exercise but is flat-bellied and firm. Of course, as she approaches thirty, six or seven years from now, her flesh will soften then sag. We each drank Sambuco with three floating coffee beans, and she drank coffee. I didn't dare.

I do not record this drinking as some laurel for hedonism, but because the alcohol gave us a distance from the afternoon, as surely as air travel would have, and during dinner we were able to see clearly what had, in Clark's office, been blurred by names (I knew some of them), and ages, and ailments. We were talking generally about morality and the distillation of its whisperings that we had confronted in the files, when Paula stopped talking, and stopped listening to me, though she watched me still as she twirled spaghetti in oil and garlic around her fork.

"Jesus," she said. "He was a script doctor."

And there it was, as though rising to the surface of a dream, the truth coming as it so often does in that last hour of drunkenness when all that is unessential falls away and suddenly you see clearly. Soon after that you are truly drunk and may not remember next day what it was that you saw. But we had it now, the truth, or a truth out of all the pneumonia, flu, strep throat, two cases of gout that had made me feel I was in the nineteenth century watching Anna Karenina's eight rings sparkle in candlelight, cancer and heart disease and strokes, an afternoon of illness and injury and their treatment recorded in Francis Clark's scribbled sentences that began with verbs: *Complains of chest pains. Took EKG*—a truth that seemed tangible and shimmering on the table between us, among the odors of wine and garlic and Paula's lipsticked unfiltered Gitanes in the ashtray: a number of girls and young women whose only complaint was fat, and whose treatment was diet and prescriptions. Speed, Paula said. That's what they get, so they won't eat. And downers so they can function. Which did not really mean he was a script doctor, for neither of us could recall whether the patients were fat or simply getting drugs. There was also the matter of his Wednesday nights, and I knew they involved a woman, or women, and believed Paula knew it too, though was too loyal to what her sex has told itself it has become to admit it, and she argued that both my age and my Greek heritage had combined to blind me as surely as the famous Greek motherfucker; that Lillian Clark's bitter and unhappy face and Francis Clark's Wednesday nights did not add up to adultery.

"She may be unhappy for a *totally* different reason," she said, waving a cool and hardened chunk of garlic bread. "Something that has *noth*ing to do with a man."

"Right," I said. "One morning she woke up and looked under the hood of her Porsche and found an engine there instead of God."

"I knew you'd see the truth. You don't know how hard it is to be a rich woman."

"A rich lovely woman."

"Yes."

"A rich lovely sensual woman."

"With a balding Greek for a lover. Yes."

"It runs in my family."

"Why don't I ever meet them?"

"Saturday."

"This Saturday?"

"There's a Greek dance."

"Will you teach me how, before we go?"

"I don't know if Wasps can learn it."

We left the epiphanic phase with Sambuco, and had a second one, and I drove carefully home, turned on the eleven o'clock news, found that I could not understand it and was drinking a bottle of Moosehead beer; so was Paula; then I remembered bringing them to the bedroom. I turned off the television and lights and we undressed and got into bed and talked for a while, about snow I believe, or rain, and forgot to make love. I woke early, at eight-fifteen, with a hangover, and got the *Boston Globe* from the front steps, and after aspirins and orange juice and a long time in the bathroom with the paper, I ran ten miles and returned sweating and clearheaded to the smells of dripping coffee and the last of Paula's Gitanes.

Beverly Strater lived on the second floor of an apartment building that had been a house, and the front door did not unlock from inside her apartment. About ten years ago, in this town, that would have been customary, but whatever was loose in the land had reached us too, a city of under fifty thousand where old people living in converted factory buildings, renting good apartments for small portions of their incomes, boasted of the buildings' security. Beverly Strater was neither old nor young, and had the look about her of a divorcee whose children had grown: that is, she looked neither barren nor discontented, had a good smile and some lines of merriment in her face, and a briskness to her walk and gestures that seemed to come from energy, not nerves. I had simply climbed the stairs and knocked on her door, and I wished she were not so accessible; I did not think she could afford thieves, and she was certainly not too old to discourage any aesthetic considerations a rapist may have. She dispelled my worries before I mentioned them, as, over tea in her kitchen, she told me about Francis Clark's gun, and that she kept a loaded .38 at her bedside, and took it with her when she went places that would keep her out after dark. Her husband had taught her about guns, and it was his revolver she had now; she had reared three children and gone back to nursing six years ago, after he died. Because of her husband's attitude—and her own—about guns, she had not thought it unusual of Dr. Clark to own one and keep it in his office. Sometimes he left the office after dark, always in the winter months of short days, and she assumed he armed himself before walking to his car.

"It's just the times," she said. "And, you see, poor man, he was right."

In winter I am condemned to sit in rooms of smoke. Beverly was filling the kitchen, and her lungs too, and watching her inhale, I shuddered. Or perhaps I shuddered at the image of Clark putting a .45 in his pocket to walk out to his car, and Beverly's seeing that as something of no more significance than wearing a hat or a pair of sunglasses. Yet I liked her. She was one of those women whom, if I had children, I would trust to care for them. I liked her stockiness, which reminded me of my mother, who was at that time visiting Greece, and reminded me also of women in a Greek village, not of a stout American. I have never held a gun and would be frightened if I did, and as I was about to tell her that, I thought of something else, of the fear and anger I would feel if anyone pointed a gun at me and what I would do if I could get that gun from him, and I said, "It may have got him killed."

"That's true too. My husband always said: Don't ever use it for a bluff. He meant—"

"I know what he meant. Did he ever use it?"

"Oh, Lord, no: he was a mailman. He had a spray for dogs. The gun was to protect our home at night."

There are days, and this was one of them, when I cannot bear the company of my countrymen. I wished Paula were not at classes. My God, you can stay more or less happy doing your work and enjoying the flesh and the company of friends until you get a glimpse of the way people perceive the world. Once in a psychology journal I read an article on suicides in New Hampshire during the decade of 1960 to 1970; there were graphs showing that suicides by women were on the rise; the two authors did not mention it, but I noticed that suicides by both women and men increased each election year. My own notion is that my neighbors to the north were incurably shocked to see the evidence of what the majority of people were not simply content with, but strove for. I often feel the same and conclude that most of us are not worth the dead trees it takes to wipe our asses one summer. I was feeling this now, watching Beverly's motherly face talking about life as though it were lived in a sod hut in Kansas in 1881 or in a city slum where teenaged criminals routinely sacked apartments.

I asked her about Wednesday nights. She was truly surprised, and she remained so, went from surprise to puzzlement and was still frowning with it when I left. Before doing that, I asked her about the girls and young women on diets. She answered absently, still trying to understand the Wednesday nights. A few, she said. He wasn't a *diet* doctor, but there were a few patients—girls—who came to him with a weight problem. I have noticed that women of the working class call each other girls, as men say the boys. I asked only one more question, at the door: "Were they really fat?"

"If they weren't, they *thought* they were. It's the same thing, isn't it?"

Paula and I met for lunch in my office, then went to Clark's. Because she does not exercise, she still had a hangover. In front of the filing cabinet, she touched me, but I shook my head, starting to explain but then said nothing, knowing I was too despondent to give meaningful words to my despondency and my dread, so muted that it was lethargic, as impossible as that sounds. But it was lethargic, my dread, and it made me think of summer and lying on the beach in the sun, so that I wanted to lie on the floor and sleep, for I was beginning to know that in simply trying to save George Karambelas I was going to confront nothing as pure and recognizable as evil but a sorrowful litany of flaws, of failures, of mediocre hopes, and of vanity. We wrote the names and addresses of the twelve, and Paula said That's what Jesus started with, and I said So did Castro, and at the sound of my voice, she said, "Are you all right?"

She stood at Clark's desk, holding the notebook, and looking at me in a way that would have been solemn if it weren't tender too.

"Sure," I said. "Let's start."

We did, in midafternoon, in the low winter sun of that Tuesday. The sun lasted through Wednesday, and that night we lay in the dark and watched snow blowing against the windows and listened to Alicia de Larrocha play Chopin preludes. We spoke to one woman on Tuesday, three on Wednesday, three on Thursday, and two Friday; then we did not need the other three. Paula rescheduled some of my appointments, mostly for tax returns and wills, work that could wait, though I felt like a gambler when we changed the appointments for wills, and since the gamble did not involve me, I felt a frightening sense of power I did not want. Wednesday morning we brought the key back to Lillian; Paula wanted to see her. But Teresa answered the door and said She is busy, and I gave her the key, looking at her brown eyes and thinking of her making Lillian's bed, and cooking her meals, and cleaning her house.

The first woman was a florist, or she worked in a florist's shop, and she took us to the office at the rear of the store and gave us coffee while the owner stayed in front with his flowers. Ada Cleary was twenty-five years old, one of those women whose days for years have been an agony about the weight of her body, or how much of it she could pinch. She looked at Paula, with polite glances to include me, as she spoke of her eight years of diets. I could not see the results, since I did not know what she looked like before she started seeing Clark a month ago. What I saw was a woman in a sweater and skirt, neither fat nor thin, but with wide hips and a protrusion of rump that looked soft enough to sink a fist into; I did not dare look at her legs, though I tried to spy on them but was blocked by the desk she stood behind. Her cheeks, though, were concave, and the flesh beneath her jaw was firm, and her torso looked disproportionate, as though it were accustomed to resting on smaller hips; or, the truth, it had recently been larger. Dr. Clark was very nice, she said, very understanding. And for the first time she was able to say no to food. It was the drugs.

"Speed," Paula said.

"Yes. And I take the others. You know, to get me down."

"Don't you worry about your head?" Paula said.

"I can't. Once I get down to one hundred and six pounds, that's when I'll stop the drugs. And see if I can make it on my own. You know: throw away my clothes, buy some new ones."

"Why one oh six?" I said.

"That's what I weighed in high school. Junior year. Before I turned into an elephant."

"What will you do without Clark?" I said.

"Oh, Gawd, find another doctor. I still have some pills left."

"Will he be hard to find?" I said.

"Oh, no. It's like sleeping pills. I've never had trouble sleeping, but a friend of mine does. You just have to shop around. Some are strict, some are—helpful."

"Understanding," I said. "I don't sleep well either."

"Oh? What do you take?"

"Moosehead," Paula said.

"Really? You don't look it."

"Sometimes," I said. "Sometimes I just read."

"He runs a lot," Paula said.

"It's all legal," Ada said. "I mean, wasn't it?"

"Sure," I said. "Good luck with the one oh six."

In the car, Paula said: "You shouldn't have looked at her like that."

"Like what?"

"Angry."

"Was I?"

"Weren't you?"

"Yes."

"Why?"

She opened her purse and went through the smoker's elaborate motions, whose rhythm was disrupted by her hurriedly lifting and pushing aside whatever things had found or lost their way into her deep purse, until her hands emerged with the pack and lighter, and with thumb and forefinger she tore open the cellophane, opened the box, removed the top foil, put it and the crumpled cellophane into her purse, and so on. I have never wanted to smoke, but I would enjoy opening those pretty little boxes, as I would enjoy filling a pipe. My brother Kosta carries worry beads, but at work he is too busy to play with them. If he smoked, he would have to pause to give his attention to the cellophane, the cardboard, the foil. I thought of telling him he should stop every half hour to play for five minutes with his beads, and opened my window a few inches. Her cigarette was American.

"Well?" she said.

"Because it's bullshit."

"What is?"

"All that dieting."

"You should feel sorry for her."

"I do."

We passed the college where she lived and, on some nights, slept.

"Describe her," she said.

"Okay."

"Well. Go ahead."

"I mean okay, I get your point."

"Do you really?"

"I don't want to, but I do."

"*You* look at women that way."

"You couldn't let it go, could you?"

We passed the Common, a small park with a white fence and scattered old trees. On Thursday nights in summer an orchestra of old men plays old popular songs and marching tunes, and old people bring their lawn chairs and listen. At other times, young people gather under the trees. In the summer afternoons they are still lifes, except for an occasional Frisbee game. I have never understood why they cup their hands and lower their heads when smoking dope, since those are the only signs giving them away to anyone passing by. They should pretend to be smoking cigarettes, but then no one cares anyway, until night when the police cruiser disperses them.

"You just had to say it."

"Yes."

"Okay."

At the Square that is not a square but a street and one parking lot in front of commercial places, I parked and we crossed the street and looked in the window of the young Greek's fish market. He waved from behind the counter where he was wrapping and weighing white fillets of fish for a woman taking bills from her wallet and wiping her nose with Kleenex. We waved and went to Timmy's.

"Does it bother you?" I said at the bar.

"Why should it? I'm not fat."

"It bothers me," I said, and big Steve Buckland came and greeted us and took our orders. Steve has a grand belly, but his chest is even larger, by eight or ten inches, and if he didn't have the belly he would look like those body builders who seem involved with their bodies to the point of foolishness, so I don't like looking at them. It gets confusing. We drank beer, then went to my apartment for the steaks we had not cooked the night before.

When I look back on that week, I see a series of female faces and gesturing hands, and I hear their voices, and I remember the constriction I felt, as though I had left the world and its parts I recognized, and was immersed in only one of those parts, and it blinded and deafened me to the others. All I could see was female flesh, all I could hear was female voices: they were intense, as from long anger; they were embittered yet resolute; they were self-effacing, with a forced note of humor; they were lyric in their plaintiveness, abrupt with considered despair; they were hopeful. Their hands held pencils, pens, cigarettes, black coffee, diet drinks, and moved in front of and beneath their faces, hovered and swooped over laps and desks, and darted to the mouth that sucked or chewed, smoked or drank. Their faces, I realized, were the faces of the obsessed. Always, behind their eyes, I could see another life being lived. They spoke to us of Dexedrine balanced by Seconal, Nembutal, or Quāāludes and, before the drugs, water diets, grapefruit diets, carbohydrates, calories, diuretics, laxatives, vomiting— every one of them but Ada had forced herself, until Clark's treatment, to vomit at least three times a week, usually more, so we assumed Ada had too, and I liked her for not disclosing that, for keeping private at least that humiliating detail, and also the other one these women did not spare us: images of frequent and liquid emptying of the bowels, whose imagined sounds and smells destroyed, for me, whatever beauty the women did have (none of them was truly fat), as well as that ideal of weight and proportion they strove for. Yet, while they turned their bodies, before my eyes, into bowels, intestines,

adipose, digestive juices, piss, shit, and vomit, there was that
other life visible in the light of their eyes. Perhaps they strode
across the room of their consciousness, graceful, svelte; or sat
naked, their stomachs flat, unwrinkled, the skin as taut as the
soles of their feet; or, with slender arms, whose only curves
were those of athletic muscles, whose flesh did not shake or
hang, they reached for steaming bowls of food and piled it on
their plates.

That week, except for the martini and Sambuco night, I
kept my usual discipline and drank only a few Mooseheads in
the evening. So I was sober all those nights after our talks with
the women, and I lay awake long after Paula slept, and the little
bastard spoke to me of flesh, of food, of dresses, of Lillian's
Porsche and my brothers bent over bows and vamps, and I
tried to shut him up with the word *vanity*, but he was persistent. *It always connects,* he said. *Everything connects. You have
only to look.* I got up to drink milk in the dark living room; I
rolled from side to side on the bed and lay still, listening to
Paula breathing, and I thought of my brothers fleeing the shoe
factory and the future my uncle had planned for them: to learn
English while they learned the work of every room and bench
in the factory, from the designer in the basement, whose ideas
were stolen from Italian shoes bought or photographed in Italy
by my uncle, or clipped from magazines, to the cutting room,
the stitching room, and so forth, to the room where women
inspected and boxed and shipped the pieces of leather that
would be the tops of shoes, and then perhaps my brothers
would become foremen, certainly not partners, for my uncle
had his own sons (has: they now own the factory), though
maybe he would have left them a share. Fled to beautician
school, then borrowed money and opened a shop and married
Greek women, lovely Greek women who bore children who
are respectful, beautiful, and well behaved, not at all like American children, though they speak English without the accents of
their parents. Anyone visiting my brothers' houses will be
given a drink and food, and always there are feta cheese and
olives, and my brothers' wives keep stuffed grape leaves and
spinach pies in the freezer. They proudly sent me through
school, and now, with love and less pride, they look at my life,

and sometimes they ask me, as the little bastard did those nights of the week of the dieting women, why was I, at thirty-three, still living in a three-room apartment (including the kitchen, with the table where I eat) and going to work at ten in the morning and taking Wednesday afternoons off and spending so much time running and fucking young girls. They are not opposed to running but that I do it during my long lunch break and so return late for the afternoon's work, nor are they opposed to the young girls but insist that I could have them and marriage and a family. I have no answers. But when they tell me I'm thirty-three, I am for moments, even minutes, frightened. It is strange: no one is Christian anymore, but every man I've known reach the age of thirty-three has been afraid that he will not see thirty-four, as if none of us can forget that the most famous death of the culture occurred at thirty-three. I do tell them I don't need more money, but they say I do, I should be investing in stock, in bonds, and buying a house, and I shiver at this and grow silent until they laugh and clap my shoulder and hug me, and I am the baby brother again, whom they care for and indulge.

The little bastard is not so gentle, and those nights he demanded answers and got none, and he kept saying *It all connects; it all connects,* as I tried to sleep and tried to read, but *Anna Karenina* took me back to, rather than away from, the women; for if she had lived now and had believed she was fat because her stomach creased, because she could pinch flesh over her ribs, because she could not wear her size eight or ten, she would have been among them, taking pills and getting through the day on black coffee and cigarettes, nibbling food while her face tautened and her heart beat faster, creeping down to the kitchen at night to eat a half gallon of ice cream, then rushing in remorse to the bathroom to jam fingers down her throat and vomit the colors of that food children and dieting women so love, if I can take as a microcosm the women we interviewed, for each of them confessed ice cream as her secret wickedness. These images of shitting and vomiting induced by laxatives and fingers interrupted me whenever, that week, I touched Paula: to teach her a Greek dance in my living room standing side by side, hands on each other's shoulders, as

I counted one-two one-two; to make love with her before she slept and I lay staring opposite the bed, at the dark window, its glass fogged and moist.

We simply happened, on Friday, to be free at two-thirty, so we drove to the public high school, whose crowded halls and rooms I had endured for four years. I parked at the front of the building. They would all come out there, to the waiting buses in line ahead of us, to the cars in the lot. A large statue of *The Thinker* was on the schoolground, between us and the building. A bell rang loudly, and as they came out, some singly, most in hurried groups, lighting cigarettes, Paula got out of the car, stopped several of them until one boy turned back to the grounds and pointed at a girl alone, lighting a cigarette in the lee of *The Thinker*. Paula went to her, and I watched them talking. Then they came to the car. I watched Paula talking, smiling; when they got closer I could see that the girl was doing neither, and as she slid into the back seat and looked at me, I thought she wouldn't, not in this car, not with us.

"Who's your father?" I said.

"Jake."

"Jake? I know Jake."

KAREN ARAKELIAN

They said they would take me home, but could we go by his office first and talk where it was comfortable so him and the girl didn't have to stay twisted around to look at me. I knew who he was, I had seen him a lot in town, but he didn't recognize me, because I kept growing up while he stayed the same. Except he had lost more hair. He drove, and I just watched his bald head and the hair at the back and sides and smoked two cigarettes. I didn't say anything, and I didn't know if I would or not in his office; I wouldn't know till it was over. But I felt like it was all over and nobody would understand what it's like when they're all so thin. Everybody, even Heidi, even though she's always talking about how fat she is, but I know it's so we'll look at how thin she is and be jealous. And we are. Anyways I am.

I think it was money. I even thought of shoplifting and trying to sell things, but after I figured out how I could do it and where, and that took hours and hours, for days and nights, a lot of time thinking about the different stores and what they had in them and where the clerks were. I even went to some of them and looked around. Then after I planned how to do it and what to take, I realized there was no one to sell it to. Because if they could afford to buy the stuff, then they didn't have to buy it cheaper from me, and if they were my friends, or people like them, they couldn't buy anything anyways.

I was relieved, but I was at the bottom again, like the times when I wanted to be dead, because the pills were working but I couldn't afford a second prescription. I had saved for the first one, and for the first visit to Francis too, and there were no jobs, not unless I quit school and worked full time, which I would do, but my parents would never let me. All of us were supposed to go to college, my Dad was very proud about that, and I could see why: he had worked so hard at that shitty place, and his father had come over from Armenia to get away from the Turks. I have heard those stories, about them killing my great-grandparents, and other stories, and I hate fucking Turks. Everyone else had gone to college, and I'm the youngest. So I couldn't get a job.

I went to Francis for my second appointment in January, when school had just started and my Christmas job at the department store was over and I was down to my last two days of pills. He weighed me; then I started crying, and he told me to get dressed and he sent the nurse out. When I was dressed he sat me down in his office and said: "You lost seven pounds. Why did you cry?"

So I told him, and I see now that's when he knew my parents didn't know I was going to him, didn't know about the pills and the vomiting. You know how they are, the doctors: they handle you so fast they hardly look at you, and even if they do, even if they touch you with their stethoscope and their fingers, you feel like they haven't. But he was definitely looking at me, and I couldn't believe it: there it was in his face; he wanted me, the first time almost anybody ever looked at me like that, anybody but punks in the halls and at parties, the first time ever that the guy was a grown man. An old one too. So I looked back. And saw that he was old but not too old. He was probably fifty or more, but he was distinguished-looking; he had a nice haircut, not too short, and blow-dried hair, dark brown with some gray at the sides and temples; and he was tall and trim, athletic-looking, probably racquetball and tennis. I knew he sailed his boat. The lines in his face must have come from the boat; they looked like outdoor lines. I watched him watching me; then I took out a cigarette, which I'd always been afraid to do in a doctor's office, and I lit it and he didn't say anything. After a while he got up and gave me his Styrofoam cup for an ashtray. A few drops of coffee were in the bottom. He drank it with cream. Then he said: "I can help you."

He was standing right in front of me, his legs nearly touching my knees, and I moved my cigarette out to the side so the smoke wouldn't go up to his face.

"Please do," I said.

"Come tomorrow night at eight."

Tomorrow was Wednesday. I said I would. He kept standing there. I finished my cigarette, blowing the smoke off to my side and watching him talk to me. We would have to be careful, he said. He could get into very bad trouble. But he could give me the pills. But I mustn't ever say a word. I nodded. Then, I don't know why, I knew he was hard. When I put out my cigarette I glanced at it. His pants stretched across its top, and it was like it was trying to push through the pants and touch my eyes.

On Wednesday night it was very big, and I knew I had never really fucked before. I had done it in the yard and in cars at parties, when I was loaded on drugs and beer. But this was slow getting undressed, and his hands weren't a doctor's anymore, they were slow and gentle and everything took a long time. He liked eating me and he stayed down there till I came; then he sat on the floor beside the couch and touched me till I was ready again. Then he put on a rubber, and for a long slow time he was in me and I came again and finally he did: when it happened to him he groaned and shuddered and cried out in a high soft voice like a girl. That night he gave me birth control pills too.

So I had all these pills to take, and I hid them in my underwear drawer where I keep my cigarettes and grass, and I should have kept them all in my purse, but I'm so careless about my purse—I keep dropping it on the kitchen table with my books, or leaving it in the living room, on top of the television or on the couch—that I was always afraid, when it was just grass and cigarettes, that my mother or father would pick it up wrong, just to move it, and everything would fall out on the table or floor: my Newports and my dope, and then it was speed and downs and the birth control pills, so everything was under my pants. Still I should have been safe. I do my own laundry and fold them in the basement and put them away.

But that night Heidi was over and we were up in my room, and I was putting away my clothes when Dad knocked on the door. I said come in. He opened the door and stood in the doorway a while, talking to us. He always liked to talk to us kids and our friends. That night we talked about school, and he said we had to work hard and try to get scholarships but that he'd see to it I went to any place I could get into. He could always get money, he said, and I was the last one, so it was easier. Then he was talking about when he went to the high school and the trouble he and the guys got into, getting wise with old Mrs. Fletcher (she still teaches English, even though we think she's senile the way she keeps reciting "Snow-Bound" every year on the first day it snows because Whittier was born here and lived here), and he and his buddies would get sent to the principal; and talking Armenian in French class; and sneaking fishing rods out of the house in the morning and walking down to the bus stop with the rods in two parts down their pants legs, so they walked stiff-legged, and when they were around the corner, they took out the rods and went to the pond—and it was all so tame and old-fashioned I felt sorry for him.

I've told him there are guards in the halls and patrolling the lavs for pushers, and he knows, because every kid in the family has told him, about kids smoking dope and drinking on the bus at seven in the morning, but it's like to him it's something that's going on, but it's out *there* somewhere, with the Puerto Ricans and Italians, but it's not here, in this nice house he's buying every month, like we have our own world here. And Goddamn me, that's when I put the panties in my drawer, while he was laughing about him and his buddies growing up. He had moved into the room by then, and was standing on the rug under the ceiling light, and what I didn't think of is how tall he is. If I were standing there, I could not see into the back of my drawer. I can't even see into it when I'm standing beside it; I have to sort of raise up and look toward the back. But he could look straight down in it. Not that he was. He was talking to us, Heidi sitting on the bed and me standing between the bed and the chest of drawers, and I suppose his eyes just naturally followed my hands as they took clothes from the bed and put them in the drawers, and when I put a stack of pants in the top drawer, all he did was glance that way, and what he saw wasn't the cellophane of grass or the two bottles of pills or the birth control pills, but the Goddamn turquoise of the Newport pack, and he stopped talking and I saw his face change; he said "Uh-oh," and I shoved the drawer closed.

"Karen," he said, and I looked at Heidi. She said later she thought it was the grass. She didn't know about the pills, none of them, and she still doesn't.

"It's for me," Heidi said. Her face was red, and her mouth and eyes were scared-looking, and I will never forget what she did for me, or tried to. Because she knows my dad has a temper, and telling him you smoke dope is like telling some of these other parents you're on heroin. "Karen doesn't smoke it," she said. She looked like she was about to cry.

Then he knew. He lives at home like he doesn't know anything but the leather factory—he's a foreman there—but he is not dumb. I wish for him and me both, and Mom, and Francis, that he was. Because then he said: "You better go on home now, Heidi."

She got her parka and was gone, looking at the floor as she walked past him; at the door she looked back, and her face was still red and her eyes were bright and wet. Then she went down the hall and I heard her on the stairs and my mom calling good night and Heidi said it too, and I could tell it was over her shoulder as she went out the door. I heard it, and then the storm door, and was looking at Dad's shoes.

"Open it," he said.

I shook my head. If I spoke I would blubber. He turned his head and shouted, "Marsha!"

Mom didn't answer. She came up the stairs, her footsteps heavy like running, but she was only climbing fast. She stood at the door a moment looking at me and at Dad's back; then she came in and stood beside him.

"She's smoking dope," he said. "Cigarettes too. Show your mother the drawer, Karen."

Then I was lying on the bed, face-down, like I had fainted, because I didn't remember deciding to do it or getting there: one second I was standing looking at them, then I was crying into the bedspread, and I knew from the footsteps and the slow way the drawer opened that it was Mom who did it. Then she was crying over me, hugging me from behind, her hands squeezed between my shoulders and the bed, and Dad was talking loud but not yelling yet, and I started talking into all that, babbling I guess, but it wasn't about Francis and me. I said that too, but it was like a small detail when you're describing a wreck you were in, telling the police, and Francis and me were just the rain or the car that stopped to help: sometimes I screamed, but mostly I moaned and cried about vomiting my dinner and hiding that from them and laxatives and having to go at school and holding it and holding it till the bell, then hurrying to the lav and the sick sounds I made in the stall with the girls smoking just on the other side of it and saying *gross gross*, and my fat ugly legs and my fat ugly bottom and my fat ugly face and my fat ugly floppy boobs and how I wanted to be dead I was so fat and ugly, and some time in there my dad stopped talking, stopped making any sound at all, except once when he said, like he was going to cry too, like Mom was the whole time: "Oh, my God."

ARCHIMEDES NIONAKIS

I said it too. I didn't say much more as I stood at the window looking from Karen to the twilit traffic to Karen again while she talked and wept and Paula's eyes brimmed over and she wiped her cheeks. Then Paula took her to the bathroom behind the waiting room, and they worked on their faces and came out cleansed of tears and made-up again, walking arm in arm. Karen was plump. But, like all those others—and I know all is hyperbolic for only eight women, nine with Karen, but on that Friday afternoon their numbers seemed legion—she was not fat.

Looking out my window at people driving home from work in the lingering sunset, the snow having stopped Thursday morning and the sky cleared overnight, I listened to Karen and thought of my brothers, perhaps the happiest Americans I know. I barely remember my father—I am not certain whether I recall him or merely have images from stories my brothers and mother have told—but my brothers remember him and the village where we lived. My father owned a small café and was also the mayor of the town, so when the Communist guerrillas came they took him with them, to the hills. They all knew him, and they said We have to take you because you are the mayor. Some months later one of them came through town and stopped at our house to tell my mother her husband was well. Kosta was ten, and my mother sent him with the man and a knapsack of food and wine, and they walked for two days to the camp in the mountains, where Kosta spent a day and a night with my father, who showed him to everyone in the camp and boasted of his son who had come to visit. It was, Kosta says, a gentle captivity. They treated my father well, and he could do whatever he pleased except escape. Kosta walked back alone, stopping at houses along the way. Later a guerrilla came to tell my mother that my father had died, probably of pneumonia, and they had properly buried him, with a marker, in the hills. She managed the café and cared for me, playing among the tables, and worried about her older sons and wrote to her brother in America to sponsor us.

So my brothers have built a business and houses, and when I go visit them or, more important, when, unobserved, I see them driving in town and I watch from the sidewalk, I know they are happy, as I do when I go to their shop and wait for one of them to trim what is left of my hair. They laugh and talk; for eleven or twelve hours a day, six days a week, they do this, and they make a lot of money from those women, as though, immigrants that they are, they had seen right away in the shoe factory where the heart of the nation was and left that bleak building and women's feet and moved up to their own building, and later their homes, paid for by women's hair. And remained untouched, unscathed: swam and skied and played tennis with their wives and children, indeed lived athletic lives as naturally as animals and never considered the burning of fat or the prolonging of life. As I run, not for my waist or longevity, but to maintain some proportion of my *homo duplex*, to keep some balance between the self I recognize and the little bastard who recognizes nothing as familiar, a quotidian foreigner in the land. My brothers watched with amusement, if even that, as their hair fell out. They celebrate all Greek holidays, as I do with them, and on Greek Easter we cook a lamb on a spit; they take their families to the Greek church, and I do not know whether they believe in God as much as they believe a father should take his family to church. They visit Greece, where now my father's bones lie in a cemetery in our village, and I go there too, having no memories save those of a tourist who speaks the language and shares the blood, so that I have no desire for a Greek household as my brothers have made with their marriages here, nor do I have a desire for an American one. So this year in my apartment I have Paula, and I have a law practice that is only an avocation, and my only vocation is running each year in Boston the long run from my father's country.

Still Karen talked, seated at my desk, leaning over it, her hands outstretched, held and stroked by Paula's. I looked at Paula sitting in the chair she had pulled up to a corner of the desk, and I thought I could tell my brothers now; it was clear to me, and I could explain it to them, could show them why I would not, could not, work twelve or eight or even six hours a day five or six days a week for any life this nation offered. I had not fled a village where I would roam without education till I died. I had simply been a five-year-old boy placed on a ship. I looked out the window again and thought of Lillian Clark and those terrible eyes and the Puerto Rican girl to free her of her work, so that she had nothing at all to do, while in the garage the steel of the Porsche drew into itself the February cold. I spun from the window in a moment of near glee, so that Karen stopped and sniffed and looked at me, wiping her eyes. But I stopped myself and turned back to the window. I had been about to tell her that I was glad Jake had done it.

She did not mention once, that entire time, the killing of Francis Clark. Nor did I ask her to. When she finished I told her we would take her home and saw at once in her eyes what I knew as soon as I had spoken: we could not do that, we could not enter or even drive to the front of Jake's home, and I felt affection and respect like love for her then, saw her as a sixteen-year-old daughter who not only loved Jake but understood him too. She would have done everything again so she could clothe herself in smaller and smaller pants and skirts and dresses and blouses, but she would have done it with more care. And I remembered from somewhere, someone, in my boyhood: *Don't shit where you eat.* It was the way my brothers ran their households, and perhaps one of them had said it to me. I told Karen that Paula would drive her to her street corner and I would phone her father. They both nodded and went to the bathroom. When they came out, I held Karen's parka for her and told Paula I would see her at my apartment.

I sat at the desk in the smoky and shadowed room—we had not turned on a light—then I looked up Jake's number, closed the book, gazed at the window and the slow cars, forgot the number, and opened the book again. His street was not far away, and I wanted to give him time to leave before Karen walked into the house. Marsha answered, and I heard the quaver of guilt in my voice and heard it again when Jake took the phone, and beneath the warmth in his voice I heard what I knew I would see in his eyes. I asked him if we could have a talk.

"Sure, Archimedes, sure. I'm on the way."

I waited outside, in the waning light now, and watched every car coming from his direction. His was large, and American, and I peered at him through the window, then got in. He drove us to the ocean. I do not know why. Perhaps it was for

the expanse of it, or some instinct sent him to the shore. But I
do not want to impose on Jake my own musing of that day:
perhaps he wanted a bar where no one knew us. He drove for
half an hour, and we talked about my brothers and his and his
sisters and his work at the factory. We did not mention my
work or Karen or Marsha or his grown children. Now and
then I looked at his face, lit by the dashboard, and his eyes
watching cars and trucks, while they stared at his new life.

He stopped at a restaurant across the road from the ocean;
on the beach side of the road, a seawall blocked our view of the
water, but night had come, and we could only have seen the
breakers' white foam. The empty tables in the restaurant were
set for dinner, their glass-encased candles burning over red
tablecloths; we went through a door into the darkened lounge
and stood for a few moments until we could see, then moved to
a booth at the wall, across the room from the bar. The other
drinkers were at the bar, four men, separate, drinking quietly.
The bartender, a young woman, came for the order. Jake said a
shot of CC and a draft, so I did too and had money on the
table when she came back, but he covered it with his hand,
said, No, Archimedes, and paid her and tipped a dollar. He
raised his shot glass to me, and I touched it with mine. He
drank his in one motion; I swallowed some and said, "I'm
defending George Karambelas."

"Yes."

"I've just talked to Karen."

"Ah."

He drank from the mug of draft and called to the bar:
"Dear? Two more shots, please."

So I drank the rest of my whiskey, and we watched her
cross the floor with the bottle and pour, and he gave her
money again before I saw it in his hand, but I said: My round,
Jake, and gave her my ten and told her to keep one. We
watched her until she was behind the bar again, then touched
glasses, and I sipped and looked at his wide neck as he drank.
Then I said: "I've been wondering about the boat."

"The boat?"

"That model. How did it break?"

"I broke it. With my fist, on the desk."

"Why?"

"How do you think he paid for it, Archimedes? You think he was a good man? An honest man? A good *doctor*?"

"No."

"That's why I broke it."

"Then what?"

"He was sitting behind his desk when I broke it. He was waiting for—you know what he was waiting for."

"Yes."

He turned toward the bar, lifting his glass.

"No," I said. "Finish first. Please."

"Okay. That's when he took out the gun. From his drawer. He took it out and he worked it, so he had a bullet in there, in the barrel, and it was cocked. You know something? I looked at that big hole in the barrel, pointed at me, and I looked at that son of a bitch's face, and I wasn't scared of that gun. I think because if I died I didn't care. I can't tell you how bad I felt. You don't know; I can't say it."

"I know."

I took our shot glasses to the bar and she filled them and he said loudly, to my back: "Archimedes. That's my round."

"I'll run a tab," she said. I noticed then she wore glasses, and in the light behind the bar was pretty, and I wanted to be home with Paula, only to lie beside her, and to sleep. I spilled whiskey on both hands going back to the booth.

"She's keeping a tab," I said.

Jake nodded, and raised his glass to mine, and I smelled more whiskey than I drank.

"He told me to leave. How do you like that? He's doing that to my daughter and giving her those pills, and he says to me, Leave. Go home. So I didn't move. I came to talk to that son of a bitch—"

"He was certainly that, Jake."

"Yes. And you know how they are, those rich doctors, all the rich people, they're used to saying leave, go home, and everybody goes. So what's he going to do, Archimedes? Shoot me? Of course not. He's got the gun and he's behind his desk, but *still* he has to listen. Because I'm talking to him, Archimedes; I'm telling him things. So he gets mad. *Him*. And he comes

around the desk with that gun, and I tell him I'll shove that
thing up his ass. Then I hit him. But, goddammit, he hit his
head. On the corner of his desk there, when he went down.
Just that once. I hit him just that once, and the son of a bitch
cracked his head. I can't feel bad. For him. But let me tell you,
since that night nobody talks in my house. Marsha and Karen,
they just go around sad. And quiet. Jesus, it's quiet. We talk,
you know; we say this and that, hello, good morning, you
want some more rice? But, oh Jesus, it's quiet, and me too.
I've just been waiting. You see, when they blamed it on George,
I knew I had to go tell them. Every night, I'd say to myself:
Tomorrow, Jake. After work, tomorrow, you go down to the
station. Then I'd go to work next day, and when five o'clock
came I'd drive home. I couldn't leave them. My family. I don't
mind being punished. You kill somebody, you go to jail, even
if he's a son of a bitch. But every day I couldn't leave my
family."

"Monday," I said.

"What about Monday?"

"Let's do it Monday. That'll give you two days to raise
bail."

He drank the rest of his beer, then leaned over the table.

"How much?"

"Probably five thousand for the bondsman."

"I can get it."

"I could ask my brothers," I said. "You might need ten,
but I doubt it."

"No. I have some family. And I have friends."

He slid out of the booth, stood at the table's end, held two
mugs in one hand, the glasses in the other.

"Well," he said. "Okay. Yes: Monday."

He went to the bar, tall and wide and walking steadily,
and I wanted to tell him not to bring me another shot, but I
could not keep that distance from him, though my legs under
the table felt weak, as if they alone, of my body, were drunk.
Then he paid her, so this was our last drink, and I imagined
Paula in the warm bedroom, lying on the bed reading her
philosophy book, glancing at her watch. When Jake sat across
from me, we raised the glasses, and I said, To Monday; then

we touched them and I drank mine in one long swallow, exhaled, and drank some beer.

"You said let's," he said.

"What?"

"Let's do it Monday. What did you mean?"

"I don't charge much," I said. "I don't charge anything at all, for a good Armenian."

"Really? You? You want to be my lawyer?"

"Jake, you'll never see the inside of a prison."

"*No.*"

"I'm sure of it."

"Really?"

"Really."

"What about George?"

"He won't be my client anymore."

"But this weekend. He stays in jail?"

"Only till Monday. What the hell: he shouldn't drink so much."

His smile came slowly and then was laughter that rose and fell and rose again as we walked out of the dark lounge, to the parking lot and the smack of breakers beyond the seawall and into his car, where pulling down his seat belt, he turned to me and said, "Come to the house and have dinner."

"Another time," I said. "I've got a woman waiting at home."

He squeezed my shoulder, reached across me and pulled my seat belt over my chest and snapped it locked, then started the car and turned on its headlights and slowly drove us home.

KURT DUECKER

SAVING THE DEAD

FROM SHENANDOAH

ᔆ

I'M THE ONE IN THE BOAT, the one in the red plaid parka gripping the oars. The anchorman will never say, "There, that's Dick Lilly," but I'm there, playing my small red part at 5:00 and 11:00. I'm either bent over the side talking to a diver or passing a cup of coffee to Lance. Or sometimes it's a long, clouded shot of me and Lance out on the empty lake, huddled against the mist. But in the end that's always my red hunting parka turned to the camera.

It's not a lake really. It's a gravel pit, hollowed out years ago by the highway department. It was close enough to the Yellowstone that they struck water and it filled in on them. I imagine it just seeped up from the bottom and through the walls. The green highway sign at the turnoff reads "Two Moons Lake." It gives up palm-sized sunfish and one or two soft bass in the summer, and seals over like a tomb in winter. My dad used to take a bunch of us out on it after most of the snow had blown off. We'd knock a tin can around with tree branches. The old man danced and slid among us, trying to ref. He never needed a whistle. His voice could push a tree over in the high-strung winter air. It was the gravel pit then. It's all we've ever called it.

This time it's a girl, a nine-year-old with straight teeth and ribbons around her ponytail. Her eight-by-ten will grow to fill the whole screen. Her mom last saw her at lunch. She'll say it eight or ten times over the air.

"I've told her, I've told Shell a hundred times, *never* to go near that pond. She knows she's never to ride her bike past Shiloh Road." The voice is frightened.

Kids don't listen. On those first nice days of spring they're listening to something else. With me it was snakes, and tadpoles, and turtles waiting out in deep water. A couple of afternoons are sunny, almost hot, and then the clouds are there, not many but enough. By morning it's bone-cold and rainy. The sheriff found her bike against a tree last night, her miniature blue license hanging from the seat—SHELLY. The news will make sure to return to that shot, even though they have to restage it.

It must be a horrid thing to find a kid's new bike late in the evening like that, propped against a tree. The mother waits at her kitchen window, hands lying confused in the cooling dishwater. The tan car pulling into the driveway with its dome breathing blue light is the messenger of God. She quick prays to it before the sheriff steps out and opens the back door or trunk. He lifts the bike out, and bent over because they're never more than a twenty-incher, he starts to wheel it towards the front door. That must kill her.

Lance called me at 5:17 a.m. The wife and I both worry over what the 5:17 call means. As she lies turned away from me I can feel her listening, eyes open, the sheet clutched under her chin. We've been getting a rash of the early rings lately. When I answer there's dead air or breathing on the end. The new boyfriend must be jealous that we're sleeping together. When I hang up she whispers to me.

"Another one?"

"A nine-year-old girl's been missing all night. They found her bike at the gravel pit. No one we know."

I go to the closet and dig out thermals, the mackinaw, and my Hermin Survivors. While I'm getting dressed Pat always makes coffee. She drops a couple of Pop-Tarts in the toaster, tunes the radio into Country Koyn, and checks for the paper. I can see her from the bedroom, sleepy and stretching on the porch. I feel like taking her back to bed. The big head of yellow hair loosens and lets go of her face. Until summer she sleeps in sweatpants and a T-shirt, then just the T-shirt and panties. Her seat hangs well in the sweats. We're usually friends in the morning. Her eyes welcome the light. They're not after anything yet, just half open and nice to look at.

"It's going to rain on you," as I step into the kitchen.

"Spring isn't easy." We agree to smile.

"Be careful," she always says when I leave. Even when I'm off to work at the regular time it's always, "Be careful."

While I'm knocking around the garage after the boat, she finishes her coffee. She might come to the picture window as I'm tying it on the station wagon, but then it's back to bed.

Even when it's raining I like the morning air, the quiet, the cold trying to climb in with you. Even on these mornings when the Rangers call I like the air. I think it's because the air's always shitty at the refinery. Refineries, they all stink like eggs.

I don't think about who's in the pit until I pull onto Lance's block. It's almost always a child, eight kids in five years (twice that many searched for) and one old man who went in after his stuck lure. They've become mixed up with the other signals of spring, meadowlarks and lawnmowers. It's gotten so the first thaw and longer days scare me.

Lance is a younger guy, a few years out of high school. He still lives with his folks—his mom's always watching from the kitchen window where she's finished making him breakfast and packing a lunch. I'll have to mooch some or stop at the Quickway for microwave. It isn't long before you notice his hands, goddamn hands. That's how he's always referring to them, "These goddamn hands!" They had to be put back together after a can of lighter fluid blew up in them. The flame climbed right up the stream from the briquets, hit the nozzle and blew. The next thing he knew his arms were candles. The skin on both of them is smooth and shiny. Patches of it seem stretched too tight over the bones. It's mostly from his ass. There's feeling and they still work like hands, but they'll stiffen up and ache after long at the oars. "These goddamn hands," he'll whisper and then cross them under his armpits to hide as much as warm them. We rarely speak up on the lake. Other than his hands Lance is a big, strong, good-looking kid. He's got shoulders like an old Ford, thick, corded forearms, and a smooth anvil-shaped face. He's okay company for this.

I pull against the curb. His mom raps good-bye on the window, and he stretches and starts across the wet grass to the car. The rain hasn't turned into much more than mist.

"Morning, Licks."

"BV." I'm Licks to all the Rangers, Licks Dicks. Lance was given Burn Victim. I don't know why men have to pass nicknames around, but they do.

"Goddamn nine-year-old girl! Hope we find her."

"Hope we don't." It's the answer you learn to give, part of a before-search ritual. It reminds us that we're looking for something we don't want to find. We find them and it's over, the real grief can settle in. And if we don't, the awful hoping goes on. Who knows what's worse?

The car whines on the wet highway. The ceiling is low and gray. On clear mornings you can make out the white veins of the Beartooth ski runs. Today the trees have returned to winter, shadowed and paled. The damp cold seeps in along the windows.

The other Ranger cars are parked in a T near a small fire. I pull my wagon in adding a fourth arm. Across Two Moons a couple of sheriff's cars, an ambulance, and the KGHL van are huddled in another small group. Fifty or sixty steps back from them has to be the parents' car. It's a fairly new Buick. A lot of businessmen types do well in Stark City and then move out into ranch-styles and pretend their riding mower's a tractor. The Rangers like to stay a good distance away from the official grief and media show. There's six of us between the four cars. We all have the shield, "Stark City Search and Rescue Ranger," sewn somewhere on our bodies. The divers, Golly Gean and Yikes, have it laminated to the breast of their wet suits. In both cases it's peeling off. Gean's father Ed is the squad chief. He deals with police and sheriff communications, paces the bank with a walkie-talkie, and nurses a cup of coffee in his Bronco. All this crap has become his life, Ed and the dead or just Dead Ed. Leroy Simms is the other ground man. He pours Ed's coffee and scurries around loose picking up the poop. Sometimes I'd like to drown him.

"What say, what say, Licker?" I don't pay much attention to him while I'm unloading the boat. He isn't worth the fart it would take to chase him away. I pass the rope back and forth through the rack, leaning out trying to keep the car water off my coat. I'll be wet and cold soon enough.

"Eddy's with the posse, telling them our game plan. Laura Soring's over there for KGHL, getting her pretty hair wet. She's got big-league knockers, Licker. I was chatting and couldn't keep my eyes off them."

Lims has deep-hooded eyes that spend most of their time pointed at women's tits and tails. He has to stare up to look me in the face, but every once in a while he'll do it. I don't feel at all like talking to him this morning.

"Eddy wants you and Beevy over off humpbank. The frogs'll work their way over to you from where Cowboy Bob thinks she went in. He's had his deputies shake the brush along the bank. No luck. You two can sit and count rubbers till they get there." A laugh the size of a bat escapes between his large teeth.

"Nice Lims, run around there and help me dump this. Watch yourself, we don't want any shit to fall out of your head. Beevy," I shout, "get the phone."

Pat says Lims is needed out there. The couple of times they've met she's kept her distance. "Any woman can feel his eyes making the rounds. But he's needed out there," she said. "His filthy mouth drones out mood music, keeps reminding all you saints where you're at and why." She called him a wastebasket for hard emotions.

"You get lots of anger, sorrow, and hate with no place to dump it, so you dispose of it in the nearest receptacle—Lims."

"Yeah, maybe," I said. She always catches me with those, the way she turns things into neat little packages. Most things I run into hit and scatter like a magpie off the grill. A clump sticks, but I never have time to pull over and collect the pieces. You can tell it's a magpie by the black and white remains.

She called her first affair, over a year ago, a bad taste in her mouth, that simple. Said I was working too much, drinking too much, and nodding off too early. It was turnaround at the refinery. We were offline and had to do a month of 7-10's to get back on. The arc of the welder sparked in my dreams. It all left a bad taste in her mouth, and she tried to wash it out with a school teacher. I chased that one down, traced his plates from the bar parking lot. It was all right out of "The Young and Restless." He was this extra-large jock that taught biology at the high school. I went over to football practice straight from work, still had my greasy coveralls and welding cap on. My face was black and shiny around the beard. I felt a little like Spencer Tracy giving it to Gable. I think it frightened him. When he saw me marching over the chalk lines he blew his whistle and sent the kids into laps. It didn't stop them from watching. He was a big boy, had six inches on me, and over-sized thighs pouring out of his coaching shorts. But I delivered the Tracy, told him if I ever saw him with Pat, or even caught whiff of a rumor, I'd weld his dick to the flagpole. All the young girls could pledge allegiance. He acted dumb, which suited his face, and I told him again, same thing, a little louder. I left him standing there in the middle of the field, his kids running in wide circles around him. It felt great. At home I stepped into the ring with Pat.

"I had to get that taste out of my mouth. He came with the pretzels, stingers and juke box."

What could I say. I told her I'd weld her shut. It didn't go over as well. The marriage had begun to smell.

The next course was a gandy dancer, tie-gang foreman for the Burlington Northern. We spoke the same language, and I rubbed his face in it for little more than a chipped tooth. I wanted bad to use the same approach with her, but once I got my hand up over her I couldn't bring it down. I tucked all the anger away for later. Now it's gone. This new voice in the early morning I don't even feel like answering. I'm afraid it might be someone I know. Maybe I'm tired of being the only one trying to save us.

The fire is pretty sad. It's more for company than warmth, hissing and struggling with the light rain. The signboards and flagsticks, tired of fighting, blacken and throw up their flame. As always, there isn't much to say. We share only Stark City Search and Rescue, and we're not close. You can't go out for beers after something like this, get to know a guy. Either way it ends there's nothing to celebrate.

The divers are sitting on Golly Gean's tailgate. Because of the black suits their swinging, white feet almost glow. The rubber fins hang in a cluster off the bedrail. The Manta tanks clank and scrape as they're hauled from the bed. Talking quietly among themselves each double-checks the other's gauge and regulator, and then fastens his partner's bottles. More and more they become twins of another animal, the soft puffy growth of hood bouncing at their necks. Soon they are transformed for water, waiting nervously to enter. We will hardly talk at all until they become comfortable in the lake. BV is busy weatherizing the walkie-talkie. His hands fumble with the plastic bags. He's talking more to himself than the divers. Coming around different sides of the wagon, Lims and I lean against my back end. Golly Gean and Yikes look up long enough to smile and say hi. BV continues to talk into the fire.

"Thermos, blankets, phone, rope, smokes, anchor . . . Yikes, you bring Cremora for your coffee? Woap, here she is. I should have brought more coat than this. It's going to get worse. A day like this, we'll probably find her. A nine-year-old girl, did you hear?"

"Ten," murmurs Lims. "Cowboy Bob told Ed ten. Too old to listen, too young to know."

"I thought they were going to fill in some of them holes last summer, slope out the floor and sand up a beach for kids along here. Goddamn death trap is what it is. They should level some of that near bottom out."

"Can't," Golly Gean breaks in without looking up. "The bottom's loose gravel. It shifts over winter. We never feel the same floor twice out there. They'd have to drain it and bank it up. It's no swimming hole for kids."

BV doesn't answer, just watches the fire. What's there to say? We all grew up swimming in the gravel pit. Across the water the small stocky figure of Dead Ed breaks from the patrol cars and circles quickly around the bank toward us. He jogs a little and then slows back to the walk. Golly Gean does it for Ed, comes out here in the cold looking for bodies, rubbing his hands in the cluttered bottom. Even drags the hook sometimes, all for the Old Man. Yikes just got caught up in it. He chased a girl here from Florida, pushed his Dodge on six cylinders halfway across the country to find her engaged. He got tight with Gean and taught him frogging. They went under a couple of times for the sheriff and checked bottom on some mountain lakes. Then Ed comes up with the idea to form the Rangers. It saved the state sending divers over from Bozeman. Neither boy could say no and took the patches he'd made up. They talk about going to Hawaii or the Caribbean, but they're still on the bank, hanging their white feet from the tailgate, every time I pull in at the pit.

BV's loaded the boat. He's got the phone, wrapped in a plastic bag, clipped to his belt. The divers' masked faces peer at us from out in Two Moons. They're full-fledged creatures of the black now, and turn their heads back and forth in the mist like aliens. I steady the boat and settle myself onto the middle seat. Kicking the orange life jackets away I clear the oars and adjust my shorts. BV's posed at the tip, ready to scrape us out into deeper water. The real rain isn't coming. It waits patiently in the lead sky stretching around us. I turn to Ed's voice. He makes a quick wave of his hand as he speaks.

"You all know where you're headed? Take her slow, Gean. Let's get it over with," and he starts for the Bronco, swinging his short arms.

"Hope we find her," as BV leans his shoulder into the boat's aluminum tip.

"Hope we don't," Ed returns without turning.

When the bottom releases us I swing the oars out, drop the left and point us toward humpbank on the other side. I begin to row in smooth, deep strokes. It's something I enjoy, the oars pressing and curling the water, its quiet response against the hull. The land begins to fade into its soft line of trees. My dad taught me to row with my breathing, to use the whole lake in a stroke. He helped me pick out the boat, the best Sears had. It doesn't fight too hard ahead or drag too much behind. It leaves a clean wake for fishing, and the bottom's fitted deep for less rock. A boat like this deserves better water. We used to take it up to Yellowtail Dam, and I've had it after browns on the Big Horn River. I even sang to Pat across it once on Mystic Lake. It was evening, the fish were rising to mayflies, and my song echoed off the mountains like a voice from shore. That was only two years ago.

The boat's the reason I got into the Rangers. I knew Ed from the refinery, not well. They needed a guy with a boat. It was after Dad died. I needed to save someone. I guess, in the beginning, I thought that's what we'd be doing, not just looking for the dead.

Lately, at the refinery, I've been spending most of my time off the ground, up among the pipes and pots. We've been welding connections, adding some elbows and blinds, and re-welding some old beads. The casual I've got with me is a good man, Jeff Kirkfleet. He's skipping a semester of school to make some fast money; a loose-fisted kid that runs after work, five miles at a clip. He's one of these new clean-living young, but I like him. The mouth isn't running all the time, and his head goes to his hands well on the job. I don't always have to look back or point. With the plant running full we shout or don't talk at all, and like me he only laughs when it's funny or dangerous. When we do have air to talk he steers it toward Zen, a mind cure that goes back to the Samurai. Most of it V's over my head like ducks, but what's stuck is that he's these two people trying to find a third, the real him. I told him if he ever draws close I'll get the boat and the grap-hook and we'll drag for him. He said he's something he's going down after alone. The stuff keeps him calm though; first casual I ever worked with that didn't seem to mind the heights. When the crane lifts us he saddles up on the bucket and watches the ground pass away. I've never learned to enjoy the high work. They say I have to do it, but I don't have to like it. I still keep the eyes straight or up. Jeff says he loves the feeling of rising, of being lifted by the big arm. He says I think too much about the falling that goes along with it. I should just keep my mind on the lift and free it from its partner.

"From the beginning it's the rise that's been the result of the fall, not bass-ackwards like most people have it. You'll rise in the end," he says.

"Tell that to the guys we've had to scrape off the base pipes," I answered. We laughed.

I've quit worrying about gas with him too. He hunts up and down the pipe for it like a weasel, putting gauge to traps and flanges. When he gives me the okay I'm not afraid to spark the welder and set to. Gas is something you never want to find, unless it's there. Three months and we haven't found a live pipe, and he still runs a good check, and keeps the hose on my sparks like it's his first time.

I've talked to Pat about him, about how fond I am of him. She calls him my Zen Master.

"Don't worry," she said. "His butterfly kite will come down some day," and then called me a trickless old dog that shouldn't always be listening to kids. She calls me an old dog at thirty-seven. I told her she's the one that's too old to be turning new tricks. I almost welcomed the evening of cold cuts and cold shoulder. One minute she tells me to grow up, the next it's old man.

Later she comes out and sits in front of the TV. "Can we talk?" She does, about how she's losing herself. I take her for granted. She's sorry she gets mean and hurts. She thinks she has to leave. "Why?" Maybe she doesn't. I'm glad she decides we'll give it some more time. We hug. I tell her I listen to the kids a lot because I have to work with them a lot. I like them, and want a couple of my own someday. I didn't buy a station wagon for the great mileage and easy handling. I tell her the young are life, their heads busting with their own guts. You just can't turn off your old songs. It doesn't seem like what she wants to hear, but she smiles. "What do we do?" I don't know why I can't talk. I search my head for answers but find nothing. I figure at thirty-two she should love me or dump me. She wants to do both.

BV splashes the anchor a hundred yards or so off hump-bank; called teenage wasteland by the kids that use it now. It's a flat gravel parking lot that ends at the water in a small cliff. It's got the usual collection of beer cans and black remains of party fires. There's an old cottonwood with some crippled lawn furniture and a gutted couch under it. With the mist all you can see from the water is the cliff. And in the water you do come across rubbers. The loose flat ones we called prick skins, the knotted ones, peter eels. I used to knot mine and then shout to it as I threw it in. "If you get out of that, we'll name you Houdini." My old man, I bet, used the same line. Today the women carry the protection. If I ever have a kid his girl will probably be the one that stops his first bullet with a manhole cover.

As we're grumbling and sipping our coffee, the front of the new Buick rolls into view on the cliff. The shiny grill catches what light there is, and you can hear the wheels on the gravel. After a minute the opening and closing of the door is heard, and a man appears at the front of the car. He stands holding the elbows of his overcoat. He looks in every direction he can and then remains still, pointed at us in the boat. We are both hunched over, hoping that he says nothing, that he'll stop and get back into the car. And he does. No matter what he would have said, I wouldn't have been able to answer him with more than a wave. I'm sure his little girl is in the gravel pit.

BV talks to himself about his latest girlfriend. The morning's dragging. The rain has arrived, sweeping in with darker clouds that push into the pale overcast. The gravel pit is alive with the rain, and as it has gotten later, I've begun to watch the water near the boat for bubbles. The divers must be close. My hands are deep inside my parka, my baseball cap tight over my head. BV's yellow slicker, bright with rain, is almost cheerful. His head is thrown back, catching the drops on his face as he talks to the low sky.

"She loves them now, likes to feel them, and feel them on her body. They're always afraid at first, afraid to touch them, to even look, but once they get past the touching phase and see they won't come apart, they enjoy the shit out of them. You know, sometimes I wish my face was messed up too. Nah. You ever been with a gimp, Licks?"

"I was with a cross-eyed lady once. We passed out on a couch together, me in my underwear, her with her clothes on. She had a Doberman, big friendly thing, but he pissed on my socks. I remember leaving them under the seat of her car when she took me home. I forced myself all evening to look her in the eye until it came natural. I decided she was very pretty. You're not a gimp, Beevy, just a little beat up. A girl will put up with a lot worse than you."

"Yeah, like you." He opens his mouth wide to the rain. "The dog peed on your goddamned socks. That's great."

"Yep, I guess he was just staking his claim, or he liked the smell of them."

"Sure." We must look funny, grinning at each other with the rain churning the water around us. "You know Carol Pottsman?" BV continues. "He picked up an old lady once, with one tit, spent the night and said it wasn't out of pity either. He was crazy for her, that night anyway. I would have jumped ship after coming up empty on one side. Think you could stare at one tit until it became natural?"

"Who knows? I bet I'd feel bad if I backed out. I imagine she'd think it was an act of mercy either way. You can't win some of those."

Air bubbles up to the surface. We both bend over to watch more float up. A diver is just below us. We become more serious, waiting for the frog to cover the floor beneath us. BV's face is tight and troubled. I've decided that's why he's here. With all his girling, and boozing and life wasting, he needs this to feel good about himself, to feel like he's got at least one foot out of hell. The bubbles become a stream and then a cluster, and then we can see the black head rising. It's the terrible moment when you're looking hard to see if the frog is bringing someone up with him. There's a second where you can't decide if you want him empty-handed or trudging up the dead. It's Yikes. He comes out of the water and throws both arms over the side of the boat, spitting out the mouthpiece and sliding up his mask. He used to cry "Yikes!" after coming out of the cold, dark water. He wasn't comfortable not seeing where he was. The eerie, closed-in feeling got to him. BV pours him a cup of coffee and stirs some Cremora into it with his finger.

"Thanks, Burny. Christ almighty it's cold down there. Settle down, teeth."

"Not much better up here. Nothing, huh?"

"Empty. There's lots of holes down there, cold and dark holes. I think I woke up some carp, but nothing. God damn waste of good equipment in this mud puddle. Gean not up yet? I went wide, thought he'd beat me."

"Hasn't been up."

Yikes sips his coffee. His teeth have quit shaking. The father, and this time the mother, have gotten out again, and stand near the Buick. They have a large umbrella. The mother draws the father's raincoat around her shoulders. None of us will look back at them. Gean's bubbles arrive fast and in a herd, with him close behind. He throws one arm up, while coughing out his mouthpiece. In the other hand is the end of his orange fly line. He reaches it out, and I grab it, tying it to the oar lock. BV is already digging the walkie-talkie out of its plastic. Golly Gean speaks quickly across the boat to his partner.

"Yikes, I need your help. She's caught up in some branches."

I hand Yikes the coil of rope, and both divers disappear, following the orange line to the bottom, and the girl.

BV has raised Ed. "Golly found her, Ed. Yep. She's caught on the bottom. They both went down. Get them all over here."

I'm busy clearing the boat, unfolding the thick wool blanket. The rain begins to darken it with small drops. At this point you feel as if you are saving someone. The feeling is gone in my hands, and I work them to get it back. As we wait for the air bubbles to return everything becomes important. I notice that BV's hiking boots are speckled with blue paint. He sees me staring and draws his feet closer, not knowing why. I am glad that we don't have kids. Pat would be either terrible or incredible during the waiting. I want to imagine she would break down in my arms. I find myself thinking a drowned child would help our marriage.

The divers are busy off below us, trying to untangle the

girl. They work slowly, unable to see each other in the dark silence. Passing signals by touch they feel for how the small body is caught and try to free her. They also treat her as if she is still alive, unhooking the clothes and releasing the arms delicately. All the vehicles hurry in a parade line along the bank. I finally hear the father shouting at us from the car. Both parents realized, as soon as I tied off the line, what it meant. It's the girl's name he's shouting, maybe even to her and not to us. He has stepped closer to the edge, leaving his wife. She is stuck to the side of the car. The father has taken his umbrella with him, and the rain now reaches her. She does not feel it. She will not yet let go of the girl and cannot come closer to see. Suddenly the father realizes he has the umbrella. He sees his wife standing in the rain and stretches his hand with the umbrella in it back to cover her. He does not go to her because he has to know what is happening. The sheriff will arrive soon and take care of them in his official way.

As the divers' air comes to us, BV and I move to the back of the boat to take the girl. The black figures become visible first, the girl's body only a white shadow or glow. She begins to take shape in their arms as they rise. We see the white legs and then the purple shoes and shorts. You don't want to see her face and concentrate instead on the red top. You know you will have to look at the face later. She bursts into clarity as they all break the water. Resting in their arms as she comes out of the rain-pocked surface into the light she seems asleep for a second, and it frightens me terribly. But I take her from the divers, and BV has her legs, and I take the small shoulders and rest her on the blanket. She is incredibly white, and we are both staring at her against the dark wool. She is now a dead child. The divers push off, moving across the water as if being reeled in. We don't cover her yet because we have to look. Each time we have to look until it becomes only a body. BV straightens her out with his clumsy hands. His face is shaking with her cold. Soon she is not there anymore, and there is just the small, empty picture that I will see again with the others. We wrap her carefully. The sheriff can uncover her for the parents, themselves and the news. After all she's what we've come out to see. But the cameras will not focus on the girl.

They'll point to the parents, so at 5:00 and 11:00 we can feel for them, see how hard they try to hold life in the body. The parents will not believe it has left, and will save both, the living and the dead, as one for a long time. God knows why we all have so much trouble giving them up.

I move to the middle of the boat and point it toward shore. Again I am glad my back is to all that is waiting. BV looks past me to the camera. He is collecting himself. He almost appears to draw calm and strength from the bundle he keeps covered against the bottom.

GERALD DUFF
FIRE ANTS

FROM PLOUGHSHARES

ᧉ

SHE HAD KEPT THE BOTTLE STUCK DOWN inside a basket of clothes that needed ironing, and throughout the course of the day whenever she had a chance to walk through the back room where the basket was kept, she would stop for the odd sip or two. By the middle of the afternoon, she had stopped feeling the heat even though she had cooked three coconut pies, one for B.J.'s supper and two for the graveyard working, and had ironed a dress for her and Myrtle. And by suppertime with Myrtle and B.J. and Bubba and Barney Lee Richards all around the table waiting for her to bring in the dishes from the kitchen, MayBelle had reached the point that she couldn't tell if she had put salt in the black-eyed peas or not, even when she tasted them twice, a whole spoonful each time.

"Aunt MayBelle," B.J. was saying, looking up at her with a big grin on his face, "where's that good cornbread? I bet old Barney Lee could eat some of that." He reached over and punched at one of Barney Lee's sides where it lapped over and hid his belt. "He looks hungry to me, this boy does."

"Aw, B.J.," said Barney Lee and hitched a little in his chair. "I shouldn't be eating at all, but I save up just enough to eat over here at your mama's house."

"Well, you're always welcome," said Myrtle from the end of the table by the china cabinet. "We don't see enough of you around here. Used to, you boys were always underfoot. I wish it was that way now."

"Barney Lee," said MayBelle, and waited to hear what she was going to say, "your hair is going back real far on both sides of your head. Not as far as B.J.'s, but it's getting on back there all right." She moved over and set the pan of hot cornbread on a pad in the middle of the table. "You gonna be as bald as your old daddy in a few years."

MayBelle straightened up to go back to the kitchen for another dish, and the Bear-King winked at her and lifted a paw, making her not listen to what Myrtle was calling to her as she walked through the door of the dining room. Maybe I better go look at that clothes basket before I bring in that bowl of okra, she thought to herself, and made a little detour off the kitchen. The foreign bottle was safe where she had left it, and she adjusted the level of the vodka inside to where it came just to the white bear's neckline.

When she came back into the dining room with the okra, everybody was waiting for B.J. to say grace, sitting quiet at the table and cutting eyes at the pastor at the head of it. "Sit down for a minute, Aunt MayBelle," B.J. said in a composed voice and caught her arm. "Let's thank the Lord and then you can finish serving the table."

MayBelle dropped into her chair and looked at a flower in the middle of the plate in front of her. It was pounding like a heart beating, and it did so in perfect time to the song of a mockingbird calling outside the window. It's the Texas State Bird, she thought, and Austin is the state capital. The native bluebonnet is the State Flower and grows wild along the highways every spring. But it's hard to transplant, and it smells just like a weed. If you get some on your hands, you can wash and wash them with heavy soap, and the smell will still be there for up to a week after. But they are pretty to look at, all the bluebonnets alongside the highway. There were big banks of them on both sides of the dirt road for as far as you could see, and when the car went by them it made enough wind to show the undersides of the flowers, lighter blue than the tops of the petals.

He stopped the car so they could look at all of them on both sides of the road, and a little breeze came up just when he turned the engine off, and it went across the bluebonnets like a wave. It was like ripples in a pond, they all turned together in rings and the light blue traveled along the tops of the darker blue petals as if it wasn't just the west wind moving things around, but something else all by itself.

He asked her if she didn't think it was the prettiest thing she ever saw, and she said yes and turned in the seat to face him. And that's when he reached out his hand and put it on the back of her head and said her eyes put him in mind of the color on the underside of the bluebonnets, and he had always wanted to tell her that. It was hot, early May, and there was a little line of sweat on his upper lip and when he came toward her she watched that until her eyes couldn't focus on it anymore he was so close and then his mouth was on hers and it was open and there was a little smell of cigarette smoke.

She could hear the hot metal of the car ticking in the sun, it was here, the only one she ever owned and that was only for a little over a year. It set high off the road and could go over deep ruts and not get stuck and it could climb any hill in Coushatta County without having to shift gears. The breeze was coming in the car window off the bluebonnets and it felt cool, but his hands were hot wherever they touched her and she kept her eyes closed and could still see the light blue underside of the flowers and the thin line of sweat on his lip and she was ticking all over just like the new car sitting still between the banks of bluebonnets in the sun.

"All this we ask in Thy Name, Amen," said B.J. and reached for the plate of cornbread. "You can go get the mashed potatoes now, Aunt MayBelle."

"Yes," said Myrtle, looking across the table at her, "and another thing too while you're in the kitchen. You poured me sweet milk in my glass, and you know I've got to have clabbermilk at supper."

Everybody allowed as how the vegetables were real good for this late in the season, but that the blackberry cobbler was a little tart. It was probably because of the dry spell, Barney Lee said, and they all agreed that the wild berries had been hard hit this year and might not even make it at all next summer unless they got some relief.

After supper Myrtle and Barney Lee went into the living room to catch the evening news on the Dumont, and B.J. put on his quilted suit and went out with Bubba and the cattle-prod to agitate the Dobermans and German shepherds.

From where she stood by the sinkful of dishes, MayBelle could hear the dogs begin barking and growling as soon as they saw B.J. and Bubba coming toward the pen. She ran some more water into the sink, hot enough to turn her hands red when she reached into it, and she almost let it overflow before she turned off the faucet and started washing. She didn't break but one dish, the flowered plate off which she had eaten a little okra and a few crowder peas at supper, but dropping it didn't seem to help the way she felt any.

She stood looking down at the parts it had cracked into on the floor, feeling the heat from the soapy water rising into her chest and face and hearing the TV set booming two rooms away, and decided she would look into the clothes basket again as soon as she had finished in the kitchen.

Outside a dog yipped and Bubba laughed, and MayBelle lifted her eyes to the window over the sink. The back pasture was catching the last rays of the setting sun, and it looked almost gold in the light. But when she looked closer, she could see that the yellow color was in the weeds and sawgrass itself, not just borrowed from the sun, and what looked like haze was really the dry seed pods rattling at the ends of the stalks.

Further up the hill yellowish smoke was rising from one of the cabins in the quarter, perfectly straight up into the sky as far as she could see, not a waver or a bit of motion to it. She stood watching it for a long time, dishcloth in one hand and a soapy glass in the other, until finally her eye was caught by a small figure moving slowly across the back edge of the pasture and disappearing into the dark line of pines that enclosed it.

That's old Sully, she said to herself, probably picking up kindling or looking at a rabbit trap. Wonder how he can stand the heat of a wood cookstove this time of the year. Keeps it going all the time, too, Cora says.

In the living room Barney Lee asked Myrtle something, and she answered him, not loud enough to be understood, and MayBelle went back to the dishwashing, rinsing and setting aside the glass she was holding. It had a wide striped design on it, and it felt right in her hand as she sat it on the drainboard to dry.

Picking up speed, she finished the rest of the glassware, the knives and forks, the cooking pots and the cornbread skillet, and then wiped the counters dry and swabbed off the top of the gas stove. By the time she finished turning the coffee pot upside down on the counter next to the sink, the striped glass on the drainboard had dried and a new program had started on the television set. The sounds of a happy bunch of people laughing and clapping their hands came from the front part of the house as MayBelle picked up her glass and walked out of the kitchen toward the back room.

She filled the glass up to the top of where the colored stripe began and took two small sips of the clear bitter liquid. She stopped, held the foreign bottle up to the light and watched the Bear-King while she drained the rest of the glass in one long swallow. A little of the vodka got up her nose, and she almost sneezed but managed to hold it back, belching deeply to keep things balanced. As she did, the Bear-King nodded his head, causing a sparkle of light to flash from his crown, and lifted one paw a fraction. "Thank you, Mr. Communist," MayBelle said, "I believe I will."

A few minutes later, Bubba Shackleford looked up from helping B.J. untangle one of the German shepherds which had got a front foot hung in the wire noose on the end of the cattle-prod, barely avoiding getting a hand slashed as he did, and caught sight of something moving down the hill in the back pasture. But by the time he got around to looking again, after getting the dog loose and back in the pen and the gate slammed shut, whatever it was had got too far off to see through his sweated-up glasses.

"B.J.," he said and waved toward the back of the house, "was that Aunt MayBelle yonder in the pasture?"

"Where?" said B.J. through the Johnny Bench mask in a cross voice. He laid the electric prod down in the dust of the yard and pulled the quilted suit away from his neck so he could blow down his collar. He felt hot enough in the outfit to faint, and the dust kicked up by the last dog had got all up his facemask, mixing with the sweat and leaving muddy tracks at the corners of his cheeks.

"What would she be doing in that weedpatch? She's in the house last I notice."

"Aw, nothing," said Bubba. "If it was her, she just checking out the blackberries, I reckon. It don't make no difference."

"Bubba," said B.J. and paused to get his breath and look at the pen of barking dogs in front of him. "I believe Christian Guard Dogs, Incorporated has made some real progress in the last few days. Look at them fighting and snapping in there. Why, they'd tear a prowler all to pieces in less than two minutes."

"B.J.," Bubba answered. "Watch this." He picked up a dead pine limb and rattled the hogwire with it, and immediately the nearest Doberman lunged at the fence, snapping and foaming at the steel wire between its teeth, its eyes narrow and bloodshot.

"That dog there," Bubba announced in a serious flat voice, "would kill a stray nigger or a doped-up hippie in New York in a minute."

"I figure you got to do what you can," said B.J., "and if there's a little honest profit in it for a Christian, it's nothing wrong with that." B.J. took off the catcher's mask and stood for a minute watching the worked-up dogs prowl up and down the pen, baring their teeth at each other as they passed, their tails carried low between their legs and the hair on their backs all roughed up. Then he turned toward his brother and clapped him on the shoulder.

"Let's go get a drink of water and talk about your business problems, Bubba. The Lord'll find an answer for you. You just got to give him a chance."

The houses were lined up on each side of a dirt road that came up from the patch of weeds to the south and stopped

abruptly at the edge of the pasture. In front of the first one on
the left, a cabin with two front doors opening into the same
room and a window in between them with a pane of unbroken
glass still in it, was the body of a '54 Chevrolet up on blocks.
All four wheels had been taken off a long time ago and fastened
together with a length of log chain and hung from the lowest
limb of an oak tree. The bark on the oak had grown over and
around the chain, and the metal of the wheels had fused together with rust.

MayBelle took another sip straight from the bottle and
stepped around a marooned two-wheeled tricycle, grown up in
bitter weeds, careful not to trip herself up. She walked up on
the porch of the next shotgun house and leaned over to peer
through a knocked-out window. Her footsteps on the floor-
boards sounded like a drum, she noticed, and she hopped up
and down a couple of times to hear the low boom again. There
was enough vodka left in the bottle to slosh around as she did
so, and she shook it in her right hand until it foamed. It didn't
seem to bother the Bear-King any.

The only thing left in the front room was a two-legged
wood stove tilted over to one side and three walls covered with
pictures of movie stars, politicians and baseball players. "Howdy,
Mr. and Mrs. President," MayBelle said to a large photograph
of JFK and Jackie next to a picture of Willie Mays and just
below one of Bob Hope. "How y'all this evening?" She took
another little sip and had a hard time getting the top screwed
back on, and by the time she had it down tight, it was getting
too difficult in the fading light to distinguish one face on the
wall from another, so she quit trying.

The back of the next cabin had been completely torn off,
so when MayBelle stepped up on the porch and looked through
the door all she could see was a framed scene of the dark woods
behind. A whippoorwill called from somewhere deep inside the
picture, and after a minute was answered by another one further off. MayBelle held her breath to listen, but neither bird
made another sound, and after a time, she stepped back down
to the road and looked at the clear space around her.

She felt as though it was getting dark too quickly and she
hadn't been able to see all she wanted. Already the tops of the

bank of pines around the row of houses were vanishing into the sky, and one by one the features of everything around her, the stones in the road and the discarded jars and tin cans, the bits and pieces of old automobiles, the broken furniture lying around the porches and the shiny things tacked up on the wall and around the edges of the eaves, were slipping away as the light steadily diminished. Whatever it was she had come to see, she hadn't discovered yet, and she shivered a little, hot as it was, feeling the need to move on until she found it. I waited too late in the day again, she thought, and now I can't see anything.

It was like the time at Holly Springs she had been playing in the loft of the barn with some of the Stutts girls and had slipped down between the beams and the shingles of the roof to hide. Papa had found her there at supper time, passed out from the sting of wasps whose nest she had laid her head against, her face covered with bumps and her eyes swollen shut from the poison. He had carried her down to Double Pen Creek, the coldest water in the county, running with her in his arms two miles through the cotton fields and the second-growth thickets until he was able to lay her in the water and draw off the fire of the wasp stings. She hadn't been able to see for six days after that, even after the swelling went down and she was able to open her eyes finally. The feeling of the light fading and the dark creeping up came on her again as she stood in the road between the rows of ruined houses, the bottle from the culvert tight in her hand.

"You looking for Cora, her place down yonder."

MayBelle lifted her gaze from the Bear-King and focused in the direction from where the voice had come. In a few seconds she picked him out of the shadow at the base of a sycamore trunk two houses down. He was a little black man in a long coat that dragged the ground and his hair was as white as cotton.

"You Sully," declared MayBelle and took a drink from her quart bottle.

"Yes, ma'am," said the little black man and giggled high up through his nose. "That be me. Old Sully."

"You used to do a little work for Burton Shackleford.

Down yonder." She waved the bottle off to the side without looking away from the sycamore shadow.

"That's right," he called out in a high voice to the empty houses, looking from one side of the open space to the other and then taking a couple of steps out into the road. "You talking about me, all right. I shore used to do a little work for Mister Burton. Build some fence. Dig them foundations. Pick up pecans oncet in a while."

"Uh huh," said MayBelle and paused for a minute. Two whippoorwills behind the backless house traded calls again, further away this time than before.

"I heard a lot about you. Cora she told me."

"Say she did," said Sully and kicked at something in the dust of the road. "Cora you say?"

"That's right," MayBelle said, addressing herself to the Bear-King and lifting the bottle to her mouth. The liquor had stopped tasting good a while back and now seemed like nothing more than water.

"She says," MayBelle said and paused to pat at her lips with the tips of her fingers, "Cora says you're still a creeper."

"She says that?" Sully asked in an amazed voice and scratched at the cotton on top of his head. "That's a mystery to me. She uh old woman. Last old woman in the quarter." He stopped and looked off at the tree line, then down at whatever he had kicked at in the sand and finally at the bottle in MayBelle's hand.

"What that is?" he said. MayBelle raised the bottle to eye-level and shook its contents back and forth against the Bear-King's feet, "That there liquor is Communist whiskey."

Then both regarded the bottle for a minute without saying anything as the liquid moved from one side to the other more and more slowly until it finally settled to dead level in MayBelle's steady grasp.

"Say it is?" Sully finally said after a while.

"Uh huh. You ever drink any of this Communist whiskey?"

"No, ma'am, Miz MayBelle. I uh Baptist," Sully said. "If I's to vote, I vote that straight Democrat ticket."

MayBelle unscrewed the lid, took a hard look at the level of the side of the bottle, and then carefully sipped until she had brought the liquid down to where the Bear-King appeared to be barely walking on the water beneath his feet.

"You don't drink nothing then," she said to Sully, carefully replacing the metal cap and giving it a pat.

"Nothing Communist, no ma'am, but I do like to sip a little of that white liquor that Rufus boy bring me now and again. Somebody over yonder in Leggett or Marston they makes that stuff."

"Is it hot?"

"Is it hot," declared Sully. "Sometimes I gots to sit down to drink from that Mason jar."

"Tell you what, Sully," said MayBelle and gave the little black man a long look over the neck of the bottle.

"Yes, ma'am," he said and straightened to attention until just the edges of his coat were touching the dust of the road. "What's that?"

"You go get yourself a clean glass and bring me one too, and I'll let you have a taste of this Communist whiskey." Sully spun around to leave and she called after him: "You got any of that Mason jar bring it in too."

"It be here directly," Sully answered over his shoulder and hopped over a discarded table leg in his way.

MayBelle walked over to the nearest porch and sat down to wait, her feet stuck straight out in front of her, and began trying to imitate the whippoorwill's call, sending her voice forth into the darkness in a low quavering tone, but not a bird had answered, no matter how she listened, by the time Sully got back with two jelly glasses and a Mason jar full of yellow shine, the sheen and consistency of light oil.

"You gone fell down again in amongst all the weeds, Miz Maybelle," Sully said, "you keep on trying to skip."

"I have always loved to skip," said MayBelle, moving through the pasture down the hill at a pretty good clip. She caught one foot on something in the dark and stepped high with the other one, bobbing to one side like a boxer in the ring.

"Watch me now," she said. "Yessir. Goddamn."

"You show do cuss a lot for a white lady," said Sully, dodging and weaving through the rank saw grass and bullnettles.

"I know it. Damn. Hell. Shit-fart."

"Uh huh," said Sully, hurrying to catch up and trying to see how far they had reached in the Shackleford back pasture. The moon was down, and he was having a hard time judging the distance to the stile over the back fence, what with his coat catching on weeds and sticks and the yellow shine thundering in his head.

He bent down to free his hem from something that had snagged it, felt the burn of a bullnettle across his hand, and recognized a clump of trees against the line of the night sky.

"I'se you," he called ahead in a high whisper. "I'd keep to the left right around here. Them old fire ants' bed just over yonder."

"Where?" said MayBelle, stopping in the middle of a skip so abruptly that she slipped on something which turned under her foot and almost caused her to fall. "Where are them little boogers?"

"Just over yonder about fifteen, twenty feet," Sully said, glad to stop and take a deep breath to settle the moving shapes around him. "See where them weeds stick up, look like a old cowboy's hat? Them ants got they old dirt nest just this side." He paused to smooth his coat around him and rub his bullnettle burn. "That there where they sleep when they ain't out killing things."

"You say they tough," said the skinny white lady. "It burns when they bite?"

"Burns? Lawdy have mercy. Do it burn when they bites? Everywhere one of them fire ants sting you it's a little piece of your hide swell up and rot out all around it. Take about a week to happen."

Sully felt the ground begin to tilt to one side, and he lifted one foot and brought it down sharply to level things out. The earth pushed back hard, but by keeping his knee locked, he was able to hold it steady. "I don't know how long I can last," he said to his right leg, "but I do what I can."

"Shit, goddamn," said MayBelle, "let's go see if they're all asleep in their bed."

"You mean them fire ants? They kill the baby birds and little rabbits in they nests. Chop 'em up, take'm home and eat'm. I don't want no part of them boogers. I ain't lost nothing in them fire ants's bed."

"Well, I believe I did," said MayBelle. "Piss damn. I'm gonna go over there and go to bed with them."

Sully heard the dry weeds crack and pop as the white lady began moving toward the cowboy hat shape, and he lifted his foot to step toward the sound. When he did, the released earth flew up and hit him all down the right side of his body and against his ear and jaw. "I knowed it was going to happen," he said to his right leg as he lay, half-stunned in the high weeds, "I let things go too quick."

By the time he was able to get up again, scrambling to find one knee, then the other, and then flapping his arms about him to get all the way off the ground and away from its terrible grip, the skinny white lady had already reached the fire ant bed and dropped down beside it. Sully moved at an angle, one arm much higher than the other and his ears ringing with the lick the ground had just given him, until he came up close enough to see the dark bulk of the old woman stretched out in the soft mound of ant-chewed earth.

"You got to get up from there, Miz MayBelle," he said and began to lean toward her, hand outstretched, but then thought better of it as he felt the earth begin to gather itself for another go at him.

She was speaking in a crooning voice to the ant bed, saying words he couldn't understand and moving herself slowly from side to side as she settled into it.

"Miz MayBelle," Sully said, "crawl on up out of there now. They gonna eat you alive lying there. That ain't no fun."

"Don't you put a hand on me, Papa," she said in a clear hard voice, suddenly getting still, "I'm right where I want to be."

"I see I got it to do," Sully said and threw his head back to look around for somebody. He couldn't see a soul, and every star in the night sky was perfectly clear and still.

"You decide to get up while I'm gone," he said to the dark shape at his feet, "just go on ahead and do it."

Running in a half-crouch with one arm out for balance against the tilt the earth was putting on him, Sully started down the hill toward the back fence of the Shackleford place, proceeding through the weeds and brambles like a sailboat tacking into the wind. About every fifty feet, he had to lean into a new angle and cut back to keep the ground from reaching up and slamming him another lick, and the dirt of the dry field and the hard edges of the saw grass were working together like a charm to slow and trip him up.

He went over the stile on his hands and knees, and the earth popped him a good one again on the other side of the fence, but he was able to get himself up by leaning his back against the trunk of a pine tree and pushing himself up in stages. There was a dim yellow light coming from a cloth tent right at the back steps of the house, and Sully aimed for that and the sounds of a man's voice coming from it in a regular singing pattern. He got there in three more angled runs, the last one involving a low clothesline that caught him in the head just where his hairline started, and he stopped about ten feet from the tent flap, dust rising around him and the earth pushing up hard against one foot and sucking down at the other one.

Barney Lee Richards lifted the tent flap and stuck his head out to see what had caused all the commotion in the middle of B.J.'s prayer against the unpardonable sin, but at first all he could make out was a cloud of suspended dust with a large dark shape in the middle of it. He blinked his eyes, focused again, and the form began to resolve itself into somebody or something standing at an angle, an arm extended above its head, which looked whiter than anything around it, and the whole thing wrapped in a long hanging garment. The clothesline was making a strange humming sound.

"Aw naw," he said in a choked disbelieving voice, jerked his head back inside the lighted tent, and spun around to look at B.J., his eyes opened wide enough to show white all around them.

"B.J.," he said, "it's something all black wearing an old long cape and it's got white on its head and it's pointing its hand up at the sky."

"At the sky?" said B.J. and began to fumble around in the darkness of the tent floor with both hands for his Bible. "You say it's wearing a long cape?"

"That's right, that's right," said Barney Lee in a high whine and began to cry. He heaved himself forward onto his hands and knees and lurched into a rapid crawl as if he were planning to tear out the back of the mountaineer's tent, colliding with B.J. and causing him to lose his grip on the Bible he had just found next to a paper sack full of bananas.

"Hold still, Barney Lee," B.J. said. "Stop it now. I'm trying to get hold of something to help us if you'll just set still and let me."

To Sully on the outside, standing breathless and stunned next to the clothesline pole, the commotion in the two-room tent made it look as though the shelter was full of a small pack of hounds fighting over a possum. First one wall, then the other bulged and stretched, and the ropes fastened to the tent stakes groaned and popped under the pressure. The stakes themselves seemed to shift and glow in the dark as he watched.

"White folks," Sully said in a weak voice and then, getting a good breath, "white folks. I gots to talk to you."

The canvas of the tent suddenly stopped surging, and everything became quiet. Sully stood tilted to one side and braced against the pull of the earth, his mouth half-open to listen, but all he could hear for fully a minute was the sound of the yellow shine seeping and sliding through his head and from far off somewhere in the woods the call of a roosting bird that had waked up in the night.

Finally the front flap of the tent opened up a few inches and the bulk of a man's head appeared in the crack.

"Who's that out there?" the head asked.

"Hidy, white folks," said Sully. "It's only just me. Old Sully. Just only an ordinary old field nigger. Done retire."

The flap moved all the way open, and B.J. crawled halfway out of the tent, straining to get a better look.

"It's just an old colored gentleman, Brother B. Lee," he said over his shoulder. "Like I told you, it ain't nothing to worry about."

"Well," said Barney Lee from the darkness behind him, "I was afraid it was something spiritual. Why was it standing that way with its hand pointing up, if it was a nigger?"

"Hello, old man," said B.J., all the way out of the tent

now and standing up to brush the dirt off his pants. "Kinda late at night to be calling, idn't?"

"Yessir," said Sully. "It do be late, but a old man he don't sleep much. He don't need what he use to."

"Uh huh," B.J. said and turned back to help Barney Lee who had climbed halfway up but had gotten stuck with one knee bent and the other leg fully extended.

"Why," Barney Lee addressed the man in the long coat, "why you standing that way with your arm sticking way up like that?"

"Well sir," said Sully and turned his head to look up along his sleeve. "It seem like it help me to stand like this." The shine made a ripple in a new little path in his head, and he had to lift his hand higher to keep things whole and steady.

"I just wish you'd listen to that, Barney Lee," B.J. said in a tight voice.

"What? I don't hear nothing."

"That's exactly what I'm talking about. Here's this old nig—colored gentleman—come walking up in the dead of night, and what do you hear from them dogs? Not a thing."

Everybody stopped to listen and had to agree that the dog pen was showing no sign of alert.

"And I thought the training was going along so good the last few days. I'm getting real discouraged about Christian Guard Dogs." B.J. sighed deeply, kicked at the ground, and coughed at the dust hanging in the air. "I don't know. I just don't know."

"However," said Sully, "what it is I come up here and bother you white folks about it be up yonder in the pasture." He swung a hand back in the direction he had come, almost lost the hold he was maintaining against the steady pull of the earth, and staggered a step or two before he found it again.

"Say it helps you to stand like that?" asked Barney Lee and shyly stuck one arm above his head until it pointed in the direction of the Little Dipper. "Reckon it helps circulation or something?"

"Didn't make one peep," said B.J. "I didn't hear bark one, much less a growl."

"Yessir, white folks, it up yonder in the pasture. What I

come here to your pup tent for." Sully's arm was getting heavy so he ventured to lean against the pole supporting the clothesline and found that helped him some. Things were tilted, but not moving.

"A few minutes ago, I was outside my house walking to that patch of cane. You know, tending to my business and that's when I heard her yonder."

"Who?" said B.J., making conversation as he looked over at the dark outline of the Christian Guard Dog pen as though he could see each individual Doberman and shepherd.

"Miz MayBelle."

"MayBelle? Aunt MayBelle Holt?" B.J. turned back to look at the little black man leaned up against the pole. "You say you heard her up in the nigger quarters?"

"Naw sir, white folks, not rightly in the quarters. She in that back pasture lying down in that fire ant bed."

"The fire ant bed?"

"Yessir, old Sully was in the quarters and she in the bed of fire ants."

"What's Aunt MayBelle doing in the fire ant bed? Did she fall into there?"

"I don't know about that," said Sully and adjusted his pointing arm more precisely with relation to the night sky. "I only just seed her in there a-talking to them boosters."

"Come on, Brother B. Lee," B.J. said and broke into a trot toward the back fence. "We got to see what's going on. Them things will eat her up."

"Thata's just the very thing I thought," said Sully, lurching away from the clothesline pole, and stumbling into a run after B.J., his gesturing right arm the only thing keeping him away from another solid lick from the ground. "I thought it sure wasn't no good idea for a white lady to lie down in amongst all them biting things."

"I'm coming, B.J.," called Barney Lee, a few steps behind Sully but close enough that the old man's flapping coattail sent puffs of dust up into his face. As he ran through the fence at the bottom of the hill, he raised an arm above his head and immediately felt his wind get better and his speed increase a step or two.

"I believe," Barney Lee said between breaths to the tilted sidling figure moving ahead of him, "that it's doing me good too. Pointing my arm up at the sky like this."

"Yessir, white folks," Sully said to the words coming from behind him, fighting as best he could against the yearn of the earth beneath his feet. It was going to get him at the stile again, he knew, but he had to live with that fact. "I just get them fat white folks to the ant bed, I quit," he said to the clouds of dust floating up before him. "You can have all of it then. I give it on up." He ran on, changing to a new tack every few feet, the pointing arm dead in the air above him, and listened to the shine rumble and slide through all the crannies of his head.

"It's gonna be hard times in the morning," he said out loud and aimed at the fence stile coming up. "It most always is."

You've got to say something to me, she said. You don't talk to me right. Now you got to say something to me.

I'm talking to you, he said. I'm talking right now to you. What you want me to say? This?

And he did a thing that made her eyes close and the itching start in her feet and begin to move up the back of her legs and across her belly and along her sides down each rib. Oh, she said, it's all in my shoulders and the back of my neck.

She let him push her further back until her head touched the green and gold bedspread, and one of her hands slipped off his shoulder and fell beside her as though she had lost all the strength in that part of her body. The arm was numb, but tingling like it did in the morning sometimes when she had slept wrong on it and cut off the circulation of blood. She tried to lift it and something like warm air ran up and down the inside of her upper arm and settled in her armpit under the bunched-up sleeve of the dress.

No, she said, it's hot and I'm sweating. It's going to get all over her bed. It'll make a wet mark, and it won't dry and she'll see it.

He said no and mumbled something else into the side of her throat that she couldn't hear. Something was happening to the bottoms of her feet and the palms of her hands. It was crawling and picking lightly at the skin. Just pulling it up a little at a time and letting it fall back and doing it over again until it felt like little hairs were raising up in their places and settling back over and over.

Talk to me, she said into his mouth. Say some things to me. You never have said a thing yet to me.

I'll say something to you, he said, and moved against her in a way that caused her to want to try to touch each corner of the bed.

If I put one foot at the edge down there and the other one at the other corner and then my hands way out until I can touch where the mattress comes to a point, then if somebody was way up above us and could look down just at me and the way I am lying here, it would look like two straight lines crossing in the middle. That makes an X when two lines cross. And in the middle where they cross is where I am.

Please, she said to the little burning spots that were beginning to start at each end of the leg of the X and to move slowly towards the intersection, come reach each other. Meet in the middle where I am.

But the little points of fire, like sparks that popped out of the fireplace and made burn marks on the floor, were taking their own time, stopping at one place for a while and settling there as if they were going to stay and not go any further and then when something finally burned through and broke apart, moving up a little further to settle a space closer to the middle of the X.

Just a word or two, she said to him, that's all I want you to say.

He said something back to her, something deep in his throat, but her ears were listening to a dim buzz that had started up deep inside her head, and she couldn't hear him.

What? she said. What? One foot and one hand had reached almost to the opposite corners of the bed and she strained, trying to make that line of the X straight and true before she turned her mind to the other line.

He moved above her, and suddenly the first line fell into place and locked itself, and the little burning spots along that whole leg of the X began to gather themselves and move more quickly from each end toward the middle where they might meet.

The buzz inside her head that wouldn't let her hear suddenly stopped the way you would click off a radio, and the sound of a mockingbird's call somewhere outside came twice and acted like something being poured into her head. It moved down inside like water and made two little points of pressure which were the bird calls and which stayed, waiting for something.

You talk to her, she said to him, her mouth so close to the side of his head when she spoke that her lips moved against the short hairs growing just behind his ear. I hear you say things to her. In the night. I hear you in the night. Lots of times.

Her other foot and hand were moving now on their own, and she no longer had to tell them what to do. The fingers of the hand reached, stretched, fell short, tried again and touched the edges of the mattress where the two sides came together. The green and gold spread moved in a fold beneath the hand, and as it did, the foot which formed the last point of the two legs of the X finally found its true position, and the intersecting lines fell into place at last, straight as though they had been drawn by a ruler. And whoever was looking at her from above could see it, the two legs of the X drawing to a point in the middle where they crossed and touched, and something let the burning points know the straight path was clear, and they came with a rush from each far point of the two lines, racing to meet in the middle where everything came together.

Say it, she managed to get the words out just before all of it reached the middle which was where she was, and he said something, but she couldn't hear anything but the fixed cry of the mockingbird and she blended her voice with that, and all the burning points came together and touched and flared and stayed.

PAM DURBAN

ALL SET ABOUT WITH FEVER TREES

FROM THE GEORGIA REVIEW

ɕ

IN MACON, GEORGIA, MY GRANDMOTHER, Mariah Palmer, was a famous teacher. She took up this career after her husband died during the Depression, leaving her with three small children to look after. From that time on, she taught English in the Bibb County schools and Sunday school at the First Presbyterian Church. Later, when the wine of her understanding had clarified and aged to her satisfaction, she taught the Bible at the YWCA, where all seats were filled, so I've heard, when her topic was the Book of John, that great gospel of abiding faith. Then, at sixty, she announced to us all that she'd signed on to teach the children of the Presbyterian missionaries in the Belgian Congo in Africa.

For days after she got the news, my mother went around worrying out loud to herself. Folding the laundry, she'd snap a towel and say, "Well, damn," as if she were determined to have her say, even if she'd already lost the argument. I overheard them talking once when my grandmother came to visit that summer before she left for Africa. They were sitting out on the screened porch, stringing and snapping beans for supper. My mother is a master at subtle persuasion. Not for her the direct attack. She prefers to sketch an outline of danger and leave you to fill in the rest. Driving by a black juke joint called the Royal Peacock Club, for instance, she had recently taken to slowing down and pointing out to me the slash marks in the black vinyl door, and the men, with hats cocked low over their eyes, who were bothering women and shoving each other around outside, and though I was only eight years old I knew that this was a piece of some puzzle that I was supposed to hold onto until I was old enough to realize where it fit and what I was being warned against.

That particular day, Mother selected her somber colors, muddy browns and greens, and with these she painted pictures for my grandmother of the lonely life she would lead over in Africa. Then she selected the darker earth tones and with these she made her a picture of an aging, ailing body, of brittle bones, a failing mind, all set against the black background of death itself. When this was over she sighed: "I've had my say, not that it makes any difference."

"Good," my grandmother said. "It's always better to get these things off your chest than to keep them bottled up inside. But I will tell you, my best beloved," she said. "I have done a lot of praying in my short and happy life and I can now report to you with confidence that I have never been surer of anything. As it happens, I have heard the clear call down deep in my soul and it is summoning me to labor in the fields far from the fleshpots of civilization."

This was good stuff. I stood there hugging myself, feeling the goosebumps run along my arms as I imagined how her eyes must look—like Moses' eyes in her illustrated copy of the Old Testament, two points of leaden fire aimed at the idolaters as they danced around their golden calf and tended their fleshpots, where fleshy women and men with small pointed beards played tambourines and writhed around together. "Fleshpots," I said to myself, and I remembered the way the fire blazed up in the trash barrel outside the door of the Royal Peacock Club on cold winter nights, throwing shadows on the black faces, and the way the whiskey bottles flashed in that light. And I wanted her to go to Africa and stay as long as she wished, as long as it took to find whatever had called her. I wanted her to go because lately I had had glimmerings in myself, intimations of some kind of destiny that was waiting for me, somewhere, with my name, Annie Vess, already written on it in big bright letters. Sometimes when I was sitting in the library at school or running in the playground or even at supper with my family, everything would get very quiet inside me and then a glowing would begin, followed by a burst of light, like a bomb going off up in the air, and I would feel that something was about to speak, to show me the way I was meant to go.

While she was gone, I kept a map of Africa thumbtacked to the wall of my room and circled her town, Lubondai, and every other place she mentioned, in red. Her letters arrived covered with stamps that featured regal black heads held high on thin necks, a white queen in her jewels, a king who looked like a walrus with his mustache and his heavy staring expression. The paper smelled sweet and dusty, the way Africa must smell, I thought, sun-warmed and lush, like hay. I imagined her writing them, alone there in the middle of the continent, in a hut late at night, with the lantern burning beside her. I saved these letters and studied them at night by flashlight under the covers before I fell asleep, speed-reading through the parts about how their houses were nice houses just like those back in the States, with plumbing and curtains and all, and about the well-mannered Christian children she was fortunate to be teaching, and hurrying on to the paragraphs that described her travels.

She wrote that she traveled by Land Rover, along roads where the vines grew so fast the driver had to get out now and then and hack the road clear. In the snapshot she sent along with one letter, the driver is naked to the waist and black as a carved onyx while she is as serene as the queen mother, her broad-brimmed straw hat lying on her lap. "On the road to Lulluraburg," the caption read, "to hear a chorus of native voices sing Bach, Handel, and Brahms." "A 50,000-acre game preserve," read another caption enclosed with a postcard that was divided into four sections and showed elephants, giraffes, lions and antelopes. "The Mountains of the Moon," she wrote, "imagine, Annie, mountains 19,000 feet high, so high that even viewed up close, they look far away." Sometimes I would dream of these places, the Mountains of the Moon and a chorus of golden lions singing as they galloped up and down the slopes.

When I showed my mother one of these letters or a postcard, she would shake her head, sigh, and say, "It certainly sounds like Mother's found what she's been looking for."

"Which is?"

She would shrug, roll her eyes. "Beats me."

I kept the faith, waiting for the day when my grandmother would come back and tell me everything she knew about clear calls and destiny. I was patient in my waiting because I believed in her. She knew things. She would not fail. She had powers that other people did not have. There is, for instance, a memory which is not a dream, which I have of her and of myself as a child in her house in Macon which will show you what I mean. In this memory, I've gone downstairs by myself at night, looking for a drink of water. The light from the streetlights comes through the tall windows and makes shapes like tall lighted doors across the floors. So I start for one and find myself standing in the corner of a room, start for another and I end up facing the wall. I've not made a sound but my grandmother comes down from upstairs, tying her bathrobe as she comes, flipping light switches until we reach the kitchen and when she flips that switch, everything is white—the enamel of the table top, the kitchen sink, the bowl of paper white narcissus just coming into bloom, her bathrobe and the ruff of white hair standing out around her head, the glass of milk she sets in front of me.

And then she lifts me and holds me so close to her face I can see the flecks of gold in her bright hazel eyes and the tiny roses etched along the gold rims of her thick glasses, and sets me down on her lap. From the shelf above the kitchen table, from beside the bowl of narcissus, she has taken down a book, the *Just So Stories* by Rudyard Kipling, and slowly, surely, as I listen to her heartbeat, and the sound of her voice humming against my back, the bewildered way I had felt as I wandered from room to room, like a small leaf floating in a cold sea of light, leaves me. And we are gone into that country on the banks of the great, gray, green, greasy Limpopo River, all set about with fever trees, where life first stirred and crawled from the mud. Where the rhino got his baggy skin, the whale his throat, the leopard his spots, where the cat walked by himself waving his wild wild tail and the humans made the first letter and then the whole alphabet. Where everything is about first causes, sources, what stirs within the seed that causes the plant to grow. "Hear and attend and listen," she reads, "for this befell and behappened and became, O My Best Beloved, when the Tame animals were wild."

As she reads and reads I drowse and float close to sleep, feel the house all around us, sleeping and dark, except for this room. And then I'm growing, I'm rising out through the roof and flying over the planet, searching until I find Macon, Georgia on the banks of the Ocmulgee River, sleeping in its grove of dark pines, and in the middle of that city, I find the room where we are reading, set against the dark like the North Star. And below the windy ocean of darkness that runs around the world, that lighted room remains.

The summer I was twelve, my grandmother came back to the States and we went to Macon to welcome her home. I had prepared for days with a notebook full of questions to ask her. What was it in your experience which most clearly answered the call that took you there? What unusual or exciting experiences did you have that give us a clue as to the differences between people? Did anything happen to you there that has convinced you of anything or shaken any previously held beliefs?

Macon, Georgia straggles along the banks of the great grave Ocmulgee River which is a broad, slow river, sluggish as its name. In the summer, the sky is always white, as though a layer of smoke hangs between you and everything you want to see, and the sun burns behind this haze like a white metal disk. "The only difference between Macon, Georgia and hell," my father said, as we drove across the bridge and into the city, "is that a river runs through Macon."

"A river runs through hell, too," I said. "If what you mean by hell is the underworld. It's called the River Styx." I knew because I had just finished reading a book called *Great Myths of the Western World* and added it to the list on my summer reading club card at the public library.

"Then I guess there's no difference at all," he said.

In the same church basement where we'd told her good-bye four years earlier, we spread the long tables with yellow tablecloths and set out platters of chicken, and potato salad, green beans, and a thickly iced cake shaped like Africa with the Belgian Congo outlined in red and centered with a small green flag in the middle of red icing that spelled out "Lubondai" to show where she'd lived. I was the one responsible for the lettering on the cake.

As I helped to set the tables, I kept one eye on the doorway and the excitement turned inside me like a bright whirligig going round and round. As I slid down the halls and in and out of the Sunday school rooms with my pack of cousins, I kept an ear tuned to the noise in the other room. To this day, I don't know exactly what I'd hoped to see, but when she walked through the door, something died in me with the sudden fading sound that a record makes when the plug is pulled on the machine. It was my grandmother, arms open wide to welcome everyone, and was she fat! She must have gained thirty pounds and she looked like a flour sack tied in the middle, with her black patent leather belt cinched tight around the waist of her gaudy blue-and-pink print dress.

I remember I tried to escape, but it was too late. She wrapped me in her flabby arms and pulled me into her bosom, where I thought I might suffocate on the smell of English Lavender cologne and Vicks Vapo-Rub. She rocked me, weeping, calling me her best beloved, the heart of her heart, the light of her life. And then I was weeping too, the whole place was weeping. She would take off her glasses, wipe her eyes, look at me, and we'd both burst into tears again. But I'll bet I wasn't weeping for the joy of seeing her again. I was weeping because I'd been betrayed. Because she'd crossed the equator and received a scroll signed by Neptune, ruler of the deep. Because she'd sailed up the Congo River as far as it might be sailed. Because she'd climbed halfway up the great Pyramid of Cheops at Giza, she'd visited the Sphinx and heard the riddle. She'd even walked the streets of Paris, France, on her way back home. Because she'd done all those things and then she'd come back fat. That was the only change, not to mention miracle, that had happened to her.

Now all she could do was argue and eat, eat and argue. She tore the paper table cloth with her pen, drawing maps and lines and arrows. This tribe, that tribe. What does the Mau-Mau uprising have to do with the one clear call? That's what I wanted to know. Meanwhile, she ate four wedges of cornbread soaked with butter, three pieces of chicken and a biscuit. She ate fresh peach cobbler topped with two scoops of ice cream. She ate after everyone else had laid down their forks. My mother said, "My God, Mother, how could you let yourself gain all that weight?"

"Daughter mine," she said. "I did not plan it that way. I became fond of the native diet which consists mostly of starch and well, these things happen in this great world of ours."

"What do they eat?" I asked, shoving the last of my banana pudding into the potato salad.

"A root called *manioc*, my best beloved," she said, fishing for another slab of cornbread. "It's like our sweet potato. They dry this manioc root and pound it into flour and they make a bread with the flour that's called *bidia*. They dunk this bread (she dunked the cornbread into the gravy boat and held it up, dripping) in palm oil gravy, and they call it food for the hunter inside."

"That's gross," I said. She laughed and I saw all the gold fillings in her teeth. While we watched slides of Africa which consisted mostly of a dozen different views of a row of mustard-colored concrete block houses, with here and there a view of the Mountains of the Moon seen through a herd of curious giraffes, I hashed over the story about the roots. There in the land of the one clear call, in the shadow of the Mountains of the Moon, they scratched in the dirt and ate roots. From that point on, I could have cared less about anything. I imagined that I was sitting up on a high bald rock, too high even for eagles to reach, looking down on everyone as they crowded close to see the treasures she'd collected—the broad-bladed knives etched with intricate woven patterns, the hammered copper crosses, the raffia baskets and carved wooden bowls and ivory crosses, the shaman's headpiece that was covered in leopard skin and had cold eyes, a fiercely sucking mouth and perfect little ears made of clay. I watched as she lined up a troop of ivory elephants in order of descending size. The smallest was no larger than the nail of your smallest finger and each was carved in perfect detail, from the flapping ears down to the moon-shaped toes. I watched as she modeled the latest fashion from The Congo—a braided straw rope with two tassels of coarse black hair attached, to be worn around the waist like a skirt.

I watched it all from my bald rock high above the valley. But when she came to my gift I would have gladly died. I was her favorite, so they said, and when she called me to the front of the room everyone turned their tender smiling silence, their tearful happiness my way. I unwrapped the tissue paper she'd pressed into my hand, and there in my palm was a wooden pin—a brown, antelope-looking creature, carved so that the hooves, horns and nostrils, even the muscles that rippled under its coat, looked real.

"Now, my best beloved," she said, "I watched the crafts-man carve it. He took great pains and I told him all about you so that he might make it especially for Annie. And that's not only beautifully carved, it's very valuable wood too," she said.

"What kind?" I felt the pin, felt along the carved muscles. My hand had warmed it and under my thumb the wood felt alive, as if the animal were about to wake up and begin breathing.

"That's called *stinkwood*, Annie," she said. At that, the whole adult chorus chuckled, heads bobbed, eyes were wiped, hands were patted and pressed, and my humiliation was complete. "Thank you, it's very nice," I managed to say. While they clapped and clapped, I stood staring at the broken strap of my Aunt Louise's sandal, at her toes that gripped the soles as though she were leaning into a wind that was blowing her backwards, or trying to. Restlessness, like an itch, began inside me. If my grandmother had corrected herself, said: "Oh, please excuse me, Annie, I have made a dreadful mistake, that's called *heavenwood*," I would not have been comforted. My mother pinned the thing to the front of my dress and I sat there, feeling itchy and hot inside my clothes, looking at my badge, that sleek animal all carved of stinkwood and gathered for the leap.

But I didn't give up. When I'd recovered a little from my embarrassment, I worked my way close to her again and asked, "How did you talk to them?"

"Who, my best beloved?"

"The people over there." I imagined sign language, shadow shows by the fire, figures scratched in the dirt with sticks, and all around, the jungle night—which was longer and scarier, somehow, than nights we knew—had gathered to listen.

"Some speak English," she said.

"Oh."

"And of course I learned a little of the Tschiluba language," she said. "It's a tonal language, not like ours."

"Say some of it."

She closed her eyes and began to speak, low liquid sounds, like music that asked questions, like a stream running fast over stones. On this tide, my hope returned. "Of course there were people who could talk for me too," she said. "They translated that language into English and vice versa. We had us a big talking party once, and, oh, was it grand."

"Do they really wear, you know, those things?" I pointed to the rope with the tassels.

"Why yes," she said. "Some do. I can't explain this to you, heart of my heart, but it's the most natural thing in the world to them, to go around like that. They don't give a hoot about some things we hold very dear. To them our bodies are the coverings we wear, *the beauty inside turned inside out*, they say."

Well, afterwards as we drove back to the motel, I turned over what she'd said like a small bead, round and polished. All that about people's bodies and what she'd called the hunter and the inside. I felt that a series of small but violent explosions had dislodged certain ideas I'd held without even knowing I believed them. I was being raised Roman Catholic because this was my father's faith and Mother, a Presbyterian, had promised to turn us over to the church in return for being allowed to marry him. At least that's how she told it. So I knew all about the soul because every day in catechism class at Catholic school we pinned her wings and studied her, worried over her condition and her future. I knew that this soul was either a rippling sheet of light, cold and distantly beautiful as the *aurora borealis*, or it was spotted with decay or even entirely dark, extinguished by sin. But whatever this soul might be, its life was not with roots or stinkwood or hunters and darkness was always its death.

The summer I was sixteen, we went to a reunion of the Palmer family in the mountains up near Highlands, North Carolina. The house, which belonged to my great aunt Martha, Grandmother's sister, had been added onto haphazardly and looked like a train wreck, a heap of boxcars lying every which way and covered with tar paper but no boards or shingles, and screened from the road by a line of cedar trees that ran straight along the road's edge. Behind this house, Scaley Mountain reared up out of the earth. You could actually go out and touch the place where the mountain came out of the ground and when the mountain threw its shadow over the house, it was damp and cold. Inside, the house was full of rooms where a person could go off by herself and think about things or read all afternoon without being disturbed.

In the valley between the mountain and the house, a small, cold stream ran so fast it made a roaring sound, as though it were angry at being confined in such a narrow channel. Aunt Martha took her constitutional there. She'd built a small dam in the stream and every morning she descended into the stream, with her hair done in braids and wrapped over the top of her head, and for ten minutes she sat on stones below this dam and let the water pelt her shoulders. Now this water was so cold that you could not breathe when you were in it and whatever parts of your body the water touched turned red and began to ache, and then went numb as cork. Nevertheless, I had decided that Aunt Martha, who was a clairvoyant, a medium and an astrologer, famous in the family for her seances and levitations, for giving somebody the heebie-jeebies at every reunion, was more likely than my grandmother to tell me what I needed to know about clear calls, souls, destinies and all the rest. So every morning just at dawn, I put on my bathing suit and followed her into the stream, and while the water poured over us like a clear cape, I gasped out my questions and she would tell me things about the psychic gifts of the Palmer side of the family, each one unique and fabulous—the gift of second sight and the ability to read destinies in the stars being first among them.

Or she would talk about what she called the spirit world and the reincarnated lives of other members of the family. My grandmother, for instance, had lived several lifetimes on the continent of Africa, which is why Martha had not been at all surprised when Grandmother had returned there since the human soul, according to Martha, gravitates toward scenes of its former unfoldings as naturally as a seed seeks the earth. I told her about the time when the idea of my search had first come to me and about those moments when I'd felt that I was bound for a destiny that no one had ever lived before. I told her about the night when my grandmother had found me and read to me and I had felt myself leave the room and fly around the planet, a disembodied spirit, searching for its home. Martha nodded as she listened. "It doesn't surprise me in the least," she said. And as I talked I imagined the clear icy water running all through me and I thought, this is how I will feel when I arrive at my destiny, this is how it will be.

Nights, the grownups gathered near the line of cedar trees beside the road to reminisce about each other. The rest of us sat around on quilts on the grass. The stories they told were about each other but it seemed to me that they all shared a common center. They were about the past but not the whole past, just special moments, those moments I was looking for, times that had been dilated somehow by a mysterious richness. Uncle Edward, they said that night, came to Macon, a scared, green boy from Statesboro, to take a job at the Bibb Mills. One day, on his lunch break, he passed the door to the weave room and looking in he saw a woman sitting with her back to him, elbows flying, working like there was no tomorrow. "Never saw her face until later," someone remembered he'd said. "Never had to." The bare light bulb suspended over her head had made the cotton dust shine in her hair, and he'd known at that very moment, as though some hindrance to sight had been struck down and he saw not just her but something essential and radiant about her, that this woman would be his wife. As it turned out, he did marry her and she died shortly after bearing him two children, but no one seemed particularly sad about that as long as they could go to the quick sweet stream of that moment when he'd first seen her and drink deeply of the life there, the life that he saw in her and cleaved to all his days, past reason, past hope. And this was the stream, I promised myself, that I would drink from too. I lay on my back and listened and watched the stars and the fireflies, which were like stars drifting down to join us, until the entire meadow and valley and sky swarmed with light.

Meanwhile, Aunt Martha sat twisting the paisley scarf around her neck, rocking so hard her chair cracked each time she rocked. Finally, Uncle Edward's story was done and he was at peace, having been hauled around to funeral services in three states before coming to his final resting place among the family in the long slope of green hillside above the Ocmulgee River. Then Martha chimed in. "Now I have an interesting recollection for us about my sister, Mariah, and about her birth long ago in the south of the state of Georgia." I struggled up from the grass, pulling the damp quilt around my shoulders. My grandmother had gone to bed early. She was dizzy, she said, from the blood pressure medicine she had to take six times a day. But it was better without her there; in her absence, her story expanded, took on important new dimensions.

Aunt Martha went on: "You know Mariah was born with her eyes shut tight as a kitten's and that she didn't open them for three days? I would give anything to know what wonders she witnessed during those three days." As she talked, she rocked and stared out past us all in a fixed way. Now we are getting someplace, I thought, this is more like it. And it seemed as though I'd been waiting for a long time to be there at that moment with Martha staring at the night with her enormous eyes as though she were using her second sight to carry her past the first layer of things and right on into the marrow. I turned my head slowly, the hair prickling along the tops of my arms, and looked where she was looking and saw only the fireflies and the shape of Scaley Mountain, darker than the sky.

"Mariah's was a special birth, attended by special signs," Martha continued. "She was born with the caul over her head." She looked at the group of us with wide, light eyes which at this moment I can still remember as the eyes of a creature staring in from somewhere outside a circle of light. "They say the caul is a sure sign that she had been granted the gift of second sight." From the line of rockers, someone protested: "Oh, Martha, go on now."

"You can't tell me it's not true," Aunt Martha snapped back. "I was present at her birth, and though I was only a small child, I remember it as though it were yesterday. The pity is that she's never developed this gift."

"But how do you know she hasn't?" I asked. Martha bent her long thin neck and smiled on me. She always encouraged us girls to use our minds and speak up when we had something to say.

"Hush now, Annie," someone answered. "Martha's just talking."

I sat up then; I sat very still. The damp quilt felt clammy against my skin so I shucked it off and stood up as if I'd remembered someplace I had to go. I ducked out through the cedars and onto the road that ran the length of the valley, pulling the cigarette I'd snitched earlier out of the waistband of my shorts. I lit up, inhaled deeply, tipped my head back and blew smoke up in a blue plume toward the stars. A gift. Martha had said there was a gift and it had to do with special powers. I held the cigarette between my teeth, put my hands on my hips and looked up at the deep blue sky. "I'm ready," I said. I thought I could hear the silence that rested there between the stars. I wondered what my gift might be. I wanted it to be clairvoyance, or something like it, because only with this gift would I be able to penetrate the layer of troubles that seemed to lie over everything like humid heat over Macon, and see into the heart of things. I wandered to the edge of the road where the rhododendron bushes grew. I stamped out my cigarette, leaned close to one of the blooms and opened my eyes very wide and stared until I started to get a headache, waiting for that flower to give up and reveal the secret of its life. I imagined that this would happen in slow motion, like time lapse photography—first the petals would unfold, then the center would break open and fall away and there inside I would see it, a star-swarming stream of pure life.

I gave up on the flower and I imagined myself going back to school with these special powers, able to tell who my real friends were and my secret enemies, able to know the secrets people keep in their hearts and to help them with their darkest troubles. And I would know what it was that Mother and I fought about all the time and why Grandmother never spoke to Aunt Rachel except in a cold and formal tone of voice and why Aunt Louise, Mother's sister, only called us late at night, and why my father could sometimes be found sitting back in the kitchen at three o'clock in the morning without a single light turned on. Behind me, something scratched lightly in the gravel. I turned slowly, full of a tingling like the light shaking of a thousand small silver bells, ready for my first encounter with the spirit world, and found one of Aunt Martha's old palsied hounds that had shuffled out after me, wagging its lazy tail. From back at the house, a screen door slammed, my mother's voice called "Annie, Annie, come in now, please." The spell was broken.

Still, for most of the rest of the night, I tried not to sleep because I had discovered that sleeping on it, as you're so often advised to do, makes some of the best feelings and strongest convictions dissolve into thin air. So, up in the Hen's Nest, a narrow room under the eaves where the women and girls slept, I tried to hold onto what Aunt Martha had said about the gifts and the way I had felt out on the road waiting for mine, as though some barrier were about to crumble and I was about to see things that no human eye could see, and no tongue could tell. As it turns out, I was right about sleep. When I woke up, it seemed, I had forgotten everything. Martha had taken her constitutional without me and gone into town, so I went looking for my grandmother instead, to ask her about these gifts she was supposed to have and why she'd never developed her own as Aunt Martha had accused her of not doing.

It was then that trouble lifted its head. I wandered through the house listening for the sound of my grandmother's voice. In the living room, a picture window looked out onto Scaley Mountain. Someone had placed an ink bottle full of violets on the windowsill, right below the teardrop-shaped crystal which Martha had hung in the window. Crystals, Martha said, are excellent conductors of the life force. I tapped it and small rainbows wobbled all over the walls and ceiling.

I found them in the kitchen. My grandmother was wiping

her eyes with the back of one hand and fanning a newspaper over the cakes with the other. My mother chopped cabbage on the drainboard beside the sink, her mouth as thin and set as the blade of her knife. Aunt Louise's name, like the echo of an angry outburst, hung in the air. I perched on the stool beside the table, grabbed a knife and a head of cabbage and began to chop. There were travel brochures fanned out on the table. They showed New England on a vivid autumn day, all red and orange, with a silver bus cutting cleanly down a road, beneath a sky so clear you might break chunks from it, the sun exploding off the windshield.

Grandmother was keen on taking fall foliage tours in New Hampshire and Vermont. Every year she went and sent us back postcards covered with lists of the colors she'd seen which sounded to me like no colors ever seen on this earth—helianthin, saffron, beaten gold—all brought to an absolute *pinnacle* of beauty in their last days of life. If Louise could just be there and see it, surely it would do her heart good, surely she would thrive in that good clean air. Surely the trip would bring her back to herself. I tried to match this vision of Louise with the woman I knew, the one who hadn't been able to come to the reunion because she had sprained her ankle or something. The Aunt Louise who sat restlessly silent at any gathering, worrying at her hands, the woman who walked as though she were a globe turning around a bent axis. Oh, no, not that Louise. My grandmother shooed her off with the newspaper. This other Louise was revived, refreshed, she was a risen Louise who laughed like a girl, who drank all the clear sweet water she wanted to drink. "Is Aunt Louise sick?" I asked.

"Just worn down, honey," my grandmother said. "She's had such a long, trying summer, you see."

"Louise has had several trying *winters* too," my mother snapped. "In fact, if you ask me, her summers and winters are getting worse every single year."

"Well, it's a good thing no one's asked you," my grandmother said. She flipped open a brochure and frowned at an autumn hillside. The newspaper swept back and forth across the cakes.

"Let's just look at some facts here, Mother," she said.

There's no stopping Mother when she's in full cry. As usual when Mother talked facts, I wanted to yell loud enough to drown her out. Her facts were always strong medicine, mixed in a dose equal to your high opinions of yourself and others. I cringed to see her number Louise's failures: the three lost jobs, the falls, the near accidents, the calls, the *collect* phone calls to my mother in the middle of the night. Grandmother hunched over, guarding something with her body.

"You're free to make of this what you will," she said. "Thank the Lord for independent minds. But Louise is my daughter. You're not there. I am. And she needs me."

"Will somebody please tell me what's wrong with Aunt Louise?" I said.

My mother fixed me with her long, contemplative stare in which she seems to be staring into a void full of the world's sadness. "She drinks," Mother said wearily. "She should be put in a hospital where she can get help."

"Her life is hard," my grandmother said, smacking the table hard with her palm. "She has a difficult life. Her husband is dead and her children are unmanageable. And Louise will never go to a hospital as long as I'm alive." She spoke these words so clearly it seemed she'd bitten them out of all possible words on the subject.

Backing away, my mother shrugged and bit her lower lip; then she began to chop cabbage, letting the blade come too close to her hand. "Louise is a wreck," she said quietly. "It's just plain cruel not to see it."

"Louise is my daughter. It doesn't matter what she is, I'm with her."

I put down my knife. "Excuse me," I said and I left the kitchen, fighting down the urge to run. I went and stood on the porch, blinking into the strong sunlight. Did Aunt Louise have gifts, I wondered. If so, what happened to them? What was it that wrecked inside you? Where did you go when you were lost, and where did you come back to when you were found?

That fall, as she had promised, my grandmother took Aunt Louise to New England for a foliage tour. And, as my mother had predicted, the trip was a disaster. The Louise my grandmother had imagined—the revitalized, healed Louise, who would find inspiration, comfort, peace, something bright in herself to match the leaves—that Louise, when taken to the mountains, vanished from the tour. She was found two days later holed up in an expensive hotel without two dimes to rub together. "The room-service tab was all for liquor, Annie," my mother said. "Louise was dead-dog drunk." Mother's cheeks were flushed, her eyes bright. When she looks that way it's easy to imagine her on a horse, leading a crusade. The story of the crisis as it developed via the long distance telephone line was this: On the morning when they came within sight of the most spectacular gorge in the White Mountains, a deep gorge with sides so thickly wooded and blazing that the air seemed saturated with color as though the world they'd come into at last were one tall flame, Louise bolted. The last person to see her reported that she was weeping. She'd checked into the resort hotel where they found her, started drinking, and—since she couldn't pay and she couldn't leave without paying—she stayed, and kept ordering out for liquor.

The ashtray on the phone stand filled up with Mother's cigarette butts as she negotiated the return of her mother and sister to Georgia. I hung around waiting for the progress reports and feeling helpless. I'd grown up believing there was always *something* you could do. She slammed down the phone: "Annie, she took Louise out and bought her a new dress and then she led her around like a little lost child, just like a little child. Can you beat that?"

I said I couldn't. It seemed some things couldn't be helped. Aunt Louise was one of them. My grandmother seemed defeated by it. She telephoned us when she got home and she said: "Louise has so much to give, I wanted to remind her of that. I thought she might see it this time."

"Well, she didn't," my mother said.

"Why didn't it help?" I asked my grandmother. I couldn't keep the anger out of my voice. After all, *she* was the one who was supposed to know about everything.

Her voice sounded tired as though she'd sunk to the bottom of a deep, hollow place. "There is something in Louise that nobody can get to," she said. "Don't ask me why."

I heard my mother take a breath. I thought I would kill her if she said anything small or mean-spirited. "Well, Mother, you tried," she said finally.

"And I will continue to do so," she said. "You can count on that."

I didn't exactly lose touch with my grandmother after that fall, but over the next six years it seemed we had to reach across a wider gap in order to make contact. There were the letters, always, and the Christmas visits when Louise wasn't doing too badly and my grandmother could leave Macon. But in the November after the reunion, Martha died, the mountain house was sold in April and after that the family split off into separate orbits, each around a different sun.

I knew my grandmother was sick and getting sicker but it didn't seem exactly real to me. I only knew that by the time I graduated from college, my grandmother was seriously ill with angina. Her life had become a series of risks. "Washing dishes or bathing," she wrote to me once, "are now gambles I must take. For my efforts, I'm rewarded with a freely drawn breath or these chest pains."

Early in July, I was visiting at home when Aunt Louise was involved in her second hit-and-run accident of the year and the judge gave her a choice: she could sign herself into a hospital for alcoholics, or she could go to jail. When my mother heard that my grandmother had consented to Louise's hospitalization, she said: "We are going to see Mother, *today*."

It was an edgy drive, a cord of silence tied in small knots of talk. We drove down through Georgia, through Thompson and Sparta, the dusty towns bunched around their courthouse squares, some with limp red and green tinsel left over from Christmas, faded and unseasonable, still wrapped around the light poles. We spoke only twice during the drive. Leaving Thompson, she said: "You be sure to tell her you're getting married."

"Of course," I said. "Why wouldn't I?" Later, when we stopped for the traffic light in Sparta, I said: "Is she very sick?" My mother gunned the engine until the fan belt screeched.

"Yes," she said. The light changed from red to green, and

she pressed the accelerator firmly. I felt as though we'd spoken to each other for the first time in years.

The apartment house where my grandmother lived hadn't changed. Neither had the hill where the building stood. Only the trees lining the sidewalk had changed, their tops sawed flat to make way for the power lines. We opened the heavy oak door that always stuck and walked inside. In the hallway, the smell of gas and bacon grease still lingered. The tea roses on the stained wallpaper were brown.

We let ourselves into her living room. It looked like one of those rooms in a museum, arranged to show the clutter and hurry of someone's everyday life. Her books, reference books, and composition books with their black and white mottled covers, were piled beside chairs, slips of paper sprouting from between their pages. Dust lay thick on every surface and the windows were clouded, streaked with dried rain. All the walls were hung with African paintings, hammered copper crosses, the shaman's mask with its leopard-skin face motheaten and mournful as the face of a derelict.

Her nightstand was covered with pill bottles, and a chart with check marks beside the hours and the names of pills hung from a string around the bedpost. She lay dozing on the bed, one arm flung over her eyes, dressed as though she were going to a party, in a lavender print dress with purple beads and earrings to match. She'd dotted her cheeks with two bright circles of rouge and brightened her mouth with lipstick. But her feet were bare, the blue veins like a forked branch all over them, the toenails thick and stained tobacco brown. I reached for my mother's hand. And as I watched my grandmother's chest rise and fall with each breath, I realized that Mother and I were matching our breathing to hers and I thought I understood a little more about what people mean when they say, "This person is alive." They mean that the circle curves, unbroken, between what is visible and what cannot be seen and you know of its existence the same way you know currents in water by watching a boat or currents in the sky by seeing the way a hawk holds tight to the wind. I let go of Mother's hand and went to the window and yanked at the dusty blinds, forced the window open as high as it would go. The sound of a jackhammer riddled the air. Still she lay quietly, breathing from somewhere high in her chest.

"Mother."

"Grandmother." My mother and I spoke at once. For a second or two, she stared at us wildly as though we were robbers. She sat up, one cheek creased and flushed, and fumbled at the nightstand for her glasses. I helped her with her slippers and then she stood up beside the bed and reached for us. She'd lost weight and her dress hung on her in folds, like a slack flag. I was her best beloved, my mother was the light of her life. She pressed her hand to her chest and began taking small sips of air.

"You sit down," Mother said, her forehead tight with worry. We helped her to the armchair in the living room and she sat heavily. "I'll make us some tea," Mother said, in her voice that gets cheerful and bright whenever she's afraid.

"Coffee for me," I said. "Black, please." Grandmother started to protest. She leaned up in her chair, then let herself go against the cushions. And I saw that she was radically changed. It was as if I'd been looking at her from the corner of my eye and had finally gotten up the nerve to look her full in the face. And for a moment, whatever hurries us along, slipping one minute into the next to make a continuous flow of time, stopped, and I had my moment of sight, though it was no gift I would have asked for. Her face looked vivid and full of light as though her expression had become a clean window, and peace itself looked through. And then, without pause or change, her face began to darken into a stillness beyond peace, beyond any power to name or know. But that light didn't just disappear—I saw it leave her. And it seemed at that moment that death was very close to us, only it wasn't silent or empty or dark. It was full of the recollection of everything I had loved about her, everything that would be lost, as though grief and love are the fruit of the same tree, the one with roots so old and tangled they can never be pulled apart.

I turned away then. I think I twisted away because she grabbed my wrist and held it. Her hand felt strong, as though she'd gathered all her strength there. "Well, sit right down," she said, "and tell me how it is."

"How is what?" I felt confused and let myself be pulled into the chair next to hers.

"Oh the wide, wide world and those who live there."

"It's about the same," I said. I rubbed her hand, felt the knuckles under the loose skin, moved my thumb over the joints.

"Now you know as well as I do that that is never so," she said. She closed her eyes, her head dropped back. I saw her face settle along the bones into that stillness. When she opened her eyes again, she looked angry and scared. "Lulluraburg," she said. She shook her head. "That name has eluded me for days."

"The place where they sang?"

She smiled. "Imagine remembering that from when you were just a little thing."

"I think there's lots I remember," I said. "Pieces of it come floating back to me now and then, like there's a place for them, you know what I mean?"

"I do indeed," she said. "I do indeed. And aren't you looking well. Your mother tells me you're just doing so well."

"Yes," I said, "yes I am." The sound of my voice was loud with cheerfulness, just like my mother's. "I'm getting married soon."

"Married?" She turned her head so quickly I thought a sound had startled her. She looked at me fiercely. "Is he a good man, and I mean day to day?" She tapped out the words on the arm of the chair with one long finger.

"Why, yes," I said. "Yes he is, as a matter of fact. How did you know? Now don't forget, the wedding's in August. I want to make sure you don't miss it. I'll drive down and pick you up, how would that be?"

"Married," she said. "Isn't that something!" She folded her arms and looked straight ahead. "The Bible says it's not good that we should be alone because if one should fall alone, who will pick him up, and if one should lie alone in the cold, who will warm him?" She picked at a loose thread on the arm of the chair. *You haven't answered my question, will you come to my wedding?* I wanted to say, but just then my mother returned with a rattle of cups and saucers, calling: "Here we are now, isn't this nice?"

I let go of her hand and excused myself. I went into the bathroom and stood at the window looking across what had been a trash-filled gully, now grown over in kudzu and wild Cherokee rose. The chinaberry tree was still standing, hung with dull gold fruit, half choked in dead limbs. As I watched, a cardinal snagged in the upper branches and began its high sweet chipping. The Ocmulgee wound by, a thick and sluggish muddy gold, and I thought of the summers I'd spent there watching the river, following it in my mind's eye all the way down till it found the Atlantic. I used to stand there imagining myself in a small glass-covered boat drifting down the river, and when I talked to her about this trip I wanted to make, my grand-mother was always ready to go. Sometimes while I helped her dry the dishes, we stocked my boat with provisions—matches in a waterproof case, canned food, a cat for good company, a map. She'd laughed. "You don't need a map."

"Well, what if the river forks?"

"Well, what if it does?"

Around five o'clock my grandmother refused for the last time to come back with us to South Carolina. "This is my home," she said. "I have work to do here."

"What work?" Mother snapped. She thrust her chin out the way she does and I saw how she must have looked as a child challenging someone whose protection she needed, whose power she feared.

"I have to prepare my YWCA classes for fall," my grand-mother said in that cold, imperious tone that allowed no words to follow.

My mother shoved a cigarette into her mouth and bustled around the apartment, bullying things into place, shoving books and papers around, slapping at the dust with a rag, stirring it up so it hung in the air. When she finished and we'd collected our things, she said: "Now, Mother, for goodness' sake call us. You just worry me to death." She laughed, her mouth open, said: "Oh well, Mother, what would we do if everybody was as stubborn as you?"

"I'm glad I have a tractable nature," I said. I laughed too.

Grandmother hauled herself out of her chair and stood

there breathing, counting, as though she were poor and every breath was a dollar she was forced to spend.

"Mother, don't come out with us, we can let ourselves out," my mother said. But she walked with us anyway, as far as the entrance to the building. I turned and waved as we walked down toward the car. "August," I yelled. "I'll come and pick you up. You'll like him, I promise, he's your type." She cupped her hand to her ear, nodded. At the car, I shaded my eyes and looked back, hoping to find her gone but she was still there, standing quietly and watching the clouds, the trees along the street in a shy sort of way as though she'd just noticed the size and silence of things. She stared at me as though she were looking for a bird in a tree. Then deliberately and clearly she said: "Good-bye," and she turned and walked back into the building.

It wasn't until four summers later, when Grandmother was four years dead and my daughter Jesse was three, that I came to a place I recognized again as a destination on some road I had been traveling though I couldn't tell you all the twists and turns that brought me there. What happened was that Mother came down with pneumonia in the middle of August. It came on her overnight while my father was away on business in Mobile and what was so frightening was the timing of it. When she called to tell me, the sky was white, the sun glared off the sidewalks, the thermometer read 97 degrees. She couldn't say just exactly what was wrong, probably nothing, or why she hadn't called one of her friends there in town, but she was having trouble breathing and she just felt, well, weak and sort of cold, not all the time, but whenever she moved around. Why, yesterday, if I could imagine such a thing, she had gotten so dizzy that she'd just had to lie down for a minute, right there on the kitchen floor. She sounded casual about it, the way you might with a stranger in the house and you calling for help and trying not to let on that you were afraid of him.

People just don't get pneumonia in the middle of August, I said to myself as I drove to South Carolina. That's just crazy. It was close to dusk by the time I made it. When I opened the door, the heat hit me like a blast of desert air. The house must have been 80 degrees. Mother had camped out under a pile of blankets on the sofa back in the den. With the curtains drawn, the room was dark as a lair, the only light came from the television set on the table just in front of the sofa. Her eyes watched me from a shadowed place way back in her head. I put my hand on her forehead; it was so hot the heat seemed to radiate from it. "What took you so long?" she asked, her voice high and wheedling as an old woman's.

"I've been on my way ever since you called, Mother," I said. "I came as soon as I could." I yanked back the curtains, cranked open the window. As the light came into the room I saw how old she looked, how scared. I saw on her face the same dimness I had seen on my grandmother's face just before she died. It looked as though her cheekbones were throwing shadows under the skin. And I felt ashamed just then, for the trust I had put in the future, the way I always looked beyond what was right in front of me, believing that my destiny was somewhere else. For that blind burrowing trust that tunneled toward some promised land where we would all arrive some-day, together and healthy and whole. For that misplaced faith in a someday when all would be well, all promises kept, all gifts given, all life lived.

"At least you're here now," she said. Her eyes closed and I pressed her hand to my cheek and held it there.

"Let's go," I said. "We're going to the emergency room right now." She was too weak to change out of her housedress but while I called her doctor to meet us at the hospital, she pulled on the fur coat my father had given her and together we went down into the August heat. There was something awful about the sheen of that healthy-looking fur wrapped around her and the way she shivered inside it as though she were shivering from a place that nothing could warm.

I called my father in Mobile. Then, for three days, while I waited for him to come home, I took prescriptions to the drug store and doled out the medicine, cleaned the house and wa-tered the flowerbeds. For some reason I got it in my head that what she needed was fish, fresh vegetables, and clear broth with lots of ginger in it. So I went to the market and bought bunches of greens, tiny lady peas and lima beans, okra and tomatoes and corn with the milk still sweet in the kernels. Every day I bought fresh shrimp or grouper or flounder, food from the ocean, with the ocean's mineral brine in the sweet flesh. "I'm going to swim out of here by the time you get through with me," she said.

"That's the idea," I said. I watched while the shadow retreated from her face. On the third day, her fever broke, her eyes cleared.

The night before my father was due back from Mobile we sat up late back in the den while a summer storm moved onto us. I was paging through back issues of *Southern Living* while Mother read, an afghan across her lap to guard against the chills that still grabbed her now and then. The air thickened and grew stuffy, bringing the charge of the storm into the room to surround us. The rain blew in scattered gusts. Then, with a stumble of thunder, the tall hickory tree just outside the window bent halfway to the ground and the windows rinsed with rain as though a bucket of water had been thrown against the glass. I held the magazine up in front of my face and tried to focus my attention on the chart on the page which showed how to schedule your fall garden chores, when to take in the gladiola bulbs, how deep to plant next spring's jonquils.

I tried to concentrate but all I heard was the rain as it rushed around the house, around the room where we sat watching, and the wind as it bent the trees and whipped the leaves. Then a gust of wind came that was so strong it made the weatherstripping hum under the door. I dropped my magazine and looked up and that's when I saw my startled face staring back from the window. At the sight of my own scared face, something gave way inside me that had been holding firm since I'd first arrived and seen how sick my mother was. Behind me, Mother read as though she did not hear the storm, as though she would read forever. But the storm was everywhere and I thought that if I listened long enough, I might hear the sound of the rain as it came into the house and ran inside the walls like a river and the sound of the house going under that river, dissolving board by board, life by life, until all had been returned that once had been given.

I bowed my head again and turned through the pages,

trying to find something that would hold my attention. And when I had skimmed through every page and looked up again, I saw myself again in the window glass and Mother behind me, with her book closed over one finger and her head turned toward the sound of the storm. And I saw that the dullness had left her face. She was well again, and unafraid.

"Some storm," she said, as though she could match it, strength for strength, blow for blow.

"The best part of a storm is when it's over," I said. Already, the storm had wheeled away to the south. The gap lengthened between lightning and its thunder. Outside, I heard the trees dripping. It was over. But when the time came, I felt no peace. I looked to my mother, trying to find comfort in her health, in the light that had returned to her face. Instead, I saw in this light everything I had ever rejoiced in, grieved over, loved. There was nothing outside it, nothing beyond. And I saw that this life I had tried to find and know and keep exists in this world in human form, and darkened by the crossing. And on the banks of that river I bowed my head, thankful for the night and the rain and the trouble, and for the darkness in which the light is kept.

Seeing Aunt Louise again is what started me thinking about all this again. I'd driven down to Macon for the day to do research in the Mercer library and she'd asked me to stop by for a visit. I hadn't seen her in years, not since Grandmother had died, so I wasn't prepared for the change in her. The Louise I remembered had been dazed and frumpy looking. But the Louise who answered the door was thin and dressed in a buff suede tunic and sweater and matching shoes. She looked thin but not starved. In fact, she looked healthy and solid, alive. I remembered what my mother had said after seeing Louise up on the dais, the guest of honor at her fourth AA birthday party. "I felt like I was celebrating right along with her," she'd said. Seeing Louise again, I felt that same kind of rejoicing, so quiet it couldn't be named, running like a stream through her life. "Louise," I said, "you're looking so well." We held each other's elbows while she considered this.

"That's because I am," she said.

Louise's place is modern and it overlooks the river. She's done it up with a lot of glass, glass shelves, glass ornaments, each set on a chosen spot and with a little pool of space around it as though everything needed room to breathe. Louise moved within a quiet space of her own. As we talked, her hands stayed calm in her lap. But it was her face that told the story. Nothing had deserted her face, not the pain and not the death. It was all there like something you could read if only you knew the language. There was the death she'd lived and the life that came after that death, all shadowed by a determination that was almost, but not quite, peace.

We sipped our coffee and traded pictures—my daughter Jesse and my husband Thomas, her grandson, William, Jr. Finally, I said: "It's getting late, Louise. Thomas and Jesse expect me for supper." But neither of us moved.

She said: "Will you look at something before you go? I found this the other day and I can't for the life of me figure it out." She hauled out her mother's African scrapbook, the one covered in woven straw and embroidered on the front with a wine-red moon, a golden sun. We flipped through the pages— past the pressed fronds and African flowers, the snapshots of the Mountains of the Moon, the scroll signed by Neptune— and stopped at a child's crayon drawing done in yellow, black, and green, of people in a jungle gathered around a snake. My grandmother was among them, the pillow-shaped person wearing black shoes and glasses. "I know that's supposed to be Mother," Louise said, "but what's that?"

"A dead snake?"

"I know that," she said. "I'm talking about the other thing."

The snake's eyes were red x's, the forked tongue lay limply on the ground. Out of its middle, an animal was rising, a cross between fox and deer with wings and a fishy smile, surrounded by a globe of light. "Oh that," I said, sorting back through the Africa stories. "Isn't that the anaconda they found that had swallowed some kind of animal?"

Louise laughed. She put her hand to her throat. "How could I forget?" she said. "Of course, that's right. The animal that was alive inside the snake." She shook her head. "Now, who do you suppose made that one up? Mother was always so serious about it, too."

"Maybe she made it up."

"Maybe she did. She was good at that." Louise's smile tightened. "She surely was."

By the time I left Macon, dusk lay thick as blue dust over the fields. It was autumn then, and in the dusty green woods the sourwood leaves had already turned a lustrous red. All the way home I thought about these things, turning them over in my mind, putting one turn next to the other, watching the road they made. It seemed like one road with many turnings and the end nowhere in sight. When I got to the outskirts of Atlanta and the traffic started picking up, I turned my attention toward home and I imagined how Jesse would look, waiting for me at the front window and how she'd rush out as soon as she saw the car coming down the street and dance around me while I unloaded the car, talking a mile a minute. "What'd you bring me," I could almost hear her say. "Where'd you go, how long did it take you? What'd you bring me?"

Well, Jesse, I will say, I have those ivory elephants that march across the mantel in single file, the big ones first, the little ones following. I have the wooden bowl with the people carved at the bottom, the ones who are passing the inlaid ivory bird from hand to hand. And now I have this story to tell, to keep her through the night and give her good dreams. I will say: In Africa, Jesse, your great-grandmother was walking beside the Kasai River one day and she stepped over a log lying across the path and do you know, that log was a snake? Yes it was. Well, that old snake lifted up its old scaly head and its eyes looked cold and dead, like the eyes of a very sad person. And this snake wanted to swallow her whole, it surely did. How did she know? She saw it in his eyes. When she saw the snake, why of course she yelled as loud as she could. And some men heard her and they ran out from the village and they killed the snake. Yes they did. They killed it, and they cut the snake open and do you know what they found? They found an antelope fawn that the snake had swallowed. It stood up trembling, Jesse, and do you know, that creature was alive? Yes. Down inside that dark old snake, it was alive as you or me.

JOHN GARDNER

JULIUS CAESAR AND THE WEREWOLF

FROM PLAYBOY

៶

AS TO CAESAR'S HEALTH, there seems to me no cause for alarm.
The symptoms you mention are, indeed, visible, though perhaps a little theatricized by your informant. Caesar has always
been a whirlwind of energy and for that reason subject to
nervous attacks, sudden tempers, funks and so forth. When I
was young, I confidently put it down to excess of blood, a
condition complicated (said I) by powerful intermittent ejec-
tions of bile; but phlebotomy agitates instead of quieting him,
sad to say (sad for my diagnosis), and his habitual exhilaration,
lately increased, makes the bile hypothesis hogwash. I speak
lightly of these former opinions of mine, but you can hardly
imagine what labor I've put into the study of this man, scribbling, pondering, tabulating, while, one after another, the chickens rise to confront a new day and my candles gutter out. All
to no avail, but pride's for people with good digestion. I bungle
along, putting up with myself as best I can. (You'll forgive a
little honest whining.) No man of science was ever presented
with a puzzle more perplexing and vexatious than this Caesar,
or with richer opportunity for observing the subject of his
inquiry. He's interested in my work—in fact, follows it closely.
He allows me to sit at his elbow or tag along wherever I

please—an amusing spectacle, Caesar striding like a lion down some corridor, white toga flying, his black-robed physician leaping along like a spasm behind him on one good leg, one withered one.

In any event, at the age of 55, his animal spirits have never been more vigorous. He regularly dictates to four scribes at a time—jabber, jabber, jabber, sentences crackling like lightning in a haystack, all of his letters of the greatest importance to the state. Between sentences, to distract his impatience, he reads from a book. Or so he'd have us think, and I'm gullible. It saves time, I find, and in the end makes no big difference. His baldness more annoys him, it seems to me, than all the plots of the senators. For years, as you know, he combed his straggling blond hairs straight forward, and nothing pleased him more than the people's decision to award him the crown of laurel, which he now wears everywhere except, I think, to bed. A feeble ruse and a delight to us all. The reflected light of his bald pate glows like a sun on the senate-chamber ceiling.

His nervous energy is not significantly increased, I think, from the days when I first knew him, many years ago, in Gaul. I was transferred to the legion for some disservice to the state—monumental, I'm sure, but it's been 35 years, and I've told the story so many times, in so many slyly self-congratulating versions, that by now I've forgotten the truth of it. I was glad of the transfer. I was a sea doctor before. I don't mind telling you, water scares the pants off me.

I remember my first days with Caesar clear as crystal. He struck me at once as singular almost to the point of freakishness. He was taller than other men, curiously black-eyed and blond-headed, like two beings in one body. But what struck me most was his speed, both physical and mental. He could outrun a deer, outthink every enemy he met—and he was, besides, very strong. We all knew why he fought so brilliantly. He was guilty of crimes so numerous, back in Rome, from theft to assault to suspicion of treason, that he couldn't afford to return there as a common citizen. (It was true of most of us, but Caesar was the worst.) By glorious victories, he could win public honors and appointments and, thus, stand above the law, or at least above its meanest kick. Whatever his reasons—

this I have to give to him—no man in history, so far as it's recorded, ever fought with such effectiveness and passion or won such unshakable, blind-pig devotion from his men. He was not then the strategist he later became, killing a few left-handed and blindfolded, then persuading the rest to surrender and accept Roman citizenship. In those days, he painted the valleys red, weighed down the trees with hanging men, made the rivers run sluggish with corpses. He was always in the thick of it, like a rabid bitch, luring and slaughtering seven at a time. His body, it seems to me, runs by nature at an accelerated tempo: His sword moves much faster than a normal man's. And he's untiring. At the end of a 12-hour day's forced march, when the whole encampment was finally asleep, he used to pace like a half-starved jaguar in his tent or sit with a small fish-oil lamp, writing verse. I wonder if he may not have some unknown substance in common with the violent little flea.

Through all his wars, Caesar fought like a man unhinged, but I give you my word, he's not crazy. He has the falling sickness, as you know. A damned nuisance but, for all the talk, nothing more. All his muscles go violent, breaking free of his will, and he has a sudden, vividly real sense of falling into the deepest abyss, a fall that seems certain never to end, and no matter what servants or friends press around him (he's dimly aware of presences, he says), there's no one, nothing, he can reach out to. From an outward point of view, he's unconscious at these times, flailing, writhing, snapping his teeth, dark eyes bulging and rolling out of sight, exuding a flood of oily tears; but from what he reports, I would say he is not unconscious but in some way transformed, as if seized for the moment by the laws of a different set of gods. (I mean, of course, "forces" or "biological constraints.")

No doubt it adds to the pressure on him that he's a creature full of pangs and contradictions. Once, in Gaul, we were surprised by an ambush. We had moved for days through dangerous, twilit forest and had come, with relief, to an area of endless yellow meadow, where the grass reached only to our knees, so that we thought we were safe. Suddenly, out of the grass all around us leaped an army of women. Caesar cried, "Save yourselves! We're not in Gaul to butcher females!" In the end, we killed them all. (I, as Caesar's physician, killed no one.) I trace Caesar's melancholy streak to that incident. He became, thereafter, moody and uneasy, praying more than necessary and sometimes pausing abruptly to glance all around him, though not a shadow had stirred. It was not the surprise of the ambush, I think. We'd been surprised before. The enemy was young and naked except for weapons and armor, and they were singularly stubborn: They gave us no choice but to kill them. I watched Caesar himself cut one in half, moving his sword more slowly than usual and staring fixedly at her face.

The melancholy streak has been darkened, in my opinion, by his years in Rome. His work load would rattle a stone Apollo—hundreds of letters to write every day, lines of suppliants stretching half a mile, each with his grievance large or small and his absurd, ancient right to spit softly into Caesar's ear—not to mention the foolish disputes brought in to him for settlement. Some starving scoundrel steals another scoundrel's newly stolen pig, the whole ramshackle slum is up in arms, and for the public good the centurions bring all parties before Caesar. Hours pass, lamps are lit, accuser and denier rant on, banging tables, giving the air fierce kicks by way of warning. Surely a man of ordinary tolerance would go mad—or go to sleep. Not our Caesar. He listens with the look of a man watching elderly people eat, then eventually points to one or the other or both disputants, which means the person's to be dragged away for hanging, and then, with oddly meticulous care, one hand over his eyes, he dictates to a scribe the details of the case and his dispensation, with all his reasonings. "Admit the next," he says, and folds his hands.

And these are mere gnats before the hurricane. He's responsible, as they say when they're giving him some medal, for the orderly operation of the largest, richest, most powerful empire the world has ever known. He must rule the senate, with all its constipated, red-nosed, wheezing factions—every bleary eye out for insult or injury, every liver-spotted hand half closed around a dagger. And he must show at least some semblance of interest in the games, escape for the bloodthirst of the citizenry. He watches the kills, man or lion or whatever, without a sign of emotion, but I'm onto him. He makes me think of my days at sea, that still, perfect weather before a plank buster.

All this work he does without a particle of help, not a single assistant except the four or five scribes who take dictation and the slave who brings him parchment, ink and fresh oil or sandals—unless one counts, as I suppose one must, Mark Antony: a loyal friend and willing drudge but, as all Rome knows, weak as parsley. (He's grown fat here in the city and even less decisive than he was on the battlefield. I've watched him trying to frame letters for Caesar, tugging his jaw over decisions Caesar would make instantly.) In short, the life of a Caesar is donkeywork and unquestionably dangerous to health. I've warned and warned him. He listens with the keenest interest, but he makes no changes. His wary glances to left and right become more frequent, more noticeable and odd. He has painful headaches, especially at executions, and now and then he sleepwalks, looking for something under benches and in every low cupboard. I find his heartbeat irregular, sometimes wildly rushing, sometimes all but turning around and walking backward, as if he were both in a frenzy and mortally bored.

Some blame the death of his daughter for all this. I'm dubious, though not beyond persuasion. That Julia was dear to his heart I don't deny. When she was well, he was off with her every afternoon he could steal from Rome's business, teaching her to ride, walking the hills with her, telling her fairy tales of gods disguised as people or people transformed into celestial constellations or, occasionally—the thing she liked best, of course—recounting his adventures. I remember how the girl used to gaze at him at such times, elbows on her knees, hands on her cheeks, soft, pale hair cascading over her shoulders and down her long back—it made me think of those beautiful altar-lit statues in houses of prostitution. (I mean no offense. Old men are by nature prone to nastiness.) She was an intelligent girl, always pursing her lips and frowning, preparing to say, "Tut, tut." He taught her knots and beltwork and the nicer of the soldiers' songs, even taught her his special tricks of swordsmanship—because she nagged him to it (you know how daughters are)—and, for all I know, the subtleties of planning a campaign against India and China. I never saw a father more filled with woe than Caesar when the sickness first invaded her. He would rush up and down, far into the night (I never saw him take even a nap through all that period), and he was blistering to even the most bent-backed, senile and dangerous senators, to say nothing of whiny suppliants and his poor silent wife. His poems took an ugly turn—much talk of quicksand and maws and the like—and the bills he proposed before the senate weren't much prettier; and then there was the business with the gladiators. But when Julia died, he kissed her waxy forehead and left the room and, so far as one could see, that was that. After the great funeral so grumbled about in certain quarters, he seemed much the same man he'd seemed before, not just externally but also internally, so far as my science could reach. His blood was very dark but, for him, normal; his stools were ordinary; his seizures no more tedious than usual.

So what can have brought on this change you inquire of and find so disturbing—as do I, of course? (At my age, nothing's as terrible as might have been expected.) I have a guess I might offer, but it's so crackpot I think I'd rather sit on it. I'll narrate the circumstances that prompt it; you can draw your own conclusions.

Some days ago, March first, shortly after nightfall, as I was washing out my underthings and fixing myself for bed, two messengers appeared at my door with the request—polite but very firm—that I at once get back into my clothes and go to Caesar. I naturally—after some perfunctory sniveling—obeyed. I found the great man alone in his chamber, staring out the one high window that overlooks the city. It was a fine scene, acted with great dignity, if you favor that sort of thing. He did not turn at our entrance, though only a man very deep in thought could have failed to notice the brightness of the torches as their light set fire to the wide marble floor with its inlay of gold and quartz. We waited. It was obvious that something was afoot. I was on guard. Nothing interests Caesar, I've learned, but Caesar. Full-scale invasion of the Empire's borders would not rouse in him this banked fire of restlessness—fierce playfulness, almost—except insofar as its repulsion might catch him more honor. There was a scent in the room, the smell of an animal, I thought at first, then corrected myself: a blood smell. "Show him," Caesar said quietly, still not turning.

I craned about and saw, even before my guides had inclined their torches in that direction, that on the high marble table at the far end of the room some large, wet, misshapen object had been placed, then blanketed. I knew instantly what it was, to tell the truth, and my eyes widened. They have other doctors; it was the middle of the night! I have bladder infections and prostate trouble; I can hardly move my bowels without a clyster! When the heavy brown cloth was solemnly drawn away, I saw that I'd guessed right. It was, or had once been, a tall, bronze-skinned man, a slave, probably rich and admired in whatever country he'd been dragged from. His knees were drawn up nearly to his pectorals and his head rolled out oddly, almost severed at the neck. One could guess his stature only from the length of his arms and the shiny span exposed, caked with blood, from knee to foot. One ear had been partially chewed away.

"What do you make of it?" Caesar asked. I heard him coming toward me on those dangerous, swift feet, then heard him turn, pivoting on one hissing sandal, moving back quickly toward the window. I could imagine his nervous, impatient gestures, though I did not look: gestures of a man angrily talking to himself, bullying, negotiating—rapidly opening and closing his fists or restlessly flipping his right hand, like a sailor paying out coil after coil of line.

"Dogs—" I began.

"Not dogs," he said sharply, almost before I'd spoken. I felt myself grow smaller, the sensation in my extremities shrinking toward my heart. I put on my mincing, poor-old-man expression and pulled at my beard, then reached out gingerly to move the head, examining more closely the clotted ganglia where the thorax had been torn away. Whatever had killed him had done him a kindness. He was abscessed from the thyroid to the *vena cava superior*. When I looked over at Caesar, he was back at the window, motionless again, the muscles of his arm and shoulder swollen as if clamping in rage. Beyond his head, the night had grown dark. It had been clear, earlier, with a fine, full moon; now it was heavily overcast and oppressive—

no stars, no moon, only the lurid glow, here and there, of a torch. In the light of the torches the messengers held, one on each side of me, Caesar's eyes gleamed, intently watching.

"Wolves," I said, with conviction.

He turned, snapped his fingers several times in quick succession—in the high, stone room, it was like the sound of a man clapping—and almost the same instant, a centurion entered, leading a girl. Before she was through the archway, she was down on her knees, scrambling toward Caesar as if to kiss his toes and ankles before he could behead her. Obviously, she did not know his feeling of tenderness, almost piety, toward young women. At her approach Caesar turned his back to the window and raised his hands, as if to ward her off. The centurion, a young man with blue eyes, like a German's, jerked at her wrist and stopped her. Almost gently, the young man put his free hand into her hair and tipped her face up. She was perhaps 16, a thin girl with large, dark, flashing eyes full of fear.

Caesar said, never taking his gaze from her, "This young woman says the wolf was a man."

I considered for a moment, only for politeness. "Not possible," I said. I limped nearer to them, bending for a closer look at the girl. If she was insane, she showed none of the usual signs—depressed temples, coated tongue, anemia, inappropriate smiles and gestures. She was not a slave, like the corpse on the table—nor of his race, either. Because of her foreignness, I couldn't judge what her class was, except that she was a commoner. She rolled her eyes toward me, a plea like a dog's. It was hard to believe that her terror was entirely an effect of her audience with Caesar.

Caesar said, "The Goths have legends, doctor, about men who at certain times turn into wolves."

"Ah," I said, noncommittal.

He shifted his gaze to meet mine, little fires in his pupils. I shrank from him—visibly, no doubt. Nothing is stupider or more dangerous than toying with Caesar's intelligence. But he restrained himself. " 'Ah!' " he mimicked with awful scorn and, for an instant, smiled. He looked back at the girl, then away again at once; then he strode over to the corpse and stood with his back to me, staring down at it, or into it, as if hunting for its soul, his fists rigid on his hips to keep his fingers from drumming. "You know a good deal, old friend," he said, apparently addressing myself, not the corpse. "But possibly not everything!" He raised his right arm, making purposely awkward loops in the air with his hand, and rolled his eyes at me, grinning with what might have been malice, except that he's above that. Impersonal rage at a universe too slow for him. He said, "Perhaps, flopping up and down through the world like a great, clumsy bat, trying to spy out the secrets of the gods, you miss a few things? Some little trifle here or there?"

I said nothing, merely pressed my humble palms together. To make perfectly clear my dutiful devotion, I limped over to stand at his side, looking with him, gravely, at the body. Moving the leg—there was as yet no *rigor mortis*—I saw that the body had been partly disemboweled. The spleen was untouched in the intestinal disarray; the liver was nowhere to be seen. I could feel the girl's eyes on my back. Caesar's smile was gone now, hovering just below the surface. He had his hand on the dead man's foot, touching it as if to see if bones were broken or as if the man were a friend, a fellow warrior.

He lowered his voice. "This isn't the first," he said. "We've kept the matter quiet, but it's been happening for months." His right hand moved out like a stealthy animal, anticipating his thought. His voice grew poetic. (It was a bad idea, that laurel crown.) "A sudden black shadow, a cry out of the darkness, and in the morning—in some alley or in the middle of a field or huddled against some rotting door in the tanners' district—a corpse ripped and mauled past recognition. The victims aren't children, doctor; they're grown men, sometimes women." He frowned. The next instant, his expression became unreadable, as if he were mentally reaching back, abandoning present time, this present body. Six, maybe seven heartbeats passed; and then, just as suddenly, he was here with us again, leaning toward me, oddly smiling. "And then tonight," he said, "this treasure!" With a gesture wildly theatrical—I saw myself at the far end of the forum, at the great door where the commoners peer in—he swept his arm toward the girl. She looked, cowering, from one to the other of us, then up at the soldier.

Caesar crossed to her; I followed part way. "He was half man, half wolf; is that your story?" He bent over her, pressing his hands to his knees as he asked it. Clearly he meant to seem fatherly, but his body was all iron, the muscles of his shoulders and arms locked and huge.

After a moment, she nodded.

"He wore clothes like a man?"

Again she nodded, this time looking warily at me. She had extraordinary eyes, glistening, dark, bottomless and very large, perhaps the first symptom of a developing exophthalmic goiter.

Caesar straightened up and turned to the centurion. "And what was this young woman doing when you found her?"

"Dragging the body, sir." One side of his mouth moved, the faintest suggestion of a smile. "It appeared to us she was hiding it."

Now Caesar turned to me, his head inclined to one side, like a lawyer in court. "And why would she be doing that?"

At last the girl's terror was explicable.

I admired the girl for not resisting us. She knew, no doubt—all Romans know—that torture can work wonders. Although I've never been an optimist, I like to believe it was not fear of torture that persuaded her but the certain knowledge that whatever sufferings she might put herself through, she would in the end do as we wished. She had a curious elegance for a girl of her station. Although she walked head ducked forward, as all such people do, and although her gait was odd—long strides, feet striking flat, like an Egyptian's— her face showed the composure and fixed resolve one some- times sees on statues, perhaps some vengeful, endlessly patient Diana flanked by her hounds. Although one of the centurions in our company held the girl's elbow, there seemed no risk that she would try to run away. Caesar, wearing a dark hood and mantle now, kept even with her or sometimes moved a little ahead in his impatience. The three other centurions and I came behind, I in great discomfort, wincing massively at every right- foot lurch but, for all that, watching everything around me, especially the girl, with sharp attention. It grew darker and quieter as we descended into the slums. The sky was still overcast, so heavily blanketed one couldn't even guess in which part of the night the moon hung. Now and then, like some mysterious pain, lightning would bloom and move deep in the clouds, giving them features and shapes for a moment, and we'd hear a low rumble; then blackness would close on us deeper than before. The girl, too, seemed to mind the darkness. Every so often, as we circled downward, I would see her lift and turn her head, as if she were trying to find her bearings.

No one was about. Nothing moved except now and then a rat researching garbage or scampering along a gutter, or a chicken stirring in its coop as we passed, its spirit troubled by bad dreams. In this part of town, there were no candles, much less torches—and just as well: The whole section was a tinder-box. The buildings were three and four stories high, leaning out drunkenly over the street or against one another like beggars outside a temple, black, rotten wood that went shiny as intestines when the lightning glowed, walls patched with hides and daubs of mud, straw and rotten hay packed in tightly at the crooked foundations. The only water was the water in the streets or in the river invisible in the darkness below us, poisonously inching under bridge after bridge toward the sea. When I looked back up the hill between lightning blooms, I could no longer make out so much as an arch of Caesar's palace or the firm, white mansions of the rich—only a smoky luminosity red under the clouds. The street was airless, heavy with the smell of dead things and urine. Every door and shutter was unhealthily closed tight.

We progressed more slowly now, barely able to see one another. I cannot say what we were walking on; it was slippery and gave underfoot. I was feeling cross at Caesar's refusal to use torches; but he was the crafty old warrior, not I. Once, with a clatter I at first mistook for thunder, some large thing rushed across the street in front of us, out of darkness and in again—a man, a donkey, some rackety demon—and we all stopped. No one spoke; then Caesar laughed. We resumed our walk.

Minutes later, the girl stopped without a word. We had arrived.

The man was old. He might have been sitting there, behind his table in the dark, for centuries. It was not dark now. As soon as the hide door was tightly closed, Caesar had tipped back his hood, reached into his cloak past his heavy iron sword and brought out candles, which he gave to two centurions to light and hold; the room was far too confined for torches. The other two centurions waited outside; even so, there was not much room. The man behind the table was bearded, not like a physician but like a foreigner—a great white-silver beard that flicked out like fire in all directions. His hair was long, un-kempt, his eyebrows bushy; his blurry eyes peered out as if from deep in a cave. Purple bruises fell in chevrons from just under his eyes into his mustache. If he was surprised or alarmed, he showed no sign, merely sat—stocky, firmly planted—behind his square table, staring straight ahead, not visibly breathing, like a man waiting in the underworld. The girl sat on a low stool, her back against the wall, between her father and the rest of us. She gazed at her knees in silence. Her face was like that of an actress awaiting her entrance, intensely alive, showing no expression.

The apartment, we saw as the light seeped into it, was a riddle. Although in the poorest section of the city, it held a clutter of books, and the furniture, though sparse, was elabo-rately carved and solid; it would bring a good price in the markets that specialize in things outlandish. Herbs hung from the rafters, only a few of them known to me. Clearly it wasn't poverty or common ignorance that had brought these people here. Something troubled my nostrils, making the hair on the back of my neck rise—not the herbs or the scent of storm in the air but something else: the six-week smell of penned ani-mals in the hold of a ship, it came to me at last. That instant, a terrific crash of thunder struck, much nearer than the rest, making all of us, even Caesar, jump—all, that is, but the bearded old man. I heard wind sweep in, catching at the ragged edges of things, moving everything that would move.

The first indication that the old man was aware of us—or, indeed, aware of anything—came when Caesar inclined his head to me and said, "Doctor, it's close in here. Undo the window." The bearded man's mouth opened as if prepared to object—his teeth gleamed yellow—and his daughter's eyes flew wide; then both, I thought, gave way, resigned themselves. The man's beard and mustache became one again, and the flicker of life sank back out of his face. I, too, had certain small reservations. The only window in the room, its shutters now rattling and tugging, was the one behind the bearded man's right shoulder; and though he seemed not ferocious—he behaved like a man under sedation, in fact, his eyelids heavy, eyes filmed over—I did not relish the thought of moving nearer to a man who believed he could change into a wolf. Neither did I much like Caesar's expression. I remembered how once, halting his army, he'd sent three men into a mountain notch to find out whether they drew fire.

I made—cunning old fart that I am—the obvious and inevitable choice. I hobbled to the window, throwing my good leg forward and hauling in the bad one, making a great show of pitiful vulnerability, my face a heart-rending mask of profoundest apology—I unfastened the latches, threw the shutters wide and hooked them, then ran like a child playing sticks in the ring back to Caesar. To my horror, Caesar laughed. Strange to say, the bearded man, gloomier than Saturn until this moment, laughed, too. I swung around like a billy goat to give him a look. Old age, he should know, deserves respect or, at least, mercy—not really, of course; but I try to get one or the other if I can.

"He keep clear . . . werewolf," the bearded man said. His speech was slurred, his voice like the creakiest hinge in Tuscany. He tapped his finger tips together as if in slowed-down merriment. The night framed in the window behind him was as dense and black as ever but alive now, roaring and banging. Caesar and the two centurions laughed with the old man as if there were nothing strange at all in his admission that, indeed, he was a werewolf. The girl's face was red, whether with anger or shame I couldn't guess. For an instant, I was mad as a hornet, suspecting they'd set up this business as a joke on me; but gradually, my reason regained the upper hand. Take it from an old man who's seen a few things: It's always a mistake to assume that anything has been done for you personally, even evil.

The world flashed white and the loudest crash of thunder

yet stopped their laughter and, very nearly, my heart. Now rain came pouring down like a waterfall, silver-gold where the candlelight reached it, a bright sheet blowing away from us, violently hissing. The girl had her hands over her ears. The werewolf smiled, uneasy, as if unsure what was making all the noise.

Now that we were all on such friendly terms, we introduced ourselves. The man's name was Vödfiet—one of those northern names that have no meaning. When he held out his leaden hand to Caesar, Caesar thoughtfully bowed and looked at it but did not touch it. I, too, looked, standing a little behind Caesar and to his left. The man's fingernails were thick yellow and carved with ridges, like old people's toenails, and stranger yet, the lines of the palm—what I could see of them—were like the scribbles of a child who has a vague sense of letters but not of words. It was from him that the animal smell came, almost intolerably rank, up close, even with the breeze from the window. I'd have given my purse to get the palps of my fingers into his cranium, especially the area—as close as I could get—of the *pallium prolectus*. Preferably after he was dead.

"Strange," Caesar said, gently stroking the sides of his mouth, head bowed, shoulders rigid, looking from the werewolf to me, then back. Caesar seemed unnaturally alert, yet completely unafraid or else indifferent—no, not indifferent: on fire, as if for some reason he thought he'd met his match. The fingers of his left hand drummed on the side of his leg. He said, with the terrible coy irony he uses on senators, "You seem not much bothered by these things you do."

The werewolf sighed, made a growllike noise, then shrugged and tipped his head, quizzical. He ran his tongue over his upper teeth, a gesture we ancients know well. We're authorities on rot. We taste it, insofar as we still taste, with every breath.

"Come, come," Caesar said, suddenly bending forward, smiling, sharp-eyed, and jerked his right hand, fingers tight, toward the werewolf's face. The man no more flinched than an ox would have done, drugged for slaughter. His heavy eyelids blinked once, slowly. Caesar said, again in a voice that seemed ironic, perhaps self-mocking, "Your *daughter* seems bothered enough!"

The werewolf looked around the room until he found her, still there on her stool. She went on staring at her knees. Thunder hit, not as close now, but loud. Her back jerked.

"And yet, you," Caesar said, his voice rising, stern—again there was that hint of self-mockery and something else: lidded more violence—"that doesn't trouble you. Your daughter's self-sacrifice, her labor to protect you—"

The man raised his hands from the table, palms out, evidently struggling for concentration, and made a growling noise. Perhaps he said, "Gods." He spread one hand over his chest in the age-old sign of injured innocence, then slowly raised the hand toward the ceiling, or possibly he meant the window behind him, and with an effort splayed out the fingers. "Moon," he said, and looked at us hopefully, then saw that we didn't understand him. "Moon," he said carefully. "Cloud." His face showed frustration and confusion, like a stroke victim's, though obviously that wasn't his trouble, I thought; no muscle loss, no discernible differentiation between his left side and his right. "Full moon . . . shine . . . no, but. . . ." Although his eyes were still unfocused, he smiled, eager; he'd caught my worried glance at the window. After a moment's hesitation, the werewolf lowered his hands again and folded them.

"The moon," Caesar said, and jabbed a finger at the night. "You mean you blame—"

The man shrugged, his confusion deepening, and opened his hands as if admitting that the excuse was feeble, then rested his dull eye on Caesar, tipped his head like a dog and went on waiting.

Caesar turned from him, rethinking things, and now I saw real fury rising in him at last. "The moon," he said half to himself, and looked hard at the centurion, as if checking his expression. Recklessly, he flew back to the table and slammed the top with the flat of both hands. "Wake up!" he shouted in the werewolf's face, so ferocious that the cords of his neck stood out.

The werewolf slowly blinked.

Caesar stared at him, eyes bulging, then again turned away from him and crossed the room. He clamped his hands to the sides of his face and squeezed his eyes shut—perhaps he had a headache starting up. Thunder banged away, and the rain, still falling hard, was now a steady hiss, a rattle of small rivers on the street. We could hear the two centurions outside the door flap ruefully talking. At last, Caesar half turned back to the werewolf. In the tone men use for commands, he asked, "What does it feel like, coming on?"

The werewolf said nothing for a long moment, then echoed, as if the words made no sense to him, "Feel like." He nodded slowly, as if deeply interested or secretly amused. The girl put her hands over her face.

Caesar said, turning more, raising his hand to stop whatever words might be coming, "Never mind that. What does it feel like afterward?"

Again it seemed that the creature found the question too hard. He concentrated with all his might, then looked over at his daughter for help, his expression wonderfully morose. She lowered her hands by an act of will and stared as before at her knees. After a time, the old man moistened his lips with his tongue, then tipped his head and looked at Caesar, hoping for a hint. A lightning flash behind him momentarily turned his figure dark.

Caesar bowed and shook his head, almost smiling in his impatience and frustration. "Tell me this: How many people have you killed?"

This question the werewolf did seem to grasp. He let the rain hiss and rattle for a while, then asked, "Hundreds?" He tipped his head to the other side, watching Caesar closely, then cautiously ventured a second guess. "Thousands?"

Caesar shook his head. He raised his fist, then stopped himself and changed it to a stiffly cupped hand and brought it to his mouth, sliding the finger tips up and down slowly. A pool was forming on the dirt floor, leaking in. I cleared my throat. The drift of the conversation was not what I call healthy.

The werewolf let out a sort of groan, a vocal sigh, drew back his arm and absently touched his forehead, then his beard. "Creatures," he said. The word seemed to have come to him by lucky accident. He watched hopefully; so did Caesar. At last, the werewolf groaned or sighed more deeply than before and said, "No, but. . . ." Perhaps he'd suffered a stroke of some kind unknown to me. *No, but* is common, of course—often, in my experience, the only two words the victim can still command. He searched the walls, the growing pool on the floor, for language. I was sure he was more alert now, and I reached out to touch Caesar's elbow, warning him. "Man," the werewolf said; then, hopelessly, "moon!"

"Men *do* things," Caesar exploded, striking his thigh with his fist. He raised his hand to touch the hilt of his sword, not quite absently, as if grimly making sure he could get at it.

"Ax," the werewolf said. He was working his eyebrows, looking at his palely window-lit palms as if he couldn't remember having seen them before. "*Ax!*" he said. He raised his eyes to the ceiling and strained for a long time before trying again. "No, but. . . . No. . . . No, but. . . ."

Caesar waved, dismissive, as if imagining he'd understood.

Their eyes met. The thunder was distant, the rain coming down as hard as ever.

"Ax," the werewolf said at last, softly, slowly shaking, then bowing his head, resting his forehead on his finger tips, pausing to take a deep, slow, whistling breath through his nostrils. "Ax," he said, then something more.

The girl's voice broke out like flame. She was looking at no one. "He's saying *accident*."

Caesar started, then touched his mouth.

The werewolf breathed deeply again; the same whistling noise. "Green parks—no, but—chill-den—"

Abruptly, the girl said, shooting her burning gaze at Caesar, "He means you. You're strong; you make things safe for children." She shook her hands as if frustrated by words, like the werewolf. "But you're just lucky. Eventually, you'll die."

"The Empire will go on," Caesar broke in, as if he'd known all along what the werewolf was saying and it was not what he'd come here to talk about. "It's not Caesar's 'indomitable will.' We have laws." Suddenly, his eyes darted away, avoiding the girl's.

"*Moon*," the werewolf wailed.

Caesar's voice slashed at him. "*Stop* that."

It was beginning to get light out. It came to me that the old man was weeping. He laid his head to one side, obsequi-

ous. "Thank . . . gods . . . unspeakable . . . no, but. . . ." His
bulging forehead struggled. The candlelight was doing something queer to his glittering, tear-filled eyes, making them like
windows to the underworld. He raised his voice. "No, but.
No, *but!*" He gave his head a shake, then another, as if to clear
it. Furtively, he brushed one eye, then the other. "Vile!" he
cried out. "*No, but.* . . ." His hands were trembling, as were
the edges of his mouth. His voice took on pitch and intensity,
the words in the extremity of his emotion becoming cloudy,
more obscure than before. I had to lean close to watch his lips.
I glanced at Caesar to see if he was following, then at the girl.

It was the girl's expression that made me realize my error.
She was staring at the window, where the light, I saw at last,
was not dawn but a parting of the thick black hood of clouds.
There was no sound of rain. Moonlight came pouring through
the window, sliding toward us across the room. The girl drew
her feet back as if the light were alive.

I cannot say whether it was gradual or instantaneous. His
beard and mouth changed; the alertness of his ears became a
change in their shape and then bristling, tufted fur, and I saw
distinctly that the hand swiping at his nose was a paw. All at
once, the man behind the table was a wolf. A violent growl
erupted all around us. He was huge, flame-eyed, already leaping, a wild beast tangled in clothes. He was still in mid-air
when Caesar's sword thwunked into his head, cleaving it—a
mistake, pure instinct, I saw from Caesar's face. Only the
werewolf's daughter moved more quickly: She flew like a shadow
past Caesar and the rest of us, running on all fours, slipped
like ball lightning out the door, and vanished into the night.

It's difficult to put one's finger exactly on the oddity in
Caesar's behavior. One cannot call it mania in any usual sense—
delusional insanity, dementia, melancholia, and so forth. Nonetheless, he's grown odd. (No real cause for alarm, I think.)
You've no doubt heard of the squall of honors recently con-
ferred on him—statues, odes, feasts, gold medals, outlandish
titles: Prince of the Moon, Father of Animals, Shepherd of
Ethiopia and worse—more of them every day. They're nearly
all his own inventions, insinuated into the ears of friendly

senators or enemies who dare not cross him. I have it on good authority that those who hate him most are quickest to approve these absurdities, believing such inflations will ultimately make him insufferable to the people—as well they may. Indeed, the man who hungers most after his ruin has suggested that Caesar's horse be proclaimed divine. Caesar seems delighted. It cannot be put down to megalomania. At each new outrage he conceives or hears suggested, he laughs—not cynically but with childlike pleasure, as if astonished by how much foolishness the gods will put up with. (He's always busy with the gods, these days, ignoring necessities, reasoning with priests.) I did catch him once in an act of what seemed authentic lunacy. He was at the aquarium, looking down at the innumerable, flickering goldfish and carp, whispering something. I crept up on him to hear. He was saying, "Straighten up those ranks, there! Order! Order!" He shook his finger. When he turned and saw me, he looked embarrassed, then smiled, put his arm around my shoulders and walked with me. "I try to keep the Empire neat, doctor," he said. "It's not easy!" And he winked with such friendliness that, testy as I am when people touch me, I was moved. In fact, tears sprang to my eyes, I admit it. Once a man's so old he's started to piss on himself, he might as well let go with everything. Another time, I saw him hunkered down, earnestly reasoning—so it seemed—with a colony of ants. "Just playing, doctor," he said when he saw that I saw.

"Caesar, Caesar!" I moaned. He touched his lips with one finger.

The oddest thing he's come up with, of course, is his proposed war with Persia—himself, needless to say, as general. Persia, for the love of God! Even poor befuddled Mark Antony is dismayed.

"Caesar, you're not as young as you used to be," he says, and throws a woeful look over at me. He sits with interdigitated fists between his big, blocky knees. We're in Caesar's council room, the guards standing stiff as two columns, as usual, outside the door. Mark Antony grows fatter by the day. Not an interesting problem—he eats and sleeps too much. I'd prescribe exercise, raw vegetables and copulation. He has an enlarged subcutaneous cyst on the back of his neck. It must itch, but he pretends not to notice, for dignity's sake. Caesar lies on his couch as if disinterested, but his legs, crossed at the ankles, are rigid, and the pulse through his right inner jugular is visible. It's late, almost midnight. At times, he seems to be listening for something, but there's nothing to be heard. Cicadas; occasional baying of a dog.

It strikes me that, for all his flab, Mark Antony is a handsome man. His once-mighty muscles, now toneless, suggest a potential for heart disease, and there's blue under his too-smooth skin; nonetheless, one can imagine him working himself back to vigor, the dullness gradually departing from his eyes. Anything's possible. Look at me, still upright, thanks mainly to diet, though I'm farther along than he is. I frequently lose feeling in my right hand.

"If you must attack Persia," he says, "why not send me? You're needed here, Caesar!" His eyes squirt tears, which he irritably brushes away. "Two, three years—not even you can win a war with Persia in less time than that. And all that while, Rome and all her complicated business in the hands of Mark Antony! It will be ruin, Caesar! Everyone says so!"

Caesar gazes at him. "Are you, my friend, not nobler and more honest than all the other Romans put together?"

Mark Antony looks confused, raises his hands till they're level with his shoulders, then returns them to their place between his knees, which he once more clenches. "You're needed here," he says again. "Everyone says so." For all his friends' warnings, I do not think Mark Antony grasps how thoroughly he's despised by the senate. Caesar's confidant, Caesar's right arm. But besides that—meaning no disrespect—he really would be a booby. Talk about opening the floodgates!

Caesar smiles, snatches a moth out of the air, examines the wings with great curiosity, like a man trying to read Egyptian, then gently lets it go and lies still again. After a moment, he raises his right hand, palm outward, pushing an invisible bark out to sea. "You really would like that," he says. "Away to Persia for murder and mayhem."

Mark Antony looks to me for help. What can I say?

Now suddenly, black eyes flashing, Caesar rears up on

one elbow and points at Mark Antony. "*You* are Rome," he
says. "*You* are the hope of humanity!"

Later, Mark Antony asks me, "Is he insane?"

"Not by any rules I understand," I say. "At any rate,
there's no cause for alarm."

He moves back and forth across the room like a huge,
slow mimicry of Caesar, rubbing his hands together like a man
preparing to throw dice. His shadow moves, much larger than
he is, on the wall. For some reason, it frightens me. Through
the window I see the sharp-horned, icy-white half-moon. Most
of Mark Antony's fat has gone into his buttocks.

"They'll kill him rather than leave the Empire in my
hands," he says. Then, without feeling, his palms pressed together like a priest's: "After that, they'll kill me."

His clarity of vision surprises me. "Cheer up," I say. "I'm
his personal physician. They'll kill me, too."

Last night, the sky was alive with omens: stars exploding,
falling every which way. "Something's up!" says Caesar, as
tickled as if he himself had caused the discord in the heavens.
His bald head glows with each star burst, then goes dark. He
stood in the garden—the large one created for his daughter's
tomb—till nearly sunrise, watching for more fireworks.

Mark Antony's been sent off, plainly a fool's errand,
trumped up to get him out of Rome. "Don't come back," says
Caesar. "Never come back until I send for you." I don't like
this. Not at all, not one damn bit. My life line has changed. My
stool this morning was bilious.

All day, Caesar has been receiving urgent visitors, all with
one message: "It would be good if tomorrow you avoided the
forum." There can be no doubt that there's a plot afoot.

Late this afternoon, at the onset of twilight, I saw—I
think—the werewolf's daughter. She's grown thinner, as if eaten
away by disease. (Everyone, these days, looks to me eaten away
by disease. My prostate's nearly plugged, and there's not a
surgeon in Rome whom I'd trust to cut my fingernails.) She
stood at the bottom step of the palace stairway, one shaky hand
reaching out to the marble hem. She left herbs of some kind.

Their use, whether for evil or good, is unknown to me. Then she fled. Later, it occurred to me that I hadn't really gotten a good look at her. Perhaps it was someone I don't know.

Strange news. You'll have heard it before you get this letter. Forgive the handwriting. My poor old nerves aren't all they might be. Would that I'd never lived to see this day. My stomach will be acid for a month.

Caesar was hardly seated, had hardly gotten out the call for prayer, before they rose like a wave from every side, 60 senators with daggers. He was stabbed a dozen times before he struggled to his feet—or, rather, leaped to his feet—eyes rolling, every muscle in spasm, as if flown out of control, though it clearly wasn't that. You wouldn't have believed what strength he called up in his final moment! He dragged them from one end of the forum to the other, hurling off senators like an injured bear and shrieking, screaming his lungs out. It was as if all the power of the gods were for an instant contracted to one man. They tore his clothes from him, or possibly he did it himself for some reason. His blood came spurting from a hundred wounds, so that the whole marble floor was slippery and steaming. He fell down, stood up again, dragging his assassins; fell down, then rose to crawl on hands and knees toward the light of the high central door where, that moment, I was running for my life. His slaughtered-bull bellowings are still in my ears, strangely bright, like a flourish of trumpets or Jovian laughter.

JANETTE TURNER HOSPITAL

HERE COMES THE SUN

FROM COSMOPOLITAN

∽

NOT AN EASY SITUATION, THIS. There are no precedents, no guidelines, and I'm nervous. I signal the waiter and order another drink, even though this is not such a great idea on an empty stomach. Am I really starving or do I just feel light-headed with apprehension? Let me think. It's 6:30 P.M., and I certainly didn't have lunch, I'm sure of that. There just wasn't time. Breakfast? Probably not. There are certain days—you know what I mean—when the body does not react kindly to the thought of food before noon.

The waiter brings my drink. It is also his task to keep things moving along in socially acceptable channels. "Perhaps Madame would care to order now?" he says.

"I'm waiting for someone."

I smile.

He smiles back, but there is no warmth in his smile. Professional civility. Probably thinks I'm cheap. Or broke. (More or less true. It always seems to show, or so one fears.) Perhaps he thinks I'm wasting restaurant table space, instead of sitting in the lounge on the other side of the potted plants and dangling mirror tiles. I imagine him thinking: She'll have three drinks and a bowl of soup, and the tip won't be worth the trouble.

Of course I have come much too early, out of nervousness. Nervous, I suppose, that I'd get a phone call suggesting my apartment instead. But why did I have to pick the Grand Hyatt, which I obviously can't really afford? For its unreality, I think. Mirrors everywhere you turn, even on the ceiling. When I look up I see excessively green Benjaminas and pink azaleas growing back down toward me like streamers from heaven. I also see the tops of cars and buses crawling like lizards along Lexington Avenue-in-the-sky, mating with the flow of sheet metal on East Forty-second Street, jamming into gridlock snarls, a dance of armored insects.

It's a little like Laundromat visions of underwear (one sees, spilling from dryers, all the secret stains and frayings), or like the furtive soles of shoes at an altar rail, their worn patches mournful as eyes gazing back at other communicants. What I am saying is this: I feel like a voyeur; I have an unfair vantage point; in watching this surreal inversion of Lexington and Forty-second, I am astonished, even oddly disconcerted and saddened, to find out how many vehicular roofs are rusted and weathered through and patched.

Speaking of Achilles' heels and of shameful secrets . . . maybe the heredity laws move backward these days. Why not? If time itself turns out to be relative, why shouldn't the genes go into reverse, and parents inherit tendencies from us?

It might be a good idea to have another drink. I raise my hand, then change my mind. Won't help at all if my speech is slurred, or if I lose track of just how much I'm revealing, or if, God forbid, I should get weepy. Won't help one bit. The whole illusion would be ruined—and one feels so responsible for the well-being of one's parents.

I do think this is one hell of an impossible situation to find oneself in. Outrageous. Totally unfair. But then again, if assigning blame for such things were simple, where would all the agony go? What would happen to the liquor business and the bartenders and the waiters in lounges?

Maybe it would have been better after all to meet in my apartment. To sit cozily on my cushions with a pot of tea or a bottle of wine and some fresh pastries on a tray on the floor. To cry together. I imagine trying to explain my apartment.

Actually, if I could blindfold guests until I got them inside, there would be no problem. It's a lovely old building, high ceilings, intricate moldings around doors and windows, and I do believe that what I lack in discretionary income I make up for in flair. There are the aforementioned brightly colored cushions, and potted plants breeding like lemmings, and of course large vistas of naked walls and oak floors and empty space. Tranquil, really, especially since I've artfully covered all the windows with opaque screens of one kind or another. The light can stream in, but not the view, which sometimes makes one think of war movies. But a lot of people live up around West 120th Street because of the rents, and I'm perfectly happy with my place.

Still, I'd rather not have to account for the burned-out shell of the building opposite, or the quantity of graffiti in English and Spanish and Arabic on our stairwell wall. Nothing remarkable about any of this, but try explaining it to a parent who has known only modest suburban living in New Hampshire. I'd rather just say I live in a very cosmopolitan neighborhood and leave it at that.

So. We'll avoid discussion of my apartment and concentrate on my work. (I came here straight out of college like everyone else, English degree in my eager little hand, literary stars in my eyes, ready if necessary to sweep floors and take out the garbage for any publishing house that would open its munificent doors just a crack. And, metaphorically speaking, sweeping floors for a publisher is about what I do, though when I write home or send brief sprightly notes to old college friends, I will admit to dropping intimations of book-launching parties and luminaries and major editorial decisions.) Oh my work makes for wonderful anecdotal conversation. Embroidered a little, it is a rewarding area of discourse, so unverifiable. Besides, everyone in publishing started out where I am, and quite frankly I don't expect to stand still for long.

What else can be said of my life? Alas. That it is positively tasteless in its lack of originality. Here I am, age twenty-two, turning heads when I walk down the street, but hopelessly committed to a forty-five-year-old married man who is never going to leave his wife and children. This is something I know with certainty, although every morning I think perhaps I am wrong; I add up all the favorable evidence, I hope there is cause for hope—and this despite the fact that I would not even condone his walking out on that other life, because it would prove something so awful about him. Every evening that he stays with me as late as eleven o'clock, my fantasies indulge in a romp of triumph and happiness.

"I can't bear it," he says, getting up to leave. "I can't bear it. I don't know what to do."

Every solitary midnight, I cry into my pillow and order my life to have a grain of common sense and pull itself together, and every fresh day I ignore my own advice.

On aesthetic grounds *alone*, I tell myself, have some class. Do you want to be a living cliché? And the answer is: apparently.

Junkie, that's what I am, living for these moments made incandescent by impossibility. Waiting for Jeff to call, waiting for Jeff to arrive, waiting for Jeff to regret he won't be able to . . . Perhaps I'm as addicted to the pain as to the pleasure. It's a highly infectious disease, and now it seems my parents have caught it from me. This is why my hands so often shake. Now, for instance. I'm always waiting, waiting. . . .

Eight o'clock, and still no sign. . . .

I'll have to order something, keep the waiters at bay. Soup du jour, I request, least expensive item on the menu. Might as well make an effort to be sensible about one segment of the evening's tab, since I'm going to be paying for both of us. That's part of my strategy. All around me, couples are leaning toward each other over their wineglasses, and there is considerable danger that I will cry into my soup—not something for which I would forgive myself. There is even an escalating risk that I will lose these few hothouse shreds of self-possession, will abandon this experiment entirely, fleeing like a swallow from winter. The waiter, finding twelve dollars on the table, will raise his eyebrows and shrug his shoulders and smirk to the bartender: One more lonely lady who got stood up. Pathetic, aren't they?

If only it were that simple. An ordinary case of agony, just one more terminal affair, so easy to handle, one knows all the ropes: Hang in and ride out the misery. But there are no guidelines for this new kind of dislocation. It's all back to front, and I suddenly decide that tonight's dinner was not a good plan, not the right strategy at all. I'm going to make my exit now, call my little sister, plot some better campaign of comfort.

Too late.

She is standing beside the maître d' as if she were a forlorn child in a new school, terrified: my mother, fifty-two years old going on ten, a total innocent in the jungle of her brave new life. When she sees me her relief is so visceral that she takes the maître d' by the arm and murmurs up at him, eyes bright as a gushing schoolgirl's—something horribly embarrassing, I just know it, like: "My daughter Reenie—we call her that, her name's Irene really—is taking me out on the town tonight. She won all the English prizes in high school and college, you know, and we always knew she'd go straight to the top in New York."

I can see the twitch at the corners of the maître d's mouth, and I want to kick him in the shins and hiss: I'll bet you never let your mother come here.

My mother has been to a hairdresser in Queens (where my aunt lives)—unfortunately a practitioner of the old baroque-swirl-and-rigid-lacquer school. She has also let my aunt talk her into wearing something new and fussy and polyester. I let my eyes flick around the room, fiercely defensive, daring anyone to snicker.

I have intended to be very cool and formal, a giver-off of confidence, but when she reaches my table I find myself standing and taking both her hands and saying (incredibly): "Mommy."

"Oh Reenie," she says, her voice quavering. "Oh Reenie, what am I going to do?"

And now I rise magnificently to the occasion. "First, Mom, you're going to order a drink and soup. And then anything else you want. It isn't often I get a chance to take my mother out on the town."

She brightens up like a child who's been sent to the principal's office only to find that she's to collect an award rather than disciplinary action. She looks around, takes in the expensive jungle and the mirrors, sees herself hundreds of times in the slicked illusion of ceiling, a pale lily of a face in a reflected frame of massed pink azaleas and the now-glittering procession of traffic lights on Lexington and East Forty-second.

"Oh Reenie!" she breathes. Meaning: At least one of us has caught at the gold ring and held it. "I was so frightened, you know," she confesses, "driving down from New Hampshire. Your father never let me drive on the turnpike, you remember. . . ." She trails off.

It would be such a relief to be able to say the usual things—"Forget that SOB, you're much better off without him"—but it would do nothing for either of us. I love my father, I know far more about his agony than my mother should ever suspect (I hope), and who am I to feel angry about the other woman, his twenty-five-year-old secretary? I may wish her a slow and painful death, but the confusing truth is, I'd probably like her. Not that I'm ready to meet her for at least a decade or so.

"And then," my mother goes on, "coming in on the subway to Grand Central Station, I was sure I'd get lost. Get off at the wrong place, or something. Bella wanted me to take a taxi, but I can't give in to that sort of extravagance. I'll have to watch every penny now. In fact, if I can't find a job in our town after the retraining course . . . Still, I do have the house, and Betsy seems to be taking it all so calmly. She's following in your footsteps, Reenie, wonderful grades. I'm so proud of her. Next year she'll be off to college, and the next thing I know she'll be joining you in New York." She pauses and then says, so wistfully that I am terrified I will burst into tears, "I must have done *something* right." It comes out as a question, a plea.

"You certainly did!" The college drama star now, I am playing Rosalind in *As You Like It,* full of warmth and confidence, the key to the unraveling of crossed destinies in the palm of my hand. "You're a *wonderful* mother. You taught us to believe in ourselves, to have courage, to reach for whatever we dreamed of. Look at what you've made possible!" I gesture vaguely at Manhattan, implying unimaginable freedom and successes.

"Did I really, Reenie?" She seems to catch a glimpse of a different image of herself in the mirrors and contemplates it with hope. "Perhaps I'll take some more courses," she says. "Once I get a job. There are a lot of things, actually, that I've wanted to do. Do you know, I had the strangest feeling coming down through Boston? That section where you have to bypass the downtown and get onto the Mass Pike, it's always terrified me, even when your father was driving. You see the chunks of blowouts, and the pileups dragged into the breakdown lane. I never expected to get through alive. And there I was, all by myself, my heart in my mouth, weaving in and out of lanes, and I felt like dancing and singing and shouting: I'm *doing* it! I'm on my way!"

She studies her hands, the hands that have miraculously steered a car through the valley of the shadow of many accidents, turning them over and back, as though they might hold some clue to the meaning of her life. "Sometimes, Reenie, I think I will be all right, even more than all right."

I reach over and take her hand. But all I am able to say is "Let's look at their pastry trolley and have a sinfully rich dessert."

Over Sacher torte, she is relaxed and expansive. "So when can I see your apartment, Reenie? You know I'd much rather stay with you than out in Queens. Cook for you for a few days, go for walks around the block together."

But I don't want to puncture any more illusions for her, I want her to believe all is perfect in my world, so I say quickly: "It would be crazy, Mom. My job is so demanding, my hours are insane, you'd be alone far too much of each day, when what you need right now is company."

"I guess you're right," she sighs. "Just a look at it, then? Just so I can picture . . . ?"

"Now, Mom, it would take us *ages* to get way up to my apartment." My smile exudes affectionate tolerance, intimates the complications of life at the top. "It's just so time-consuming getting from A to B in Manhattan. Do we really want to waste time in the traffic when we can be relaxing and talking here?"

She succumbs. To my indisputable grip on life. To the wine and dessert. To the after-dinner brandy, which moves through her veins like a sunrise of new plans. She is flushed, animated, speaking of possibilities and adventures.

When I put her into the taxi, giving the driver his fare in advance, she makes him wait while she opens the door again and gets out to hug me. "It's such a load off my mind, Reenie, you can have no idea, to know you are absolutely all right." And then she says shyly, coyly: "Don't be so busy for too many years, darling. I mean, you have to take time out to fall in love, to find the right man."

Just as though her life told her that this was the perfect answer to all dreams.

Gently I coax her back into the taxi, lean through the window, and offer archly: "There's a man in the wings, it might go somewhere, you never know. But I don't want to rush things."

"Oh no," she says quickly, suddenly taking back into account a welter of recent evidence. "Don't rush things. Be *awfully* cautious." But in spite of herself, her face is dreamy with pleasure. "Oh, I'm *so* pleased, Reenie." The taxi begins to move, and she leans out the window, calling back, "But if you ever need me—sometimes things go wrong, just little things, it's natural, and you might want advice—I'd love to, you know, just *be* here if you ever need . . ."

Her face, pale and wistful, grows smaller and smaller. When the taxi is out of sight, I wrap my coat tightly around me and wait for the uptown bus. It's so awful, I think, so unfair, that people as innocent and vulnerable as my mother get thrust out into the cruel world. Parents, these days, are a great source of anxiety to their children. Fortunately we've been through it all, we're tough, we're learning to cope.

And on the bus, heading back to my apartment where I will wait, sick with futile hope, for Jeff to call, I think: There's always this about life. There's no obsessive anxiety so great that it can't be muted and displaced by another one. This strikes me as deliciously comic, and I smile at my reflection in the window. Then, quite suddenly, I visualize my mother, tense with fear and determination, hurtling around the turnpike rims of cities. *I felt like dancing*, she had said. *I'm doing it. I'm on my way.*

Epiphany.

There is no other word for it. I am gripped by an unexpected sense of exhilaration. As though the phone has rung and it is indeed the voice one most passionately wants to hear. But it is the resilience of the human spirit that has seduced me. No one is chained to misery, I think. One doesn't need mirrors and fakery.

I positively run from the bus stop to my apartment and dial my aunt's number in Queens.

"Mom," I say. "Listen. On second thought, I *would* love to have you stay with me for a while. We can be, you know, comrades in arms. Actually there's—well, I'm fighting a few uphill battles myself. If you won't mind."

"Oh Reenie, I did want to so much. And I don't mind a bit about the Upper West Side. In fact, I think it's terribly exciting."

So whom did I think I was fooling?

"See you in the morning," I laugh.

For some reason I feel like dancing. The phone rings again. Of course. I forgot to give her precise directions.

But it is Jeff.

For just a second, vertigo and indecision strike, and then I say calmly, with fond regret: "I'm sorry, Jeff, I can't. I'm seeing someone else tomorrow." There's a time and a season for everything, I tell him quietly. A time for pain, and a time for learning, and a time for endings.

He is incredulous. Stricken. How can I do this to him?

"Thanks for everything," I say gently, and mean it. I hang up quickly before my resolution wavers, and unplug the phone from the wall.

Freedom, I think, breathing deeply: Here I am.

And then I *do* dance, weaving between my cushions and my potted plants, while my old Beatles record belts out "Here Comes the Sun."

LISA INTEROLLO

THE QUICKENING

FROM SEVENTEEN

꙳

THE INSIDE OF WOOLWORTH'S is swimming-pool green. I breathe in the smell of the store—hand soap, face powder, plastic, skillet grease—in short, anxious puffs. I an seven and moving along the first aisle searching for my sister Patty, four years older than I, who baby-sits me each afternoon with her friend Rebecca. They have trained me to shoplift, and I have caught on well, exceeding their expectations. The first aisle, lower than the others, reaches chest-high on me. There are eyebrow pencils and artificial nails and false eyelashes encased in clear, hard plastic. And lipsticks: True Red, Proposal Pink, Warm Toast. I hurry on to the next aisle, where I see that the store manager, a man in green, has caught my sister and Rebecca and is scolding them. I walk up to them, and he holds me gently by the shoulders, squatting down to look in my eyes. "You shouldn't play with these girls. They're very bad girls," he says. I nod, feeling he is somehow right about them, although I can't say why. My underpants are full of lipsticks.

Next, I remember Easter week and a storekeeper and my mother both staring down at me. "Turn out your pockets," my mother says, and her voice seems to come from a long way away. I pull on the pocket of my turquoise stretch pants, and out comes a long, multicolored, bunny-shaped balloon. Even though I put it there just moments earlier, I feel surprised, almost mesmerized, by seeing it, as if I were watching a magician drawing scarves out of his sleeve. As we leave the store, my mother says, "I'm never coming shopping with you again."

My mother is always tired. She has varicose veins, migraines, three children, and a job at the Social Security office—all of which exhaust her. All except my brother, that is, who is one year younger than me and seems younger. "Boys mature slower," my mother repeats defensively, explaining why he never matches the grades I made the previous year at school. George has curly brown hair, bright dark eyes, and a beguiling smile. His shoulder blades jut out beneath his T-shirt, since he has a tendency to eat a few forkfuls of dinner, then push his plate away with a bored sigh. We all eat his favorite foods because he won't eat at all if they aren't served. My sister and I, both more robust, call him Runty. We don't see our father much. On weekdays, he rarely comes home before we're in bed. On those days, we carry our dinner plates into the shadowy living room and watch TV. But when he is home, he likes us to eat together at the kitchen table. These meals tend to have a cramped, tense quality; George, especially, hates missing programs, and the rest of us are not in the habit of making table conversation. Afterward, we all scatter while my father heads for the living room, drifting cautiously around as if it were the waiting room of a doctor's office and any moment might bring an unpleasant diagnosis. His shyness makes me nervous. Sometimes—though I know better now—I used to think he was mad at me. "Oh, no, of course not," my mother would reassure me impatiently. "You know how he is."

When I am twelve, I take a test and win a partial scholarship to Kingston, a small private school for girls on Fifth Avenue, far from our apartment. My brother and sister stay in nearby parochial schools, where most of our friends in the neighborhood go. Occasionally, I stand in the gym at recess, remembering my old school—how it had no cafeteria and long folding metal tables had to be set up each day at eleven on the varnished planks of the gymnasium floor and how steaming meatballs were served on big round metal plates and the room smelled of sneakers and sweat. The boiler hissed; voices roared.

At Kingston, our behavior reflects not only on us but on the school itself. Charity is stressed. Not the petty sort of charity that consists of giving a few pennies here and there. That, in fact, is frowned upon as insignificant, meaningless. A grander, vaguer, philosophical charity is encouraged. We certainly don't fritter away time praying for indulgences; we think about issues. Our religion classes are called Philosophy/Theology, or simply P.T. And to stress their importance, they are taught by the principal herself, Mrs. Medford, a handsome woman whose well-groomed hand any parent or alumna might shake and be reassured. In one P.T. class, Mrs. Medford explains this subtler form of charity by saying, "I obviously don't expect you girls to go and give your allowances away on 115th Street and Amsterdam Avenue."

I feel my face heating up like a warm bath. Amsterdam and 115th: That's near where I live, that's where the post office is; that's not a bad neighborhood. I decide to tell her, to raise my hand and say, "That isn't a bad neighborhood. The people there wouldn't *want* your money." But she moves along to another subject. When the class is dismissed, four girls gather around her with questions about the exam. I linger on the outskirts for a minute, then turn and leave the room.

In the eighth grade, everyone is exchanging turquoise friendship rings. I trade mine with Andrea Spencer—a tall, quiet girl with flame-colored hair. Andrea doesn't make trouble, and all the teachers like her for this but also because her family were killed when their BMW missed a turn near Ajaccio. Now she lives with an aunt in an apartment with long dark corridors near the school. During the summers, she visits relatives from her father's side in England. She went on a camping trip with them once, she told me, and her cousin Kevin—who's our age—got inside her sleeping bag for five minutes. Sometimes when I'm in bed with the lights out, listening to the late subways creep along the el, I think about being in England for the summer and having no parents or brother or sister anywhere and meeting the unknown, daring Kevin.

The next year, Susan Doherty comes into our class from a school that doesn't go past eighth grade. Susan, whose black bangs tickle her eyes, has more classes with Andrea than I do; once I overhear her telling Andy, "You're so beautiful, you should try to become a model." At lunchtime, the three of us walk one block to a delicatessen to buy Tab. My eyes sweep around quickly, and I slip a yellow package of chewing gum into my pocket. Outside, Andy and Susan have already started strolling toward school. I catch up with them, breathing harder than I should. "Look what I got," I say, punctuating the sentence with a wire-thin, conspiratorial smile. "You didn't!" Susan shrieks instantly. I smile again, and we all chew gum.

I steal frequently after that, and Susan joins me, although Andy never will. She waits outside. One snowy day in February in the same delicatessen, Susan and I each drop round red Gouda cheeses into our woven shoulder bags, which everyone at school is using. We exchange glances, each taking another cheese and then another. No one notices. The store is noisy, smoky, and warm, the fogged windows blocking a view of the street. When we get outside, Andy's face has turned red and blotchy, and she looks angry. Susan and I are keyed up. We insist on heading over to the park despite the cold. Andy refuses and turns back toward school, but we go on alone against a freezing wind. On Fifth Avenue, we stop at a bench to unload the cheeses. My numb fingers stumble over the red cellophane. I bite through the red wax, spit it out, and bite into the cheese. Susan takes another cheese and does the same. The cold is appalling, the street almost silent. I take another cheese, abandoning the first. Bite, spit, bite. Swallowing hurts: I take another bite. "Let's get rid of these cheeses," Susan says in almost a whisper. Standing on the bench, the wind searing my thighs, I hurl the cheeses, one after another, into the empty park. They sail over the wall in sharp arcs, sinking into the new-fallen snow. In class that afternoon, my mind keeps going back to those wasted cheeses. I compose a riddle for Susan, neatly writing it on a part of a sheet of loose-leaf paper. It reads: "What did the man say to the judge after he stabbed someone with a knife? Answer: I used the knife for evil, but it was meant for Gouda . . . ho, ho, ho." I watch Susan unfold the note, study it, and then—finally!—get it. Her suppressed laugh sounds like air rushing out of a balloon.

Susan and I don't talk about stealing, we just do it, more and more. Soon, I recognize every feeling—and every gradation of every feeling—that arises in the process of taking something. An inexplicably pretty object sets everything in motion. From the moment my eyes settle on it—whatever it is—I know I'm going to go for it. This first impulse is unpleasant, because unyielding: There is no backing down. It is followed by a quickening: of the pulse, the heart, the senses. These last play tricks. Voices become more acute but seem to come from far away. Colors—all colors—turn distractingly rich. Afterward: relief, release, a rush of pleasure, a certain increasing grayness, which disappears instantly once another inexplicably pretty object is spotted.

Boutiques, bookstores, gift shops, pharmacies—all these we frequent when a change in school policy allows students to leave the school during free periods to "explore the cultural offerings of the city." Our hauls become larger, our methods brazen.

In a sprawling unisex clothing store, a young salesman with a downy mustache shows me to a fitting room. Whenever I glance at him, he's looking at me with dark, flashing eyes. He doesn't count the hangers but checks to see that every dress has one. I hear Susan outside talking to him, saying she doesn't need clothes. "Do you have a boyfriend?" he asks. I pull the curtain open. Four dresses and four hangers. "Walk fast," I say outside, ignoring her "Did you get anything?" We round the corner onto Eighty-ninth Street. The dress is in my purse. The hanger inches lower and lower down my back, finally clattering onto the sidewalk. Her laugh: air escaping from a balloon. I scoop the hanger up fast. I break it in half, the thick plastic raking my hand as it splits with a cracking sound. I throw it into a narrow alley. I begin laughing hard. My hand is bleeding.

"See this shirt," I say to my mother, holding a turquoise silk blouse. "I got it on sale." She is lying on her bed reading *The Fan Club*. I try it on for her. The color makes my skin glow as if I were immersed in a motel swimming pool on a sunny day.

"It's nice," she says, fingering the sleeve, "soft."

"Eight dollars," I say, "reduced from twenty-five." She doesn't ask where I bought it.

"Where did you get this?" asks Mr. Donnelly when I give him a heavy picture book with color plates, entitled *The Life of Mozart*. He's a tall, thin young man with pockmarked cheeks and ironic, smiling eyes. Susan often says that with his talent, he could have been a lot more than a music teacher in a girls' school.

"I ripped it off from Stanley's," I say.

"Stanley's," he repeats slowly. "That guy's a friend of mine. I have a charge account there."

"So? Take it back if you don't like it. Tell him *you* took it."

My voice is firm. For him, things are perplexingly complicated, much too complicated to act on. He muses to our class all the time about questions that have never been satisfactorily answered: Did Süssmayr finish the Requiem in D minor as Mozart had intended? Could Chopin have triumphed in "larger" areas of composition? Dilemma was his charm, also his undoing. "He's obviously thrown his life away," Susan often says decisively. And I don't know whether to agree or disagree, so I say nothing.

It is spring and junior year. The season has arrived unfairly early, in February, and signs of it are everywhere: that smell of rain and wet turf, even on blocks far from the park; that pitiless, diffused light. The season's aching promise disturbs me. What is the future? Senior year, college, the rest of life. I imagine you have to be thin, blond, and confident to meet spring on equal terms.

"Want to go for a walk?" Susan asks on this certain February morning and I know what that means and I go along. The street is crowded with shoppers, workmen, and women pushing pudgy toddlers along in strollers. A redhead in the distance looks just like Andy—no longer a regular companion of ours—but as she comes closer, she becomes a stranger.

We stop before an old-fashioned drugstore with a display of trusses in the window. The store is dark and cool inside, with a comforting medicinal smell. The long aisles are lined with shampoos, lotions, bubble baths, and intriguing tonics. In a large glass display case, hairbrushes and tortoiseshell combs are pinned onto red velvet like rare butterflies mounted in a museum.

"Can I help you girls?" asks the old man at the counter, poking his head out from behind a giant cash register. He looks daffy. He has wispy flyaway white hair and a matching flyaway goatee. His voice cavorts high and low as he talks, each syllable a surprise. I'd never trust this guy to fill a prescription.

"I'd like a bottle of contact-lens wetting solution," says Susan. This is always kept behind the counter for some reason. He putters off to get it, and Susan turns to me, pitching her eyes upward. While she waits, I turn into one of the aisles. A few other customers glide noiselessly, almost reverently, along as if they were in a house of worship and the shampoo bottles were sacred statues. Susan joins me in a moment. We walk to the end of the aisle, where there is a rotating rack with packages of foam curlers, aluminum clips, eyebrow pencils, and other objects hanging from it. She turns the rack, and it, too, moves without a sound, without creaking. We stand close together with my shoulder bag, an open pouch, dangling between us.

Susan says in a low, apologetic voice, "I have no purse." Unwillingly, my senses sharpen. I track the movements of the noiseless, gliding customers, the fey pharmacist, and his assistant, a large, bespectacled saleswoman. The gentle, almost imperceptible tug on my shoulder is Susan dropping something in my bag.

Suddenly, something begins to go wrong. It happens rapidly, with points merging in awful combination, control slinking helplessly away. I stand fast, paralyzed, flooded with a strange visceral recognition of what is approaching. It starts innocently: The large, no-nonsense saleswoman moves up the aisle parallel to us on her rounds. There, she is corralled by a reedy, elderly woman wearing a purple turban who demands, in a snobby, self-amused drawl, to know why the store has stopped carrying a certain brand of laxative that she has been purchasing here "for the past two hundred years." This is funny, and the saleswoman's glance veers—unpredictably, really—to see if anyone is overhearing and sharing the joke. She spots us. If she weren't standing exactly where a sliver of space joins the two aisles—the point where the shelves leave off and the rotating rack begins—there would be no problem. But she is, and that is all it takes. Very quickly she sees—or senses with absolute certainty—that something is amiss, that Susan's hand is in my bag.

Her mood changes palpably. She begins moving toward us, dodging the turbaned customer.

"Get those things out," I hiss to Susan, looking straight ahead.

Tug. Tug.

"Get those things out."

"They're out."

"Get them out."

"They're out."

I don't know what she put in or whether to believe her or whether she found everything—half the time, I can't even find my wallet in that bag. There is no time to check, though; the saleswoman has reached us, her face sweaty and severe.

"What are you girls doing?" she demands.

"Just looking," I hear myself answer in a curiously detached voice. Inwardly, I am in a state of emergency. There is a heavy pressure on my chest, as if a pine tree had fallen across it, pinning me down.

"What do you have in that bag?" she asks, her eyes straining to see inside it, sure of what she saw, yet doubting it, mainly because of my steady voice. There is a pause. My eyes falter downward, but I quickly pull them up to meet hers: shrewd and medium-brown behind wire-rimmed lenses.

"Were you stealing something?" she asks directly.

"No!" I sound shocked, slightly offended. She doesn't fall for it but doesn't know what to do, either. By now, the other customers have formed a silent, threatening ring around us. The pharmacist breaks through the ring, his face working as if he were maneuvering a bicycle through heavy, unyielding traffic. The saleswoman is appreciative of this supportive audi-

ence but also flustered by it. She plows on with a determination
to triumph that I admire in spite of myself.

"If I ever catch you girls stealing in here again . . ." Her
voice trails off in search of the appropriate threat.

"We're going," I say breathlessly, falling short of the
intended huffiness, then adding irrelevantly, "We have a class."

The saleswoman's eyes settle on the Kingston emblem on
my blazer.

"I'm going with you," she announces suddenly. "I think
we should all have a talk with your principal. I don't know
what you girls are doing out roaming the streets at this hour,
anyway."

An approving murmur runs through the ring. A moment
later, the three of us are marching along the street toward the
school, an unlikely, stony-faced tribe. The absurdity of the
situation bothers me, despite my nervousness. I consider running, but that would be an outright admission of guilt. Anyway, she could just come to the school and identify us. And
prove what? Nothing. Worse still, she might come bounding
after us and make a scene, which would be mortifying. I don't
even dare check my purse. She is walking behind me, watching
me.

Mrs. Medford is in conference with Mr. Donnelly when
we arrive. I see Donnelly—his head bobbing earnestly as he
talks—through the glass partition dividing the principal's office
from the reception area, and my queasiness swells. How many
times had I hoped to bump into him accidentally in the halls,
skimmed my eyes over the crowd to give chance a nudge? I
rarely spotted him. But there he is now, at the worst possible
moment. The saleswoman is telling Medford's assistant the
matter is "urgent."

We are shown in. Mr. Donnelly rests his ironic eyes on
the three of us. The saleswoman introduces herself to Medford—
who responds with a cold, polite nod—and begins to explain
what happened: She caught us stealing something in her store,
makeup or something—but someone put something in my bag—
and then when asked about it, we denied it, quite rudely, and
she doesn't even know what we're doing roaming the streets at
this hour, anyway.

Her explanation is garbled. I feel bad for her. She, too, has lost her nerve before Medford's supercilious confidence. They are opposites, I see now. She is a commonsense right-and-wrong woman. Medford, you never know what she believes, but she is always well-dressed and soft-spoken and quietly impressive. And this is her office, her terrain, painted pale yellow and gray in understated cheeriness, not the dark, old-fashioned drugstore. And they don't like each other.

Medford smooths her gray hair. She leans forward in her chair, looking first at Susan, then me, then the saleswoman, with an intent, pondering gaze. She picks up a felt-tipped pen, taps its point twice on her desk, puts it down. She pauses, looks at us again, and says, "What do you girls have to say?"

"We didn't do anything," says Susan.

"No," I murmur. "I don't know what she's talking about."

Mr. Donnelly clears his throat.

"These girls are students of mine," he says slowly, looking significantly into the saleswoman's eyes with a kind, nearly pleading gaze. "They've been under a lot of pressure lately—they're preparing for the college boards. I'm sure they didn't mean to be rude to you. They've always been good—" he pauses—"forthright students."

Medford takes it up, on a haughtier note.

"Frankly, Miss—what did you say your name was?"

"Olafson."

"Miss Olafson, I'll have to stand by our girls in this case. They have very good records. And they are not out of the building illegally. We have a program here that permits that. It's been highly successful and was recently written up in an educational journal. I think you'll find, if you ask around, that this school has a very good reputation."

And as if to demonstrate this, she says to me, "Vicky, give me your bag."

I feel that pine tree again, bearing down hard on my chest. I press my legs together to keep them still and hand her my bag.

Woven out of thick Greek wool, the bag has a black, gray, and red geometric pattern. It looks out of place in Medford's hands. She would never own anything like it. She grips the rim of the bag with both hands, thumbs on top, and squints inside. Then her hand and wrist disappear into it. She takes out my wallet and puts it on her desk. She reaches in again: a copy of *The Great Gatsby*. Then a hairbrush. And a bus pass. My pen.

"That's it," she says, surveying the objects. "Everything."

Miss Olafson's lips move to the verge of speech. She hesitates, as if reconsidering. Her face looks moist and reddened. Then an outburst: "That can't be it," she says. "That just can't be it."

She reaches across the desk, grabs the bag, and plunges her hand inside, pressing it to the bottom. "That can't be . . . I saw . . ." Her eyes widen seriously as she touches bottom, as if she has discovered something. She has—that there is nothing inside.

When she speaks again, her voice is different, faltering. "I . . . uh . . . we have a lot of problems with kids shoplifting. And I guess in this case, I may have overreacted."

"I quite understand," says Medford graciously. "That happens to all of us."

Our little gathering disperses. Susan gives me a we-have-a-lot-to-talk-about look and then runs downstairs to get books from her locker. I take a few slow steps next to Mr. Donnelly. Classes are going on; the halls are deserted.

"Well," he says, looking ahead down the corridor. "Aren't you going to say anything?"

"Like what?"

"You might tell me what happened—though I can pretty much guess. Or even thank me for helping to get you out of that jam."

"Thank you," I say curtly.

He laughs softly. We walk along in silence.

"You know," he says, after what seems a long while, "you're getting a bit old for this sort of thing. I wish you'd cut it out."

"Maybe that's what I planned to do," I say.

"I certainly hope so."

"Why?"

"I don't know," he says. "I guess it's because I like you and would hate to see you screw things up for yourself. Or other people, for that matter—I don't think you feel too good about dragging that woman in here."

"I didn't drag her. She followed us."

"Whatever," he shrugs. "I'm not interested in quibbling. I just think you should consider putting your energy to some use. Other than stealing makeup."

"Like what?"

"You figure it out," he says quickly. "You're smart."

He stops talking, as if trying to catch and hold a thought that keeps slipping forward and away from him like a minnow. I look at him, picturing how he might look on a hot summer beach: white and serious, with a book on his towel, watching the water, the bathers shouting and raging in the water. I think of Susan's harsh pronouncement on his life and still can't—don't—endorse it. The bell rings. I make out one, two, voices behind us. Then others coming from the opposite direction. The din builds.

"Look, I have a class," Mr. Donnelly says now, in a louder voice. "But I'll just say in passing that I think it takes more guts to develop yourself than to . . ." The end of his sentence drowns in the growing wave of voices.

At three o'clock, I leave the school building without books or my coat. The sun is gone, and it is February again. The wind throttles me. I close the top button on my shirt, draw my blazer closer, and begin to walk, thinking with faint guilt, "I won't wait for Susan today, I'll call her later." I walk fast, though without destination: to Lexington, then downtown, not toward home. Ten, twenty blocks, and I am less cold; thirty, and the housewives carrying groceries have become working women and men with briefcases. Under the eerie, bright fluorescent light of a counter restaurant, I stop and order coffee. The first black draft scalds my throat. I cup my hands around the thick ceramic mug and wait, then look up and into the mirror facing me: I am there with long, strong brown hair, wild now around my shoulders; a round face, still babyish but possessing a flushed prettiness; eyes dark and direct—honest (yes!) and alive-looking, with a certain liquidy sparkle.

Outside, I buy the *Times*. I rarely read the newspaper. But

I feel good casually pressing the coins into the vendor's palm. Who knows? There may be something of interest in it, I think, folding the paper into the offending shoulder bag, satisfied to find that it doesn't fit completely, that it sticks out.

I walk on, and as I walk, I feel a certain exhilaration grow inside me, a familiar quickening of the pulse, the heart, the senses. The lavender of a nearby store awning is distractingly rich. The singsong wail of a passing siren sounds at once acute and oddly distant, as if coming from farther away. Unsettled, I resist the old sensation, unbeckoned this time. But as it stays on, it reveals itself as different, a harmless euphoria, gentler and less frantic than the one I have known: The wanting is gone.

The man and woman walking ahead of me wind their arms around each other's waist and dip, as one, through a restaurant door. On the avenue, a crowded blue bus sighs to a stop. A lovely, cold evening: I think I'll walk home.

JANET KAUFFMAN
HARMONY

FROM VANITY FAIR

∽

IT'S SATURDAY AGAIN. Sherry sits on the floor beside the refrigerator, her bare legs flat against the tile. She's telling me she likes sex. She's fairly general about it, but enthusiastic. "It's good when it's like swimming," she says, and she pushes her arms through the air a little. "Everything going easy, your shoulders in and out of the water, and what you're doing keeps you afloat and keeps you going. And another body, swimming along, nothing opposite about it, playing right along and rolling— Vicki, it's better than any daydreaming. You can touch everything."

Upstairs, in the kids' room, I hear something crash, not a serious noise though, and some scrambling and stirring follows, not silence, so Sherry just stays where she is and so do I. I'm in the low-slung canvas chair beside Sherry's table of plants. Polly and Hal, Sherry's kids, pretty much take care of themselves now. I'm not here as the baby-sitter. Since school's over, I just stop in sometimes to talk to Sherry, or she calls me up to go someplace. And Saturdays, every week, we spend together. Sherry talks about everything, and she tells me whatever she thinks. Apparently, she thinks I should hear the good side of sex. No matter what she's got hold of, Sherry acts as if she experiences some kind of special pleasures. The trouble I have is, I don't know if she's lying. Sherry might be lying. In February she told me she liked Februarys. And it's true that I saw her one afternoon cut up a hard blue plastic backyard sled; she scissored it into shoe-shaped footsies and super-glued them onto her sneakers and onto the good rubber boots of her kids. With branches as poles, the three of them walked out onto the iced-over drifts to shoe-skate the neighbor's field. It didn't look easy. But she said she enjoyed it.

I'm not sure what makes real, acceptable proof. I wish I could just take her word.

Sherry says Jeff is a complex man. She says to me when I cackle at that: "Vicki, the man is no oaf. You watch out, Vicki," she warns me, and her palms smack her knees, and her frown lines cave in, "you'll end up with one handsome bastard after another."

Then, with her kids tearing into the room and running around the kitchen table, Sherry gets up, pours me some white wine in a juice glass; she brings out the gutbucket she made with a washtub and mop handle, and while I drink and while her kids drum the chair seats, Sherry sings me her favorite song, which she made up, she says, for the sake of women everywhere in the world. "And that means you and me, too, Vicki," she adds. Like we are all poor souls, starting over at A-B-C. Anyway, she is interesting to watch, and I'm getting to like this enough to join in for the last two lines. I'm good at harmony.

I say, "Write a song for men, too, why don't you?"

"Can't be done," Sherry says.

Sherry believes she makes herself clear, with what she calls "demonstrations," which I would call good times you plan. When I baby-sat for her, she left notes saying, for instance: "Demonstration for Polly and Hal—Take dough from baggie in crisper. Sculpt a self-portrait. Don't explain. *Use your fingers.*"

I did what she said. Apparently, not explaining made it a demonstration.

Sherry has thick brown hair. Each strand is separate and crinkled. Her hair stands out from her head, as if she's got herself over a sidewalk grate where a steady air is rising. What I like best about her is the gap between her front teeth, which are skewed out a little, and the two sharp frown lines between her eyebrows—because otherwise she'd be very beautiful. She has dark-green eyes, like the green you sometimes see in coal. She says she is thirty.

For the last year Sherry's been living with Jeff, a ceramist and a half-mute. He is a tall person, with flat cheekbones and blue eyes stretched out beneath blond eyebrows; his chin has a cleft down the middle which makes his face look like it's being torn apart from the bottom up. I pity him. He looks, I swear, like an infant smashed and stretched very suddenly into an old man.

Sherry says they stay together because things are good; sex is good. That wouldn't keep me, I don't think, even if it was the truth.

She tells me that when Jeff sleeps, he throws pots, and treadles the wheel, pumping his foot faster and faster until he runs out of breath and swings back an arm as if he's angry and is slinging the pot out the window. He's too calm in the daytime to suit me. I don't like his ideas of conversation: he refuses to talk about the weather, or food. He denies the fact that his mother still does his laundry once a week, which she does.

It's a dishonest house, is what I think.   .

"He pays attention," Sherry told me the day Jeff was moving in and we were cleaning out half of her closet. "He pays attention."

"To what?"

"To skin. To the body."

"What if he doesn't know anything else?"

"He knows clay."

"And what if he doesn't know anything else?"

"Vicki!" she said, stuffing brown socks, two blue Arrow shirts into a black garbage sack for Goodwill. "What the hell do you want?"

She sat down on the bed. She pulled me by the wrist and held all the fingers of my left hand in her palm. "Now shut your eyes," Sherry said. I shut my eyes. "Jeff does this." She took my fingers, one at a time, and let them slide through hers as if she were blind, or measuring, or slipping invisible rings off and on. All of her fingers felt like lips.

"There," she said. "He's no oaf."

She let go of my hand and it fell against my thigh like somebody else's hand, weighty again.

Okay, that kind of touch is something to think about. But I think there should be more to a man than good touching, so why won't Sherry tell me? Honest to God, I work at these things. I ought to learn something from Sherry, or from someone. My mother's no help, but I don't expect it from her. She is a fine but closemouthed woman; she's glad enough that Sherry's the one to deal with me. My mother doesn't know it, but Sherry knows it—I've had sex, more than a couple of times. And with guys I liked. There's been interest in it, but it was nothing as smooth as swimming, and I've decided to put it off for a while and wait for some real excitement.

The best time I remember, at least the most comfortable, was at Harold's, when I rubbed him up for a while, and that was that, and he rubbed me, too, like a long-armed mechanical man, for as long as it took. The TV was going, and I watched him watching the Lansing news, from the school-board report right through the weather. We were under the influence, the weatherman said, of a low-pressure system in the Upper Peninsula.

"Never mind about the right man," Sherry tells me. "You keep your eyes open, Vicki."

I have my own thoughts about how Sherry keeps her eyes open—she blinks, looks right on through everything, and ends up watching the sky. She won't put curtains on any windows. And she tells me she's always had trouble sleeping, which I believe. She was beaten up by her father once and lost her hearing in one ear. "It brought me completely to my senses," she brags. When that happened she left home, and she's lived with several men, which she's mentioned in connection with ashtrays or stitches or stealing. She had Polly and Hal; she was married twice. Oafs, I suppose—lousy touchers.

So far, with the baby-sitting, I've picked up this kind of thing: recipes for rice dishes, plenty of kids' games, a little about anthropology, which is the subject Sherry studies at MSU. These aren't items that Sherry thinks of as learning, however. I agree with her there. I'm interested in learning, for instance, if she knows what she's talking about when she says she enjoys sex. When she says she enjoys life.

Sherry will have her degree at the end of the summer and she wants to move to Chicago in the fall. If she leaves, Jeff plans to "digress," as he calls it; he'll try out Detroit, "the hotbed of potting," he says, looking serious and sad, with a hand on each side of his chin, his eyes straight on Sherry.

Given the uncertain future, Sherry and I have been spending Saturdays this summer together, hunting up "Beautiful Views of Jackson." It's a real project. Sherry puts a red-headed pin in the map taped to her kitchen wall whenever we come back with a place we can both agree is a beautiful view. She complains about how mapmakers always make the wrong kind of maps, showing only obvious features. The Fourth of July we were checking a map for the way out to Napoleon to see the fireworks. "Who wants a map of animal trails?" Sherry pointed to the intersection of First and Morrell. "They could put in grazing patches, rocks. Shelters. We'll make a *meaningful* map, Vicki," she said, and that's how these Saturdays started.

I wouldn't have believed you could put together a meaningful map of Jackson, but it hasn't been going too badly. So far, we've stuck in six pins. In the last survey *Life & Living* took of Michigan cities, Jackson came in last, as the worst place to live, and Sherry said, "Naturally. Nobody sees the beautiful views." I agree with that. What they point out downtown are a couple of banks and a couple of steel buildings and two blocks of potholed mall. The Penney's store has three floors but, even so, what they do is stack jeans on two tables in the basement, by the wall display of pillows and bedpads, honest to God. There's one piece of sculpture in front of the Sheraton, but the men come in from an underground parking lot, up the elevator, to register, and nobody sees the front entrance except for the walk-ins. How many walk-ins do you get at the Sheraton?

We decided against marking objects and points of interest on our map: the sculpture is big and listed in the books; the four-trunked elm on Fourth Street is a commonplace; and Little Mary's Grave with the carved, sexed cupids is public, junior-high knowledge. I went there like everyone else in eighth grade, a moonless night, to touch the cupid. You touch the granite cupid of the opposite sex until you shiver, which isn't long for anybody, and Sherry says the chill is still half of Jackson's idea of orgasm.

She said skip it.

She wants larger views. She wants each pin to mark a place you can sit and sit for a long time and not get tired looking. She gave me instructions about finding angles where the light is especially good, where buildings come together in interesting ways, where colors of plants and smells and everything combine to make some whole thing worth looking at. The first red pinhead on Sherry's map was the view from a slab in the vacant lot opposite Francis and Cortland, where a bricked-up six-story building marks the end of the mall. Four stories up, a mission church from around the corner has painted its name in huge blue cursive letters. You sit on the slab and you see the bricks and the blue letters, and the morning sun's on your back.

Last Saturday, at the edge of a swamp by the railroad yards, Sherry said, "In the fall, Vicki, you'll want to have places like this. Show your boyfriends. It'll be a good test."

"For what?"

"For your boyfriends!"

"You bringing *Jeff* around to these views?" I asked.

"Vicki, you're sly," Sherry said. "You're a sly one."

She picked a cattail right where she was, bent the stalk, and sailed it off. "Sometimes they fly back," she told me. She held both hands at her eyes for shade. "Like a boomerang," she said.

That I don't believe. At all.

From where we were in the swamp, we could see the back end of the railroad yards, the hulk of the old roundhouse, and a good bit of debris from the place—bent rails, a box of rusty spikes, miscellaneous metal—heaped at the edge of the water. Farther behind us, across a stretch of reddish, slimed water, was one of the largest muskrat houses I'd ever seen, a structure of sticks maybe six feet wide and about as high. On top, two turtles soaked in the sun, shining like coins.

"From where they are," Sherry said, "it would be a view. What do you think?"

"I suppose," I said, balking. Which I am good at, having learned that much in school.

I tramped around, looking for other ways to get the whole panorama of two dozen tracks, the gutted roundhouse, with plenty of swamp in the foreground. But I had to agree she was right. Over the water, the view would be better.

Sherry took off her shoes and started in.

Just about then, some clown from the railroad yards, far away, blew a goddamn whistle and started toward us.

"Hey! Hey, you, there!" he was yelling, or yelling something. He jumped on a stack of crossties and I could see a bright red cap, a beard, a red shirt, and light pants. Then he was coming at us again.

Sherry called to me, "Get over here. Move it."

She was already somehow across the water. Her light-blue jeans were a mess from the slime, which must have gone nearly up to her waist, and there she sat, dripping, on the muskrat's heap of branches and sticks, shaking her hands and arms, drops flying all around.

One thing with Sherry, you don't get much choice. I didn't even pull off my shoes for fear of underwater metal. I didn't breathe; I didn't want smells to deal with, too. I just strode in, with my lips tight together, and sloshed along. It wasn't pleasant. But it also wasn't too far across. Sherry gave me her hand and I was perched up on top of the muskrat house beside her with room to spare.

The view was a good one. The railroad man, a slash of red in the cattails, was a nice touch.

He could see we were just sitting there doing nothing, but he came along anyway. Pretty soon, he stood like a cop at the edge of the water, a silver whistle around his neck; he puffed himself up, and when he breathed, his lips rolled up, pink, like something alive moved in his beard.

"You looking for something?"

"No," we both said.

"You ladies hunting a man, that it?"

I stuck out my tongue.

"Sure!" said Sherry. "Come on over."

"Watch it now, girlies. I'll get the whole crew out here and that'll be something to see." He had his hands on his hips, like a coach.

"You go, we go!" Sherry called back. "Come on over. One man is plenty."

Honest to God. I just looked at her. You liar, you crummy liar, I thought.

"Trespassers, ladies, don't give out orders," the man said. He smiled, openmouthed, through the beard. "*I'm* the one says do we use cuffs or not."

With one hand, he reached around into the back pocket of his pants.

"What'll it be?" he said. "You slip on across, or I handle this some other way?"

It was hot in that stinking swamp, hot as a foreign country. My jeans were steaming. The man kept smiling his open-wide smile and didn't once take his eyes off Sherry.

Sherry pulled herself up a little and hunkered there, like she wanted her good ear closer to him, for quiet conversation. But she kept the baby talk going.

"Come *here*. There's a great view."

Well, he laughed at that, the black hole of his mouth sending up noise, and he swung an arm around. The hand was missing the thumb. I could see the stump, pearly, glistening.

"You're the view, lady," he said to Sherry. "I got you right in my eye. Say I cuff your feet, how far do you think you'll get?" His voice dropped. "You nod to trouble, you got it."

Sherry stood up, and there were small sticks and brown streaks of mud on her shirt sleeves. I thought she was going to help him in. But she pointed: "What happened there to your thumb?"

The man leaned far over, as if for some reason he had to bend down to see his thumb. The toes of his boots pressed into the wet. When he stood up, his lips went shut in a pink line.

"Lady," he said, "you want this simple or not?" The man was across twenty feet of water, alone and clean and thumbless, and you could tell he was less and less happy about it.

"I want you over here," Sherry said, serious as when she called her kids. "I'll comb your hair, honey—look." Sherry combed her hair upward with her fingers. Some of it stayed standing up. She bent over me, and she demonstrated again, with my hair, what her combing could do. Her fingers pulled through my hair and I could feel hot air reach right to my skull bone. Sherry recited him a list of what she would do, and it was quite an accounting. "Vicki won't mind, will you, Vicki?"

"Ha."

"Sure. Vicki's no kid."

Sherry'd say anything once she saw that she was in charge. She isn't subtle. But she knows how far a person will finally go, and which direction. She sets things up, Sherry does.

"You lose your thumb in the yards?" Sherry asked the man. "In Korea?" She'd guessed his age, I bet; anyway, I had.

The man just stood there, looking at her. I heard a redwing blackbird trilling nearby.

"Korea," the man said, calm. "And the tip of the little finger."

He held his hand up; he pulled the shirt sleeve back, and I could see it was true.

Sherry sat down, cross-legged, on the muskrat house. "I have all my fingers," she said.

The poor man was standing, just standing, at the edge of the water in his red shirt.

"You live around here?" he asked.

"No," Sherry lied. I'd call it a lie.

"Too bad," he said. "I'd walk you home." And that's when he turned and went back the way he'd come.

That swamp closed in. The sun was straight overhead and the water was flat, burning. The muskrat house, it turned out, was not built for human weight and the mess had sunk quite a way into the water, spreading sticks out on all sides, the middle squashing.

Sherry lay back like a woman on a beach, even so. She pushed her hair back from her face and shut her eyes. I could see that the sun was hurting her eyes through the lids; she was squinting, and her face was filled with lines, and I could see her setting her eyes up under the eyelids, up and slightly back. She breathed as if she were comfortable. As usual. Behind me, I heard the redwing again, its throaty gargle, closer than before. Sherry sat up and turned herself around, to look out that way, too, where there was nothing to see but flat greenish swamp-land to the horizon. We could have been looking out over China; we could have been in the rice fields trying to figure something out.

"This a view this way, Vicki?" she asked me.

"No."

"Well," she asked next, kind of harumphing, "was he an oaf?"

"Jesus! What do you mean? He was almost as bad as you!"

"Vicki, look," she said, quiet, but straightening up, and folding her hands the way a kid folds them up to pray at the table. "Think about his hands. Vicki, I'm serious—a man who's lost a thumb is worth some attention. To start with. Vicki, I swear."

"What if he'd stomped right on over?"

"He'd have walked us home."

"Ha!"

"It's the truth," she said. And that's all she said.

We worked our way out of the swamp, across the west end of the yards, and out onto the sidewalk of Page Avenue, me making squishing footprints and splattering drops that went dark for a second on the pavement before the heat took them, and Sherry making sucking noises with her cheeks. When we got to her place, we stuck a pin in the map, and Sherry poured some wine and handed it over as if it capped an afternoon when she'd proved something to me. Something simple: life is sweet; life is incorruptible. She thinks she's living proof. I swear she has figured out how to ignore nine-tenths of all she knows.

Honest to God, she can stretch a view. I think it's a pity. She doesn't expect enough. She'd love a body for thumblessness, Jackson for a swamp, and probably the rest of life for that.

She wears me out. Today I just want to take it easy. I don't want to have to make up my mind, or say true or false.

Sherry is twirling with Polly around the kitchen, faking a sour face; she sees I'm not much for moving out of the chair. We haven't decided yet where we're going. Sherry's idea is to head toward the bus station and take the back alley to Paka Plaza; she thinks that whole area has possibilities. By the end of summer, she wants a good map, and I tell her we'll have it.

We will.

But today I hope we stay put.

Sherry says I am easy to read, so she'll probably say next, "Vicki, let's just sit around." I don't even care if she calls it some kind of event—which she will. All I want to do is take her gutbucket out on the back step and strum a couple of old tunes.

JAMES HOWARD KUNSTLER
THE RISE, FALL, AND REDEMPTION OF MOOSKI TOFFSKI OFFSKI

FROM TENDRIL

"I AM MOOSKI TOFFSKI OFFSKI, Sultan of Bungwah, Caliph of Poona, Archduke of Soodna, Tsarovitch of the Imperial Russian realm, so what else is new?"

The author of this speech, delivered to a full-length mirror in the bedroom of a Manhattan apartment, was an eleven-year-old boy named Jeff Greenaway. Since he had finished his homework—a "report" on the state of Iowa, its history, products, official song, et cetera; plus two pages of fractions in the odious math workbook—and since there were fifteen minutes remaining before *The Untouchables* television show would come on the air, Jeff worked on his latest comedy routine. He was an accomplished mimic and the accent sounded a lot like Nikita Khrushchev, who had recently visited New York in order to bang his shoe at the U.N.

Jeff rehearsed telling several jokes, first in his normal voice, then in his Mooski dialect, and the second time around they sounded so hilarious he could barely finish them. He tried to imagine the circumstance where he might do his routine for Wendy Waldbaum, whom he adored, and sweep her off her feet on gales of laughter. The ultimate triumph, of course, would be to somehow get on *The Ed Sullivan Show* and take her by complete and overwhelming surprise. But Jeff realized that he was unlikely to get on the show, at least for a few years, and by then he and Wendy would be in different schools. Then again there were the "talent shows" held in the school auditorium where the children sought refuge at recess on rainy days. Impromptu affairs at first, they had become boringly predictable as the school year wore on. Barry Goldblatt would amaze the audience at the piano with "The Theme from the Million Dollar Movie," after which Bobby Bedrosian would play "Me and My Shadow" on his cornet. Richard Schnabel, the class dork, would do his birdcalls. After that it would all go downhill. Jeff had mixed feelings about debuting in such company. New acts always had to wait until after the established ones took their turns. By the time he got up there, the crowd would be ready for blood. What if they didn't get the jokes? What if the jokes weren't any good? Wendy Waldbaum wouldn't be caught dead talking to him. He'd have to move to a new city, change his name . . . !

Jeff approached the mirror and examined himself. Gazing with dismay at the image, he decided that short arms and legs might be fine for comedy, but they were no help at all in the romance department. He thought of his rival for the affection of Wendy Waldbaum, Lee Talbot, and how Talbot towered at least a foot over him. *How's the weather up there, Lee?* he would ask on line, as Mrs. Snipes's class moved in formation down the hall toward the gym. Lee would pretend to laugh, but it was obvious he simply didn't get it. Jeff loved the fact that Talbot didn't get it far more than he liked the wisecrack itself. Then, during the game of "bombardment" that comprised the daily gym period, Jeff would fire volley after volley of big rubber balls at Talbot, seeking not merely to eliminate him from the game, but to ring his bell, to cause brain damage, if possible. Once, he nailed him right between the eyes and Talbot sank to his knees on the varnished hardwood floor like a gut-shot Indian. Mrs. Snipes put a moratorium on "head-hunting" after that, but the rule was unenforceable. ". . . I couldn't help it, Mrs. Snipes, honest . . ." What Wendy Waldbaum saw in the big jerk, Jeff couldn't begin to imagine, but they'd been spotted together buying tickets at the 86th

Street RKO theater one recent Saturday by Jay Skolnick, who was not known to lie about such things.

Jeff stepped closer to the mirror and smiled as if at a photographer. His teeth were very large, and he noticed a similarity between his smile and the expression on the muzzle of the alligator that adorned the polo shirts his mother bought for him.

"Frank Nitti traveled all the way from Chicago to New York for the sole purpose of exterminating Lee Talbot," Jeff declaimed in his best Walter Winchell voice. Then, he turned on the TV at the foot of his bed and watched that week's episode of *The Untouchables* in which Special Agent Elliot Ness sent yet another batch of Italian-American miscreants to that great speakeasy in the sky.

Noon recess at Public School Number 6 on Manhattan's upper east side was surprisingly informal. Patronage of the school cafeteria was strictly voluntary, and most of the older children, the 5th and 6th graders, scorned it for the liberty of the playground and the streets. Lunch could be gotten, for instance, at the Copper Lantern Coffee Shoppe across Madison Avenue, where a hamburger, french fries and a cherry coke cost $1.03 plus tip. An equally nourishing, if not exactly wholesome, lunch could be had for half that price from the Sabrett hot dog man who parked his pushcart on 81st Street every day. A squat, furtive, melancholy figure dressed in a grimy quilted jacket and a laborer's hat with three earflaps which he wore in all weathers and all seasons, and with stumpy, permanently blackened fingers (the stains etched in tiny cracks of his skin like scrimshaw), the hot dog man spoke a language which not even Jeff Greenaway, with his love of mimicry, could identify. But there was not much to go on, for the hot dog man never said more than the two words *mustard* and *saurkraut*, which he pronounced "moostahrokrot" and posed in the interrogatory.

Now, on this particular noon, a blustery March day when newspapers blew down the avenues like tumbleweeds, Jeff went off by himself at lunch hour in foul and turbulent spirits. That morning, he had overheard Lee Talbot describe his 12th birthday festivities, upcoming this Saturday. First, Talbot's father, a bigshot Broadway attorney, would be taking Lee and a horde of his so-called friends to the matinee of *The Sound of Music*. From there they would proceed to the F.A.O. Schwarz toy store on 59th Street where Lee would be given 12 minutes to grab everything his heart desired. Finally, the group would debouch up Fifth Avenue to the Talbot duplex for a birthday party with cake, ice cream, soda, and favors.

As far as Jeff was concerned, it was obvious that the whole purpose of this party was to impress Wendy Waldbaum. In the first place, Talbot didn't have any friends, just acquaintances who liked to play with his slot cars and mooch candy off him. It was Talbot, in fact, who had given Jeff his first insights into the true nature of the political mentality. (Talbot was "president" of class 6-B, meaning he got to sit up at the teacher's desk and lord it over everybody while Mrs. Snipes visited the "powder room.") In any case, the prospect of this party—to which he had been pointedly *not* invited—filled Jeff with loathing and nausea.

All morning long he had done nothing but stare diagonally across the room at Wendy, so demure in her green jumper with the red tights. From the angle where he sat, Jeff could see inside the bib front of her jumper where a little mound of budding breast swelled beneath her white cotton turtleneck. The sight of it made him half-mad with a desperate yearning he could not quite account for. He had started out the year with no more interest in girls than in math. For the last several months, however, since Wendy had moved her desk to its present site, Jeff had slowly begun to acquire an interest in Wendy Waldbaum that seemed, at times, utterly consuming.

He would haunt the corner across the street from her building at 85th and Park and try to guess which of the 400-odd windows on each side belonged to her apartment. One Saturday, he waited six hours—hiding behind the trash bins in the alley of a Catholic school across Park Avenue—for Wendy to emerge from the canopied entrance, just to confirm that she had an existence beyond P.S. 6. But she never did appear, and Jeff subsequently learned that she had been skiing in Vermont with her parents that whole weekend.

Then, one abnormally mild afternoon in February when

everyone was lining up in the playground to return to class from recess, Jeff found himself paired with the black-haired, brown-eyed, inexpressibly beautiful Wendy and, on an impulse that he would rue for weeks, reached for her hand, leaned close to her ear (her hair smelled like the florist's shop on 83rd Street), and whispered, "I love you."

She recoiled from him, not reproachfully, but with a look of pained bewilderment on her face, those dark eyes searching every inch of him as though she were trying to understand how he fit together, and then she said, quietly, in a voice that was not unkind, "But I don't love you." The three flights of stairs from the playground to the classroom were the longest climb of his life. But what really confused him was that she continued to hold his hand the whole way up, as though consoling him for his terrible humiliation. His love for her, therefore, not only went on undimmed but reached a new and blinding degree of intensity.

And so, having overheard the demoralizing details of Lee Talbot's upcoming birthday bash, and having spent the morning in a torment of gazing and longing, Jeff bought two hot dogs with "moostahrokrot" from the Sabrett man and then headed toward the Metropolitan Museum of Art a block away, to look at the old swords and armor and to try out his Mooski routine on one of the guards.

In the days before art began competing with showbiz, department stores and bigtime sports for the tourist dollar, the Metropolitan Museum of Art would be well nigh deserted late on a dreary Friday afternoon in March, especially the great, gloomy, Gothic hall where the white and black knights perpetually faced off, lances bristling, on rearing plaster-of-Paris chargers. It was here, among the echoes of chivalry, that Jeff found his captive audience, a nervous young Negro security guard, so thin that his uniform looked as stiff and bulky as a suit of armor, and with a downy mustache which, contrary to its intended effect, actually made him look younger than his 21 years.

"Hello, guardski. I am Mooski Toffski Offski, official

Russian tourist, from Babooski, Sovietski. Could you tellski meski which way to the mumski?"

"Say what?" the guard said.

"Mumski, deadski."

When the guard still failed to understand, Jeff lay down at his feet on the marble floor, crossed his hands over his chest and sucked in his cheeks to convey the idea of ghoulish emaciation.

"You can't do that here," the guard said. "Come on, get up."

So, Jeff got up and began circling the guard in a lurching, limping gait, dragging one leg stiffly and holding both arms out as he had seen various types of the undead do in a host of movies.

"Tana leaves!" Jeff croaked hoarsely. "I must have my tana leaves . . . !"

"If you don't go away, I'm gonna have to call my supervisor."

Jeff added a disgusting snorfling noise to the act, a sound halfway between a rooting pig and a man dying of tuberculosis.

"Get out my face, boy!" the guard finally exploded in exasperation.

Jeff loped across the great hall crying "Sanctuary!" and disappeared through an arched portal into the world of the high Renaissance. He counted the tryout a resounding success, and thus cheered up, made his way through the art of the ages back toward the main entrance. Just short of the lobby, he paused to visit the reconstructed tomb of the Pharaoh. The exhibit was set up so that one entered a narrow stone passageway enscribed with hieroglyphics, taken from a real mummy's tomb, and thus experienced what it must have been like for the art plunderers who emptied the great troves of Egypt. Jeff liked it especially for the acoustics. It enhanced the effect of any of the accents he was proficient in—Mooski, Dracula, Quasimodo, Walter Winchell, Amen-ho-tep. He stepped under the lintel guarded by a bas-relief of the jackal-headed god Anubis, and had only taken a few steps when he detected the echo of somebody weeping within.

It frightened him for a moment, until he remembered that he was not in a real mummy's tomb, but a museum in the middle of the biggest city in the world, and then, curiosity bolstered, he advanced down the passageway and turned a corner. There, in her camel hair coat, face to the hieroglyph-covered wall, was Wendy Waldbaum. Having gazed at her from so many rearview angles that he knew the back of her head as well as her face, Jeff recognized her at once. Uncertain what to do, afraid to reach out and touch her, yet unwilling to skulk quietly away, he decided the most polite thing would be to clear his throat.

"*Ahem.* . . ."

Wendy glanced furtively over her shoulder at him, her face swollen with misery.

"What's wrong?" Jeff asked.

But seeing him only added indignity to her anguish. She tore herself away from the wall, wedged past him in the narrow corridor (he could smell her tears), and ran out of the tomb. Jeff did not follow. His own emotions were in a tumult, and he sensed somehow that to inflict himself on her would only make matters worse. When he emerged from the tomb, she was not in the lobby; when he left the museum, she was nowhere to be seen on Fifth Avenue or 82nd Street; and when he returned to Mrs. Snipes's class at one o'clock, she was absent from her seat and did not reappear.

During the course of that afternoon—an hour of geography in which Lee Talbot held forth smarmily on the wonders and virtues of the state of Texas, and a final hour of the detested fractions—Jeff slowly came to the conclusion that whatever had driven Wendy Waldbaum to the mummy's tomb in tears and desolation was directly attributable to that lumbering, toothy, would-be Texan whose initials were L.T. They burned themselves into Jeff's brain like a smoldering brand. When the bell rang at five minutes to three, and the boys and girls put on their coats and lined up, Jeff had half a mind to push Talbot down the stairwell. But he refrained, and also checked an impulse to shove Talbot in front of a Madison Avenue bus, once they got out on the sidewalk. After all, Jeff tried to reason logically, he ought to make sure that the big jerk really was to blame before doing anything that might land him in the electric chair.

After school, he returned to the museum, thinking that perhaps Wendy might be hiding in another part of it. But though he searched the place high and low—from the 17th Century bedchambers in the most obscure corner of the American wing, to a sepulchral gallery of Etruscan sarcophagi on the ground floor, rear—he encountered no sign of her. Still trying to puzzle the matter out, he returned briefly to the hall of antique weaponry and savored a vision of the havoc that a thirty-pound iron mace could wreak on the person of Lee Talbot. He imagined Talbot hacked with a halberd, cleaved in twain with a battle-ax, blindsided with a broadsword, and shot with so many crossbow bolts that he looked like a porcupine.

On his way out, Jeff crossed paths with the thin Negro security guard again.

"No trouble, you," the guard warned him, sternly pointing an index finger.

Jeff just smiled.

He got home to the apartment on 79th Street between Park and Madison at four-thirty. His parents were going to the theater that night.

"Not *The Sound of Music*, I hope," Jeff remarked to his mother as he ransacked the kitchen cabinets for a snack.

"No, *The Threepenny Opera*," she informed him. "Say, what's wrong with *The Sound of Music*, incidentally?"

"Mom, it's the stupidest play on Broadway. Only a complete moron would go see it."

"The Strombers adored it."

"They must have brain damage, then."

"Jeffrey!"

"Promise me you'll never go see it."

"Don't you think six Oreos are enough, young man?" She took the package away from him and put it back in the cabinet. "Alma's coming over to cook your dinner and to . . . to . . . ."

"Go ahead, say it."

". . . to be with you."

"To babysit, you mean. Yaagghh! I'm eleven years old, for crying out loud. I'm going to be twelve in September!"

"We can't leave you here alone, darling."

"Why not? Whaddaya think I'm going to do? Burn the building down—?"

"I don't have time for this, I don't have time," she chanted in a not-entirely-playful singsong. "Look, we'd just worry about you, okay. Starting in September, no more babysitters. I promise."

"Promise you won't go see *The Sound of Music.*"

"I swear by all that's holy, I will not see that abominable play, ever. Happy?"

"I've got a lot on my mind, Mom," Jeff muttered and shuffled out of the kitchen.

There were three phones in the apartment. The one Jeff customarily availed himself of was in the den that doubled as a guest room. Here, his father kept all his tennis trophies and the reference books they needed to complete the crossword puzzle in the Sunday *Times.* The room was paneled in dark wood and its single window thickly draped. Jeff liked it for many of the same reasons that he liked the mummy's tomb in the museum—it was easy to forget you were in the middle of the biggest city in the world.

Though he had already done this once or twice before, Jeff looked up the name Waldbaum in the Manhattan telephone directory. Eighty-three of them were entered, but only one of them, a Harvey Waldbaum, was listed at 1014 Park Avenue, the very building Jeff had staked out from behind the Catholic school's ash cans, and so Jeff had every reason to believe that the seven-digit number printed beside Harvey Waldbaum's name could feasibly connect him, via the magic of electricity, to the object of his heart's desire. He held the phone handset until it was clammy with sweat and the dial tone turned into an angry klaxon, like an air-raid siren. He slammed the receiver down, breathing shallowly, his mouth as dry as a mummy's. He repeated this bungling operation almost a dozen times, having gotten as far as the sixth digit once before chickening out.

At six o'clock, his mother barged into the den, looking quite lovely in a dark skirt, shimmering blue silk blouse, and pearls, with a fur coat over her arm.

"I'm meeting Daddy for drinks at the Edwardian Room,

pussycat," she said and stopped to kiss him on the forehead. "Say, are you all right?"

"Sure, I'm all right."

"Alma's here."

"Hot diggity dog."

"Who are you trying to call?"

"I'm not *trying* to call anyone," he said irritably. "If I wanted to call someone, I'd call."

"I suppose so," his mother agreed with a sigh. "Well, 'bye, darling."

She floated out of the room on a stately cloud of *Joy de Patou*. As soon as the door closed behind her, Jeff snatched the phone back out of its cradle and dialed all seven digits. The first ring at the other end had as much terrifying potency as the whine of the dentist's drill before he inserts the tip in an inflamed tooth. The second ring seemed to physically scramble Jeff's brain and he doubted he would even be able to speak when someone answered, let alone remember his name. By the third ring he had entered a psychological wasteland as vast and empty as the Sahara desert, where there is no hope for the stranded wayfarer, nor any hope of hope. But, on the fourth ring, a strange rapture of almost religious dimension began to well inside him. And on the fifth ring, practically delirious with relief, Jeff toppled back into the yielding cushions of the convertible sofa. Nobody was home. Most particularly, Wendy Waldbaum was not home. After that, he let it ring and ring and ring, gleefully allowing the phone to violate the silence of the empty Waldbaum apartment.

Alma the babysitter prepared Jeff's hamburger to his exact specifications ("burnt to a crisp on a buttered English muffin with Velveeta melted on both halves") and gave him permission to take the sandwich into his room, as he requested. He turned on the TV. A program featuring candid interviews with movie stars, taped at their own Hollywood homes, was in progress. An oleaginous actor of the Latin persuasion, known for his portrayal of cads in second-rate feature films, was explaining his philosophy of matrimony at poolside. Jeff hurled objurgations at him in his Mooski accent. Meanwhile, a movie about romantic villainy starring Wendy Waldbaum and Lee Talbot began to flicker on one of the silver screens deep inside Jeff's head. He pictured Talbot taking Wendy out on the town: hamburgers and onion rings at Prexy's, where the food was delivered on electric trains; then the two of them at a Broadway show (the vile and execrable *Sound of Music*—he had no idea what it was about, so he imagined a stage full of clashing tympani, xylophones, bassoons, blaring horns, assorted screeching strings, like a symphony orchestra in the throes of a revolution); then Talbot escorting Wendy into F.A.O. Schwarz and flinging money at the obsequious clerks; finally, Talbot luring Wendy to the Metropolitan Museum of Art, seizing her by the shoulders and kissing her right on the mouth!

Jeff shook his head to disperse the horrifying fantasy. The actor on TV had been replaced by a woman dressed as a plumber selling drain cleaner. That had to be it, Jeff thought: Talbot had taken her to the museum that lunch hour and done something disgusting to her in the mummy's tomb!

After that, and for the next three hours, Jeff labored in a veritable blur of activity. First, he cut his leather briefcase up into strips, pointed at one end, and stapled these strips around the waistband of a pair of his summer camp shorts so that it ended up resembling something akin to a Roman foot-soldier's battle tunic. Next, he carefully clipped the collar off one of his blue oxford button-down shirts, cut off the sleeves just above the cuffs, and scissored the remaining sleeves into long fringes. Finally, the *pièce de résistance,* he chopped the brim off one of his father's hats, fashioned two great horns out of shirt cardboards, and fastened them to the crown with tufts of colored yarn hanging off the tips. By the time *The Twilight Zone* came on the air (a grim little tale featuring Mickey Rooney as a washed-up, alcoholic ex-jockey living in a miserable furnished room and waiting for the Angel of Death to knock on his door—it finally appears in the guise of a nine-year-old girl), Jeff stood before the full-length mirror in full regalia. The effect was impressive. At eleven o'clock, promptly, Alma came to his room and told him to get ready for bed, and for the first time in several years, to her vast astonishment, Jeff did not utter a peep of protest.

*   *   *

On Saturday morning, his father invited him to come along on a ride to Mamaroneck to inspect a sailboat he was thinking of buying, and to his father's surprise Jeff begged off, citing a "report" on dinosaurs he had to get done for school by Monday. "I could get left back," Jeff explained gravely, and his father agreed that he had better see to it, then.

At one o'clock, his mother went off to do the galleries on Madison Avenue and meet one of her fellow-mothers for lunch at a French place. As soon as he heard the elevator door close, Jeff changed into his costume. He could tell by looking out the window at the pedestrians bundled up on 79th Street that it was another blustery day out, so he put on his ski pajamas under the fringed shirt and battle tunic. He decided it looked even better that way. Finally, he helped himself to one of his mother's raincoats, a plain tan poplin model that came down to his ankles, thus concealing his warrior's outfit. He stuck his horned helmet in a Bloomingdale's bag and left the apartment.

At 78th Street, he ducked into the candy and newspaper store and purchased a pair of those plastic eyeglasses that come complete with bushy eyebrows and a fake nose. He put these in the shopping bag with his helmet. To avoid any chance encounter with his mother, he swung over to Fifth Avenue and began the trek downtown, walking on the Central Park side of the street. He reached his destination by two o'clock. From his seat on a stone bench in front of the Pulitzer fountain on 59th Street, Jeff could surreptitiously observe all those who entered the F.A.O. Schwarz toy store diagonally across the street. The Grand Army Plaza swarmed with college men checking their watches as they waited for their dates. The horse-drawn cabs were lined up in seedy splendor along 59th Street, and though Jeff wanted desperately to go over and pet the horses, he made himself stay on the bench and watch the toy store entrance. Time crept by with agonizing slowness. One hour. Two. Several people sat down on the other end of Jeff's bench, lingered awhile to watch the passing spectacle, then left. One of these was an elderly gentleman, fastidiously attired in a worn brown overcoat and shiny brown brogans.

"Say," Jeff asked him, "do you happen to know what

time the matinees of the Broadway shows get out on Saturday?"

The old man shrugged his shoulders.

"Have you seen *The Sound of Music* by any chance?" Jeff inquired further.

The old man shook his head.

"Don't go, even if someone gives you free tickets. It stinks."

"You are a critic?" the old man spoke for the first time, his voice thick with the dialect of Eastern Europe. Hearing it had an electrifying effect on Jeff.

"You are Sovietski?" he asked excitedly.

The old man recoiled, wincing.

"Sovietski!" Jeff insisted. "Sovietski Ruski, like meski: Mooski Toffski Offski!"

The old man got up off the bench, spat on the ground, and walked stiffly away. Jeff would have felt chagrined by the encounter, but he had hardly fastened his gaze back on the entrance of F.A.O. Schwarz when whom should he spy before its bountiful windows but Lee Talbot, all dressed up in a tie and Chesterfield coat, hair plastered slickly down, along with a handful of schoolmates, all of them led by Talbot's towering, cigar-chomping father. Jeff got up and crept over behind a chestnut peddler's smoking pushcart. He was already shivering with anticipation.

The Talbot party remained in F.A.O. Schwarz for more than a half hour, then emerged absolutely loaded down with boxes and bags. They mustered briefly at the corner, then started north up Fifth Avenue, Talbot's companions burdened like native bearers on an African safari. Jeff followed them stealthily up the Central Park side. In a little while, they turned into a canopied entrance between 64th and 65th. Jeff waited fifteen minutes, then crossed Fifth Avenue and approached the doorman, an imposing figure in his gilt-frogged green uniform.

"Is this where Lee Talbot's birthday party is?" Jeff asked in his most retarded-sounding voice.

"Seven-E," the doorman said gruffly and let Jeff in. The elevator was down a long, carpeted corridor lined with gilded, marbleized mirrors, far fancier than his own building. Jeff turned up his collar. The elevator operator was an ancient, white-haired Irishman whose head was permanently cocked to one side by arthritis. He was not much taller than Jeff.

"Seven," Jeff told him in a firm, rather froggy fake voice.

"Goin' ter see the birthday boy, are ye? Got yer present?"

Jeff hoisted up the bag to show.

"He come in through here a little while ago like the Aga Khan," the elevator man muttered acidly. "Well, here we are, sonny."

Jeff stepped out into the seventh floor hallway, his heart racing. The door to 7-E was directly across from the elevator, and the elevator man waited for him to ring the doorbell. Sounds of merriment could be heard within. Jeff thought he would have a heart attack waiting for the elevator man to get lost. He turned and smiled.

"Yer a shy little lad, aren't ye?"

Jeff nodded his head. Just then, the elevator buzzer sounded and the old man was constrained to depart, leaving Jeff alone in the hall. When he was gone, Jeff raced frantically around the hall trying to find the fire stairs, then ducked inside. Panting with fear, he removed his raincoat and dumped it on the landing. He put on the helmet and magic eyeglasses, took a deep breath, and went forth to the door of the Talbot apartment, ringing the bell for two full seconds. Footsteps on a hardwood floor could be heard within. The door swung open, held by a glamorous blonde in a puffy skirt. Far beyond her, amid heaps of paper and cardboard boxes, and a table laden with cake and sodas, was Lee Talbot in a blue metallic pointed party hat that made him look like the world's richest pinhead. He was surrounded by his fawning cronies.

"Why, look Lee, another one of your friends is here," the woman announced brightly, then said to Jeff, "What a cunning costume."

Jeff stalked past her, ignoring the compliment, until he was ten feet away from the great horseshoe of sofas where Talbot and his friends were assembling his booty of new playthings. Talbot's mouth tried to form a smile, but it was a cracked, uncertain thing.

"Who is it?" he asked timidly.

"It is Mooski Toffski Offski," Jeff replied, his voice grow-

ing louder and more shrill with every syllable, "Sultan of
Bungwah, Caliph of Poona, Archduke of Soodna and Tsarovitch
of the Imperial Russian realm. I have come to take my
vengeance!"

"It's Greenaway!" Bobby Bedrosian cried.

In a matter of perhaps fifteen seconds, an interval that
would live in his memory and imagination as an eternity, Jeff
bounded around the room amid cries and shrieks and alarms
and the original cast recording of *The Sound of Music*—which
just happened to be playing on the hi-fi—grabbing Talbot's
birthday presents, his chemistry set, his gleaming new brass
alcohol-fired miniature steam engine, his microscope kit, his
electric train, his upgraded slot-car set, his telescope, his electric
football game, his Frank Nitti machine gun, his drum set, his
plastic models of the U.S.S. Enterprise and the Cutty Sark, et
cetera, et cetera, et cetera, and to the horror of all present,
most particularly Lee Talbot, began hurling these things against
the rose-colored walls of the apartment, concluding with the
upending of an eleven-pound marzipan-bedizened birthday cake
right on top of the stupefied Talbot's pointy-hatted head.

Of course, he tried to get away via the fire stairs, but he
was nabbed by Talbot's father before he could make it back out
the front door.

The ensuing thirty-six hours were glum and embarrassed
ones for the Greenaway family, his parents left to try to explain
their offspring's deplorable conduct—and to settle for damages
before the courts were notified. All told, it ended up costing
Jeff's father in excess of $300, the same day he had shelled out
$1,000 on the down payment for a 25-foot motor-sailer. Jeff
remained sequestered in his bedroom, visited, at first, only by
silent adults bearing food trays. But he remained strangely
placid throughout the ordeal. Deep inside, his heart throbbed
with glory. He accepted the possibility that his parents might
disown him and he even made plans for running away to Iowa,
a state whose products, history and waterways were familiar to
him. He figured that he could learn all the words to the state
song on his way out there, and that it would help him get into
the better sort of orphan asylum.

Then, early Sunday evening, his father came to see him, sitting on the edge of the boy's bed while Jeff hugged his knees in his padded swivel desk chair.

"Why did you do it, son?"

"Love," Jeff said.

"What did he say?" Jeff's mother asked her husband when he returned wearily to their bedroom.

"He says, 'love.' "

"Love? What could he possibly mean by that?"

"I don't know," Jeff's father sighed. "Well, he's eleven. That's almost a person."

Somewhat later, Jeff's father went back and told his son what had been decided:

"We're sending you to a special private school next year," he said quietly, "where you have to wear a uniform and they make you work very, very hard."

The cloud over Jeff took an exceedingly long time to lift. Suspicion and recrimination lingered for weeks, not only within his family but among his schoolmates. The story of his crazed exploit was the talk of the upper grades at P.S. 6; and even among the children, whose sense of acceptable comportment is highly elastic, he was treated a little standoffishly, as though he were a walking bomb that might go off at the slightest provocation.

Then one day in early May, it began raining buckets five minutes after the boys and girls were let out for the noon recess. The auditorium, therefore, was opened up and very shortly filled to capacity. Mr. Peevis, a fourth-grade teacher on recess duty, soon organized a rainy-day talent show, and Barry Goldblatt led it off at the piano with a rendition of "My Favorite Things," a song from (unbeknownst to Jeff) *The Sound of Music.* He was followed by Bobby Bedrosian ("Life Is Just a Bowl of Cherries") on the cornet, and Richard Schnabel, who had added a whole program of wild animal cries to his formidable repertoire of birdcalls. A newcomer, Raymond Hosner, tried to sing "I'm a Yankee Doodle Dandy" but forgot the words; Esther Grubka related the heartwarming saga of her family's recent audience with the Pope; and Joseph Fucci, prime candidate for the soon-to-be-vacated role of official 6th-grade dork, performed a dance that had to be stopped by Mr. Peevis on account of incipient lewdness. It was at this juncture, with seven minutes left to the bell, that Jeff took his turn.

He peered at the audience from the cleft behind the heavy velour curtain, then stepped out to the forestage. A thrill of recognition crackled across the audience, not necessarily of the approving kind.

"I am Mooski Toffski Offski . . ." he declared loudly. A great roar of laughter swept up at him like a warm, friendly breeze and drowned him out. The younger children especially squirmed in their seats with delight. While they laughed, Jeff duckwalked up and down the apron of the stage, as he had seen Groucho Marx do in several movies. This too provoked gales of laughter. He noticed Lee Talbot get up and leave. When the noise subsided, he told a joke about the kamikaze pilot who signs up for tango lessons. The audience ate it up, even though they laughed in the wrong places. He followed this with a dramatic vignette out of *The Untouchables*, Jeff acting out the voices of all the principal characters himself: Elliot Ness, Big Al Capone, Frank ("The Enforcer") Nitti, a flapper. This earned laughs throughout and a smattering of applause. He wrapped up the routine with a joke about Adolf Hitler meeting Superman in heaven. The cheers and clapping that followed would have guaranteed him an encore, but the bell rang and the children were instructed to line up by class.

Jeff climbed down from the stage and fought his way up the aisle to his classmates. En route, many of the other children slapped his back or touched him, saying things like, "Nice goin', Mooski." He was still in a daze when he felt someone take his hand and looked to his left to discover Wendy Waldbaum beside him.

"You were great," she said.

Mr. Peevis yelled at everyone to start marching out of the auditorium. Wendy held his hand all the way up the stairs. His heart fluttered inside his chest like a bird in a cage. On the third floor landing, Wendy leaned over and whispered in his ear, "Meet me at the museum after school."

"Where?"

"You know where."

He remained in a transport the rest of the afternoon, oblivious to the recital of state capitals, the voyages of Ferdinand Magellan and the boggle of fractions. For two hours, the highly musical name *Wendy Waldbaum* reverberated through his skull like the notes of a heavenly choir. At five minutes to three the bell rang and Mrs. Snipes's class filed downstairs to the exit.

It had stopped raining. Jeff waited on the corner of 82nd Street thinking that he and Wendy might walk the block up to the museum together, that perhaps she would like to hold his hand again. But she paid no attention to him and skipped uptown on Madison with a crowd of her female classmates. Jeff considered the possibility that she had been playing a practical joke on him earlier, but his life had grown so consistently absurd in recent months that he felt immune to further disgrace. So, he walked up to the museum alone and went directly to its heart, the mummy's tomb.

Twelve minutes later, when he had given up all hope and was about to leave, she came to him. Her eyes, her mouth, the little brown mole on her cheek, seemed to him utterly original elements of beauty, previously unknown on the planet Earth.

"I heard about what you did at Lee Talbot's party," she began directly.

"Oh . . . ?" Jeff replied, gazing into the stone floor and mulling over the costly escapade. A moment later he looked up at Wendy and, a smile spreading across his face, said, "It was great. It was worth it. You should have been there."

"You know why I was crying that day in here?"

"Because of him: Lee."

"No. My parents are getting divorced. I found out the night before."

"Oh . . . ? Oh, God. Divorced—"

"It's okay. Well, it's *not* okay. But *I'm* okay now. Only, we're moving, my mom and me, to a whole new state."

"Not Iowa by any chance?"

"Connecticut."

"Oh. I've been there."

"It's real New Englandy."

For quite a while neither of them said anything.

"My parents are sending me to this special punishment school next year," Jeff finally broke the silence.

All of a sudden, he felt her incredibly warm body press against him. His spine touched the wall as her lips touched his, soft and slippery, her hair like flowers. Jeff's heart seemed to fly up to his throat, then out of his very body.

"Hey," he said breathlessly when she pulled away, "do you want to run away with me and move to Iowa?"

"What's in Iowa?"

"Oh, it's great there, Wendy," Jeff told her, taking her hand and leading her out of the mummy's tomb. "They've got corn, soybeans, oats. The state flower is the wild rose. I'm learning the state song now. Herbert Hoover was born there."

BETH NUGENT
CITY OF BOYS
FROM THE NORTH AMERICAN REVIEW

ᔑ

MY LITTLE SWEETHEART, SHE SAYS, bringing her face close enough
for me to see the fine net of lines that carves her skin into a
weathered stone, you love me, don't you, little sweetheart,
little lamb?

Whether or not she listens any more, I am not sure, but I
always answer yes, yes, I always say, yes, I love you.

She is my mother, my father, my sister, brother, cousin,
lover; she is everything I ever thought any one person needed
in the world. She is everything but a boy.

—Boys, she tells me. Boys will only break you.

I know this. I watch them on the street corners, huddled
under their puddles of blue smoke. They are as nervous as
insects, always some part of their bodies in useless agitated
motion, a foot tapping, a jaw clenching, a finger drawing
circles against a thigh, eyes in restless, programmed movement,
from breasts to face to legs to breasts. They are never still, and
they twitch and jump when I walk by, but still I want them. I
want them in the back seats of their cars, I want them under
the bridge where the river meets the rocks in a slick slide of
stone, I want them in the back rows of theaters and under the
bushes and benches in the park.

241

—Boys, she says, don't think about boys. Boys would
only make you do things you don't know how to do and things
you'd never want to do if you knew what they were. I know,
she says, I know plenty about boys.

She is everything to me. She is not my mother, although I
have allowed myself the luxury of sometimes believing myself
her child. My mother is in Fairborn, Ohio, where she waits
with my father for me to come home and marry a boy and
become the woman into whom she still believes it is not too
late for me to grow. Fairborn is a city full of boys and parking
meters and the Air Force, but most of all it is a city full of my
mother and in my mind she looms over it like a cloud of
radioactive dust. If I return it will be to her. She is not why I
left, she is not why I am here; she is just one thing I left, like
all the things that trail behind us when we go from place to
place, from birth to birth and from becoming to becoming. She
is just another breadcrumb, just another mother in the long
series of mothers that let you go to become the women you
have to become. But you are always coming back to them.

Where I live now is also a city full of boys, and coming
here I passed through hundreds of cities and they were all full
of boys.

—Boys, she tells me, are uninteresting, and when they
grow up, they become men and become even more uninteresting.

I know this too. I see how boys spend their days, either
standing around or playing basketball or engaged in irritating
persistent harangue, and I can draw my own conclusions as to
what they talk about and as to the heights of which they are
capable and I see what they do all day, but still I want them.

The one time I pretended she was a boy, she knew it
because I closed my eyes and I never close my eyes, and I
imagined it was a boy there doing that, soft tongue between my
thighs, and when I came she slapped me hard.

—I'm not a boy, she said, just you remember that. You
know who I am and just remember that I love you and no boy
could ever love you like I do.

Probably she is right. What boy could love with her slipping concentration; probably no boy could ever achieve what

she lets go with every day that comes between us, what she has lost in her long history of love.

What I do sometimes is slip out under her absent gaze. —Where are you going, what are you going to do, she says, and wallowing in the luxury of thinking myself a child, I answer Nowhere, nothing. In their pure undirected intoxicating meaninglessness, our conversations carry more significance than either of us is strong enough to bear, together or alone, and I drag it out into the streets today, a long weight trailing behind me, as I look for boys.

Today, I tell myself, is a perfect day for losing things, love and innocence, illusions and expectations; it is a day through which I will walk and walk until I find the perfect boy.

Where we live, on the upper west side, the streets are full of Puerto Rican men watching women. Carefully they examine each woman that walks by, carefully they hold her with their eyes, as if they are somehow responsible for her continued existence on the street. Not a woman goes by untouched by the long leash of their looks.

Oh, they say, Mira Mira sssssssssssss. In their eyes are all the women they have watched walk by and cook and comb their black hair; all the women they have touched with their hands, and all the women they have known live in their eyes and gleam out from within the dark. Their eyes are made only to see women on the streets.

Where we live, on West 83rd and Amsterdam, there are roaches and rats, but nothing matters as long as we're together, we say valiantly, longingly. Nothing matters, I say, stomping a roach and nothing matters, she agrees, her eyes on a low-slung rat sidling by in the long hallway toward the little garbage room across from the door to our apartment. I told the super once that if he kept the garbage out on the street, perhaps the building would be less a home for vermin.—What's vermin, he wanted to know.—Vermin, I told him, is rats and roaches and huge black beetles scrabbling at the base of the toilet when you turn on the light at night. Vermin is all the noises at night, all the clicking and scratching and scurrying through the darkness.—No rats, he said, maybe a mouse or two, and maybe every now and then you'll see your roach eggs, but I keep this place clean. Together we watched as a big brown-shelled roach tried to creep past us on the wall. Neither of us moved to kill it, but when it stopped and waved its antennae, he brought his big fist down in a hard slam against the wall. He didn't look at the dead roach, but I could hardly take my eyes off it, perfectly flattened as though it had been steamrolled against the side of his palm.—Maybe a roach here and there, he said, flicking the roach onto the floor without looking at it, but I keep this place clean. Maybe if you had a man around the house, he said, trying to look past me into the apartment, you wouldn't have so much trouble with vermins.

I pretended not to understand what he meant and backed into the room. Rent control is not going to last forever in New York, and when it goes and all the Puerto Ricans have had to move to the Bronx, we will have to find jobs or hit the streets, but as long as we're together, as long as we have each other. —We'll always have each other, won't we, she says, lighting a cigarette and checking to see how many are left in her pack.

—Yes, I always say, wondering if she's listening or just lost in a cigarette count. You'll always have me, I say. Unless, I think, unless you leave me, or unless I grow up to become the woman my mother still thinks is possible.

Today is a day full of boys. They are everywhere, and I watch each of them, boys on motorcycles, in cars, on bicycles, leaning against walls, walking, to see which of them in this city of boys is mine.

I am not so young and she is not so old, but rent control is not going to last forever, and someday I will be a woman. She wants, I tell myself, nothing more than me. Sometimes I think she must have been my mother, the way she loves me, but when I asked her if she was ever my mother, she touched my narrow breasts and said, Would your mother do that, and ran her tongue over my nipple and said, Or that. Would your mother know what you want, Sweetheart? I'm not your mother, she said, I stole you from a mattress downtown, just around the corner where all the winos lie around in piss and wine and call for help and nobody listens. I saved you from that, she says, but I remember too clearly the trip out here, in the middle of a car full of people full of drugs, most of them, and I remember how she found me standing just outside the porn theater on 98th and Broadway and she slipped me right from under the gaze of about four hundred curious Puerto Ricans. —Does your mother know where you are? she said. I laughed and said, My mother knows all she needs to know, and she said, Come home with me, I have somebody I want you to meet. When she brought me home, she said to a big man who lay on the couch watching television, Tito, this is Princess Grace, and Tito raised his heavy head from the end of the couch and said, She don't look like no princess to me.

I never thought much of Tito, and she never let him touch me, even though our apartment is only one room, and he was sick with wanting it from me. At night after they'd done it just about as many times as anyone could, she crept over to me on little cat feet and whispered into my ear, Sweetheart you are my only one. As Tito slugged and snored his way through the nights, we'd do it at least one more time than they had, and she would sigh and say, Little sweetheart, you're the one I wanted all the time, even through all those boys and girls that loved me it was always you that I was looking for, you that I always wanted.

This is the kind of talk that kills me, this is the kind of talk that won me, in addition to the fact that she took me in from the hard streets full of boys and taxicabs and cops and everywhere I looked the hard eyes of innocence turned.

What it felt like with her that first time was my mother come back and curled up inside me, giving birth, so that I came out of her at the exact same second that I moved closest into her center.

The long car pulls up to the sidewalk and I bend to see if it has boys in it. It is full of them, so I say,

—Hey, can I have a ride.

—Hey, they say, Hey, the lady wants a ride. Where to, they ask.

—Oh, I say, wherever.

I look to see where they are heading;—Uptown, I say and the door swings open and I slide in. The oldest boy is probably sixteen and just got his driver's license and is driving his mother's car, a big Buick, or Chevrolet, or Monte Carlo, a mother's car. Each of the boys is different, but they are all exactly alike in the way that boys are, and right away I find the one I want. He's the one who does not look at me, and he's the oldest, only a couple of years younger than me, and it is his mother's car we are in.

—How about a party, they say, we know a good party uptown.

—Let's just see, I say, let's just ride uptown and see.

Sometimes I wake up to see her leaning on her thin knees against the wall that is stripped down to expose the rough brick beneath the plaster. I dream that she prays to keep me, but I am afraid that she prays for something else, a beginning or an end, or something I don't know about. She came to bed once and laid her face against my breast and I felt the imprint of the brick on the tender skin of her forehead.

She herself is not particularly religious, although the apartment is littered with the scraps of saints—holy relics of one sort or another; a strand of hair from the Christ child, a bit of fingernail from Paul, a shred of the Virgin's robe. They are left over from Tito, who collected holy relics the way some people collect lucky pennies or matchbooks, as some kind of hedge against some inarticulated sense of disaster. They are just clutter here, though, in this small apartment where we live and I suggested to her once that we throw them out. She picked up a piece of dried weed from Gethsemane and said, I don't think they're ours to throw out. Tito found them and if we got rid of them, who knows what might happen to Tito. Maybe they work is what I mean, she said; I don't think it's spiritually economic to be a skeptic about absolutely everything.

When Tito left, his relics abandoned for some new hope, she was depressed for a day or two, but said that it was really the best for everybody, especially for the two of us, the single reality to which our lives have been refined. Tito said he was getting sick of watching two dykes moon over each other all the time, though I think he was just angry because she wouldn't let him touch me. I was all for it, I wanted him to touch me. That's what I came to this city for, to have someone like Tito touch me, someone to whom touching is all the reality of being, someone who doesn't do it in basements and think he has to marry you, someone who does it and doesn't think about the glory of love. But she wouldn't have it; she said if he ever touched me, she would send me back to the 98th Street porn theater and let the Puerto Ricans make refried beans out of me, and as for Tito, he could go back to Rosa, his wife in Queens, and go back to work lugging papers for the *Daily News* and ride the subway every day and go home and listen to Rosa talk on the telephone all night, instead of hanging out on street corners and playing cards wth the men outside the schoolyard. Because, she said, because she was paying the rent, and as long as rent control lasted in New York she would continue to pay the rent and she could live quite happily and satisfactorily by herself until she found the right sort of roommate; one, she said, fingering the shiny satin of Tito's shirt, who paid the rent.

So Tito kept his distance and kept us both sick with his desire and when she finally stopped sleeping with him on the bed and joined me on the mattress on the floor, even Tito could see that it wasn't going to be long before he would have to shift himself to the floor. To save himself from that he said one day that he guessed he was something of a fifth wheel around the joint, huh, and he'd found a nice Puerto Rican family that needed a man around the house and he guessed he'd move in with them. I think he was just covering for himself, though, because one day when she was out buying cigarettes, he roused himself from the couch and away from the television and said to me, You know, she was married before, you know.

—I know that, I said, I know all about that. How she pays the rent is with alimony money that still comes in from her marriage, and I know all about that and Tito wasn't telling me anything that I didn't know, so I looked back at the magazine I was reading and waited for him to go back to the television.

He kept looking at me, so I got up to look out the

window to see if I could see her coming back and if she had anything for me.

—What I'm trying to say, he said, What I'm trying to tell you, is that you're not the only one, not you. I was the only one once too, the one she wanted all those years; I was the one before you and you're just the one before someone else.

I could see her rounding the corner from 83rd and Broadway and could see that she had something in a bag, doughnuts or something, for me. I said nothing but looked out the window and counted her steps toward our building. She was reeling slightly, and leaning toward the wall, so I guessed that she must have had a few drinks in the bar where she always buys her cigarettes. When I could hear her key turning in the lock to the street door, I went to open our door for her and Tito grabbed me by the arm and said, Listen, you just listen. Nobody is ever the only one for nobody, don't kid yourself.

I pulled away and opened the door for her and she came in, cold skin and wet, and I put my face in her hair and breathed in the smell of gin and cigarettes and all the meaning of my life.

The next day Tito left, but he didn't go far, because I still see him hanging out on street corners. Now all the women he has known are in his eyes, but mostly there is her, and when he looks at me, I cannot bear to see her, lost in the dark there. Whenever I pass him, I always say

—Hey, Tiiiiiiito, Mira Mira, huh? and all his friends laugh, while Tito tries to look as though this is something he's planned himself, as though he has somehow elicited this remark from me.

One day I suppose Tito will use the key he forgot to leave behind to sneak in and cover me with his flagging desire, his fading regrets, and his disappointments, and she will move on, away from me; but rent control will not last forever in New York, and I cannot think ahead to the beginnings and the ends for which she prays.

The boys in the car lean against one another and leer and twitch like tortured insects and exchange glances that they think are far too subtle for me to understand, but I've come too far looking for too much to miss any of it. We drive too fast up Riverside, so that it's no time before the nice neighborhoods become slums full of women in windows and bright clothing slung over fire escapes, and salsa music laid over the thick city air like a layer of air all itself. Like the sound of crickets threading through Ohio summer nights, it sets the terms for everything.

—So, one of them says to me, so where are you going, anyways.

—Well, I say, Well. I was thinking about going to the Bronx Botanical Gardens. The Bronx Botanical Gardens is no place I'd ever really want to go, but I feel that it's important to maintain, at least in their eyes, some illusion of destination. If I were a bit more sure of myself, I'd suggest that we take the ferry over to Staten Island and do it in the park there. Then I could think of her. When we went to Staten Island, it was cold and gray and windy; we got there and realized that there was nothing we wanted to see, that being in Staten Island was really not all that different from being in New York.—Or anywhere, she said, looking down a street into a corridor of rundown clothing stores and insurance offices. It was Sunday, so everything was closed up tight and no one was on the streets. Finally we found a coffee shop near the station, where we drank cokes and coffee and she smoked cigarettes while we waited for the boat to come in.

Lezzes, the counter man said to another man sitting at the counter eating a doughnut. What do you want to bet they're lezzes?

The man eating the doughnut turned and looked us over and said

—They're not so hot anyways, no big waste.

She smiled and held her hand to my face for a second; the smoke from the cigarette she held drifted past my eyes into my hair.

—What a moment, she said, to remember.

On the way back I watched the wind whip her face all out of any shape I knew, and when I caught the eyes of some boys on the ferry, she said, not looking at me, not taking her eyes off the concrete ripples of the robe at the feet of the Statue of

Liberty just on our left, What you do is your own business, but don't expect me to love you forever if you do things like this. I'm not, she said, turning to look me full in the face, your mother, you know. All I am is your lover and nothing lasts forever.

When we got off the ferry, I said, I don't expect you to love me forever, and she said I was being promiscuous and quarrelsome, and she lit a cigarette as she walked down into the subway station. I watched her as she walked and it seemed to me to be the first time I had ever seen her back walking away from me, trailing a long blue string of smoke.

Something is going on with the boys, something has changed in the set of their faces, the way they hold their cigarettes, the way they nudge each other. Something changes when the light begins to fade and one of them says to me

—We have a clubhouse uptown, want to come there with us?

—What kind of club, I ask, what do you do there?

—We drink whiskey, they say, and take drugs and watch television.

My boy, the one I have picked out of this whole city of boys stares out the window, chewing at a toothpick he's got wedged somewhere in the depths of his jaw, and runs his finger over the slick plastic of the steering wheel. I can tell by his refusal to ask that he wants me to come.

This, I suppose, is how to get to the center of boys, to go to their club. Boys are like pack creatures, and they always form clubs; it's as though they cannot help themselves. It's the single law of human nature that I have observed, in my limited exposure to the world, that plays and plays and replays itself out with simple mindless consistency: where there are boys there are clubs, and anywhere there is a club it is bound to be full of boys, looking for the good times to be had just by being boys.

—Can I join? I ask. This is what I can take back to her, cigarettes and a boy's club; this will keep her for me forever, that I have gone to the center of boys and have come back a woman and I have come back to her.

—Well, they say and smirk and grin and itch at themselves, Well, there's an initiation.

The oldest of the boys is younger than me, and yet like boys everywhere, they think that I don't know nearly so much as they do, as if being a woman somehow short-circuits my capacity for input. They think they have a language that only boys can understand, but understanding their language is the key to my success, so I say, I will not fuck you all, separately or together.

My boy looks over at me and permits himself a cool half smile and I am irritated that he now holds me in higher regard because I can speak a language that any idiot could learn.

Between us there are no small moments; we do not speak at all or we speak everything. Heat bills and toothpaste and dinner and all the dailiness of living are given no language in our time together.

I realize that this kind of intensity cannot be sustained over a long period of time and that every small absence in our days signals an end between us. She tells me that I must never leave her, but what I know is that some day she will leave me with a fistful of marriage money to pay the rent as long as rent control lasts in New York, and I will see her wandering down the streets, see her in the arms of another, and I say to her sometimes late at night when she blows smoke rings at my breasts, Don't leave me, don't ever ever ever leave me.

—Life, she always says to me, is one long leavetaking. Don't kid yourself, she says, Kid, and laughs.—Anyways, you are my little sweetheart, and how could I ever leave you and how could I leave this—soft touch on my skin—and this, and this.

She knows this kills me every time.

Their clubhouse is dirty and disorganized and everywhere there are mattresses and empty bottles and bags from McDonald's, and skittering through this mess are more roaches than I thought could exist in a single place, more roaches than there are boys in this city, more roaches than there are moments of love in this world.

The boys walk importantly in: This is their club, they are
New York City boys and they take drugs and they have a club
and I watch as they scatter around and sit in chairs and on
mattresses and flip on the television. I hang back in the doorway and I reach out to snag the corner of the jacket my boy is
wearing. He turns and I say

—How about some air.

—Let me just get high first, he says, and he walks over to
a chair and sits down and pulls out his works and cooks up his
dope and ties up his arm and spends a good two minutes
searching for a vein to pop.

All over his hands and arms and probably his legs and feet
and stomach are signs of collapse and ruin, as if his body has
been created for a single purpose and he has spent a busy and
productive life systematically mining it for good places to fix.

I watch him do this while the other boys do their dope or
roll their joints or pop their pills and he offers me some; I say
no, I'd rather keep a clear head and how about some air.

I don't want him to hit a nod before any of it's even
happened, but this is my experience with junkies, that they exit
right out of every situation before it's even become a situation.

—Let's take the car, he says.

You are my sweetheart, she says, and if you leave me, you
will spend all your life coming back to me. With her tongue
and her words and the quiet movement of her hand over my
skin, she has drawn for me all the limits of my life and of my
love. It is the one love that has created me and will contain me
and if I left her I'd be lonely, and I'd rather sleep in the streets
with her hand between my legs forever than be lonely.

In the car, the boy slides his hand between my legs and
then puts it on the steering wheel. A chill in the air, empty
streets, and it's late. Every second takes me further into the
night away from her; every second brings me home. We drive
to Inwood Park and climb the fence, so that we are only a few
feet away from the Hudson.

—This is nothing like Ohio, I say to him, and he lights a
cigarette and says

—Where's Ohio.

—Don't you go to school? I ask him; Don't you have to take geography?

—I know what I need to know, he says, and reaches over to unbutton my blouse. The thing about junkies is that they know they don't have much time, and the thing about boys is that they know how not to waste it.

—This is very romantic, I say, as his fingers hit my nipples like a piece of ice; Do you come here often?

What I like about this boy is that he just puts it right in. He just puts it in as though he does this all the time, as though he doesn't usually have to slide it through his fingers or in between his friends' rough lips; he just puts it in and comes like wet soap shooting out of a fist and this is what I wanted. This is what I wanted and I look at the Hudson rolling by over his shoulder; this is what I wanted but all I think about is the way it is with us; this is what I wanted but all I see is her face floating down the river, her eyes like pieces of moonlight caught in the water.

What I think is true doesn't matter any more; what I think is false doesn't matter any more. What I think at all doesn't matter any more because there is only her; like an image laid over my mind, she is superimposed on every thought I have. She sits by the window and looks out onto West 83rd Street as if she is waiting for something, waiting for rent control to end, or waiting for something else to begin. She sits by the window waiting for something and pulls a long string through her fingers. In the light from the window, I can see each of the bones in her hand; white and exposed, they make a delicate pattern that fades into the flesh and bone of her wrist.

—Don't ever change, I say to her. Don't ever ever change. She smiles and lets the thin string dangle from her hand.

—Nothing ever stays the same, she says. You're old enough to know that, aren't you, little sweetheart? Permanence, she says, is nothing more than a desire for things to stay the same.

I know this.

*   *   *

—Life is hard for me, the boy says. What am I going to do with my life? I just hang around all day or drive my mother's car. Life is so hard. Everything will always be the same for me here in this city; it's going to eat me up and spit me out and I might as well have never been. He looks poetically out over the river.

—I wanted a boy, I say, not a poet.

—I'm not a poet, he says, I'm just a junkie, and you're nothing but a slut. You can get yourself home tonight.

I say nothing and watch the Hudson roll by.

—I'm sorry, he says. So what. So I'm a junkie and you're a slut, so what. Nothing ever changes. Besides, he says, my teacher wants me to be a track star because I can run faster than anyone else in gym class. That's what he says.

—Well, that sounds like a promising career, I say, although I can imagine the gym teacher's cock pressing against his baggy sweats as he stares at my boy and suggests after-school workouts. Why don't you do that?

—I'd have to give up smoking, he says, and dope.

Together we watch the Hudson roll by and finally he says

—Well, it's about time I was getting my mother's car home.

—This is it? I ask him.

—What were you expecting? he says, I'm only a junkie. In two years I probably won't even be able to get it up any more.

—Look, I say, coming in and walking over to where she sits by the window. Look, I am a marked woman. There is blood between my legs and it isn't yours.

She looks at me, then looks back at what she was doing before I came in, blowing smoke rings that flatten against the dirty window.

—Did you bring me some cigarettes, she says, putting hers out in the ashtray that rests on the windowsill.

—A marked woman, I say. Can't you see the blood?

—I can't see anything, she says, and I won't look until I have a cigarette. I give her the cigarettes I bought earlier. Even in the midst of becoming a woman, I have remembered the small things that please her. She lights one and inhales the smoke, then lets it slowly out through her nose and her mouth at the same time. She knows this kills me.

—Don't you see it? I ask.

—I don't see anything, she says, I don't see why you had to do this.

She gets up and says, I'm going to bed now. I've been up all day and all night and I'm tired and I want to go to sleep before the sun comes up.

—I am a marked woman, I say, lying beside her, Don't you feel it?

—I don't feel anything, she says, but she holds me, and together we wait patiently for the light. She is everything to me. In the stiff morning before the full gloom of city light falls on us, I turn to her face full of shadows.

—I am a marked woman, I say, I am.

—Quiet, she says, and puts her dark hand gently over my mouth then moves it over my throat onto the rise of my chest. Across town, no one notices this, nothing is changed anywhere when she does this.

—Quiet, she says. She presses her hand against my heart and touches her face to mine and takes me with her into the motherless turning night. All moments stop here, this is the first and the last, and the only flesh is hers, the only touch her hand. Nothing else is, and together we turn under the stroke of the moon and the hiss of the stars and she is everything I will become and together we become every memory that has ever been known.

ILENE RAYMOND
TAKING A CHANCE ON JACK

FROM MADEMOISELLE

ം

NINA WALKS THE THREE BLOCKS from the subway to her house, thinking of Jack. All day long, as she sits checking copy for the Federal Register, she deliberately blocks Jack from her mind. But the second she shuts her office door behind her, says good-night to Merrilee and starts down the twelve flights of stairs, a step she takes to keep fat from collecting on her thighs, Jack pops into her mind. Even after six years of marriage he still has the power to wipe everything else from the inside of her head and leave her with nothing but him.

If Jack knew how much time she spent thinking about him, he would be surprised. He would tell her to stop, that things would improve on their own with time. Yet ever since Jack was fired from his public relations firm a year ago, all he does is sit around the house tending his plants and fish. On occasion he drops a résumé into the mail. She wonders if he ever means to work again. All of Nina's girlfriends tell her that she is crazy to put up with such behavior, but she defends Jack, tells them he is looking for a job and that a job is hard to find.

"Not *that* hard," says Amelia. Nina has lunch with Amelia twice a week at Woodard & Lothrop. They have had lunch together on Tuesdays and Fridays for three years. For two-and-a-half years, Amelia has dominated the conversation. She is thirty years old and has been married three times. Her first husband was her high-school math teacher. Her second was a law student named Craig who dropped out of law school after the first year to play minor-league softball. They never fought. Even when she got angry with him, he refused to argue. If Amelia was particularly furious, she would walk into the kitchen and punch thumbtacks into the pasteboard wall. When they left their apartment, the wall looked like a bad case of chicken pox. Amelia said, "All marriages leave scars."

Amelia's third marriage is on its fifth month, and she is still in bliss. Nina is happy for her friend, but has learned to weigh her advice.

"Practice makes perfect," Amelia tells her, stern.

"You've got to shop around to get the right fit," Amelia instructs.

Nina lets herself into the apartment. Jack is singing to the transistor radio propped against the kitchen window. He is making Chinese food. On Thursday nights he watches a Chinese cooking class on public TV and on Friday nights he always practices the newest lesson. Since he has been unemployed, Jack has developed such hobbies. A tankful of tropical fish—kissing fish and electric elephant fish—swim circles in their living room. African violets line the bookshelves beneath eerie purple light. He has reorganized the kitchen, color coding the cabinets for dishes, pots, utensils. Nina can't find anything in her own kitchen anymore, but she thinks that if it keeps Jack busy and makes him feel useful, it's okay with her.

"Sweetie pie," Jack calls from the kitchen. Oil sizzles in the wok, his knife jumps along the cutting board. She walks in and kisses him on the back of his neck.

"How was your day?" he asks.

"Slow." She knew he would ask this question. He has asked this question for 365 days now. She would like to change the subject, to have him talk about himself, to tell her what he is feeling. It bothers her that he doesn't seem to mind that he hasn't found a job in a year. His unemployment checks ran out six months ago and her own salary as an editorial assistant is stretched far too thin. They gave up movies in March; her lunches with Amelia are next. Amelia and Timmy, her new husband, asked them to go skiing over Christmas, but the car payments are overdue. Not to mention their dwindling bank account. Yet she worries about putting too much pressure on Jack.

Jack rubs two jalapeño peppers with thumb and index finger, springing tiny golden coins from the red casing. She studies him. His skin is rosy. He has lost weight. He stirs broccoli and snow peas into the oil, then lifts the lid on the pot of steaming brown rice. Setting dishes on the table, he arranges chopsticks and wineglasses. He reminds her of the housewives in the soap commercials. He has become the perfect hausfrau. He shops every day.

She has a vision of him carting a basket on his arm filled with loaves of crusty brown breads and creamy cheeses. The liquor store where he buys wine is on the corner. The tropical fish shop is two blocks away. There is a florist for plant fertilizer on Wisconsin Avenue. Jack has become the nurturer, while she is just another fish or plant waiting to be fed. She realizes that in a year Jack has not had the need to go beyond the four-block radius of their house. She watches him closely, to see if she can spot any changes. He looks up from his set table and grins.

"Let's eat," he says.

After Jack clears the table, she sits in the living room, reading the *Post*, while he does the dishes. At lunch Amelia had said, "You're a young woman. You deserve more than that." When they finished eating their salads, Amelia walked Nina down to the lingerie department and made her select three teddy outfits of filmy black lace. In the dressing room she inspected Nina intently, making her model them front and back, selecting the one that cut the highest across her thighs and the lowest across her breasts.

"Open his eyes with that, I'll bet," Amelia said, waving her credit card at the counter. Nina blushed as the saleswoman handed her the package, and Amelia laughed. After her second divorce, Amelia offered Nina her wardrobe of negligees from her first and second marriages, saying that they carried too many memories. She spilled them from a cardboard box: red lace, peach silk, pale blue net with ivory straps. Nina thanked her but didn't accept them. There was something wrong, she thought, about making love or sleeping or brushing your teeth in someone else's nightgown. It was too intimate, too exposed. She and Jack haven't made love in at least three months. They tried for a while, but it just wasn't right between them.

Amelia talks in detail about positions and postures. She tells Nina how she and Tim have made love at least three times a day since the first day they met in Kansas City. They met in the Hyatt Regency hotel lobby, when Amelia was working as a troubleshooter for the Internal Revenue Service. Tim was separated then. Amelia wasn't. Tim has a four-year-old daughter. The little girl is coming to spend next summer with them. The thought makes Amelia nervous.

"I don't know how to act around children," she says. "It's not like I'm a mother, you know."

"Amelia's little stepdaughter is coming to visit," Nina calls to the kitchen. She thinks it's good therapy for Jack to hear about the world. She gets no reply. The water is running in the sink. She walks to the kitchen doorway, still holding the newspaper.

"Amelia says that she and Tim are happy. She thinks this is the real thing." Still no answer. Jack is over the sink, arms up to the elbows in bubbles. She tiptoes behind him, meaning to take him by surprise, but then sees that his face is wet. He is crying, standing there in the kitchen, tears running down his face. He turns to look at her and she sees his eyes are red and swollen. The radio plays a Rolling Stones song and Nina is possessed by a need to run. She doesn't want to think about Jack anymore.

Pushing the teddy set into her arms, Amelia had said, "You have to keep men on their toes, otherwise they get bored."

Nina turns and goes out the front door, leaving Jack behind.

A wind blows across Twenty-fifth Street, stirring trash and leaves. Nina walks toward Pennsylvania Avenue, at first not certain where she is headed. She passes old men on stoops, sharing a bottle of wine in a paper bag, spitting and smoking. She walks across the avenue and into a corner bar. The first person she spots is Leon, an editor from work. He is sitting across a table from a busty blonde with large violet eyes and pink lips. Leon is married with four children and when Nina walks in he bends his head, then changes his mind, looks up, and smiles right at her.

"Nina," he says. He holds out his hand. "Come join us." He doesn't introduce the woman. Nina smiles at him, hoping her smile says, I won't give you away, and shakes her head no.

"I'm going to sit at the bar," she says. She orders a vodka tonic, then walks to the pay phone and puts two dimes in the slot. Amelia answers on the fifth ring.

"I'll be right there, honey," Amelia says. Her breathing is hurried, off. "I can't say I'm surprised."

Nina returns to the bar to wait for Amelia. Her heart beats hard behind her chest wall. She wants to call Jack, but won't give in. It's time for him to stand on his own feet, she thinks. She finishes her drink and orders another. She's tired of supporting him. Her anger expands into a bubble, painful to touch.

As she is about to order her third vodka, a young man, no more than twenty-two or twenty-three years of age, sits down on the barstool beside her. He lifts three olives from a beaker behind the counter and lines them in a row along the bar.

Nina watches him. He must have been desperate to pick her from among all the obviously single young women at the bar. That isn't positive thinking, though. Amelia said positive thinking was essential. It brought you out of yourself. Amelia said that if you wanted to be attractive to men, you should walk around thinking sexy thoughts. It made you glow. She had read that in a magazine. They taught it to airline stewardesses. Nina shuts her eyes. All she can see is Jack.

"Guess which one had an unhappy childhood," the young man next to her says. Nina turns. He points to the olives. "Okay," he says, when he receives no answer, "let's talk music." Slipping a cigarette from Nina's pack on the bar, he slides it between his fingers. "Don't you find Elvis Costello's voice the perfect expression of rage in our time?" He has a cleft in his chin and a dimple in his left cheek when he smiles. Nina ignores him. He stops smiling.

"Somedays I think I'm turning into my mother." He trades her cigarette for a cocktail swizzler. "Too neurotic, Sam," he admonishes himself. He studies the swizzler, then leans toward Nina. "The survival shelter is in the basement," he says. "We don't have to touch or anything."

Nina searches the bar. Amelia is still not there. Leon is kissing the blonde's fingernails one by one. On his desk at work sits a photograph of his four little girls: Katy, Christine, Lilli and Suzanne. His wife, Connie, gave the office a Halloween party last year, wearing her old Girl Scout uniform from fifth grade, which still fit. Leon came as a diver from the Chappaquiddick Bridge, wearing goggles and flippers and a button that read: "I'm Dead for Ted." The little girls paraded in Connie's old prom gowns and high heels. They ran up and down the stairs giggling at the adults in Hawaiian grass skirts and false noses. "I feel my life passing before my eyes," Connie confessed to Nina as they watched the pale pink and yellow skirts of her dresses flutter through the bars of the banister.

Nina isn't ready to go home. She wants to wait for Amelia. But the young man seems unbalanced, a little hysterical, ready to go off, and she's not in the mood to take on another set of problems. Opening her pocketbook, she motions to the bartender for her check.

"Okay," the young man sighs. "I'll tell you." He points the swizzle stick at the middle olive. "If you guessed olive number two, you were wrong. He's off to law school. Straight A's. Well adjusted." Nina concentrates on counting change for her drinks. She leaves a tip. The young man doesn't stop talking.

"Number one, now," he continues. "She's an M.B.A. Harvard, of course. Procter & Gamble, Lever Brothers, they all want her." He moves his attention from the olives to Nina's eyes, then back to the olives. Even she has to admit: He has persistence. And a certain charm.

"Not impressed by money," he decides of Nina, talking to the bar. She shrugs her coat onto her shoulders. "Very healthy. Not to mention unusual."

For the last time, Nina looks for Amelia. She lifts up her pocketbook. The young man abandons the olives and watches her. His eyes are a dark green. Amelia's men were always dark and sensual. They approached her in shadowed hotel lobbies and crowded dining rooms, with offers of candlelit dinners and unlimited expense accounts. Temptations were everywhere, Amelia claimed, if you knew where to look for them. Her lovers brought her perfumes bearing names of famous designers and sent flowers from exotic cities. She went out one night of her six-year marriage and got an olive nut. Nina begins to laugh. She laughs until even Sam, who she is certain is crazy, starts to look nervous. Removing her coat, she drops her pocketbook to the floor and orders a Scotch. A fresh cigarette in hand, she turns to Sam.

"It's number three, right?" she asks.

Sam doesn't respond at first. Then he grins. The dimple resurfaces. "Nope," he replies. "It's olive number four. A very dark horse." He plucks olive number four from the top of the olive beaker, then sweeps the well-educated olives over the counter to the floor.

"Nothing personal," he says to Nina and leans toward her. "But could I pay for that drink?"

Over the past hour and a half, Sam has told Nina that he once played piccolo with the Juilliard String Quartet, that he is a vegetarian by birth and that he is studying for his C.P.A. exam. She decides to believe the last and forgive the rest. After her second Scotch, she excuses herself and walks to the pay phone, where she dials Amelia's number. It rings four times before Nina hangs up.

Sam is folding a piece of newspaper left on the bar into a paper hat. "No one wears hats anymore," he complains as Nina sits down. He pinches the peak into a sharp point. "My father wears a hat every day to work," he says. He works closely and carefully, reminding Nina of a small child. He considers the paper hat before him, thoughtful.

"My father *is* a hat," he muses. "A Stetson in the fast lane." He shoots a quick grin at Nina.

Nina is watching, but not listening. She is wondering why she didn't want Amelia to answer the phone.

"God, women are hard these days," Sam says. He stops working with the hat and looks at Nina. "One bad joke and"—he snaps his fingers before her eyes—"a guy doesn't stand a chance."

Nina smiles at him. "Not true," she says. She reaches into her pocket and pulls out a tissue. Feathering the tissue into shredded ribbons, she fastens it to the brim of the paper hat. Once you could tell a lot about a person by signals like hats, she thinks: Firemen wore red helmets, businessmen wore fedoras. Or rings: Women and men wore wedding bands and went home with their husbands and wives. She considers Amelia and Leon. She does not think of Jack. And then it hits her: For the first time in a year, she is not discussing Amelia's love life; she is not thinking about Jack's unemployment. It is like a vacation.

"All of Paris is clamoring for my designs," Sam whispers into Nina's ear. "But I refuse to do ready-to-wear." He lowers the hat onto Nina's head, considers the fit, then tilts the hat until the feather of tissue obscures her vision. "You've got to take certain risks to get ahead of the pack," he says, and putting his hand at her waist, leads her to the dance floor where other couples waltz to the jukebox that plays by the stairs. Amelia is probably caught on the Metro. Or maybe she isn't coming at all. Nina leans into Sam's arms, letting him support her weight.

The lights are dim. Leon passes and throws Nina a sly, all-knowing look. Touché, Leon, Nina whispers to herself. She doesn't care. Safe in Sam's embrace, she sways to the music. Sam is taller than Jack and to meet his height she dances on her toes. It makes her feel like a little girl. Under the camouflage of the hat, she shuts her eyes. A year and a half ago, before Jack lost his job, they talked about having a child. They were at Rehoboth Beach in July, and Jack, tanned and smelling of coconut oil, woke her from a catnap with kisses and said, "Let's tempt fate," but she shook her head no and refused to forget her diaphragm.

Amelia taught: "No babies. One, they ruin your legs forever, and two, you'll never get anyplace with a kid hanging around your neck like a stone."

Nina moves back in Sam's arms. His eyes glow. His lips are a minute away from a kiss. She leans in, reaching her face toward his.

An unfamiliar hand grasps Nina's shoulder. A stubby girl with large black eyes and a fat twist of braid cuts in. She regards Sam with obvious ownership. Sam shrugs and says, "Ticket to ride, miss?" The girl glides Sam to a dark corner in the back of the room.

A night on the town for my young friend, Nina thinks, standing on the dance floor alone. She sways to the music, staying with her own thoughts, trying to imagine what it would be like now if she had gotten pregnant. She rubs her stomach. She imagines a baby's fine hair, the new eyes surrendering to light. She feels the child borne from her body, turning her inside out. Crouching to the floor, she looks to see if the child is a boy or a girl, but finds only the paper hat, fallen from her head.

"Lady." A man who has been standing beside the bar since she first entered is at her side. "Lady, you drunk?"

Nina looks at the hat, then at the man. Tears block her vision. She accepts the man's extended hand and he leads her to the bar.

"Set her up, Frankie," the man says to the bartender. He regards Nina, then Sam across the room.

"There's lots of fish in the sea, dearie," he observes.

The woman who has been sitting beside him, in a three-piece suit and ragged fingernails, lets out a sharp laugh. "Good Lord," she says. "I don't know where you store those pearls, Clyde."

Nina stares into her drink. Alone, she calms. Amelia is definitely not on her way. Nina's reason for waiting is gone.

"You need a taxi?" Clyde calls to her as she heads for the door. Nina shakes her head no.

"I know my way home," she says, and steps into the night.

Outside, headlights strobe Pennsylvania Avenue, illuminating St. Stephen's Church. Taking off her high heels, she runs her shoes along the iron grillwork fence surrounding

Columbia Hospital. At Rehoboth Beach, she and Jack necked in an iron-grilled gazebo under a full orange moon. "Corny but sweet," Sam would say. "Très sensual," said Amelia.

In the living room, Jack is asleep on the sofa, one leg dropping off the edge to the carpet. The blue square of the television set lights the corner. The fish swim in clouds of bubbles and algae. The African violets shimmer beneath their purple halo. Jack's hands cup his crotch.

Moving as quietly as she is able, Nina perches beside her sleeping husband. She strokes his hair, holding her breath. He'd never know how close she'd come to kissing Sam. He wasn't ever going to know. Amelia either. Nina stares at his ruffled hair, his parted lips. She shuts her eyes and remembers the first night they made love, outside in a park near Philadelphia. The sky was gray-pink, and when they finished, Jack grabbed his chest and said, "Does your heart ever hurt?" and Nina, sure that those were Jack's last words, planted a kiss so immediate and unthinking and heartfelt onto his lips that later he said he was certain that she had brought him back to life.

Of course, Jack wasn't dying, but at that moment she had known that if he had died she might not have wanted to live and decided right then and there and without thinking at all that she was going to take a chance with Jack.

Nina puts her hand into her pocketbook and draws out the paper bag containing the teddy set. The rustling wakes Jack. He shifts. He smells like sleep.

"Would you look at this?" she asks him. He sits up and blinks, adjusting his eyes to the light.

BOB SHACOCHIS

REDEMPTION SONGS

FROM ESQUIRE

"These songs of freedom [are] all I ever had."
—Bob Marley

§

GLASFORD HAD BEEN ON EDGE NOW FOR DAYS.

"De whole friggin world on top of us, boy."

"Daht is so."

Glasford and Fish were in the Crabhole, a two-seat rum shop owned by Momma Smallhorne. In these two chairs they sat, an oil drum between them for a table, each man facing the open side of the shop, wisely studying the lights of Georgetown in the distance. A kerosene lamp burned beside their bottle on the drum.

"Ahnd de whole world friggin us too, ya know."

"Yes, daht's so." Fish's nature was to be agreeable.

Glasford did not speak with undue anger or bitterness. His words were confident, as if he had finally discovered the exact methodology he would use to overcome his oppression. Fish, as always a composed soul, a man hard at work on understanding the world, provided an ear blessed with patience.

"We is like rocks on de bottom of de sea," Glasford continued. Each word was carefully enunciated in a low, raw voice. "Cahnt move, cahnt go nowheres. Lissen, like rocks we is, ahnd everything else swimmin by."

"Yes, daht is so too," Fish replied matter-of-factly. "Look, gimme a smoke."

Glasford made a show of searching his pockets. "I have none," he said, and then called to Momma Smallhorne, "Momma, bring two cigarettes."

Momma rose up slowly from her cot behind the counter, troubled by arthritis. From a single carton of Marlboros on the empty shelves of her shop she took a pack and spent some time removing the cellophane with her crippled fingers.

"Save me a step, child."

Fish got up from his seat and gave her ten cents for the two cigarettes. When the fuss was over, Glasford spoke again. He spoke forcefully, although the only sounds to compete with him were the creaks of their overrepaired chairs, Momma's hard breathing in rhythm with the soft notes of the sea along the beach, an occasional car racing to Georgetown along the surfaced road behind the shop.

"We must do something," said Glasford. Then he was silent, waiting for Fish to agree. Fish smoked his cigarette, puff after puff, enjoying it.

Finally Fish looked around. "Momma, bring de dominoes," he said.

"No, Fish. I tellin you, mahn, no dominoes tonight. We must do something."

"What cahn fellahs like us do?" Fish asked. Glasford frowned into the night, his face beyond the cast of the lamp. The man's insistence had teased out Fish's curiosity. There had been similar conversations between them ever since Glasford had returned from the States a few weeks ago. But now, somehow, tonight, Glasford was creating a sense of movement, a line of potential. "What cahn we do?" Fish repeated.

"Pray, now ahnd always," Momma Smallhorne croaked. She had started out on the journey to bring them the box of dominoes.

"Momma, be quiet," Glasford snapped at her. "Is mahn's talk we makin."

Fish looked at his companion again. They had been friends all their lives. There were no secrets, no mysteries between them, until Glasford had gone to the States. Glasford had his face set the way he set it when he wanted people to know that he was a warrior and bad news to anybody who bothered with him. That made no sense to Fish. There was no one to scare but Momma Smallhorne, and even the devil had given up on her.

"How you lookin so dangerous, Glahs boy?" The veins in Glasford's neck reflected the thick light as they swelled. Fish watched the glow race up and then subside with each powerful throb.

"Dis mornin I wake up ahnd see a mahn burnin weed on his piece of land so he cahn plant some cassava. I tell myself, Glahsford, you been waitin ahnd waitin, ahnd now de time come."

"How you mean, bruddah?"

"I see in dis weed burnin how God trew down Babylon. For de great day of His wrath has come."

"Amen." Momma Smallhorne kept herself ready to punctuate the word of God wherever she encountered it.

"Come out of Babylon, my peoples, lest you share in her sins, lest you receive of her plague."

"Amen."

"Glahs," Fish said. "Doan get Momma excited."

"The Queen of Whores will be utterly burned wit fire. Great riches have come to naught."

"Daht's true. Amen."

"Ah. Ah, I see," said Fish, nodding his head in understanding. "I didn't know you could scripturize so. You must get a callin, Glahsford?"

"We comin to a time of prophesy realization. Salvation reality."

"Upon dis rock you shall build a church," Fish said. He was enthusiastic about the idea of a theatrical Glasford, sowing fine language from a pulpit.

"Hallelujah," cried Momma Smallhorne.

"Mahn, doan play the arse. Is revolution I talkin now."

"Oh ho," said Fish. The tone in Glasford's voice had been condescending and Fish was offended. "Is Natty Dread I sittin wit. Johnnie Too Bad. Mistah Castro."

Glasford stood up. "Momma, we leavin," he announced.

Fish watched him disappear up the path that led to the main road. He finished the rum in his glass, and then the rum Glasford had left behind in his. He recapped the bottle and stood up also. Momma was just returning the box of dominoes to its customary spot beneath an unframed cardboard picture of Queen Elizabeth. He didn't want to trouble her further so instead of placing the bottle on the short counter for her to retrieve, he leaned over and put it away himself.

"Momma, you want company wit de light?"

She shook her head no and lay back on the cot.

"Good evenin, Momma," Fish said. He blew out the kerosene lamp and followed after Glasford on the path.

Glasford was in the bushes a few steps off the path, shielded from the nearby road. Fish saw the flare of a match and let it guide him to his friend. On his heels, Glasford crouched forward, sucking a cigar-sized splif he had just rolled.

"We is bruddahs, true?" Glasford asked, not bothering to look up.

"True."

"We is de same, you ahnd I."

Fish did not believe this was quite true but he said it was so anyway, not to humor Glasford but to avoid obstructing his point. There was a change taking place in Glasford. In island life, any change in anybody, the motivations, the possible consequences, was worthy of a lot of talk. Glasford inhaled, and inhaled still more, until a coal like a fat red bullet burned between them. Then he blew out so much smoke that he was lost behind it.

"Mahn, come to town wit me tonight," Glasford urged Fish.

Fish did not have to answer immediately because Glasford had passed him the ganja. Going into Georgetown with Glasford meant having to buy Glasford his beer and having to pay cash for it. At least Momma Smallhorne allowed him credit. And it meant giving up the bed of Althea, a woman he had been recently courting. Fish was not eager to make such a sacrifice.

"I cahnt do so, bruddah. My seed pointin me in de next direction."

Fish had discovered certain truths about his life that made him feel solid and steady. The most significant, the easiest to understand, was this: women made him happy. He didn't even consider this much of a discovery until he noticed that for so many other fellows, the opposite was true: women made them unhappy, women transformed their spirits, confused them, gave them their first breath of hatred.

The caresses, the smells, the closeness, the slick warm wetness, the words and thoughts he could only share with a female, these ran like a nectar through Fish's life. Some women were spiteful toward him because he had so many lovers, but he told himself simply that love had made him a free and honest man. When he made a baby with one of them, he did not run away as if he had committed a crime, but divided his spare time as best he could among the households. When he could not give them a few dollars, he gave them fish or conch, turtle meat, mangoes from a tree on his small property, and sometimes pretty shells or a long feather for the children to play with.

"Fish, come wit me tonight."

"Mahn, why you so in-trested in town? Daht's a bad spot, a place daht just eat de money right from a fellah's pocket."

"Come wit me," Glasford repeated, "come wit me," as if he were under a spell.

"Look here, why you need me?"

"For bruddah-hood."

"Bruddah-hood? Mahn, daht cahn wait till mornin."

"For witness."

"Witness! What, boy, you puttin youself on trial?"

"Bear witness to de lion."

"Glahsford, I feel you strivin, mahn. You lookin close at somethin I cahnt see."

"You cahnt hear me now, Fish. I speakin de language of Jah Rastafari."

"How you cahnt speak a level daht make some sense to a guy like me? You might as well be monkey ahnd me jahckass. Daht's no bruddah-hood."

"Tell me, what dese words mean—guerrilla ahction, Babylon ahfire, ahnd Jah's people in liberation?"

"Mahn, who you? You a Jamaicahn fellah now?"

"As yet I find no boundary to corruption, ya know. Dis place deviled up too, same as Jamaicah."

Fish scratched his head, thinking the matter over. Althea offered him sugar, Glasford wanted him to take salt.

"One mahn wit vision is ahll it must need to make a bettah world," Glasford added.

Fish sucked his teeth. "Daht's a simple line. You makin a joke."

"I jokin? *Me?* You come see, see how I joke."

Fish smiled without discretion. "Mmm," he said. "Mmm," as if he were savoring the dialogue, the smoke, the temptations now upon him. Glasford was blowing a big wind, talking a lot of movie house shit. But Fish would kick himself tomorrow if there was a show and he had missed it.

"Dere's a womahn callin my name," Fish said.

"Womahn must wait."

Fish stood up with a grunt and an exaggerated sigh so that Glasford would know of the sacrifice he was making for brotherhood.

It took a long time for Glasford to flag them a ride into town. Fish kept his distance from him on the side of the road, turned away as if he were just about to walk on, the visor on his cap pulled down toward the bridge of his flat nose. He was uncomfortable begging anything from a fellow he didn't know. Now, if a friend drove past, he would wave his hand as hard as Glasford, but who could tell in the dark who was friend and who was not. This attitude had much to do with the second piece of knowledge Fish had learned during what he called his *self-studies*—the hours he spent alone fishing on the sea. It used to be, a few years ago, that he worked as a crew member on one of the sport fishing boats that were charted out to tourists. He didn't mind the work, but it wasn't worth the extra dollar a day to endure a boss. In fact, given the type of boss he had, and kept having as he moved from job to job, it made more sense to sleep in the rain and starve. To suffer under the hand of God, that was one thing. It was the hand of his fellow man that Fish could not abide.

This thinking led to a third truth that completed for Fish the extent of his destiny: a man's life was not to be perfect, but that was not to be worried over until other people pressed you with responsibility for that fact—a wife, a boss, salesman, politician, or preacher.

It didn't matter whose life was better, as long as his was the way he wanted it. Two years past, with no particular ambition in mind, he had signed a piece of paper that put him in the middle of the cane fields of Okeechobee County, working like a mule, swallowing enough dust to bury himself in, his forearms scarred from the sharp leaves of the cane.

He thought vaguely that in America he would see how the white people lived, live that way for a while, and then decide which life was better—island or Stateside, black or white. But in Florida, in the labor camps and fields, he never got close enough to a white person to talk. The rest of the fellows there were all Antiguans or Virgin Islanders, or dark, dark fellows who didn't know English. The women who came along with the laborers enjoyed the spectacle of men fighting over them. Fish, for the first time, felt lonely, bottled up. At night on his bunk, he relaxed only with thoughts of the warm blue Caribbean sea. He needed the sea as much now as when he was a boy spending idle days on the piers of Georgetown, studying the water for hours at the spot where his fishing line cut through the surface and connected him to another world. When he had earned enough money to build a catboat of his own, he left Florida with no regrets.

Glasford had been to the States, too.

The States, Glasford said when he returned, *was baptism, was education.*

You ahsk how it was in New York, mahn? What, you doan know, nobody tell you so? No jobs, everybody have a blind eye to sufferin. You come today ahnd de fellah daht come yesterday tell you to go away, ain't have no place left for you. Ahll de West Indian people dere does be up to tricks. You cahnt trust you muddah. Ahll de woman too *busy.* White people afraid to look by you. Cahnt even have a piss witout trouble. Mahn, dis de sulfurous heart of Babylon.

"So how you not get rich in de States like my bruddah Granville?" This was not Fish talking, but another guy in Momma Smallhorne's a few weeks ago when Glasford had first returned.

Glasford rolled his eyes. "Mahn, what you say, you ignorant? I beg everywheres for a job. I weep ahnd pull up me shirt. Look at dis, I say. My belly cavin in. I has nuthin to eat for six days now. I will work ahll day for a piece of bread, please. Dey point a big gun at me ahnd chase me away. Den de cops see you in Manhatten where ahll de white people does live ahnd work in dese big prick buildins, ahnd dey beat you wit sticks, ya know. So how a mahn sposed to get by? You tell me. Den dis white bitch tycoonness find me. I will give you a tousand dollahs to please me, she say. I take de money ahnd poke she, but den I run away because she disgust me so."

Fish had laughed trying to picture Glasford running away from a white woman with money.

"Mahn, you realize a tousand dollahs doan pay one month's rent in New York?"

"Yes, daht's so," said Fish to the other guy. He had heard some mention of that same information.

"See, what I tell you," Glasford had said, glaring at the other fellow. "Den it get so cold ice covah me face. I tell meself I dyin now, goodbye. I fall to de street. I look up at de sky—I cahnt see it. I see only dese buildins, mistah, goin up into de air, where ahll dese bigshots does rule de world like dey in heaven. De hell wit dis, I say. I'm no mahn to give up. I is resistin. I crawl back to Brooklyn. An old Auntie take pity on me ahnd give me plane money home. I escape, I escape de dragon."

"Uh-huh!" the other fellow exclaimed, beginning to appreciate the magnitude of Glasford's adventure.

"Daht's a nice piece of story, Glahsford." Fish chewed thoughtfully on an orange, analyzing all that Glasford had said, separating what could be true from what could not. New York City was a hard place—everyone knew that. Somehow Glasford had done okay, though. He strutted off the plane in soft, pretty shoes, new Levi's with a crease ironed into them, a shiny brown shirt that Fish knew he hadn't owned before he went north, his hair wilder and longer. Strapped around his wrist he had one of those little cassette units with a good AM/FM radio in it. On the other wrist, pinching his flesh, was a thin gold bracelet that seemed too small for a man the size of Glasford.

Glasford had made out. He had done okay. Something had happened, though. Whatever it was, it made Glasford start talking like a warrior.

Glasford's calm, sardonic voice: "So Fish, you believe I makin a story, eh?"

"Nah," Fish said. "I'm only sayin my ears find an in-trest in de ahccount."

"My bruddah Granville," the other guy mused. "I thinkin now he must be a very lucky fellah to be gettin by so in de States, sendin us money each month."

"Lucky!" Glasford used the word like a whip. "Daht is *bull*shit."

"Come, Fish. Come."

Fish shuffled over to the car and lowered himself in. Glasford slapped him lovingly on the thigh. *Brotherhood.*

Fish suspected the uselessness of it all, but he got in the car anyway, uncomfortable, embarrassed to look at the driver once he saw it was no one he was familiar with. He stared straight ahead, stared directly at the government license pasted to the outside of the glovebox without realizing what it was. A car passed. In the light that melted through the interior of the old Ford, Fish suddenly focused on what it was before his eyes. He leaned forward onto the front seat to shout at the driver.

"Stop. Mahn, what de hell you doin pickin us two boys up?"

The driver tapped the brake reflexively but then let off, continuing down the road toward town.

"Mahn, stop. We ain't payin no taxi."

The driver turned to look at them. He seemed quite used to taking his eyes off the road. The three were only dark outlines to each other.

"Look, doan worry wit daht," the driver said. "I just now comin from me suppah."

The fellow sounded friendly enough to Fish so he sat back

uneasily. "Okay," he said. "Watch de road. We nuthin special to look at."

Fish could tell the fellow was okay just by the way he nodded and moved and drove—fast, but not out to be fastest. He was an older fellow, probably one of the first drivers around when the hotels were built. His car was clean but coming apart.

"Um hmm," Glasford grumbled. It was a sinister sound. Nobody else said anything.

"Um hmm." Glasford again, only louder. Fish couldn't figure it.

"Um hmm."

Fish wasn't going to pay attention. There was no sense answering a voice that proposed trouble you didn't want. He hoped the driver knew as much. But then the driver was bending around again, his elbow on the top of the seat.

"Here now," he said to Fish. "Why dis guy *um hmm* so? What's on his mind?"

Fish didn't want any sort of conversation. The best policy was to let a man make whatever speech he cared to, and forget about it if it wasn't your concern. Glasford tapped him conspiratorially on the knee.

"Fish, you think you have de proper attitudes and mentalities to be a bourgeois fellow like dis taxi mahn?"

"How you expect me to ahnswer daht?" muttered Fish.

"What you fellahs up to?" the driver turned once more to ask.

"We is de Black Knights," Glasford said. His arms were crossed on his chest and he talked scornfully. Fish looked at him in horror.

"Black nights," the driver said, nodding his head.

"You heard of us?"

"No."

Silence. Fish made himself stone-hard. They were less than a mile from the edge of town.

"You doan hear word of us?" Glasford persisted.

"No."

Silence. They slowed for a stop sign, floated through it into shantytown.

"We is revolutionaries, ya know."

"Oh," the driver said with less interest.

"Revolutionaries," Glasford repeated. He made each sylla-ble sound bittersweet in his mouth.

"Oh," the driver said. "I first thought you must be some music group."

"No, no," Glasford explained. "We is de words to de music. We is de livin words."

"Oh."

Fish interrupted this nonsense. "Drop us at de corner, please."

The car stopped. Fish jumped out. Glasford remained in his seat for another minute, continuing his talk.

"We must change our ways ahnd work togeddah."

"Okay," the driver said.

"You is wit us, taxi mahn?"

"Sure, big noise," the driver answered. "I just give you a free ride."

"Ahlright, ahlright," Glasford said as if he had fixed a deal. "Maybe someday we give you a good job, Mistah Taxi Mahn." He slammed the car door behind him and joined Fish, his feet springing lightly off the pavement, a high swagger that Fish couldn't help but admire.

There was not much action on the street. Glasford saluted the few limers and layabouts with a raised fist. They turned their heads to nod tentatively.

"Bruddahs," Glasford declared.

"Yeah," some of them called back. They stepped past a few nice houses, gated and barred, protected from the street by cement walls, and then onto a block alive with hucksters and kids, shops angry with light and noise, trash and stink scattered through the gutters.

Once they entered Billings Road Fish guessed where Glasford was headed. His mood sunk. The Ethiope was a discotheque-bar, too big, too expensive. You had to be a king-pin to feel right there. Or carry a gun—same thing. Fellows bothering you to buy weed at Miami prices or talking a big sell on pills that made you dizzy, or pills that made your thoughts jerk too fast for your brain. The girls stayed tight against the moneymen, or one of the high-rolling tourists they sometimes talked inside the door. Fish preferred smaller places, safer people, booze that only cost what it was worth.

A bouncer that was all heft checked the entrance. Glasford knew him.

"Steam, my bruddah, out de way. We comin through." Glasford tried to push by him. The bouncer grabbed his shoulder.

"How you gettin so cocky, boy? Put in me hand a dollah, quick."

Glasford pretended not to hear. "Steam, bruddah," he said with an earnest expression. He placed his own hand on the hump of the doorman's shoulder, so that the two of them formed a box, facing off each other like wrestlers. "Which title sound bettah to you—Black Knights or Black Brigaders? Knights sound too schoolboyish?" Glasford attempted to step inside the entrance but Steam restrained him.

"Doan talk shit," Steam said. Fish didn't like a man who had such a smile, a smile that let you know you were underfoot and easily squashed. He moved back on the sidewalk, from distaste as well as for his own protection.

"Put a dollah in me hand quick." The smile was fading.

"What happened, Steam?" Glasford protested. "I nevah pay a dollah before."

For a second Steam glared at Glasford's hand on his shoulder. "Dis a new policy to keep away a cheap, mouthy niggah such as you," he said. Glasford's eyes shrank and locked into Steam's, so he couldn't see, as Fish did, the bouncer reach with his free hand behind his back and pull a gun from his belt. He laughed as he slid it up the outside of Glasford's pants, into his groin. Glasford didn't have to look down to know what Steam was pressing into him. The pistol was small, almost nothing, in Steam's massive hand.

"Fish," Glasford said coolly. "Bring a dollah."

Without knowing the seriousness of Steam's threat, Fish had no choice but to pass over a bill from his pocket and then—he had not expected this—another for himself. The gun was lowered and tucked away. Steam's posture flaunted his disregard for danger, his amusement with his own power, as if he were trying to squeeze himself up to beast-size.

"So Glasford," he said. "How come it's so long since I see you? How Momma Smallhorne keepin?"

Fish was outraged. "Mahn, what kind of fool are *you*?" he demanded of Steam. The doorman blinked and grinned benevolently, finished with his big joke and now oblivious to any ill feelings he had created.

"Doan be so touchy," he chided as Fish and Glasford, who was now laughing nervously at the game Steam had played, passed by him through the entrance into the shiny fluorescent oasis of the *E-T-OPE*. The vibrations of the crushing music were like the pressures of rough water against Fish's body, the invisible surging of the bass guitar, the swift tugs of the high notes, then a sucking release as the music stopped and a deejay searched for another record.

"Dey fix dis place up nice since I last come," Glasford observed.

On the plywood and concrete walls, shimmering under the electric voodoo of black lights, were unfinished murals of lions' heads and serpents, naked women and seven-spired marihuana leaves, demons and tribal warriors, and everywhere, even on the floor, the three-bar cake of primary colors—red, yellow, green—of the flag of Ethiopia. Some of the images were crude, some elegant, some elaborate or simple. Apparently, customers were free to add to the art as they wished. Cans of Day-Glo spray paint were abundant along the walls.

"Beautiful inspiration," Glasford said. He penetrated the crowd and Fish rejoined him minutes later at the bar. Once again the music had detonated. Fish stared at the clothes of the dancers that glistened, pale sheets of flashes like phosphorus churning at night in the sea.

"Buy me a beer," Glasford yelled.

"Look, slow down wit dis revolution. It costin me dearly."

Glasford seemed to hear only the one sweet word he was operating off of. "Dis beast too big to confront straight on," he said. "Its heart too hard for weapons to pierce. We must take bite by bite ahnd cripple it so. Zimbabwe take a bite. Cuba take a bite. Nicaragua take one, too. Soon a new world will grow on de ruins of Babylon."

"Um hmm," Fish snorted. "I tell you, daht Steam is de first guy I lock up in dis new world."

Glasford acted surprised. "What! No, he's a good fellah. He knows how to handle heself."

The bartender brought them bottles of stout which Fish, when he heard the price, paid for reluctantly. Glasford slumped forward into the music in a trance. A drunken woman, clutching a can of spray paint in one hand, a drink in the other, bumped into Fish. Without apologizing, she had him hold her glass, and Fish watched suspiciously as the woman bent down, kicked off her sandals, and sprayed them a blazing green.

"Girl, you crazy?" Fish said.

"Me?" she answered seductively, looking him up and down. "How you know *what* I am?"

Fish's natural response to women was to be flirtatious. He felt he was drawing her into his charm when Glasford interfered.

"Here now, Fish," he remarked. "Doan distract youself wit dis womahn. Lissen to de music."

As far as Fish was concerned, this was bad advice. He turned back to the woman, but she was brusquely removed from his side by a scowling fellow with eyes like small blue light bulbs in a tarry face. Before the man could drag her back to the dance floor, she thrust her can of spray paint into Fish's hand.

"Discipline your mind to de music." Glasford regarded him fretfully and continued. "Lissen to dese prophets ahnd doan be foolish."

"I hear dis sound ahll de time."

"Yes, but you doan lissen, Fish mahn. You keepin a message from youself."

Because he didn't understand what Glasford wanted from him, and because he was irritated that his friend could talk so big and behave so small, Fish wandered away, surveying the images and slogans on the walls. He looked at the paintings, at the can of spray paint in his hand, and began spraying, first a tentative line, then a curve that sagged from both end points, next a perpendicular line rising from the first, then the sweep of a sail, until he had outlined the catboat built with his own sweat. The way it shined so mightily in the dark pleased him. Since the spray can was only good for broad, bold strokes, he signed the name of the boat, *God's Bread,* in the sky above the mast, so that another fisherman would know it was his. Then, under a squiggle of waves, he sprayed ugly sharks and pretty fishes. When he stood back to appraise his work, Glasford was there.

"Daht's a nice picture. Look, cahn you buy me a next beer?"

"No."

"How you mean *no?* We is bruddahs. We look out for each oddah."

"Dis rich place take ahll me money."

"Ya know, Fish, dis a very sad country if two good men such as we cahnt drink ahnd eat as we need."

"Daht's true."

Glasford took the can of paint from Fish. He shook it violently and began to spray slogans along the wall, disregarding the work of other painters.

BLACK POWER!!!

BABYLON FINISH!!! He ran out of paint on the hook of the *F* but soon found a fresh can.

MORE WORK FOR PEOPLE!!!

"Glasford, if it's work you want, come wit me in de boat."

"Doan talk foolish, mahn. You missin de point."

Fish didn't see the point. Instead, he was bored.

But Glasford had inspired himself. "Okay, let's go," he ordered. "I cahnt hold meself back now. I ready to ahktivate." He marched toward the exit, gripping two cans of spray paint as if they were pistols and he were a desperado. Without much hurry, Fish trailed after him.

Fish never came to town much at night. Once he came for medicine for one of his babies, once for a cockfight, several times to play poker with an old uncle and his cronies. But generally Fish had no business in Georgetown, and no interest in its activities, designed more for foreigners than for the people of the island.

Glasford armed Fish with the second spray can and led him up the alleys, through the streets and across the promenades, commanding "Revolution, Revolution," in his raw, heroic voice. The fellows out and about stared, turned away smirking, or raised their fists in solidarity, observing Glasford painting the slogan BLACK POWER in pink paint on the walls and windows of Georgetown.

Eventually Fish said, "Here, Glahsford, tell me something. How you writin BLACK POWER so? You think Halston ahnd dem fellahs in Parliament is pink like de words you sprayin?"

"No, no, Fish. You doan catch de music, mahn. *Black* significates the Holy Jah, ahnd *Power* symbolize his lovin sword of vengeance. You see now? I must only write dese expressions to set dis message through de blind eyes of de Ministers of Corruption."

Fish wondered if Glasford knew what he was talking about. He himself had no message to deliver to anybody, so alongside each incident of Glasford's work he would write the wobbly name of one of the women he loved: Margareet, Rita, Alvina, Lemonille.

They had infiltrated the city to its core: the hotels, the casinos, the government houses. As they sprayed their paint freely on the perimeter wall that enclosed one of the popular gambling resorts Glasford explained his forthcoming strategy to Fish. They would bust into the casino, he said, and grab the wealthiest white bitch in sight. They would hold her for ransom, and they would demand from the slaves at government house a plane to fly them to Havana. Once they were in Cuba, they would train with Castro's freedom fighters until—

"Doan stop on my account."

Fish looked over his shoulder. There, his legs spread out in a military stance, a nightstick clenched firmly in both hands, was a cop. Fish smiled extravagantly in an attempt to minimize any notion the cop might have that Fish was a threat to anybody.

"I say, gentlemen, doan stop on my account wit dis beautification program."

Glasford was just turning to acknowledge the man's presence when the cop struck them both—*tunk tunk*—so quickly
with the nightstick that Fish had to think about what had
happened before he could recognize the pain of the blow on his
elbow.

"I say *doan stop*."

"Mahn, what de hell." Fish raised his arms for protection.
Glasford was not intimidated. Before he could be stopped, his
can of spray paint was level with the policeman's nose.

"You ugly bitch," Glasford snarled. In an instant the cop's
round black face blossomed pink. "Dere, you mudhead. Now
you a pretty pink-face boy in truth."

Fish was stunned, thrilled. His knees shook. Glasford was
finally getting somewhere, behaving such a way to this bigshot,
letting him know how people were tired of cops all the time
molesting a fellow who wasn't bothering a soul.

"Run, Fish. Fly."

Glasford threw his can at the policeman but missed. The
two friends raced halfway down the block before they heard
the muffled pops of a handgun behind them. They turned a
corner, following the high wall studded with broken glass
along its top, turned another corner, then slowed cautiously as
they approached the bright entrance to the resort's compound.
A guard in a flamboyant colonial costume narrowed his eyes at
them.

"We has a message for dem fellahs in de band," Glasford
explained loudly, out of breath. "We comin right back."

"Wait a minute, you."

"Get out of me way," Fish yelled, shoving the guy aside.
He was suddenly furious. The man might have the power to
prevent his escape. The cop back on the street might beat him
and lock him up. How easy it was for a quiet fisherman such as
he to so quickly become an outlaw.

They sprinted down the drive and across the lawn to get
behind the huge glittering block of the hotel. Then they could
cut down toward the bay shore, which Fish knew would lead
them into the darkness and safety of the harbor. He looked
beside him at Glasford, legs and arms pumping frantically. He
would never have guessed this lazy guy could run so fast.

Fish was seething with militancy. Dis water rough but I cahn manage, he thought. As if he were in a movie, music—the sort of music Glasford was always barking about—began a crescendo that soon enveloped them. They poked through a tall hedge of hibiscus into what surely must be Babylon. The lawn was dazzling with party lights and torches. White folks, hundreds of them, jerked about like land crabs to the din of the reggae being cast at them by five arrogant musicians on a raised platform. Native servants in tuxedoes, their hands gloved in white cotton, delivered drinks and food on silver trays throughout the crowd. At the end of the lawn, toward the darkness of the sea, a goat was roasting slowly over an open-pit barbecue.

"Keep runnin. Doan stop." He glanced at Glasford and nodded fiercely. This was not an environment they could lose themselves in.

After his recent persecution, Fish loathed the gay scene he found himself in the midst of and wanted to mar it somehow. He thought he was feeling for the first time the brotherhood of Glasford's emotions, the new community of spirit that the music prophesied, the spirit and its rage. They pushed their way rudely through the dancers, deaf to the protests and small threats, but Fish was not blind to the fear their presence sponsored. At the shoreside fringe of the crowd, Fish's passion boiled up into a wicked impulse, and the wickedness made him laugh, at least to himself, and his laughter frightened him but he could not stop. He raised the canister of spray paint he had gripped tightly all the time they had been running.

"Look out. Look out. Get away," he shouted. "Is a bomb I have."

There were screams from women. As the news swept through the crowd, the dancing stopped although the music didn't. People struggled to back off from where Fish stood. Fish watched them move away, fascinated that they were responding to him. He shook the empty spray can at them and then pitched it into the barbecue pit. Glasford had halted to hear his proclamation and stood for a second with his mouth wide open.

"Holy Christ, Fish. What de hell craziness is dis?"

Most people had abandoned the dancing patio and were

grouping at the casino's doors, watching Fish to see what would happen next. The lawn around the roasting goat was clear. The aerosol can exploded with a noise like a truck back-fire, scattering the coals of the barbecue pit out a few yards as a cloud of sparks ballooned into the clear sky. Fish watched as the red embers swelled up, for an instant more radiant than the stars, and felt a small sadness in himself. The slogan he had painted didn't mean much to anybody.

Glasford whooped victoriously. "De Black Knights strike," he said.

They ran along the shore through the shadows of a grove of Australian pines. They kept going to where the lights began again near the harbor, the two of them loping between the few cars on the docks, crouching unnecessarily until they were positive no one followed. Finally they walked out bravely into the open, down along the pier toward the public anchorage where the yachts and sailing ships and some sport fishing boats tied up.

"We need money," Glasford stated. Fish could only sigh. He was weary and wanted the comfort of Althea.

"A hungry mahn must satisfy heself."

"Daht's true."

They proceeded aimlessly down the pier. It was late but the anchorage was filled with boat sounds: rigging slapping against masts, bilge pumps switching on automatically, splat-tering oily water into the bay, the creaking strain of anchor lines. Not many lighted portholes, though. No people around. Fish was ready to reverse direction and start home when Glasford leaped quietly from the wooden pier onto the deck of a sail-boat. He snuck along the cabin and disappeared into the cock-pit. Fish heard him trying to force the cabin door and felt his loyalties to Glasford begin to split. Fish liked boat people. No matter how well outfitted they were, their good grace was always a question of their courage and their luck. Pirates and princes were equal, their brotherhood undeniable, on the sea. He wished Glasford had shared a day of fishing with him. An island man shouldn't ignore the sea.

Glasford hopped back to the pier. "Shut up tight," he whispered.

"Glahsford—"

"Come, come." He darted onto another boat but a dog began barking from below deck, and a light flicked on. Fish was off the pier by the time Glasford caught up with him. They walked along the city wharf. There was nothing Fish wanted to say. The triumph at the casino already seemed the secondhand boast of a street hooligan.

They were coming to the end of the quay. There were no lampposts here and the air smelled fresher. A piece of moon had appeared over the eastern waters and hung in the sky like a fish scale. Glasford was still acting sneaky.

"Pssst. Fish, look." Glasford held a finger to his mouth to forewarn silence.

From the cleats on the quay two nylon lines ran over the edge and down toward the blackness of the water. To see what was below, Fish had to step up next to Glasford. At first glance the motorboat was nothing unordinary. Big but not so big, no cabin, nice-size engine pulled up and locked. It didn't take so much to buy a boat like this one—lots of fellows had them.

What was a surprise to Fish was to see on the exposed floor of the boat, at each end, two twisted piles of, what—sheets or light blankets—and to see a tennis-shoed foot, a white ankle, protruding out from one pile, and the round featureless shapes of heads under the bedding, shrouded from mosquitoes and the distant lights of the pier. Toward the stern, placed flat near one of the sleepers, was a large suitcase. If the people on the boat were tourists, they were a type Fish had never encountered before. Most visitors to Georgetown were decidedly less adventurous than this.

He didn't have to see Glasford's face to know what was on his mind. Fish felt ambivalent but vaguely curious again, noting how easy it was for Glasford to exploit the vulnerability of the sleepers, as if Glasford were a ghost capable of pranks but not of harm. Sitting himself on the lip of the wharf, extending his legs carefully until they rested on the motorboat's gunnel, Glasford seemed so adept with the stealth of his movements that Fish realized his friend had a talent for what he was doing.

Glasford put his hand on the back of the pilot's seat to steady himself, stretching until his other hand found the handle of the suitcase. He tried to ease the suitcase up noiselessly, but his position and the slight rolling of the boat made the task difficult. A scraping noise made Fish's blood move. Glasford stopped in slow motion as if he were underwater. But then he snatched the suitcase up and braced himself to toss it over to the quay. As Glasford corrected his balance Fish saw a white man's head pop wildly out from under the blankets, saw the shock pass through the muscles of the man's face, and then the grimness and determination freeze in as the man bolted upright and grabbed Glasford from behind. Glasford's mouth opened in astonishment. An instinctive pose of innocence and victimization came into his expression. Fish would have roared in delight at Glasford's not-guilty plea if at that moment the suitcase hadn't slammed into his shins and knocked him backward. He gaped down at its plaid surface as though he didn't know what it was.

"Take it up, Fish. Run!"

Glasford's voice was full of dread. The white man wrestled with him. Through the force of their struggle, they heaved themselves into the water. Fish was about to turn and flee, but he paused just long enough to see the other sleeper awaken. A woman. She was pretty in the sort of bare, hard way white women were. The confusion on her face intrigued him. He wanted to stay and look at her but with the immunity he had felt when she was still sleeping. Her hand desperately patted through her covers until she found a pair of eyeglasses. With her sight came a flush of horror. Fish grabbed the heavy suitcase and started running.

He hadn't taken more than ten quick steps before the woman began to weep and call after him in a wet voice.

"Please come back. Please. Oh God, you've taken everything I own."

Fish kept going, but he couldn't run fast enough to get past the despair in her voice.

"Please, please," she wailed. "All that's in that bag is our clothes."

Each of her sobs seemed to add more weight to his feet. What the hell was he doing on this dock, with this suitcase in his hand, running away from a helpless woman who was miserable on his account while Glasford and a white man were thrashing each other in the bay? Fish didn't have much sympathy for the troubles of other people—his own were enough for him—but he was always alert to the needs of a woman. He slowed down and then stopped altogether, unable to work his legs.

Once stopped, he didn't know what he should do. He remained motionless, the suitcase on the street, as if he were waiting for a bus. Glasford finally hoisted himself out of the water, a dark fearsome sea-thing flopping onto the quay. He spotted Fish and staggered forward, gasping and spitting, water squishing around in his leather shoes.

"Daht womahn crying a big tragedy, Glahsford. How cahn we go on so?"

"He try to kill me!" Glasford shrieked. Fish had never heard Glasford sound so offended. He stood there pounding water from his ears. "She trickin you, boy," he argued angrily. "Ahll dese rich people does cry a storm when dey lose a penny."

Fish wasn't prepared to discuss the matter any further. He spun on his heels, lifting the suitcase, and walked back to the dock. The white man, who by now had hauled himself back into the boat, looked blood wild as Fish returned the suitcase to him. Once he had his property back, the mistrust went from his face and he shook his head in wonder. He was younger than Fish and his longish hair stuck to his cheeks and forehead.

"Brother," he said, "you are twice crazy. What if I had a gun? You could've gotten killed, a decent guy like you. You'd be dead right now."

Fish was shamed by the truth of what the fellow was saying. Robbery without a gun in such circumstances was ignorant. To avoid the man, he looked at the woman, her eyes expressing gratitude and a forthright curiosity that somehow made him feel proud and countered what the man had said.

Maybe there was a better reason for bringing the suitcase back but Fish had no appetite to search for it. The world had become melancholic and too romantic.

Glasford had swaggered up, tough and unrepentant, once there was no obvious danger in doing so. "I know how hard it is for you people in the islands," the white man was saying. "But you're going to get killed if you keep doing this." He paused as if to judge them. "Look," he continued, digging into his wet pants, "here's twenty bucks I'd like to give you, you know, for bringing the bag back."

. Fish had no interest in the money but Glasford snatched the bill from the white man as soon as the fellow's hand came out of his pocket.

"You lucky dis time," Glasford said to the man below him in the boat.

There were no cars on the road. Not even a stray donkey they could hijack into service. Glasford wanted to wait for the ride he knew would come but he caught up with Fish when Fish went ahead without him, trekking the long miles back to Momma Smallhorne's. She was already up when they arrived at dawn, a fire sparking in her cookshed, baking soda bread and warming yesterday's coffee.

"I suppose you hear by now," the old woman clucked at them. "I just receive de news. Scamps blow up Richmond Park. Is dead white people everywhere. Dey place a bomb in a poor billy goat. My God, when dis wickedness goin stop?"

Momma seemed happy to have a big story to work with. Fish didn't want to spoil it for her just yet by telling her the true account. They eased themselves gratefully into Momma's two shaky chairs and had her bring a pint bottle of rum and biscuits. Glasford poured and drank and appeared revitalized, though his eyes looked dead.

Fish's exhaustion bled itself back into a pool of sadness. He was sure that the woman in the motorboat would have liked him if she only knew what sort of man he was, that he was a man who had discovered truths in his life and tried to live by them. *Don't take from me what I wouldn't take from you.* That's what she had cried to him. It struck a nerve, even if he couldn't be certain that she indeed lived that way herself.

"Fish, drink up, you fallin behind," Glasford said. "What, you sleepy? A guy like you daht blows up white people?" It was a joke but no light came into Glasford's eyes to support it. Fish knew he was being mocked.

Fish's bed was three minutes down the road and he wanted it, but his mind was carrying on against his will and would allow him no peace. Yes, it was true in many ways that he and the people around him were, as Glasford had said, like rocks on the bottom of the sea. What gave a man cause to rise up, Fish didn't know. Glasford on the gallows, Glasford in a limousine, surrounded by flags and personal bodyguards and beautiful women. How much did it matter? A rock had lost its gravity and was lifting toward the surface. Fish could only see the emptiness left by its passage.

Glasford was starting his talk again. Next time, he was saying, we get a gun.

BRENT SPENCER

THE SMALL THINGS THAT SAVE US

FROM THE ATLANTIC MONTHLY

THE FIRST TIME I SAW EASY, he was standing next to his tractor in the middle of the road, a one-armed man kicking one of the big back tires and then slapping at it with his hat. I pulled over to give him a hand. It was a small tractor, an old gray Ford, so we just rolled it onto the shoulder. The whole thing seemed to be held together with bent coat hangers and electrical tape.

I drove him back to his farm. He had about forty head of cattle on twenty-five acres that sloped into a shallow valley. The top ten acres were fenced off and full of timothy, tall and shimmering in the wind. The rest was pasture and woodland. He didn't seem worried at all about the tractor. But then, it wouldn't start for some thief any easier than it had for him.

I stayed for supper, though at first Joan, his wife, seemed nervous at having a stranger in her house. Their boy, Jimmy, must have been the quietest four-year-old on record. We had chicken, mashed potatoes, and peas, but Joan didn't seem to mind that he mainly ate slices of buttered bread.

Easy was the kind of man who likes to run the talk at supper.

"Those cows of mine are stupid on purpose," he said. I remembered thinking they were strange-looking when I first noticed them. Big dull eyes, and smaller than any cows I had ever seen. They were full-grown yet stood no higher than my waist.

Easy said, "All the smarts got bred out of them so you can raise them in a smaller space. They fatten up fast too, and don't eat much. Meek as your maiden aunt." From the window I could see them crowding up against the closed barn door, waiting for him to let them in.

Easy was Frank Nagle. He had brown shaggy hair that looked like he cut it himself, in the dark. He and Joan were thirty, thirty-five. She was taller than Easy by a couple of inches. She wore faded jeans and one of his old flannel shirts that had seen too much work and washing. The colors were faded and the cloth was limp and threadbare, but it brought out her beauty. She had a generous look that told you that the things you said mattered to her.

Easy's right arm had got chewed off in a corn picker a couple of years earlier.

He said, "It was one of those things you warn everybody else about, and then all of a sudden you just can't believe it's happening to you."

I could see Joan tense up as she listened to a story she must have heard many times. The memory made Easy massage the stub of his arm.

"Some cobs got caught in my picker," he said. "I went back to knock them free. Didn't turn the thing off first. It grabbed a corner of my cuff and pulled my arm in. When I reached in with the other arm to yank it free, I lost a few fingertips on that one. I was lucky not to lose that arm too. Caddy Leboux, my neighbor, he came running when he heard me screaming. I guess I'm lucky he was out in his field shooting snakes. He says he found me jammed up against the picker, with my arm being clawed to pieces inside. I was unconscious by then. He says the picker wouldn't let me fall. Just held me there by the arm. I got my name because I can do things easier with one arm than most can with two."

"Except when it comes to cleaning up after himself," Joan said.

After supper he and I went out on the back porch and

drank, looking out over his farm, watching the evening come
down. He said that once a month he visited a cousin in West
Virginia. He called it his "moon run." Moonshine. We left the
porch light off to keep the bugs away. Barn swallows had built
a nest in the space above the fixture. They liked the warmth
when the light was on, Easy said. We'd watch one or the other
come dipping up the long slope toward the house and then
swoop above us to the nest. All evening it was like that, sitting
in the dark, drinking Easy's moon.

We got to talking about what he wanted to do to the farm.
How he was going to get a bank loan so he could fence in more
pasture and buy more of his "mini-cows." We were talking
about how hard the work would be. And maybe it was that, or
the drinking, or just the good feeling I had sitting there, but I
offered to stay and help out if he wanted.

He looked at me a little suspiciously and took a pull from
the bottle. "If it's money you're after, there isn't any," he said.

I told him I was only after food and a place to stay. Then
he was quiet for a while.

"Let's sleep on this," he said. "See if it sounds good
tomorrow."

In the morning he showed me the shack. "You can fix this
place up any way you like," he said.

It was about a hundred yards below the house. Two
rooms attached to a small potting shed. Easy said he used the
place when Joan kicked him out of the house. He would come
down there to poison his liver and argue with the empty
rooms. The shack was a wreck, but the light in the field was
pure luxury. Country light. Clean. I could hear the birds
circling through the trees. The wind hissing in the long grass.

One room had a cot, a moldy chair, a woodburner, and a
stack of wood against one wall. The kitchen had a Formica
table and two lopsided chairs with rusty legs. It had an electric
stove that didn't work and a sink that wasn't hooked up. But it
also had a truckload of canned food stacked on wooden shelves.
I got used to heating cans on the woodburner. Easy built the
shack as a place to hole up if the Russians dropped the bomb.
But when Caddy Leboux told him about radiation, he gave up
on the idea.

The commode was in the potting shed, right by the green-house windows. At least it worked, though after a while I noticed that the grass downhill was more lush than it should have been in August. The place had mice and a few snakes. A woodchuck lived under it. Sometimes I'd go into the kitchen in the morning and there it would be, staring at me. Then it would just waddle back to the potting shed and under the house.

Easy and I got on well together, with me doing the heavy work and him dealing with feed suppliers and the bank. His farm was not a money-maker, but he was serious, he had plans. And little by little, we thought, we could turn the place around. Those huge farms you see, they're all science. A small farm like Easy's is a record of the farmer's life. Sometimes it's a record of the failures and mistakes and accidents that make a life. So it was important for us to do things right. The farm was a kind of fresh start for Easy. He had bought it two years earlier, when he and Joan had married, using inheritance money he hadn't already drunk or gambled away. He liked to say that Joan's love saved his life. It embarrassed me whenever he said that, the sentimentality of it.

Winter came in early October that year, and money got scarce. One evening Easy and Joan started yelling and stomp-ing around the house. I could hear some of it all the way to the shack, maybe because of the way sound carries over snowy ground. Maybe because misery carries over any ground.

I heard her say, ". . . cows . . . loser . . . farm . . . lunatic."

Then his voice, louder: ". . . beat me . . . I'll be damned . . ." I heard doors slam and glass breaking. The TV came on loud. Some goofy cartoon voice singing, "Take good care of yourself, like your friend Shamu!" Then the TV went off, and I didn't hear anything for a long time.

A little later I was near the house, burning some trash in the barrel. All that time Jimmy was out playing in the snow, rolling it around in snowballs that kept falling apart. He looked like a little blue astronaut in his snow gear. He was talking and singing to himself, words I couldn't make out. The barrel of trash was in full blaze. I poked at it with a broom handle so it crackled and roared. Sparks shot up in bright showers, and fell on the snow. It was late. It had been quiet for a long time.

When I looked up, I saw Easy and Joan standing on the back porch, with Joan clinging to him a little like she was hurt, like he had beaten her and it was all she could do to stand up. But then I thought she might be holding on to him to keep him from flying apart. She was crying a little with her head against his shirt, stroking his chest. There were tears in his eyes too. They stood there a few minutes on the porch in the cold, staring off down the hill. I could see him hold her close and kiss her hair without taking his eyes off the darkness. Then he called the boy to the house, his voice weak and raw. The boy walked toward them and climbed the back steps slowly.

When you're four years old, I think, the world goes on pretty much without you. You find the safe places where you can. He climbed those stairs like an old man coming home from a long day of field work. His house was safe again, for a little while at least. The three of them went back inside. The upstairs lights came on, and after a time went out again. There was nothing left but the night and the snow and flames spraying into the cold wind.

We had a few warm days late in October, and I was digging postholes for Easy, getting things ready for the new fencing he would string. Digging postholes was one thing a one-armed man couldn't do. He was off at the Agway and the bank. I went up to the house for a cold beer and found Joan at the sink, with her hands in soapy water, just staring out at the farm.

Her windowsill was full of cuttings in jelly jars. Coleus. Wandering Jew. Swedish ivy. We got to talking. We talked like farm neighbors in a back field. Later, when I thought about it, I thought it might have been the signs of hope those cuttings represented, the late-afternoon light sloping through the windows, Joan's hair shining in that pale gold light: we make up stories to carry ourselves through the longest nights, and this is mine.

We made love like old friends who thought they'd never

see each other again. Slow and solemn love. Later, we talked. Easy was her second husband. Frank, she called him.

"I was first married to Big John, Jimmy's father. He was small and spiteful. He had corns on his vocal chords from screaming at wrestlers on the TV."

I was lying on my back, listening to Joan, listening also for the sound of Easy's pickup. Already the feelings that had made it all seem so natural were starting to fade. I think she knew that, and that's why she kept talking.

"Big John worked in a heat-treating plant. Anchor chains, gun barrels, cam shafts, and the like. It was a dangerous job. Furnaces that heated up to eighteen hundred degrees. Sometimes an oil bath would burst into flame. Blow out every window in the place. Two men died there, and he was one of them. He was walking along an I-beam and slipped off into a vat of caustic soda. When I'm feeling truly mean about the past, I like to say all they could fish out was his rodeo belt buckle. But the truth is he survived, at least for a while. He swallowed some of that slop, though, and died later from pneumonia. I gave him a wake the next day." She rolled so she was leaning on her elbow, looking down at me with her loose hair shading her face. She said, "The day I married Frank, my heart was in my mouth. Without him, I would just turn into some kind of character."

When Easy's pickup pulled in next to the house, I was back in the field, chopping at the ground, feeling cheap and lonely. Beyond the fence line, over in Caddy Leboux's woods, I could see rusty tin cans and loose trash fluttering. I thought about how what had happened would drive Easy and me apart before we even got a chance to know each other well. Joan was sweet and strong, and I loved her in a way that afternoon, but I thought I had ruined all our lives.

I don't know a thing about cattle. Before the snow I used to watch them grazing in the field like slow freight trains crawling west. The cowbirds sat on their shoulders or hung in swarms overhead. Nothing bothered those cows. Easy was right about how stupid they were. I ran a water line to the field and attached a noser. It took all one afternoon to show them how to nuzzle the paddle to get fresh water.

They'd walk the fence, looking for a break into the wild grapes on the other side. During storms you could see them huddling under the lean-to Easy and I built, staring out at the rain. The lean-to was nothing but sapling trunks and sheets of tin, but it was sturdy. Then the cows got the notion that they could scratch an itch by rubbing against the roof supports. Each day that roof was more and more crooked. Someday, I figured, it would come right down on them.

When Easy couldn't get his price for the cows, he decided to keep them through the winter. Lots of farmers did that, kept cattle, siloed grain, waiting for a better market. But there was the extra cost. We had a barnful of hay, some corn. Feed, though, all that extra Super Fit-n-Fresh—that was expensive. Easy didn't get his price because the buyers said there wasn't enough meat on the new breed. They said the cows were all bone. But Easy didn't see it that way. He would keep those cows, he said, until he found a buyer who wasn't out to cheat him.

Things began to fall apart when the feed started running out. At night I'd hear the cows groaning and butting the barn door. They thought they'd graze the field, I guess, but they couldn't with two feet of snow on the ground and more falling all the time. Pretty soon the grain was gone. I pitched plenty of hay to them, but they needed more than that to keep up their body heat. They kicked at the pens when they saw the hay dropping down. Big whucking kicks that splintered wood. Later, as they passed the silo on their way to the field, they'd lick the feeding auger, but when they saw it was no use, they stamped the ground, tails switching like whips.

One evening a couple of weeks later I noticed some of them hadn't come back to the barn. Three of them were lying against one another in the lean-to. It didn't look like they had the strength to make it up the hill. That night the temperature dropped to twenty below. By morning they were dead. For days I saw them lying out there. I hoped the drifting snow would cover them up, but no. The other cows wouldn't go near the lean-to. More died, in the field, in the lane that went down to the field, in the barn. Easy couldn't work or do anything. He had gone to all the feed suppliers in the valley, but his credit was stretched to the limit and the bank wouldn't give him a break. He just sat on the porch all day in the cold, drinking moon and staring at the cows as if they had betrayed him.

It was one of those days when the sun is so bright and the cold so cutting that you can hardly stand it. From the window of my shack I could see Jimmy coming toward me, dragging a red plastic sled behind him. When I went outside, I could see that he had loaded it with kindling, a piece of rope, a few handfuls of snow, other trash. He stared up at me, and then said, "He says to give this to you."

The note said, "Let's fall by The Farmer's and do some damage."

When I looked back at Jimmy, he was almost crying. His voice was like a prayer. He said, "You're hurting my shadow." I stepped away from him. His small shadow lay sprawled on the snow, its chest caved in by my footprints.

When I got to the house, Easy was coming out the door.

Joan followed, saying, "You were my hope against hope. Do you hear? I thought . . . But look at us, Frank. Look at us."

Jimmy had followed me up the hill and was emptying the heavy sled onto the snow, singing quietly to himself.

Easy threw things into the back of his pickup. Rope, stray lumber, a sack of rock salt. It was as though he wanted to hear what she had to say but he didn't want to appear to be listening.

He said, "Don't lay it all on me, Joan." He said her name as if it were a dirty nickname. He stomped around the truck, kicking it, banging his fist against it. I remembered the first time I saw him. As we climbed into the pickup, he kept saying, "I'm bitched! I'm bitched!"

Joan was at my window. I rolled it down. "Talk to him, Evan," she said. "Knock some sense into the pigheaded cripple." She pushed off the truck and went back into the house. Easy pumped the gas hard and swung into the road.

When we were away from the house, he looked at me and broke out laughing. "Pigheaded cripple! I love that woman!"

At the Farmer's Inn we drank a few beers and threw some darts. Easy's shots kept hitting the wall.

He said, "It's a rag-arm, but it's the only arm I got. Let's say you won. Anyway, the soup here's a killer, and I'm hungry."

We each had a bowl of split pea. A few farmers were sitting around with their caps pushed back on their heads, sipping beers and wiping their faces with their hands. They nodded at Easy as if they knew his trouble but weren't going to be the ones to bring it up.

"Sure, my head's hard," Easy said to me. "I'm a pigheaded cripple! After this is all over, I'm going to have to get me a new nickname. Pig. That'd be it, I guess.

"You know what I miss?" he said, looking down at his empty sleeve, his voice softening. "I had the prettiest little dragon tattoo. Right about there." He touched the sleeve where his forearm had been. "Isn't that the damnedest thing? I miss my tattoo."

I was eating my soup and watching the old woman behind the bar. She was wide in the hips and took her time.

Easy said, "This is a good bar. Never saw a single drunk here. Gerry, there, is really something. Saved me many times in the bad old days. Helped me face up to a few things."

I thought about Joan and that afternoon months before. "You don't know me very well, do you, Easy?" I said.

"I know your work," he said. "You learn a thing about a man when you see him work. That's enough for me."

"I could be escaped from prison or something," I said.

"I thought of that," he said. "At first, when you said you wanted to stay on, I thought you might rob us blind. But then I thought, what've we got to steal?"

"I appreciate that," I said.

"You married, Evan?" he said. "It's none of my business, but you have a look. You married?"

"Not in the eyes of the law," I said.

"Not in the eyes of the law. Now that's sad as can be. When you came to the farm, I told Joan I figured you were broke down. She said your car looked fine to her, and I said no, it was more than that. That's all we needed to know. She trusts you the same as me."

"You shouldn't trust me," I said. "Easy," I said, "there are things people do. They don't mean to, but they do them. Later they're sorry, but the harm is already done."

"You planning on robbing us after all?" he said. He was scraping his spoon at the green sludge on the bottom of his bowl.

"You're not listening to me. I've done something I'm ashamed of, and I have to tell you."

Easy looked up then and sipped his beer. I could see his eyes going over me.

"A little while ago," I said, "I was working in the field. I went to the house for a beer. Joan and I got to talking."

"That woman of mine is a great one for talking. Sometimes she'll be quiet for days. And then it's like a dam burst—everything just rushes right out."

"Easy," I said, and for the first time it seemed like a foolish name to say.

"She takes her time thinking about a thing. She'll talk about it only after she has it figured out in her mind. She's deeper than me, and I admire that."

"Easy, something happened between Joan and me that afternoon."

"I know, I know," he said quietly. "You spent time together." He was looking down at the rings of wetness his bottle had made on the tablecloth. He ran his hand through his shaggy hair. He looked tired.

"I'm sorry, Frank."

He said, "Only Joan calls me Frank. Nobody else."

I said, "I wish it never happened. I wish we didn't have this standing between us now."

"When Joan told me, first I was mad. Then I cried. I thought it meant she was leaving me. But she said no, that it was just something that happened, naturally, between friends. She doesn't lie to me, Evan. I know enough to listen to her. I'm not that pigheaded. I used to be a drunk and a runaround. I know that life—do the worst and don't get caught. Joan settled me down. She opened my eyes. If you're sorry because you hurt me, well, that's one thing. To that I say, I'll live. But if you're sorry it happened, that's something else. I don't really think that's true. Do you?"

I don't know how to account for the calm in some people. I wasn't anything to him. Easy was a one-armed man watching his life fall apart, and I was the stranger who stole his wife away one afternoon. But we spent several more hours in The Farmer's, talking and laughing about bills that were past due, money beyond our reach, and the string of useless postholes I had dug.

By the time we got home, the evening was setting in. We stood awkwardly near the steps of the side door. He gripped my shoulder. There was a lot of strength in that hand. Then he moved his rough palm up against the side of my neck and held it there.

"Oh, Evan," he said. He said it like a lover, the way a woman says your name in the dark when the stars are right, making you forget how much you fear her.

I said, "Easy, this afternoon, before we left, I heard Jimmy out here. You know how he sings all the time? Well, I finally heard what he's singing: 'Cows are brown, cows are gray, cows are in the field all day.' "

Easy looked off at the dead cattle lying in the field and shook his head. "That's not fair to him. He shouldn't have to see that. What have I been thinking?"

Earlier that day, as Easy and Joan argued, Jimmy had kept quietly breathing his chant in and out. His junk scattered on the snow was the most important thing in his life at that moment—an empty cigarette pack, a saucer, old clay pots and medicine bottles . . .

"We got unfinished business, Evan."

I hooked up the backhoe and drove the tractor down the icy, rutted lane that ran along the far edge of the farm. Easy rode with one foot on the axle and the other on the backhoe, so I drove as slowly as I could. The tractor almost shook itself apart as it lurched and slid over the hard ground. Twice the engine died, and in the silence I could feel the presence of the dead cattle lying in the field beside me. The clouds were faint scraps of shadow far away, and the stars were beginning to show.

In the darkening field beside us we could see a half-dozen or more cows in plain view, like mounds of freshly turned earth. Snow had swept high against them. The coats of the long dead had lost their pigment. Shreds of gray fur covered the snow around the bloating bodies. The wind scattered bits of it into the air. Heavy black birds had settled on some, worrying the carcasses. As they landed, their broad, oily wings snapped viciously.

Halfway down the lane I turned to Easy and yelled over the engine, "Let's dig it in the woods, okay?"

He nodded his head a few times, but I'm not sure he heard me. I wanted the grave to be hidden, so I drove to a clearing deep among the trees. It was darker there and seemed colder, despite the windbreak of pine, cedar, and laurel. Easy walked off into the trees. He must have figured he wouldn't be much help, and that probably embarrassed him.

I set to work on the grave, but every time I brought the backhoe against the icy ground, the tractor's engine strained and choked and nearly died. I gave it a little more gas, shifted into the lowest gear. Nothing worked. Finally, cold and angry, I yanked the prong of the throttle toward me, ripping it over its notched metal scale. The engine roared with the rich gasoline, the backhoe bit into the ground, but then sour black smoke began to pour from the engine, the roar became an aching metal shriek, and the whole thing shuddered into silence.

I jumped down and cursed myself and the tractor. My feet were cold, my breath came in plumes. The stars glowed weakly over the bristle of trees at the edge of the clearing.

I heard Easy's voice from deeper in the woods. I thought he would yell something about burning out the engine, but he was calling for me to bring the wire cutters.

I climbed over some fallen trees and stepped across the narrow stream that fed the pond. I couldn't move quickly, because of the rocks and roots hidden beneath the snow.

When I got to Easy, he was standing near the border fence, rubbing the back of his neck and moaning a little. One of the cows had become caught in the barbed wire that ran between Easy's place and Leboux's.

Easy said, "At first I thought it might be a boulder, the woods are so dark. Then I saw it clear. Then I knew."

It had tried to push its head between the top two strings and step through, but it had fouled itself and fallen into the wire. The posts on either side strained and creaked with the weight.

Easy said, "I feel so awful. This is all my fault."

I said, "It was an accident, Easy. It just happened, that's all."

The cow had not died right away. It must have struggled against the sharp wire with the last of its strength. I could see long, twisting grooves in the flesh, and blood standing as thick as jelly in the open wounds. The carcass was pitched forward, with its head hanging just a few inches above the dark, crusty snow. One string of wire had caught under its long jaw, and held it like a strap. One hind leg barely touched the ground, the other was splayed and twisted by the wire. Both forelegs were bent and bound against the stomach.

"We got to cut it free," Easy said.

I said, "It's dead. That won't do any good."

He turned to me. His face was rashy and swollen from the cold. "We can't leave it like this," he said.

I set the metal jaw of the wire cutter against the wire, near the cow's head, and snapped it through. It sprang into spiky coils as the body fell forward onto the ground.

The cow was still alive. It gave a long screaming moan of pain, and then struggled to stand. One hind leg was still hung up in the wire. The other kept slipping on the snow. Its eyes were wide and white. I could see its fat black tongue behind its bared teeth. Then it slammed its bloody head back into my chest.

Easy said, "Oh my God, my God . . ."

The cow screamed again, a rising groan of terror. It tried to shake its hind leg free but couldn't. Just then its forelegs buckled and the cow crashed down for the last time. It didn't move, but when I bent over it, I could see one eye rolling in its socket, then trembling, and then congealing to ice. The cow lay there on the bloody snow, finally dead.

There was nothing we could do. We left the tractor and the cow, and made our way back through the woods toward the open field and home. When we got to the stone wall at the edge of the field, we sat down. Easy kneaded his stump and stared.

He said, "What was I thinking when I bought those cows? They're none of them any good."

My lungs burned and my ribs ached from where the cow had hit me. I said, "That tractor's a piece of junk too."

"That tractor's a '49 Ford. It's a classic," he said. "You just got it all gummed up."

"I think I ruined it," I said.

"No, no. We'll just give it a good swift kick in the morning. That's the thing about a classic."

"I hope you're right," I said. "I hope we can get them buried."

The shadows of clouds crossing the moon floated over the field.

"This is a terrible thing," Easy said. "I sure messed things up good. Some farmer I am. Some kind of farmer."

"Look," I said. "You can see the house from here." It was just over a mile away, and I could barely make out the lights in the windows. But it was like the sudden light you find sometimes in deep woods. All you expect is darkness and shadow. Then, just where you're going to set your foot, a shaft of sunlight or moonlight pours through the pines. It's a small thing, but it makes you think you should keep walking.

Overhead, the night hardened around its cold stars. Maybe there were things he could have done. He could have sold off some acreage or unloaded the cattle at any price. But there really wasn't time. And anyway, that didn't matter. The only thing that mattered was the way he and Joan stood on the back porch that night, clinging to each other, while out there in the dark their dreams were dying.

What happens happens. The day rises and the night falls. Troubles turn on you before you bat an eye. "Should have" and "could have" don't count. Your house is in flames and the world is made of ice.

Easy stood and said, "I'm never going to be the same."

But he was wrong. He would be all right. Easy would let the small things save him. Days of sun and sweet breezes. Late afternoons full of birds streaming into the trees. And other shadows on other nights, as deer climb down from the high ground to the stream in moonlight.

TREVANIAN

THE SACKING OF MISS PLIMSOLL

FROM REDBOOK
FIRST PUBLISHED IN DUTCH BY
TOINE AKVELD IN CONJUNCTION WITH
THE TREVANIAN POETRY PRIZE.

ᔆ

THE PROBLEM WITH MISS PLIMSOLL was that she was plain.

Of course Matthew Griswald had more and better reasons than this for deciding to give her the sack. The last Titan of American Letters and sole legatee of the Paris School of the Disenchanted, he shared the public image of himself as a deeply sensitive creative animal, a tough word-merchant with depths of pain and feeling just beneath the surface of his crisp, heroic style. And no sensitive, heroic man would fire a woman who had continued to work for him through the three years of the Great Drought when he couldn't write anything worthwhile, just because she wasn't pretty. That would be heartless and, worse yet, juvenile. And if there was one thing no one would dare accuse Matthew Griswald of, it was . . .

Take for instance the way Plimsoll had of dealing with his guests. She didn't openly disapprove of the newsprint and television creatures who affirmed their fleeting importance by letting it drop that they had been invited to one of his famous parties, but she pretended not to be impressed when he happened to mention one of them, communicating her irritating apathy by a dry, "Oh, really?" or a yet more deflating, "Is she someone I should know, sir?"

Come to think of it, she wasn't all that clearly impressed by him, either. Not that he expected or wanted people to fall into ecstasies of adulation over him. By no means. But he had, after all, achieved a certain literary prominence meriting a certain deference, and there were times when Plimsoll treated him almost as though he were a gifted child. And if there was one thing no one could say of Matthew Griswald it was . . .

Then there was her habit of arriving at his flat each day so businesslike and full of solemn purpose that he never dared to tell her he had decided to take the day off to recover from a hangover, or just because he was feeling lazy; and her very presence forced him to grind out his daily quota of words, whether he wanted to or not.

These annoyances of long standing constituted a justifying climate for his decision to give her the sack, but the impelling reason was that she was so relentlessly plain! Christ, she even lacked the arresting quality of ugliness, the overwhelming sublimity of the awful. Her plainness was so pervasive that her entering a room had the aesthetic effect of two pretty girls leaving.

He felt his public image demanded a secretary who was, if not ravishing, at least desirable and cute. And the last epithet to come to mind in describing Plimsoll would be "cute," a word he never used in her presence, lest the clear intelligent eyes behind her round steel-rimmed glasses rake him with a glance of frigid scorn. She did not like people and things that were "cute." There was no nonsense to Plimsoll, you had to grant her that. She had a brisk, no-nonsense stride, and a perfectly articulated voice, and a no-nonsense way of working that combined efficiency with the deadening calm of a laboratory.

Matthew Griswald scrubbed his white whisker stubble with his knuckles as he padded out from the kitchen, barefoot and with a coffee mug in his hand, to survey the flotsam of last night's party. Something between a sigh and a groan escaped him. He hadn't had any intention of throwing a party; it had just happened; and before he knew it the place was full of smoke and talk, and everybody was drinking his booze and stroking one another's egos and butts. And now the place was a ruin, and he was left with the jagged edges of a hangover that cut the backs of his eyes when he moved his head too quickly.

It was *always* like that! He was forever doing or being what other people expected him to do or be, and ending up lumbered with things he neither needed nor wanted: like most of the women he dutifully swived, like the fatiguing machoism of his media image, like . . . Plimsoll!

He dropped off his thick terry bathrobe and stood in his shorts, his breasts and stomach pendulous and flabby beneath the heavy varnish of sunlamp tan that leathered his skin. With a shuddering sigh, he steeled himself against the torture of his morning exercises, despite the sour taste in his throat and the leaden pain behind his eyes. The first sit-up brought a dizzying thud of blood to his head, and he lay back with a martyred moan.

"Oh, God." He covered his face with his hands. Why did he subject himself to this daily torture? Was it his fault that the reading public insisted on identifying him with the athletes and warriors and white hunters he wrote about?

Well, let's get on with it! Up you go! Thirty-five of the best!

One . . . two . . . three . . . oh, hell . . . four . . . five . . . six . . .

It seemed he was always doing things he didn't want to—a slave to his own image. He had been elevated from a top-selling adventure novelist to a cult figure among New York critics and midwestern academics who spewed out articles concerning the layers of meaning within his deceptively simple and tough style. For most writers the attention would have been a stroke of good luck, but it almost cost Matthew his career, because he made the mistake of reading what they wrote about him and believing it. For the three terrible and bewildering years of the Great Drought, he had found himself trying to write in the style of Matthew Griswald . . . and failing.

Fourteen . . . fifteen . . . Oh, Christ! Where was I? . . . Ah . . . Twenty-one . . . twenty-two . . .

Fortunately for his finances, if not his craft, the critics and academics had invested their reputations in him, so it turned out that his biggest sellers, his best money and even his Pulitzer

prize all came during the years when he was constipated with
efforts to write like himself.

. . . Twenty-seven . . . twenty-eight . . . To hell with it!
Enough!

Matthew had never been an original intellect, but he had
an original temperament, and he was always a lucid critic of his
own work. One afternoon, six years ago, after reading over
that day's output of self-emulation, he sat staring through the
pages until the room had darkened into evening. With no
histrionics, he had taken up the nearly finished manuscript and
dropped it into his wastepaper basket. Somewhat more theatri-
cally, he drank a bottle of whiskey in two hours and got so sick
that he had to spend four days in a hospital, after an undigni-
fied session with a stomach pump. For a year after that, he didn't
write a word. Lost and terribly frightened, he made an ass of
himself with drinking and scrapping and women, much to the
delight of the news-famished media. In the end, it was his fright
that saved him. It was either get back to writing or suicide.

As a symbol of making a fresh start, as a sort of geo-
graphic punctuation mark between phases of his life, he left
New York for London, where he took a flat and began working. He cut his drinking down and entered into a routine of
regular eating and exercise. Every day he ground out a self-
imposed number of pages, abjuring the old, monosyllabic,
staccato style and the worn-out idiom of the he-man with
deeply hidden pain. At first, things went very badly. Like the
trapeze performer who lets go of the bar before the swing is
within reach, he abandoned one style before he was master of
the next and he fell into the void. In seeking to avoid the
trivial, he found himself creating the tedious. He had never had
much to say, and now he had lost the ability to say it.

But he continued to pour out the words: bad words, dumb
words, stupid characters, ridiculous stories—all of it going
directly from the typewriter into the wastepaper basket, all of it
rejected at the moment of creation by his unforgiving critical
sense, the one talent that had not withered during the Great
Drought. His money began to run out, and he survived on the
little checks his agent sent from reprint and residual rights. So

he forced himself to work harder, hiring a literary secretary to free himself from the petty business of cleaning up copy. Someone—he no longer remembered who—had recommended a first-rate secretary at a publishing house, a woman who was fascinated by his writing and might work cheap.

And that was how he began working with Miss Plimsoll, who was everything a secretary should be—everything but pretty. She was efficient and unobtrusive, and soon she began to handle the correspondence with his useless agent and those readers who still sent occasional letters. She took care of his flimsy finances and kept his ever-shrinking social calendar. She even did minor editorial work, cleaning up fuzzy passages and deleting repetitions or little lapses in logic.

All this freed his time and energy and he entered the most frantic period of the Great Drought, devoting himself totally to a grueling work rate that, even if it failed to recapture success, at least dulled his panic with the anodyne of fatigue.

Little by little his style began to gel. Occasionally a page would not be dropped directly into the wastepaper basket. A story was published; then another. He won a minor award for a piece about himself when he was a young writer in Paris. He started a novel and then went dry. But the encouragement he received from his agent, together with gloomy financial prognostications from Plimsoll, made him keep at it, flogging out the words with no certainty that anything was working. But as he licked the drafts into shape his critical sense told him the writing was good . . . and getting better.

The book was a modest success, and its appearance gave the critics a chance to fill up their columns with comparisons between his earlier style and this new one. "The Graying of Matthew Griswald" became a fashionable topic at academic cocktail parties. Of course, the book never reached the top of the best-seller charts. The heroic era of American letters had passed, replaced by soap-opera novels about career women seeking fulfillment through self-discovery and musical beds, written by ex-literary agents whose skills lay in deal-making and who spent more time on television talk shows than at the typewriter.

But a film came from his novel; then another novel followed; and his short fiction was in demand everywhere. The Great Drought was broken, and his life returned to the rhythms it had had before. His flat became a center for the social luminaries of London: young talents on their way up, older talents scratching to stay where they were, Beautiful People who viewed uselessness as a social talent, media creatures who were famous for being famous, the samplers, the hangers-on. Parties sprang up of their own volition, always in his flat and always at his expense, and more often than not he ended up in bed with one of the literary ladies or one of the cute young things who migrate to such gatherings. He found that he could reduce his desperate work rate to only four or five hours a day, easily half of which was dictating answers to letters and requests into his tape recorder, while Plimsoll cleaned up the latest pages of a tale.

For the next four years he worked within a routine articulated and limited by the presence of Plimsoll, who never altered a degree in energy or attitude. He grew more relaxed; his waist and eyebrows thickened as his hair thinned and his beard whitened. But Plimsoll never changed. Always a tweed skirt and starched white blouse with a high neck; the long, meatless legs; and an expression that seemed, even in repose, to combine patience with rebuke, particularly when she arrived, as she would this morning, to find the litter of a party strewn around the flat. And her attitude toward the women who sometimes lingered into the morning was one of arctic politeness.

Naturally Matthew resented this. And he resented the fact that he never felt free to take a day off because Plimsoll's appearance at the door would act as a silent recrimination against his laziness. But above all he resented her being so remorselessly, so unregenerately plain! It was as though she did it on purpose.

Just last night he had been stung by the persistent ribbing of two of his guests, a much-lauded playwright who was a pet of the critics, who mistook his obscurities for profundity, and the woman he lived with, a popularizer of history whose editor-wrought books sold well because of her family connections and the vigorous exposure she was given by the lickspittle dons of the BBC. This pair's inane teasing had been based on the contention that all writers slept with their secretaries (or, if not exactly "slept with," at least used them casually to relax from work tensions). Many of his guests had met the cool and infinitely proper Miss Plimsoll, and they found hilarious the image of Matthew Griswald, father of the Hard Man School of Writing, grinding away on the razor-sharp pelvis of Miss Plimsoll.

That was it! It was time to be rid of Plimsoll. He could easily manage his own revisions and corrections . . . or whatever the hell it was Plimsoll did. All he needed was someone to handle his calendar and respond to letters from readers, and any good typist could do that, even a cute young thing with no more brains than a racehorse.

In ten minutes—Plimsoll was never late—she would arrive at the flat, glance at the debris of the party with her infuriating expressionlessness, draw from the oversized attaché case she had begun to affect lately the cleanly retyped pages of yesterday's output and put them on his desk for pencil corrections. Then she would sit in her little straight-backed chair and start to deal with his correspondence while he pecked out that day's ration of work on the old portable typewriter that he detested because it was forever breaking down but that had become so much a part of the Griswald mystique that every visitor wanted to have a look at it.

Such was the inflexible routine. But this morning he must find an opportunity—and the courage—to interrupt it and inform her that her services would no longer be required.

Maybe it would be best to write her a letter . . . keep the whole thing from becoming personal and sticky. That wouldn't really be cowardice. It would simply be handling a nasty chore in the most dignified way for all concerned.

What reason would he give for sacking her? I'm sorry, Plimsoll, but you have a sharp pelvis? I'm sorry, kid, but your round glasses and lack of a chin are beginning to affect your typing speed?

No, the letter idea was stupid. After all, he'd have to dictate it to her, and that might cost him something in the way of emotional distance. The best excuse for being rid of her would be that they didn't get along. Maybe that's what he should do—find fault with her for a couple of weeks so she woudn't be surprised when he finally said that their constant contention was making it hard for him to work. Say! Maybe if he found fault persistently enough, she'd quit of her own will. He'd be hurt and shocked, but he'd try to understand, and he would——

He heard her key in the apartment door, which then closed with a precise click. There was silence while she returned the key to her purse before entering the living room. God, she even closed the door tidily!

"Mr. Griswald," she said as she entered and crossed to her little desk. She greeted him that way every morning, the slight, interrogative lift at the end of his name serving in place of "good morning."

"Damn it, Plimsoll! . . ." he began. But although his feelings of irritation were genuine enough, he couldn't think of anything specific to complain about.

"Sir?" she asked rather distantly as she opened her bulky new attaché case with crisp movements and drew out the packet of yesterday's work retyped, tapping it on her desk to make the edges smooth and perfect before setting it beside his battered portable. "Sir?" she asked again. "Is something wrong?"

"Damn it, Plimsoll! I was working something out in my mind, and you come bursting in here and drive it all away!"

She turned and looked at him with just a hint of surprise in her frank, intelligent eyes. Then she turned back to the desk and collected the messy pages he had ground out yesterday. "Oh, I'm sure it will come back to you, sir," she said over her shoulder.

". . . sure it will come back to you, sir," he iterated in a singsong chant that he instantly regretted as a bit infantile. "It frigging well won't come back to me! It's lost now!"

She paused in the task of scanning his throwaway mail and looked at him, seeming to measure his mood. "Are you feeling ill, Mr. Griswald?"

"Feeling ill" was her euphemism for "hung over," and Matthew answered that he was not "feeling ill" and it was none of her damned business anyway.

She smiled thinly. "Perhaps not, sir. But you are a little

tetchy this morning." She dropped the junk mail into the wastepaper basket and began opening the other letters, reading them with her rapid, vertical scan and setting them on her desk in order of urgency. "Oh, here's a letter from Mr. Gold. It concerns details of the transaction he'll be telephoning about this afternoon. You do recall, I hope, that he will be calling from New York at" . . . she tipped up the pendant watch that was her chest's only ornament ". . . at one o'clock our time."

"Of course I remember. The bloodsucking bastard."

"That's hardly fair, sir. Mr. Gold is an honest man, and he stuck by us through our difficult times."

"There's no such thing as an honest agent. Certain people have a warp in their DNA spirals that makes them become used-car dealers or politicians or literary agents. And what's all this about *our* difficult times?"

"Just a manner of speaking, sir," she said. "Shall we go over your calendar?"

"No, forget it," he growled. "Where in hell is Mrs. What's-her-name? This place looks like a pigsty!"

"It does, rather," Miss Plimsoll said in a tone so expressionless that Matthew felt free to take it for arch. "But I'm afraid Mrs. O'Neil won't be in. She telephoned me this morning to say she was feeling a little off."

"A little off? Off what?"

"Her feed, presumably. Although from a slight slur of diction, one might be forgiven for assuming that she's off the wagon as well."

"You disapprove of drinking, don't you, Plimsoll."

"I disapprove of anything that prevents a person from doing his or her work, sir."

"But particularly the vices, eh?" He was becoming frustrated with Plimsoll's cold-blooded disinclination to rise to battle.

She looked at him from behind her steel-rimmed glasses and smiled wearily. "To which vices are you referring, sir?"

"The usual lot. The Big Seven. Sloth, greed, envy, chastity— how do you stand on the vice of chastity, Plimsoll?"

She returned to making little notes in the margins of the letters she would be answering this morning. "If one chooses to view chastity as a vice, sir, one has the reassurance that it's one vice modern society is managing to stamp out. Ah!" She held up an envelope. "We have an invitation from Somerville, my college at Oxford. Would you be interested in delivering a lecture next month?"

"On what subject?" He sat down at his desk with a heavy grunt.

"Let me see . . . On 'The Anti-Hero in Literature and Society.' "

"What are they offering?"

"Ah . . . expenses and a banquet in your honor."

"Screw 'em."

"I assume I may paraphrase that in my reply?"

He wasn't sure if she was trying to be amusing or if she was being snide. "I never got a college degree. I was kicked out of two colleges."

"Yes, sir, I know. The University of Wisconsin and Northwestern."

"Right. And I never majored in literature, either!"

"I am aware of that, sir. In letters to American academics I have often cited your view that studying literature is, to a real writer, what analyzing horse droppings would be to a stallion."

"I never said horse *droppings,* Plimsoll. But you studied literature, didn't you?"

"I read modern letters, yes. In fact, my major essay was a stylistic analysis of your early work and——"

"But you ended up a typist. There you are, Plimsoll. Some people lay eggs while others nibble at omelets."

She smiled. "I'll confess to nibbling my share of omelets, sir, if you'll confess to laying your share of eggs."

Matthew had the impression that he had not won that round cleanly. With a frown he buried himself in the work of reading Plimsoll's neatly typed transcript of yesterday's output while she dashed off answers to the morning's mail. So routine and unimaginative were the letters from readers and so long had she worked for him that she was able to reply in an imitation of his style that was close enough to let him get away with just signing or, in rare instances, adding a P.S. in his own hand.

His concentration kept straying from the manuscript because this Plimsoll business was itching in the back of his mind.

"Well, what about you, Plimsoll?" he asked out of a long silence.

"Sir?" Her voice was distant, her attention riveted on the letter she was typing.

"We were talking about the deadly sin of chastity."

She was used to his fragmented way of communicating when he was working. "Are you asking what I think of it, sir?"

"I'm asking if you're guilty of it."

She was silent for a moment; then she changed the subject, asking, "Have you decided what you're going to say to Mr. Gold when he calls?"

"Bloodsucking fifteen-percenter!"

"Mr. Gold has proved himself a very devoted friend."

"Devoted to profit. Let's get back to your chastity. What shape is it in, Plimsoll? Unassailed? Assailed but well defended? Assailed but not within the last decade? Still intact?"

"I confess that I don't see any impelling reason for us to be discussing my chastity, sir." There was a crisp reticence in her tone.

Ah! A chink in her frosty armor at last.

"I'm not asking on behalf of my own libido, Plimsoll. I'm working up a character not unlike you. And I was wondering how she would respond to a sexual advance."

She turned from her work and looked directly at him. "I am surprised that you would be introducing a character like me, Mr. Griswald. You usually populate your novels with women of a more obvious sort."

"Contrast, Plimsoll. I want to establish a character alongside whom the ordinary woman would seem to be a panting houri."

"I see." There was alum in her voice.

"Well?"

She drew a sigh and folded her long, thin hands in her lap. "Very well, sir. To begin with, I do believe that chastity is a most desirable quality in a woman—indeed, in any person. A lack of chastity indicates an absence of self-esteem. And it has been my observation that the promiscuous are either seeking to deny an unstated accusation, or attempting to find companionship and warmth at its most biological and least compassionate level. Coitus for them is a prelude to hand-holding; fornication, an avenue to conversation. But I do not equate chastity with celibacy. I see nothing unchaste in making love when one loves . . . even if that love is the product of gossamer circumstances and not an enduring relationship. Have I responded fully enough to your question, sir?"

"My frigging cup runneth over!" He returned to scanning yesterday's work. But after no more than a minute he lifted his head. "How old are you, Plimsoll?"

She emitted a slight sigh that seemed to ask if she were ever to be allowed to get on with her work. "I am forty-one years old, sir."

"Forty-one. Ten years younger than I am. And already you're standing aside from life, an observer rather than a contestant."

"I have never wanted to be a contestant, actually, sir. Which is not to say that I've never wanted to be a participant."

"You can't participate unless you're willing to be a contestant. Life's a battle; readers are fickle and stupid; agents are thieves; friends are sponges. Life, Plimsoll, is a contact sport." He rather liked that phrasing, so he made a note of it in a little notebook he kept for the purpose. When he looked up, he found Plimsoll watching him evenly.

"May I ask what is wrong, Mr. Griswald?"

"Wrong? Wrong in what way?"

She lifted her thin shoulders. "Well, you seem to be bristling with antagonism this morning. And I have the impression that you are bent upon embarrassing me . . . even hurting me."

"Nonsense. That's one of your problems, Plimsoll. You're too sensitive." He knew this was the moment to tell her he had decided to give her the sack, but he recoiled from the unpleasant task.

"Is it really nonsense, sir?" She looked at him evaluatingly for another moment. "Oh, very well." And she returned to her work.

*   *   *

Oh, hell, he thought. His chance to get this business over with was slipping away. "Ah . . . actually, Plimsoll, there is something on my mind."

"Oh, sir?" Her attention remained on her work.

"Yes. Yes. To tell the truth, I've decided to . . ." He knew he was going to lie, as he always did in awkward social circumstances—more for the sake of the other fellow than for himself, to be sure.

She left her finger on the page to mark her place and looked up at him, her eyebrows raised. "You've decided what, sir?"

He cleared his throat. "Look here, Plimsoll. I'm beginning to burn out with this routine. I'm sick of cranking out a couple thousand words every day, every day. I need a break. A vacation. And I've been thinking about the South of France."

"That's a wonderful idea, sir. And perhaps you're right. Perhaps a change of scene and a reduction of your work rate would do you a world of good. But, of course, you mustn't stop writing altogether. We both know the danger in that. The juices stop flowing and the style becomes a bit heavy, and——"

"Never mind my damned juices!"

"The season has already begun, so I'll have to get cracking to find someplace pleasant but not overrun with visitors." She smiled self-deprecatingly. "I'm afraid my French is a bit rusty. I've been told that my French is typically British: accurate in grammar but frightful in accent. Still——"

"Hold it! I didn't say *we* were taking a vacation. I said *I* was."

"Oh," she said with a soft catch of her breath. "I see." A slight flush reddened her long throat. "I didn't mean to be presumptuous. I naturally assumed that . . ." She smiled bravely, but Matthew could have sworn that her eyes were damp. Then she took a quick breath and continued in a businesslike tone. "And what do you have in mind for me to do while you're *en vacances*, sir? I assume I shall act as a sort of letter drop, unless you want to deal with all the trivia of——"

"Listen, Plimsoll. The fact is . . . Well, you see, I'm not sure I'll be coming back to Britain at all. It's still all up in the air. And even if I do return to London, it won't be the same as before. I plan to reduce my work rate permanently. I can afford a little more leisure and I think I've earned it. Maybe I'll find a place in the country somewhere. I haven't made up my mind exactly, but in any case I won't be needing a . . . well, certainly it would be a waste of talent to use a person like you just to answer a few letters and . . . that sort of thing."

As he spoke her eyes widened slowly. Her spine straightened and she seemed to grow taller in her chair. "Are you discharging me, Mr. Griswald?"

"Oh, now, I don't think I would put it that way, exactly."

"Oh? How would you put it, sir?"

"Well, it's not as though . . . Look, I've already talked to the people down on Queen Street and they're dying to have you back," he lied. "In fact, just the other day I was——"

"I'm not interested in returning to the publishing world, sir," she said firmly.

"What? Oh, well, that's your own affair, I suppose. I just thought that——"

"Sir? Excuse me for interrupting you, but would you mind terribly if we didn't discuss this further just now? I have a good deal of work to get out this morning. And I confess that I find this subject rather . . . unsettling."

He shrugged. "Whatever you say. But it's something we have to face sooner or later."

She nodded, closed her eyes and took a deep breath; then she returned to composing a response to a letter from a woman reader in Minneapolis who had suggested, not very obliquely, that if the Great Man ever found himself in St. Paul, she would be delighted to be of service.

More than half an hour passed in taut silence broken only by the staccato clicking of Plimsoll's typewriter. Matthew kept his head down, pretending to be absorbed in work. He couldn't understand why she was reacting in this childish way. All this unexpressed resentment. All this accusing efficiency. All this hysterical silence!

"I need a drink," he grumbled, and he rose to get himself a glass of burgundy. He didn't really feel the need of a drink, but he wanted to let her know that this wasn't all that easy for him either.

"Look at this place! I don't know why that damned Mrs.
. . . What's-her-name can't manage to get in to clean up. God
knows I pay her enough!"

Plimsoll did not respond. She rolled the last of the letters
from her typewriter and added it to the stack for his signature.
Then she turned her chair toward Matthew's desk, composed
herself and folded her hands in her lap. "I believe there are one
or two things I should like to say to you, sir."

"Oh? Really? Well, all right, let's have it." He was glad
she didn't intend to accept her firing without complaint, as
exposing himself to her vitriol would diminish any sense of
guilt he might have felt over the business. He carried his glass
of wine to his desk and sat down heavily. "Fire away, Plimsoll," he said with a martyred sigh.

"Before I 'fire away,' sir, I should like to remind you
again that Mr. Gold will be calling from New York in"—she
tilted up the pendant watch on her bosom—"in approximately
two hours."

"Forewarned is forearmed . . . the frigging bloodsucker!"

"I believe your unkind and unjust evaluation of Mr. Gold
provides us with a useful starting point for what I have to say
to you."

"Just so the starting point isn't too far from the finish line."

"I shall do my best to be succinct, sir." She compressed
her lips and composed herself for what he feared would be a
lengthy tirade. "I should begin by telling you honestly that I
have always considered you to be one of the most gifted writers
of our age . . ."

"I have never heard a setup line more pregnant with its
'however.' "

She smiled tightly. "However, I also consider you to be
the most self-centered and ungrateful man I have ever met. You
don't care in the least for other people. Mrs. O'Neil has cleaned
up after your silly, profligate parties for six years and you've
never even bothered to learn her name. Mr. Gold carried you
through your most difficult years and yet you constantly refer
to him as a parasite. And I, who have worked with you and
supported you for these many years . . . Tell me, Mr. Griswold,
do you know my first name?"

"Your first name?"

"My first name."

"Well, it's . . . All right, so I don't recall it at this moment! But I'm sure you have one. Coming from the poor-but-snide ranks of the fallen leisure class, no doubt every inexpensive luxury was showered on you, including a first name. Indeed, I wouldn't be surprised if, in an orgy of eponymous prodigality, your parents even gave you a middle name as well . . . What in hell are you smiling at?"

"Nothing important, sir. I've always been amused by your rather Victorian habit of retreating behind sesquipedalian barriers when you're stung. It's a charming tic, really. Particularly in a man noted for his leanness of style—don't you agree?"

"No, I do not," he grumbled.

"Pity. One of your saving graces has always been your sense of humor, your appreciation of the ridiculous, even in yourself. Without that you would have been quite insufferable."

He stared at her. "You are certainly making it easier for me to give you the sack without remorse. What in hell did you mean by saying that Gold carried me through the Great Drought . . . if anything?"

"No doubt Mr. Gold would be displeased to know that I told you, but I think I should, nevertheless. First I should explain that Mr. Gold and I have carried on a friendly and rather extensive epistolary relationship for many years now, the subject of which has been you."

"You've been exchanging letters behind my back?"

"Without your knowledge, sir. But I wouldn't say behind your back. At this very moment there are persons talking to one another in Tibet without your knowledge, but surely you're not so great an egotist to assume they are doing it behind your back."

"I hate nit-picking."

"Oh? Tell me, sir, do you recall how you managed to survive the period when you couldn't produce anything you considered—quite rightly, I may say—worthy to go to a publisher?"

"Of course. I lived from month to month on a trickle of money Gold sent me from residuals, foreign rights, reprints—

that sort of thing. A trickle from which he wrung his percentage, you can be sure. So what?"

"There were no residuals."

"What? What the hell are you talking about?"

"No residuals. No foreign rights. No reprints. You were, not to put too fine a point on it, a drug on the market—although that simile has perhaps been vitiated by the current popularity of drugs in our culture. In publishing circles there was a joke about your work which, while a little off-color, makes the point rather well. It was said that most publishers would rather fail a Wassermann than accept a manuscript from you. I confess that I was quite furious the first time I heard the remark."

Matthew was silent for a time. "Are you trying to tell me Gold sent that money out of the goodness of his granite heart?"

"Just so, sir. And because he had faith in your talent. But above all, because he was sorry for you."

"Sorry for me? Sorry for *me*?" He stood up, the blood pounding in his temples. "That presumptuous, arrogant son of a bitch was sorry for me? Well, I'll give him something to be sorry about. When he calls this afternoon, I'm going to fire his ass!"

Miss Plimsoll squinted her eyes and tilted her head to the side. "No . . . I don't . . . think so, sir."

Matthew's face stretched with mock wonder. "I beg your pardon?"

"I don't think you're going to give Mr. Gold the sack, sir." A slight smile creased the corners of her eyes. "Any more than you are going to give it to me." She rose and opened her oversized attaché case. As she drew out a large stack of papers, some quite rumpled and old, she said, "Perhaps you have wondered why I began bringing so cumbersome a case with me a couple of months ago, sir."

"Frankly, I hadn't spent much time worrying about it."

"No, I suppose not. To do so would indicate an interest in others."

"If you're accusing me of not spending my nights pondering the weight and size of Miss Plimsoll's attaché case, I plead guilty. O-oh! Wait a minute! I get it. Plimsoll's written a novel. And she wants me to help her get it published—as conscience money for giving her the sack. Don't believe that crap about everybody having a novel somewhere inside them, Plimsoll. There are two kinds of people in the world: the storytellers and the audience members. And you are an audience member. You are the prototypic audience member. No, thanks. I don't want to read your damned manuscript. I'm not interested in the precious wordsmithing of someone who has never lived, never made a mistake, never laughed, never loved!"

"Oh, I have been in love, sir," she said, evening the pages of manuscript by tapping them on her desk.

"Oh, really? Plimsoll in love. It's an image as arousing as a hip bath in ice water. And what poor bastard was the recipient of this uniquely modest gift?"

She spoke in a quiet, matter-of-fact tone. "You, sir."

"Me?"

"But that is neither here nor there just now. What I want you to do is read at random through this material. I think you'll find it——"

"Me?" Then his eye fell on the top sheet of the manuscript. "Wait a minute! What the hell's going on here? This is *my* work!" The stack contained both Plimsoll's neatly retyped copy and his first-draft material, full of X-ings-out and penciled marginalia. She had firm instructions to burn his originals after copying them. This was done to protect his reputation as a natural stylist whose first draft was practically galley-perfect—a myth that he had not originated, but one he treasured as a part of the Griswald mystique.

"Now, why don't you read through some of that manuscript, Matthew, while I make——"

"*Matthew?*"

"—while I make us a nice pot of tea."

"I don't want any lousy tea!"

"As you wish. I shall make some for myself, then. No, on second thought I think that I'll have a glass of your excellent burgundy."

"My burgundy?"

"Just read the manuscript, Matthew. Whatever I may think of you as a compassionate man, I have total faith in your gifts as a critic."

While Plimsoll sat at her desk, her legs tightly crossed, sipping her wine, Matthew read, scanning quickly at first with an attitude of martyred boredom. Then his frown deepened as he read with a growing—and chilling—fascination. She had made many small changes in his wording, little deletions and additions, slight rearrangements of phrase, no one of them very significant in itself, but in total effecting the difference between the lean and the barren, between foreshadowing and redundancy, between the evocative and the obscure. He could not quite define the change brought about by her pruning and grafting, but it had to do with density and celerity. In a way of speaking, a minute of reading his original seemed to last seventy seconds, while her version had forty-second minutes. In sum, that which the world recognized as the Griswald style existed in Plimsoll's copy and was absent from the tangled, rather muddy original.

His stomach went cold. He set the manuscript down and stared out the window before his desk, his eyes blurred. For many years he had known that he lacked the qualities of excellence he admired in other men. He could never be a good father, he was too egoistic; it wasn't in him to be a good husband, he was too much the taker and too little the giver; even his lovemaking was based more on tactic than emotion. And as for courage . . . he hadn't climbed those mountains without professional help; he hadn't shot those lions without a back-up man covering him; the only thing he had done quite alone was to be photographed in appropriately battered costume. For years he had admitted to himself that if he were not a good writer, he would be nothing at all. And now . . .

"I think I know what you're feeling, Matthew," Miss Plimsoll said softly.

"Do you? Do you really? You have no idea what a consolation that is to me!"

"There is something you must understand. I could not have written those novels and stories alone. It's you who have the creative imagination, the experience, the sense of pain and laughter, the pantheon of unique and fascinating characters.''

"I'm delighted to have been able to contribute a little something.''

"What you lost during the Great Drought was . . . style. And that is what I have provided. Please don't feel miserable. We have been a team for some years now, a *belle équipe,* but it's always been you who possessed the inspiration and the dynamic energy. I've admired those things in you . . . loved them in you, actually.''

"I don't want to hear about it," he moaned.

"I know this is unpleasant for you. You've never been exactly avid to know the truth about yourself. You've always allowed the views and values of others to define you. So it's inevitable that the truth comes to you with pain . . . as it comes to the heroes of our novels.''

He reached forward and rubbed his palms along the sides of his battered old typewriter in a kind of tactile good-bye.

"I was quite content with my silent and invisible role, you know," she continued. "I even cherished helping you the more for the knowledge that you were unaware of it, and happy to be so. I had every intention of going on like that forever. But I have seen something growing in your attitude toward me for the past month or so." She smiled thinly. "You're nothing if not transparent, Matthew.''

"Please don't call me by my first name.''

"I have always called you Matthew . . . to myself. I have known for more than a month now that you were steeling yourself to be rid of me. At first I was stung by the unfairness of it. But then I realized that you were as helpless in this as you are in other things. So I decided to take matters into my own hands, for your good as well as for mine.''

"All that doesn't matter now. It's all over. I suppose you intend to do an exposé story about this? 'Matthew Griswald's Secret Collaborator'? You could make a bundle with it. It's the kind of thing the snot-nosed provincial reporters from Toronto would salivate over.''

"Nothing could be further from my mind, Matthew.''

"What *is* on your mind, then?''

"What I propose is that we continue our association."

His eyes narrowed with chary mistrust. "You really mean that? You're willing to go on just like before?"

"Well . . . not exactly as before."

"Ah! I should have known. What is it you want?"

"I have reached an age when one must consider one's future."

"Money. Is that it?"

"Security is more important to me than money. And I believe that security would best be assured if we were to marry."

His eyes widened. "Marry? You and me?"

"Your shock is not terribly chivalrous, Matthew. It's a solution I've considered in moments of reverie for some years now."

An almost unthinkable possibility grew in Matthew's mind. "You are speaking of a marriage of convenience, aren't you? A marriage that insures your financial future and gives you some of the social advantages . . . the parties, the media events . . . all that?"

"I don't foresee all that many parties, actually. And I must tell you that I have no intention of entering into a marriage that is a sham confected for purely financial reasons."

"Let me get this straight. Are you saying that we—that you and I . . . would . . . ?"

"Just so, Matthew. We shall work together; we shall travel and amuse ourselves together; we shall cherish one another; and we shall . . . satisfy one another."

"Satisfy. I see. And I suppose the relationship is to be monogamous?"

"Oh, yes, indeed, Matthew, most strictly monogamous. You will never know how I have been hurt by the mindless women I've found here in the mornings, all rumpled and smelling of sleep."

He nodded, a bit dazed. "And that's the deal, is it? If I want your help, I have to buy the whole package."

"That—as you rather indelicately put it—is the deal."

He drew a long, shuddering sigh and turned again to the stack of manuscript on his desk. He reread two pages of his first-draft material, then Plimsoll's neatly typed revision. He tossed the papers aside and looked again at Miss Plimsoll, his eyes squinted in appraisal. You have to admit that she has a nice complexion. And her hands aren't all that bad. . . .

"It's true, isn't it, that the characters and the situations are all mine. All you do is tighten the style a little. What you might call 'stylistic packaging.' "

She smiled. "That's all I do, Matthew."

He nodded. "Ah . . . tell me, Plimsoll. Are you any good in the sack?"

A slight flush rose on her throat. She tipped up her pendant watch and glanced at it. "We have an hour and twenty minutes before Mr. Gold calls. That should be adequate time to investigate the matter, I should think."

As they crossed toward the bedroom he asked, "By the way, what the hell *is* your first name?"

"I'll tell you afterward."

GAYLE WHITTIER
TURNING OUT

FROM TRIQUARTERLY

ِ

"PLIÉ!" The pink and black line at the *barre* drops down.

"Relevé!" The line lifts, more unevenly.

I am scrabbling for leverage, parts of my forgetful body tilting out of art back into nature. At last, late, I rise too on a brilliant point of pain. I am upheld mostly by the sinew of my mother's gaze. From across the hall she stares fixedly through me to the ideal daughter alive only in her dangerous maternal mind. Inside my staved toe shoe, a specific pressure reopens last Saturday's blister.

"Plié!" We begin again.

The hands of the schoolroom clock on the far wall have frozen at two of twelve. If I watch they will never move. But when I look away, "Time!" Sergei dismisses us. Although we dance in spellbound, mispronounced French, we begin and end Group Ballet in a wide-awake and daily English.

"Time!" As the clock's hand darts across noon, the mothers discreetly check their watches to make sure of every paid-for minute. They smile, if at all, only at their daughters. They are as still, as grim as the face of a priestess casting bones.

My own mother wears even disappointment well. "Go *on*, Bonnie, take your toe shoes off. We haven't got all day." A

towel, the admonitory smell of Lysol, come towards me. "Well,
go *on*."

Turtle-shaped, my foot sticks, then springs suddenly free,
the toes still invisible inside their protective "bunny pads."
Worse is about to come. However gently I peel these cusps
away, moist strands of rabbit fur clump where my flesh has
oozed or, sometimes, yielded blood. Hair by hair I draw off
the whistling pain. "Ow-w."

"Shh."

"Well, it hurts."

"I know it hurts. Here," she slips me the phial of iodine
powder. "Be brave." But she is gazing elsewhere. "Just look at
Gillian, will you. That girl never stops."

Away from the *barre*, Gillian, our class hope, poses in
command of all the eight anatomical directions of the dance.
Fatigue has not touched her. Her body arches and her torso
tightens for a final budburst. She unfurls upward in a perfect
entrechat; tries the circumference of space, a *cabriole*. Then the
whole staff of her body blossoms, deft porcelain, ivory, not
our common stuff. She turns and returns in the gyres of an
almost endless *pirouette*. Faster she spins, the boundaries of the
legs going; faster, her bright hair streaks into her scarf. Faster,
she revolves, *spotting*, fixing an air-mark before her. Above the
blur of arms and skirt and legs, her face seems still: she has
been beheaded, reassembled by magicians.

"Well, Gillian shouldn't be in Group, it's not good for
morale," my mother's judgment falls.

Now Sergei has paused to watch. Our elderly pianist re-
vives too, scattering a few rosy bars of "Amaryllis" into the
blank air of the studio. Even the other students watch, observing in her the reason why they practice every day, what they
will turn into if they do.

"Your *plié* will do," my mother turns away, "but only
because you're helped by gravity. But you'll have to work on
élévation," a great discipline in her voice as Gillian leaps, *grand
jeté, grand jeté, grand jeté*. Then Madame, massive caryatid,
emerges from the office in her magenta satin class dress, flame-
thrower hair, thighs muscular with varicose grapes. Gillian, her

raddled face says, has more than *placement, extension, line,* those brief commodities: Gillian has a future.

Applause, dropped beads, and "Bravo!" dries up quickly among the odors of talcum and sweat. Gillian resumes her place among us. Madame smiles and beckons to her mother.

"Marie Ravert may be my best friend," my mother tells the walls, "but sometimes I think she's just a *stage mother* after all!" For it is understood that Gillian dances to fulfill her mother's "ambition," while I, more penitentially, dance for Grace. "Shh!" My mother strains to hear what Madame Orloff is saying. The word "exceptional" unrolls towards us; next, magic names, "New York . . . London," ascend to "Rome, perhaps," and consummate in "Paris, the Ballet Russe!" All the mothers start, look up as if they have heard their own names called.

But Mrs. Ravert's short arms crowd over her bosom. Her head bows no, no, no.

"You must get the money *somewhere*! *Borrow* it!" Now Madame booms whole sentences across the studio, but Mrs. Ravert's shoulders bend towards humiliation on a pulse of No, I'm afraid not, No.

"Why, the girl's a *natural*!" Madame informs everyone in earshot. "*Steal* if you have to, but get it somewhere! *Kill* for it!" she carries herself away, all Slavic extravagance. "*Kill*!"

"If there's one thing I can't stand, it's favoritism," my mother says. I sprinkle the iodine powder on my blister and wait for the reassurance of a local burn. "Bonnie, fluff your hair, it's stuck to your head."

"I can't help it."

"Group Class for *now*, then," Madame gives up on a hyperbolic gesture, you-can-see-what-I'm-up-against, to everyone who cares to watch. "But it's a *shame*!" On "shame," she turns towards us.

"Hold still while I tie it back with a ribbon, anyway," my mother says. "I wish you wouldn't twitch so."

Then it is certain. Madame is approaching us, a half-smile wired to her face. Is she going to ask *us* for Gillian's lesson money? I wonder.

"Mrs. Brent, could I see you a moment . . . ?"

"We're already paid up through next month. I've got the receipt right here. . . ."

"Oh, no. No, that's not what I wanted to talk about. In my office, please? You too, Bonnie. This concerns you."

We follow her at a distance. People are leaving now, and the studio resumes its great emptiness, to be filled by other classes today and, on Wednesday nights, the Bingo games they hold here.

"I bet she's giving you the 'Sugar Plum Fairy,' what do you want to bet?" my mother hisses. "Now act *surprised*, Bonnie."

In the smaller side room, over a table strewn with snippets of costume fabric, hundreds of younger Madames look down from glossies on a red velvet board: Madame as Pierrot, with rakish melancholy, hand under chin, and painted tear; Madame as a large-featured Giselle in Black Forest bodice; and, of course, Madame as the Dying Swan.

"Mrs. Brent, I've made myself *sick* over this, just *sick*," her accent slips as she begins.

"What is it?"

"But I believe in being frank, I owe it to you, it's your investment, after all. There is"—her hand surrenders the room to fate—"no other way."

"But what's the matter?" My mother's Sugar Plum Fairy smile lingers, dead, on her face.

Madame, steadying herself, gazes into the wall of mirrors opposite us. Before them, a light oak *barre* runs prairie smooth. This is where I danced until my father "put his foot down," before I discovered, in the cheaper democracy of Group Class, the lie of my talent. This is the room for private lessons. Our glances meet in triplicate on the silver surface of the mirror.

"Where should I begin?" Madame wonders. Plunging, "It's my *sad* responsibility to tell you, Mrs. Brent . . ." the truth flows free, "that Bonnie's future in ballet is . . . well, *limited*. Believe me, I am sorry." Madame's hands ward off a protest my stunned mother cannot, as yet, make. "Truly sorry."

"What exactly do you mean by 'limited'?" she asks at last.

"You know," Madame sidesteps, "even *two* years ago she was nudging the height limit for a ballerina." She smiles hurriedly. "Bonnie's not exactly prima ballerina *size,* if you see what I mean."

In the mirror, my mother sees what she means, and I do too, my random, changing flesh flashed back at us.

"Oh, she's *shot up.*" My mother cannot deny it. "But she won't keep on growing, will you, Bonnie. Anyway, I have no *illusions.* She may not become a first dancer, but I'm not a *stage mother* either. As far as I'm concerned, there's nothing wrong with the *corps de ballet.*"

"My dear." Madame takes my mother's hand. She clears her throat of something worse. "I'm afraid Bonnie would unbalance the line even *there.* Exactly how old *are* you, Bonnie?"

My answer and my mother's intertwine.

"I'm sure she's reached her full height. I reached *mine* early."

"Fourteen last April," I confess.

A *faux pas.* In the Dance, your exact age is never calculated. "Teen," especially, evokes panic, for everyone holds her breath as you skid across the perilous mud of adolescence, Nature finger-painting you with hormones, blurring the artful line of years of lessons. For many Mothers of the Dance, a daughter's change of heart or bone may synchronize with their darker "changes of life." We dance in a time of endings.

"Only *fourteen!*" Madame seizes on it. "What, some girls keep on growing until they're *eighteen!*"

We all close our imaginations, not quite fast enough, against the spectacle of me, a dancing giantess of eighteen, demoted, year by year, from the Ballet Russe to the sideshow.

But my mother rallies. "You don't mean to tell me that it's only a matter of *size,* do you? Didn't you say it yourself, last year, Bonnie has *talent*? How can you have talent one year and not the next?"

"All my students have talent. I never accept a student who doesn't," Madame testifies. "But talent's not the whole picture. There's structure, too. With *les petits rats,* the babies, who can tell? The older ones . . . well, one needs light bones, strict muscles, a long torso, *so,* and . . ." A complicated gesture cancels me out. "Time decides. What more can I say except that I am truly, truly sorry . . . !"

The fact upon her, my mother flattens into a chair. "You mean she should *stop dancing*?"

"Did I say that? Did you hear me say that, Bonnie? Of course not." Madame laughs palely. "Haven't I always said that Bonnie's the most . . . most *industrious* dancer I've got. She *will dance*!" Color and confusion brighten my mother's face. "She should just shift to tap, that's all."

"Tap." The sentence is pronounced. All of us know that ballet is *the* Dance, an art, unlike the dazzling, double-jointed trickery of tap dancing, or, one more fall below, acrobatic "routines" and "baton lessons."

"Oh, she'll be *striking* in tap, just look at her! Why, a few weeks of private lessons and she'll catch up in time for the Christmas recital."

"Private lessons? Oh, I don't know. . . ."

"Wouldn't you like a solo, Bonnie?"

"Who, me?"

"A solo spot," Madame promises, right hand raised to the portrait of Pavlova. "I give you my word . . . *if* she applies herself."

"A solo in five months? Is that really possible?"

Madame looks offended. "Do I know my own business or not?"

"Of course, of course. I didn't mean to suggest . . ."

"I accept your apology," Madame declares, her accent now back in place. "Now, what would be a good time for this little one's new lessons? Thursday? Friday?"

"Either. Well, Thursday."

"I hope we can fit her in." Madame consults her big ledger. "Four-thirty? Five? . . . And you can apply the Group Lessons already paid for, *of course*. Bonnie, you are a very fortunate young lady. Practice every day now, don't disappoint us."

"Oh, don't worry. I'll see that she does."

"And thank you, Mrs. Brent, thank you for being so *reasonable*. You would not believe some of the people I have to deal with!" She rolls her eyes for heavenly help.

"Stage mothers." My mother understands.

Madame starts herding us out of her office. "One of these

days," she consoles my mother, "you'll have a swan there. You'll wake up and see a *swan!*"

We emerge beside the sign INSTRUCTION MUST BE PAID FOR IN ADVANCE. The next hour's crowd of mothers and daughters swarms around us on their way to Group Tap. Theirs is a noisy, glossy craft, carried in round red or black patent-leather hat boxes. One tiny five-year-old wears, despite the heat, a leopard-skin coat. The Mothers of Tap have hard, bright faces, red nails, lips wide with Revlon's Fire and Ice.

Mine is a small, very elegant mother who has made a lifework of her good bone structure and her Good Taste. Good Taste directs that petticoats match skirts in one of three colors only: black, white, and beige. Good Taste defines the brief season for white shoes (not before Memorial Day, not after Labor Day); it even measures and colors the rim of our company china, which may be white or cream with a "classic" gold border, but painted flowers only if they are "dainty." Daintiness, in fact, is one reason my mother has befriended Mrs. Ravert, whose humility is rubbed smooth and small like a pebble, and whose Scots accent my mother thinks "refined." Also Mrs. Ravert wrestles skittishly with many small, but manageable, worries, a good sign in a good mother. "Oh dear, I hope Gillian doesn't become too *American*. Her manners put me to shame! What do *you* think, Ida?" and "Oh dear, Gillian uses so much slang I hardly understand her! Ida, what . . . ?"

The staircase clears. Marie and Gillian Ravert are waiting for us in the vacant entry below.

"Now just smile," my mother directs, sotto voce, "as if nothing's happened. There's no reason to be ashamed. Everybody knows only one or two girls ever make it."

"Only one or two will make it," Madame warns the mothers ritually. Each nods, though disbelieving that she has not earned, with her ambitious love, with the hard-saved dollar-fifty's for Group or the three dollars for a private lesson, a daughter's opportunity. Most of the mothers look plain and overworked, starved, like Mrs. Ravert, on American dreams. A startling number of them have, by some special curse, hatched peacocks, the challenge of uncommonly pretty daughters. Only my mother and I upend expectation. She walks, concluded, in a fading and ungiven legacy of beauty. I, it is charitably understood, am "still growing," not quite done.

"Only one or two" explains why silence so often covers the older students like a purifying snow. Yes, Barbara Cross actually tap-danced on the Ted Mack Amateur Hour, remember? And Judy Scolini *almost* got on the Ed Sullivan show with her Toy Shop ballet. But where are they now?

"I *heard* Barbara met somebody in New York, she got married."

"Is he rich?"

"I *heard* he's a millionaire!"

Of course. Because in every mother's mind fame flows to roses, red, red for the blood-pulse of the audience and for the passion of strangers. Millionaires all lined up outside the stage door just about to open. And if the scholarship dancer should come home quietly, failed, or pregnant, if she should be worn down to selling tickets, "Only one or two will ever make it. . . ." We have always known.

Outside Madame's studio, late summer thickens, bright and alkaline.

"I'm so embarrassed, Ida. I suppose everybody *heard*," Mrs. Ravert murmurs.

"*I* didn't. What did she have to say?"

"Well, she said Gillian ought to have private lessons, the way she used to." She adores Gillian with her eyes. "She says she's *talented*, a 'natural.' "

Gillian walks with us milkmaid-sweet, apple-breasted, arms a graceful birthright, joints that must move on golden pins, not bone. Her feet turn out without being commanded. She steps over the sidewalk cracks without a downward glance.

"I just don't know. What do *you* think, Ida? Do *you* think she's got talent?"

"Anybody can see that."

"What did she say to *you*, Ida? Madame."

"Exactly the same thing. Madame told us Bonnie's talented."

"You don't say!" Mrs. Ravert's amazement checks itself diplomatically.

"I do say. She's been watching her and she's decided

Bonnie's got a distinct talent for tap. Fix your barrette, dear, it's slipping."

"Tap?"

"That's where the *real* money is, you know, like Eleanor Powell, vaudeville . . ." she finds at last, "the Rockettes! Not in ballet."

"Bonnie *is* quite a strapping lassie."

"She's not big, she's statuesque. Bonnie's a long-stemmed American beauty."

"Hey, Bon." Gillian's elbow cuts into my side. "You really gonna do tap?"

"I guess so."

Gillian's jaws move up and down, *plié, relevé*, on her chewing gum while she considers this. "Well, Jeez Louise," she says.

"Of course I'm just thrilled!" my mother's voice is practicing behind us. "Tap's so much more natural. Did you know, Marie, that ballerinas never menstruate?"

"They don't? Oh, that can't be true, Ida, is that true?"

"It certainly is. I read it in the *Reader's Digest*. It's from starving themselves all the time, that's why."

"Imagine that!"

Gillian pushes me ahead of our mothers' lowered voices. By now Mrs. Ravert is or soon will be confiding how her husband came home drunk again and hit her—"right here" —her nylon glove touching her cheek as if to reimprint it with the color of the bruise. "You ought to just *walk out*," my mother will advise, as usual. And Mrs. Ravert will agree that yes, she knows, she should leave that man, she *would* leave him if it weren't for the children, the children. . . .

Gillian walks faster. "Guess what! Guess who asked me out?"

"Who?"

"*Fred Vargulic!* He's a *senior*! It was right after Earth Science, he comes up to me, see, and he goes, 'You wanna go out next Saturday?' 'I dunno,' I says, real cool, 'why should I?' He says, 'I might take ya 'round the world, that's why!' "

"Where're you going?"

"The *drive-in*. Only my mother," she giggles, "she thinks

it's a dance. They say Fred likes to French kiss." She is distracted, for a moment, by a passerby's stare. People often forget their manners in the face of such unexpected beauty.

"Bonnie! There's our bus!" my mother calls.

"So if anybody asks you, say it's a dance, O.K.?"

"O.K."

"We'll have to run for it!" my mother warns, running already. Lost girlhood strives inside her stiffening matron's body. She bunches up her skirt against the wind. Her hair whips out weed tall, a graying ashblond paradox around her profile, fine and eroding. Still further down, pink laces of an invisible corset hold in the first dark place where once we blended into common flesh, a mother and a child. She runs awkwardly, wholly *en terre*. She runs to make me come true.

"You almost missed it, lady," the driver complains, impatient as she sorts out change. "I ain't got all day." My mother drops the exact fare for two into the slot and turns to find seats together for us.

From our window we watch Gillian, unhurried, unperturbed, ascend the steps to the bus. A veil of glances falls over her, and she smiles. The driver smiles back, turning her dollar into coins, lingering a little over her hand. The light changes to red, but no one cares. Time has paused for her.

"Beauty like that," my mother says, "it's a burden."

But I do not believe her. The faces of everyone, both genders, young and old, smile or stare in wonder at Gillian, the way sunflowers track the sun.

"I only hope Gillian's *grateful* for what her mother's trying to do for her. She's taking in *wash* to pay for those lessons."

"Other people's wash?"

"Yes. You've seen all those baskets of it, haven't you? Did you think it was *theirs*? Personally . . ."—she settles a summer hat on her curls—". . . I've always had a suspicion she was a *housemaid* back in Scotland. There was *some* scandal, that older husband and all . . . I bet Gillian's a *love child*!" She nods at her own thoughts. "That would explain it."

"Explain what?"

"Why she's so beautiful. I mean, otherwise it's really a *mystery*, isn't it?"

Gillian's loveliness, surely immoral, poises hummingbird static and swift in my mind. "She's going out with Fred Vargulic. He's got this awful reputation!"

"How's that?" She is asking herself whether her hat looks right.

"He puts his tongue in your mouth when he kisses. Yuk."

"There!" My mother stabs her hatpin through the straw. Below the lacy brim her face shadows with remembered beauty. "Let's get going, Bonnie, I just dread this, but we better get it over with."

That afternoon we—Gillian, her mother, me, mine—all sit on the scratchy, royal-blue, velvet seats of the Bijou Theatre while the matinee performance of *The Red Shoes* lurches, whirrs and skips from frame to frame. Before us Moira Shearer leaps up close, wafts away, at the commandment of the camera. Once, the projector jams, the picture clots to a stop, "Ohhhh!" Our disappointment brings it back in pink and purple burned spots to the exhaled relief of the mothers and Gillian's small solitary cheer. "Yeah!"

But Gillian is bored. Her flawless hand browses steadily from the popcorn box to her mouth, up and down, keeping its own time over the romantic crescendos of the movie score.

"Hey, Bon, you want some popcorn?"

"No thanks."

"Yeah, I shouldn't either. Gotta watch my figure. . . . Guess what! Didja hear about Marsha Norris?"

"No."

"She *went all the way.* Honest! I got it from Marge Donaldson and Marge, she got it from Marsh *herself.* So it's true all right."

"Who with?"

"Chuck Schultz. They're getting married, Marsha says, maybe this Christmas. A Christmas wedding."

"Shh!"

"But how old is Marsha?" I ask quietly.

"She's sixteen, a girl can get married at sixteen in this state without her parents' wanting her to, it's the law. . . ."

"We are here to watch this movie, not to listen to you," my mother announces as if to strangers.

It's the dénouement. Poor Moira Shearer drops suddenly, still in her demonic shoes, before the machinery of an oncoming train. The impact jars through the women, doubling on their shocked and indrawn breaths. Mrs. Ravert cups a cry back into her mouth. "Oh, look at that, Ida!"

Against a soiled pavement the dying dancer's fractured legs splay, still *en pointe*. Wind plays at the corolla of her skirt. The pale-pink gauze of her stockings darkens to the sound of Mrs. Ravert's weeping. She is sopping up tragedy in her fresh handkerchief, saved for this moment.

"Hey, Bon, where can you get stockings like that?" Gillian nudges me. "Do you know?"

"Quiet, girls!"

Out of the dancer's legs a darkness keeps flowing. It seeps through the pearly silk of her stockings. It stains the light satin of the Red Shoes. Blood, but moving more gently than blood really moves, and fading from black to purple to a thoughtful blue, the color at the heart of a poppy. *"Take off the Red Shoes!"*

We leave the theater, silent, for the glare of half-deserted Sunday streets.

"Wasn't it *sad*, Ida? I thought it was very *sad*."

"There are sadder things," my mother understands.

Mrs. Ravert tries to gather up all her feelings in something poetic—"She danced herself to death!" Her glance seeks out Gillian, tender, bewildered, watchful. "Oh, ballet is a cruel art, isn't it," she says, "but it's so beautiful. Isn't it beautiful, Ida?"

"This sun is giving me a headache," my mother answers.

"Did I tell you, Ida, I'm taking Gillian to Scotland next year? To my sister's in Aberdeen, to study?"

"You told me, Marie."

Gillian smooths the petals of her nine-gored skirt over crinolines. She sighs, mildly exasperated, then draws me back to confide, "Bon, guess what! I got into Secretarial. Next year I get to take typing, Typing I."

"I thought you were going to Scotland, to your aunt's."

"Maybe. Maybe not." But in the shimmer of her brilliant eyes, sky color bound by darker blue, slyness cannot take hold.

"Your mother says."

"Yeah, well. My mother works real hard and everything, you know? I mean, she's really sweet. But she's not too practical, know what I mean?" She blows a pink, fruit-scented bubble. "If you take Secretarial, you can always get a job. . . ." The bubble rounds out dangerously, but just before it bursts, she sucks it back in. "I'm gonna get a job and save up for my wedding. I already got the gown picked out, *you* know," she taps her skull, "in my head. White satin, or white velvet if it's winter. My cousin, she wore blush pink. You can wear ice-blue, too, only people don't, much. Anyway, I want real lace, not fake, down here on the neckline and on the train. A *six-foot* train. Sleeves cut like so. . . ." Her hand describes a fallen triangular wing, vaguely medieval. "What about *you*, Bon? What's yours like?"

"Maybe I won't even get married."

"Sure you will. Everybody does, almost. And I wanna have three kids . . ." She pauses, almost conscious of a golden pollen of male glances. ". . . no, four, real close together, *you* know, so's they can be friends. Two girls and two boys. Well, a boy, a girl, a boy, a girl," she conceives them on her fingers. "I'm gonna call the girls Dawn and Candy. Do you like 'Dawn' and 'Candy' for names? I don't know what to call the boys, though. I guess their father can name them."

The light changes to green just as we catch up to our mothers. Sinking into the softening asphalt, we four stride forward as if to merge with our images, closing in from the plate glass window of a furniture store across the street, in Darwinian enigmas. Somehow Gillian came from her small, speckled mother, a glorious mutation. But in me my mother's silver blondness has been thrown back to mouse-brown. A triumphant moment has declined. We both know this as she walks forward in her reconstructed dignity, and I walk in my body of original sin.

"Turn, dear." I turn. "A little more." I turn a little more.

Mrs. Arcangelo talks around a slipped moustache of straight pins, held tight between pursed lips. She is fitting my costume, but her mind is on her masterpiece. "It's got hundreds of tiny little rhinestones, each one I got to sew by hand. 'Starlight effect,' that's what they call it. 'Starlight.' "

"I'm sure it's beautiful." My mother fingers the expensive slipper satin of a half-made sleeve.

"*Mrs.* Ravert, she's working extra just to help pay for it. Well," the seamstress lowers her voice, "she'd have to, it's costing over *two hundred dollars*!"

"Two hundred dollars!"

"And that's not counting *my* work. Well, it makes you wonder. . . . Turn, dear." I turn for her. ". . . what with all the starving people in the world! But Mrs. Ravert says it's an investment, the girl's dancing the Dying Swan and only the best dancer gets to do it. It's in a ballet . . . now, what did she call it? Blank? A ballet blank?"

"*Blanc,*" my mother corrects. "It means all in white."

"That's right. Well, Gillian! You could put your two hands right around her waist and touch your fingers, she's such a dainty little doll. They're taking her to Scotland, to study. . . ."

"Hold still, Bonnie. You're making it harder for Mrs. Arcangelo to do her work."

A straight pin just misses me, waist level. Mrs. Arcangelo turns, too, on her massive knees, and sets her yardstick up from the floor to my thighs. "Look at that, it's got to come down another quarter-inch! When is she going to stop growing?"

It is night; my mother is tired, but, "Bonnie's a long-stemmed American beauty," she defends me. "We expect *her* to audition for the Rockettes someday. When she's older, of course."

"What's that?"

"You never heard of the Rockettes? Why, they're famous for precision kicking. All over the world."

"Mmmm."

By now I know Mrs. Arcangelo's rhythm and turn without being told.

"You have to be over five foot seven just to try out for them!"

"My, my." Mrs. Arcangelo sits back on her haunches, finished.

"If you ask me, that waist's still not quite long enough," my mother reflects.

"There's nothing left to let down. Just step out of it, dear."

"Careful, Bonnie, don't step on the hem."

Almost negligently, Mrs. Arcangelo picks up my shed splendor, and I stand, unmasked before myself in her oval mirror, a startled, biscuit-colored shape in a cotton slip, slouched between girlhood and whatever else is coming.

"Beautiful material," she says, "a pleasure to work on."

"That's the best satin money can buy. Bonnie, put your clothes on, you'll get sick for the recital." A suffocating cape of Black Watch pleats snaps shut on me until, with one sharp tug, my mother lets me breathe again.

"That Ravert girl, now . . ." I emerge to see Mrs. Arcangelo sketching in air, "she's got a cap of feathers, each feather's threaded on separately with a *seed pearl* at the base. . . ."

"Put your coat on, Bonnie, it's late. When's our next fitting?"

Outside, after the bitter wind, we settle onto the cold seats of the car. She starts rummaging in her purse: makeup, bankbooks, comb.

"Where's my pocket calendar?"

"The recital's the twenty-second, Mom." Who does not know his date of execution? "Eight o'clock. The Moose Hall."

"Oh, I know *that*. But when's your next period? The twenty-fourth? Later?" she hopes.

"I'm not sure. I don't know."

"What do you mean, *don't know*? Don't you keep track?"

"What for? It always happens."

"Bonnie, you're hopeless. Now where's my calendar? I didn't leave it home, did I? Did you see me leave it somewhere, on the kitchen counter maybe?"

"I *think* it's January second."

"That's next *year*, thank heaven. You wouldn't want to ruin your costume. . . ." We swing out into the November night. "Your *father*, of course, he doesn't understand anything. Wait'll I tell him what *Gillian's* cost."

My costume has already spoiled a dinner. "*Forty-five dollars!* What the hell, do you think I'm made out of money, Ida?"

"It'll last forever."

"Sure, in the attic. Half a week's pay packed up in a goddamned box!" Above my head the swords of failure poise: an outgrown metallic-gold tutu I wore two Christmases ago, as a Marigold in the Waltz of the Flowers, also last year's tulle skirt, dirty-white, to turn me into a Snowflake.

"I just don't have forty-five bucks."

"Use some of the vacation money."

"Oh, Ida."

"Please? It would make me happy."

"No, it wouldn't, but sure, go ahead, take the shirt off my back."

"I'm very surprised at you, John, denying your daughter like that. Bonnie's talented. In just four months she's gotten a solo routine."

"Solo racket."

Now every afternoon between four and five, to the ratchety Voice of Music victrola, I practice without hope. It is like lying, to drag the cargo of a half-willing body through my Military Tap, cleats scratching the linoleum, eyes on the slow redemption of the clock. Where ballet required lightness, *ballon*, tap demands crispness, firecracker smiles, "bounce." To make me bouncier, my mother bobs my hair and ties it up in rags, but within moments it too falls limp.

"More life! Put more life in it!" She drives me, a dying horse, to the outpost of performance. "All right, all right, start over. Start from bar thirty." And when the phone rings, "Tell Gillian you can't talk long, you're working on *your* routine."

"Bon, listen." Gillian's voice comes to me conspiratorily soft. "I gotta see you. I've got something to *tell*. You won't *believe* it!"

My mother replaces the needle on the record. A few vacant grooves turn while Gillian urges, "After rehearsal tomorrow? O.K.?"

My mother gestures that time is up.

"Sure. I can't talk now."

My march starts. "Hey, is that yours?" Gilian asks. "Is that your music?" and starts singing,

> " 'Oh be kind to your web-footed friends!
> 'For a duck! may be some! body's moth-er!' "

"Bonnie, hang up."

"I've got to go."

> " 'And if you! think that this! is the end . . .
> Well it is!' "

Gillian hangs up first.

In bed that night the first black sweetness of my sleep breaks open. A dot of light is widening inside me. I lie still, as if listening, as it feathers, turns. A ribbon of cramp winds upwards through my belly. I swing out of the covers to start for the bathroom.

Outside it has been snowing, it still snows, wide steady flakes like petals falling off a peony. A seam of chill runs at the baseboard. Even the braided rugs feel cold to my bare feet. But from beyond my half-opened door quick air stirs in my parents' room. They are not asleep, but speaking softly, their voices distinct in the night darkness.

My mother's yields, "Oh, I'm not *blind*, you know. I can see it's over. Madame's right."

"Maybe she's wrong."

"She's right." The whole hall grows colder at the soft sound of weeping.

"Hey, it's not the end of the world."

At my window the georgette curtain lifts and falls in a current of thin heat. Below it, the radiator spits, then whistles. Perhaps I should make a noise, call out for somebody, stop them, my instinct for self-preservation tells me.

"You take things too hard, Ida honey. If you'd just stop wanting so many things, you'd be happy."

"Like you?"

"Well, yes, I guess I am, happy."

"No, ever since I knew you, you've been *contented* with what you have. Not like me. Sometimes it really makes me wonder."

Inside me fresh warm blood slips. Then out of a calm too good to last, her girl's voice, downy with wishes, speaks, "John," his name.

"What is it, honey? Let's get some sleep."

"John? What if we had another baby?"

"What?"

"I'd like that, wouldn't you? Wouldn't you?"

My father lengthens a silence around the house, its lonely shape in winter night. "Oh, Ida, we're too old for all that stuff."

"I am not, I'm not too old. John, we could start all over."

"Is that a threat or a promise?"

"Don't laugh at me."

"I'm not laughing, honey. Honest. Everybody likes to dream," he says. "It's nice to think about, anyway."

"I've always wanted another baby," my mother's voice rounds, rises in the darkness. "I always wanted to try again."

"Let's go to sleep now."

"John?"

"Let's go to sleep."

For a while I sit on the edge of the mattress. Brightness slips past the window shade. The dancer in the Degas poster on my wall blurs into a snowflower. At last water retreats banging down the radiator pipes, so that even the small heat vanishes. My bare feet have gone mineral-cold. I pull myself between the bedsheets, cold too now, draw my legs up into a smaller self beneath the wide, indifferent quilt.

They must be sleeping now. Blindly, my heart tells itself over and over. If I don't get up, by morning the sheet will be stained. "I always wanted to try again." If I do get up, my mind will work on what I overheard. Still bleeding, knowing it, I fall asleep.

"Dress" rehearsal, everyone in old leotards anyway, "Hey,

Bon," Gillian leads me to the back of the auditorium, glances
around for eavesdroppers, and announces, "This is *serious*.
First you gotta promise never to tell. Like *swear*. . . ."

"Swear."

I gesture over my heart.

"Promise? O.K., then. *Well* . . ." She tries to delay dramatically, but her pride races forward. "*Well*, Fred and me, we
went all the way the other night."

"You didn't!"

"I did." Off and on her starry eyes blink. "Well, we're
really in love, *you* know, so it's all right and everything."

"It's *not* all right." Doesn't she know about V.D. and
Pregnancy, my mother's big deterrents? "What *happened*? Did
he get you drunk?"

"You shouldn't never drink," she admonishes, "it's bad
for your skin." Her gum clicks and sloshes in excitement. "We
just, uh, couldn't stop, *you* know." She chews faster, new
juiciness.

On stage the baby swans, Beginners' Class, troop out in
their soft bottoms and soft shoes, the random shoreline of our
Swan Lake.

"But he won't *respect* you," the third reason Not
To comes to me, "I mean, no boy really wants a girl somebody's . . ."

"Nobody's laid me, only Fred. Besides, your mother just
says that so you won't. You know mothers."

Slowly I recognize that I am in the presence of an initiate,
a living sourcebook. "Did you bleed much?"

"I didn't bleed at all. I bet they lie about that, too, huh?
But I got worried, maybe Fred thought I'd been with somebody else, before, you know? I didn't say nothing. I just hoped
he didn't notice."

From the stage Madame makes a scooping gesture toward
Gillian.

"Hey, I gotta go."

"Wait. Does it hurt?"

"A little. Yeah." She half-turns her graceful back to me;
it's her cue. "But, *you* know," her hand leads my glance down-

ward to her feet, their perfect turnout, the slender pink cylinders of her toe shoes, "not as much as *this. . . .*"

Recital night, someone has strung dressing rooms with flannel-blanket walls behind the Moose Hall stage. Decibels of laughter and trouble travel the central aisle. Unseen nerves snap to tears. The curtain's up. Excitement burns among us.

"Hold still." My mother strokes solemn pigments on my face. A towel tied around the neck protects my glossy soldier's costume. Above it, her compact mirror shows me in savage colors, desiccated peachskin base, woad-blue shadow, a lipstick orange enough to turn my teeth yellow. Not for me the wing-swept ballerina's eye, the cold still red dot for a tear duct. In the small space between what my mother draws and the lines of my naked cheekbones, I feel a thin yet absolutely crucial margin, by how little I miss being beautiful. My mother's fingers move, electric with determination.

"Mom, I feel sick."

"That's just nerves. Hold still." She squints. Her sharp fingernail pares off a minute edge of paint. Up close her face terrifies my own, lipliner generous around her mouth, pores craterous with rouge. Resemblance hardens into me. "Don't look anywhere and don't blink, Bonnie, it'll smear." Then my eyes are on.

They have clamped me somehow into the white satin dress with its boy's bodice. My flesh pushes against Mrs. Arcangelo's French seams, a squash growing through rock.

"*Please* hold your stomach in." Her hands flatten her own to show me how. "If you don't, you'll look pregnant. And don't sit *down*, you might rip a seam."

"But I feel funny. Honest."

"Stage fright," she heads me off. "Everybody gets it. It's a good sign," though she knocks on the nearest wood, a cigarette stand upholding blocks, jars and sticks of makeup, its own Chinese-red lacquer peeling off.

"I think I'm getting the curse."

"Oh, you're not due for a week yet, *more*." Briefly her face clears into candor. "Please just don't get sick now, Bonnie, this means so much to me. Just keep calm, will you, and do a good job? Just this once?"

Applause, a slow match striking, comes to us through the blankets. "O.K." The aisle makes way for three belly dancers in sparkles and finger-chimes.

"Who's on now?" she whips back the flannel wall to ask them. "Nina Martin? Nina's your cue, Bonnie! You go on after Nina! Now get out there," she rights one of the purple plumes on my helmet, "and break a leg!"

Behind the hot must of the velvet curtains, I stand breathing in all the other performances of that and other nights. Overhead the pulleys creak, the curtain lifts enormously on a socket of hall. I am poised on my chalk-mark, a white X center-stage, saluting hundreds of invisible onlookers, families and friends, while the moment crawls on and on and on. In the crescent of the footlights one dead spot interrupts the ring. "Never look right at the audience!" I remember. Because if you do, your own fear and commonness stare back.

In the stage wings my mother's presence keeps getting bigger and bigger with everything she has to lose. Her hands are fixed slightly apart, as if she holds some breakable commodity, and she starts counting—numbers whisper across the boards, "One, and, two, and . . ." my march rasps in its grooves, "three, and, four AND. . . ." my foot takes over from her. In a noisy rush of turns, I come alive. There is the first naked awkwardness, the fear of tripping or forgetting, then my "routine" meshes with my body, takes me in.

Gradually I dance the rows of seats into shape out of the darkness. Out of the darkness wildflower faces come up, solitary, to the now-and-then blue dart of a camera pinning me to this place and this moment forever.

Hurtling out of every turn, I sight my mother. She mouths, "Smile! Smile!" Her hand tightens my salute. Her arms are waving "Arm movements!" and with the startling gesture of a woman garrotted, "Head *up*!" By the finale she is flailing too, and as the curtains close on our farewell smile a loud, obligatory slap of applause says it is over.

"Oh, baby, I'm so proud of you!" she tells me, but she wilts into tears. I touch my own face to see if the makeup has come off. On one satin cuff an orange stain recalls my last salute.

"Now clean up and come down and sit with us . . . it's Row B, seats six and seven."

"O.K."

In my cubicle I rub my skin fiery to cold cream everything away except my simple, earlier face. Aftermath flattens out in me like the end of a birthday, like the daily texture and pallor of the street clothes I will be putting on for the rest of my life. Headed toward the audience, I walk past islands of ballerinas waiting for their cues.

"Bonnie!"

In the wings Gillian twinkles, two hundred dollars worth of light leaping and staying among the subtle rhinestones in her skirt. On her perfect, floral face worry hesitates, accepts the diminished form of puzzlement.

"Oh, Bon, am I ever scared!"

"You? *You've* got stage fright?"

"It's not that." Her eyes assess the cygnets on stage, pretending to swandom in uneven *bourrées*. "Denise's out of step again," she says, "as usual." While I am looking, "I'm *late*, that's what's the matter."

"No, you're not. It's not even your cue."

Her violet eyes roll upward. "*Late. Late*," she repeats, " '*my aunt was coming for a visit*' and she's *late*. You *know*?"

"I bet it's the recital. It's made you nervous or something."

"Oh, no, it's not. I'm real regular, Bon. And anyways, there's other . . . signs."

"Signs?"

"Oh, Bon." She lowers her eyes in perfectly practiced shame. "I'm *expecting*."

It is the worst thing a girl could do, but even that, I sensed, you could do with talent, skill of some sort. "You're not?"

"Yeah. I'm sure. I got knocked up."

"Who?"

"Fred, who else?"

"Are you sure?"

Her glance shows damaged trust. Did I think she was one

of those girls who "didn't even know the father?" Did I think she was an amateur?

"Does your mother know?"

"Bon, really. I mean, Fred and me, we'll tell her later. We're gonna get married right away, so it's O.K. Just don't say anything, promise?"

I start to cross my heart but the gesture feels foolish, childish. "But she'll find out. What about Scotland? What about the Dance?"

"Well, I'm certainly not gonna *dance* anymore!" Gillian puts on a matron's indignation.

"Oh, Gill."

"You gotta quit sometime, I mean, look at Madame." Her face pouts and she begins to cry, though carefully, a little wad of Kleenex damming up the tears to keep her mascara from flowing. "No. This is the last time."

From the stage a sharp crack of applause finishes the little swans.

"Oh, Gillian, that's awful."

"What?" The little cygnets, Beginners' Class, giggle past us and she pulls back to preserve her fluted skirt.

"It's awful, you not dancing again."

"Oh. I mean, what I'm *really* worried about is maybe this could hurt the baby, mark it or something?" We hear the restless public murmur of the audience. "Well, me next," she says. "Cross your fingers, huh?"

"O.K."

Daintily Gillian pulls out a pink nubbin of gum and sticks it to the frame of the stage. A moment later she has assumed her place at center stage, legs effortlessly in the fifth position, arms *en couronne*.

In Row B I wedge past my mother's knees and sit between her and Mrs. Ravert, Seat 7, as the first bars of the Dying Swan draw a hush across the audience. On stage a wide confetti of pink and blue spotlights combine, settle on Gillian. The sweet soreness of her beauty, recognized, stirs in me, in everyone who watches. On our many drawn breaths she comes to motion.

Light plays on her rhinestones, bees on the living skin of flowers. The drafts catch and turn the feathers in her swan cap, until she trembles into something more than human, like us but also winged.

Beside me my mother holds in her disillusioned lap, eyes bravely forward, like a schoolgirl undergoing punishment both rigorous and undeserved. I reach for her in the darkness and am surprised by the readiness of her answering grip. We sit hand in hand.

From the audience a ripple, half cooing, half regret, says that Gillian, in a *temps d'ange*, has taken a bowman's arrow and now is slowly folding back into mortality.

In a few moments now she will sink into the sharp shape of a swan's outstretched throat, trembling to her silent death. The space between perfection and applause will seal her off. Then, resurrecting on the beats of acclamation, higher, higher, she will rise and curtsy, will make her *révérence* to Madame, the throats will fill up with "Encore!" as Sergei offers her an armful of red roses. "Encore!" until the dream cuts some other onlooker to the heart, roots there, and it begins again.

Downbent, my gaze catches the gleam of patent leather, Mrs. Ravert's cushiony small feet crammed into the pony hooves of her new shoes. She wears opaque elastic stockings, new too. Between the lapels of her Sunday suit, a cheap lace quivers. Her gloved laundress's hands are moving in small, possessed gestures to the music of her daughter's body on the stage. But I am afraid to look higher, to witness her face in all its bright intensity, the stale hair netted in a dancer's knot. Motherhood is the cruel art. If I look I will have to see her spirit burning in her eyes, the rapt and unsuspecting love of the only innocent among us.

ABOUT THE AUTHORS

Robert William Antoni is the recent recipient of a James Michener Fellowship and is writing a novel in Trinidad. "Two-Head Fred and Tree-Foot Frieda" is his first published story.

Margaret Atwood is the author of five novels including *The Edible Woman, Surfacing,* and *Life Before Man.* She is the author of eight books of poetry, a short story collection, and children's books. She lives on a farm near Allston, Ontario with her husband and daughter.

Martha Bayles's reviews, essays, poetry, and fiction have appeared in *Harper's, The New Republic, The New York Times Book Review,* and elsewhere. She is currently the TV critic for the *Wall Street Journal* and has recently completed her first novel, *Boston Common.* She is married and lives in Washington, D.C.

Michael Covino's first book of fiction, *The Off-Season,* has just been published by Persea Press. He is also the author of a book of poems, *Unfree Associations.* He lives in Berkeley, California, where he writes for the *East Bay Express.*

Andre Dubus recently retired from a seventeen-year teaching position at Bradford College. He is the author of a novel, *The Lieutenant,* a novella, *Voices from the Moon,* and four collections of short stories, the most recent of which is *The Times Are Never So Bad.* Next year, David Godine will publish a fifth story collection, *The Last Worthless Evening.*

Kurt Duecker lives in Montana and is at work on his first novel. This is his first published story.

Gerald Duff has published two collections of poetry, *A Ceremony of Light* (1976) and *Calling Collect* (1982), and a novel, *Indian Giver* (Indiana U. Press, 1983). "Fire Ants" comes from his longer work, *Graveyard Working,* and he is currently completing another novel, *That's All Right, Mama.* He has served as editorial advisor to *The Kenyon Review,* and he is academic dean at Rhodes College in Tennessee.

Pam Durban grew up in South Carolina. Her fiction has appeared in *The Georgia Review, Ohio Review, TriQuarterly,* and *Crazyhorse,* among others. She is the winner of the 1984 Mary Roberts

Rinehart Award in Fiction. "All Set About with Fever Trees" is the title story of a collection recently published by David Godine, Inc. She lives in Athens, Ohio and teaches at Ohio University.

John Gardner is considered by many to be one of the most important literary figures of recent decades. He is the author of nine novels, two collections of stories, children's books, an epic poem, as well as non-fiction books on the work of Geoffrey Chaucer and on fiction writing. In 1982, he died in a tragic motorcycle accident. "Julius Caesar and the Werewolf" was his last published story.

Janette Turner Hospital is an Australian who now divides her time between Boston and a small town in Ontario. Her short stories have appeared in *The Atlantic Monthly*, *The North American Review*, *Mademoiselle*, *Canadian Fiction*, and others. Her first novel, *The Ivory Swing*, won Canada's $50,000 Seal Award. A third novel, *Borderline*, has just been released in the U.S., Canada, the U.K., and Australia. She is currently writer-in-residence at MIT.

Lisa Interollo was born, raised, and currently lives in Manhattan. "The Quickening" is her first published story and was a winner in *Redbook*'s Fourth Young Writer's Contest. A graduate of Columbia University's School of Journalism, her non-fiction has appeared in *Cosmopolitan*, *Newsday*, *The Washington Post*, *The Los Angeles Times*, and other publications.

Janet Kauffman was born in Lancaster, PA and now lives in Michigan. She is the author of a book of poems, *The Weather Book* (Texas Tech Press), and a collection of short stories, *Places in the World Where a Woman Can Walk* (Knopf). A novel, *Collaborators*, will be published by Knopf in the spring of 1986.

James Howard Kunstler lives in Saratoga Springs, NY. His stories have appeared in *Playboy*, *Penthouse*, and *Cosmopolitan*, among others. His fourth novel, *An Embarrassment of Riches*, was recently published by Dial Press.

Beth Nugent lives in Iowa City. She was the second-prize winner of the *Redbook* Young Writers' Contest for 1983. Her stories have appeared in *The North American Review*, and *Mademoiselle*, among others.

Ilene Raymond grew up in Wallingford, PA. She is a graduate of Brandeis University and received an MFA from the University of Iowa Writers' Workshop. Her fiction has appeared in *Mademoiselle* and *Playgirl* magazines. At present, she teaches fiction writing at Penn State University in State College, PA, where she lives with her husband and is at work on her first novel. "Taking a Chance on Jack" won a 1985 O. Henry Award.

Bob Shacochis's first book, a collection of short stories, *Easy in the Islands*, was published in 1985 by Crown. He has been the recipient of a James Michener Fellowship and an NEA Fellowship. His stories have appeared in *Esquire*, *The Paris Review*, *Playboy*, and *Tendril*, among others.

Brent Spencer grew up in the Wyoming Valley of northeast Pennsylvania and is a graduate of the Iowa Writers' Workshop. He is currently completing his first novel, *A Wilderness of Monkeys*, for which he won the James Michener Award. This is his first published story.

Trevanian, writing under several pseudonyms, writes fiction, filmscripts, Welsh tales, Basque tales, and scholarly contributions in the fields of Aesthetics, Law, Theology, and Classical Studies. This story was originally published in the Netherlands by B.V. Uitgerversmaatschappij in association with the granting of the annual Trevanian Poetry Prize in Amsterdam.

Gayle Whittier has published fiction in *TriQuarterly*, *Ploughshares*, *Ms*, *Primavera*, *The Massachusetts Review*, *Carolina Quarterly*, *South Carolina Review*, *Storyquarterly* and in *Pushcart Prize VI*. She is currently director of the creative writing program at SUNY Binghamton. Her work includes a novel and other short stories.

ABOUT THE EDITOR

George E. Murphy, Jr. is the editor of *Tendril* Magazine, an independent literary journal, and is the editorial director of Wampeter Press, Inc. He is the author of a book of poems, *Rounding Ballast Key* (Ampersand Press, 1985), and a children's book, *Teddy: A Christmas Story*. He is also the editor of two anthologies, *The Poets' Choice: 100 American Poets' Favorite Poems*, and (with poet/biographer Paul Mariani) *Poetics: Essays on the Art of Poetry*. In 1983, he won the New York Contemporary Press Poetry Prize. In 1985, he was awarded the Joseph P. Shaw Award from Boston College for distinguished contributions to contemporary literature. He currently lives in Key West and is working on a novel and compiling *The Key West Reader: An Historical Literary Anthology*.